She reaches into the box and pulls out a pebble, a pink marbled pebble picked up off a faraway beach a lifetime ago.

I hold out my hand and she drops it into my palm. The familiar contours are comforting, even though my heart aches at holding it again.

I promised to treasure it, and I have for many years. I still do . . .

Kathryn Hughes is the internationally bestselling author of *The Letter, The Secret, The Key, Her Last Promise* and *The Memory Box*.

Her novels have been translated into 28 languages.

Kathryn lives with her husband near Manchester and has a son and a daughter.

To find out more about Kathryn,
visit www.kathrynhughesauthor.com, follow her on Twitter
@KHughesAuthor or find her on Facebook
at www.facebook.com/KHughesAuthor.

By Kathryn Hughes

The Letter
The Secret
The Key
Her Last Promise
The Memory Box

THE KEY

'A wonderful, enthralling story; one that I didn't want to end'
Lesley Pearse

'A heartbreakingly powerful read'
Sun

'Unputdownable with a twisting plot'
My Weekly

'A fabulous read'
Woman's Weekly

'A must-have'
Sunday Express

'Impeccably researched'
Daily Mail

'An intriguing and emotional tale with some surprising
twists that will keep the reader absorbed throughout.
Another winner'
People's Friend

'Shocking, stirring'
Woman

'A very atmospheric, heartbreaking and intriguing read that
will shock and surprise you'
Alba in Bookland

THE SECRET

THE LETTER

THE
MEMORY
BOX

Kathryn Hughes

REVIEW

First published in 2021 by
HEADLINE REVIEW
An imprint of HEADLINE PUBLISHING GROUP

First published in paperback in 2021 by
HEADLINE REVIEW
An imprint of HEADLINE PUBLISHING GROUP
7

Cataloguing in Publication Data is available from the British Library

ISBN 978 1 4722 6595 1

Typeset in Garamond MT by Palimpsest Book Production Ltd, Falkirk, Stirlingshire

Printed and bound in Great Britain by Clays Ltd, Elcograf S.p.A.

Headline's policy is to use papers that are natural, renewable and recyclable products and made from wood grown in well-managed forests and other controlled sources. The logging and manufacturing processes are expected to conform to the environmental regulations of the country of origin.

HEADLINE PUBLISHING GROUP
An Hachette UK Company
Carmelite House
50 Victoria Embankment
London EC4Y 0DZ

www.headline.co.uk
www.hachete.co.uk

This book is dedicated to the thousands of real-life 'Candices' who work so tirelessly in our care homes, especially during the most challenging of years.

1

2019

White rabbits. Those were the first words I uttered this morning. For as long as I can remember, I've said those two words on the first day of every month. It's supposed to bring you good luck, and even though that might sound crazy, today's my one hundredth birthday, so who knows?

Some people call my living so long a miracle, but I think it's more likely preordained from the minute we're conceived rather than a triumph of human spirit or a medical marvel. Or anything to do with rabbits. It was always meant to be this way. When I was twelve, the doctors said I'd be lucky to see twenty. I've outlived them all. I've given fate a helping hand along the way. Looked after myself as best I can. I don't do things to excess, but I don't deny myself too much either. I have a vanilla slice every now and then, a quarter of jelly babies, that sort of thing. Well, you're a long time dead, after all. I've heard some folk credit their old age to a tot of whisky each night. 'Just a wee dram,' they'll say, even though they've never been anywhere near Scotland. I prefer the odd gin myself. Bog-standard gin, none of this new-fangled stuff. I believe there's one flavoured with rhubarb and ginger, if you can believe that. Anyway, fate, destiny, call it what you will, here

I am about to clock up a century. You don't need to worry, though. Ancient I may be, but I still have all my marbles. I'm not one of those unreliable narrators. You can trust me.

The room's normally tastefully decorated, all soft caramel, taupe and fern, with squashy sofas that give you a giant hug as you sink into them. Tonight, though, it's garlanded with pastel-coloured paper chains, the sort kids make in primary school. I suspect they've been made by members of the Craft Club. Three silver balloons, a number one and two zeros, gently sway above the air vents. Black-clothed tables are sprinkled with glittery stars, which some poor soul will have to clear away in the morning. They'll be stuck in the carpet until Christmas, no doubt.

In the corner, a four-tiered cake towers over the makeshift dance floor, way too many candles anchored in the icing. This is Frank's doing; only he could come up with such an ostentatious offering. We'll be eating Victoria sandwich for weeks.

Can you picture a hundred-year-old woman, I wonder? I'll furnish your imagination with some details if you like. Let's see now. My once honey-blonde hair is now silver, but you've probably worked that bit out. Granted, it's nowhere near as thick as it used to be, but what there is of it is cut into what Candice informs me is a 'graduated messy bob'.

The skin on my hands is translucent and spangled with liver spots, the blue veins clearly visible. Hands are always a give-away. Hands and neck. Arthritic knuckles mean my rings will have to be cut off my fingers when I eventually shuffle off, and beneath my nail polish (yes, really), my ridged nails are yellowing. I won't go all lyrical on you and try to find a word to describe my eyes, because nobody has ever been able to

2

decide if they're blue or green. Depends what mood I'm in. There's a slightly cloudy look to them these days, though.

People say I'm lucky with my complexion, and I suppose some of it *is* in the genes, but I'll let you into a little secret. I've been using a special cream on my face for nigh on eighty years. Down on the farm when the cows' udders became sore and cracked, we used to rub on a thick, calming unguent. Yes, you read that right. My secret to good skin is chapped-udder cream. You're welcome. I'm fortunate with my teeth as well. Oh, they're not as white as they once were, obviously, but at least they're still in my mouth and not in a glass beside my bed. Back in the day, I used to stick my finger up the chimney and rub soot into them. I've never shied away from using a bold lipstick either. Well, why not accentuate your best feature? The colour I'm wearing tonight is Ruby Woo by somebody called Mac. Candice bought it for me. I hope it wasn't too expensive, because she doesn't earn a lot. She bought me a five-year diary, too. The optimism of youth is staggering sometimes.

I'm wearing a plain black immaculately tailored dress. That level of couture doesn't come cheap, let me tell you, but fortunately the two old dears who work at the charity shop have no idea what they're doing. A tenner they wanted for it. A tenner, I ask you! Now, I'm not one for ripping off charity shops, so I gave them thirty and left them dithering over what to put on the newly naked mannequin.

I'm looking around the room, scanning faces for those I recognise. I'm not even sure who all these people are, and don't like to ask. It's my guess they've been drafted in from somewhere to make up the numbers. Some people will go anywhere for a free buffet. The lights have been dimmed, but I can still make out Frank over in the corner, sitting in a wing-backed chair.

Frank's my best friend in here now. He only moved in a few months ago, and at first he was a bit distant, but I won him over in the end. I give him a little wave and he doffs his imaginary cap in return. What else can I tell you about him? I can't say he's the nicest person on the planet, because I haven't met everybody, but I'm confident he would make the podium. He's devilishly handsome, with his geometrically manicured moustache. I think he must use a ruler and nail scissors to get that Errol Flynn effect. His eyes are still as blue as a cornflower and his hair's thick, white and wavy, as though it's been piped onto his head by a Mr Whippy machine. I'm rather envious of his hair. He's young, too, somewhere in his eighties, so obviously I'm too old for him. In any case, I'm not his type. Frank was with his Ernest for fifty-eight years, married for the last four. He even took Ernest's surname and they were known as Mr and Mr Myers. That's true love, that is.

For some inexplicable reason, the music has been cranked up to a foundation-crumbling volume and has a dreadful bass I can feel deep inside my ribcage. It's as though someone is stamping on my chest. I shan't moan about it, though. If there's one thing that shows your age, it's asking folk if they can turn the music down.

My fingers fumble with the gold clasp on my patent leather handbag. It's just like the one Her Majesty carries. I often wonder what she has inside hers. A quarter of lemon sherbets, or some Polo mints for the horses, perhaps. After all, she doesn't need to carry money or house keys, but it's always with her, tucked into the crook of her elbow, never out of her sight. She's sent me a card, you know. It's a picture of herself in a canary-yellow suit with the obligatory matching hat. She's pleased to know I'm celebrating my hundredth birthday and sends me her best wishes. She looks good for her age too.

Oh, watch out, Candice is coming over. She has her fingers in her ears and tuts towards the ceiling.

'Hello, Candice.'

'Who *are* you talking to, Jenny? I've been watching you muttering away to yourself. First sign of madness that is, talking to yourself.'

'Oh, I'm just reflecting, love. Don't go fretting about me.'

'I've asked them to turn that racket down a notch. Now, can I get you a refill?'

'Go on then, you've twisted my arm. I'll have another glass of that fizzy stuff.'

'Your lipstick's bleeding a little. Hang on, I'll fix it with me tissue.'

She dabs her grotty tissue onto her tongue then wipes it round my mouth as though I'm a sticky little kid. She means well, but I'm perfectly capable of fixing my own lipstick, thank you very much. I'm not being unkind, honestly. Candice is a sweet girl and I'm rather fond of her. I know this job's only a stopgap for her. She's desperate to do some beauty course or other, and she seems to be the main breadwinner in her household. She lives with her boyfriend, who sounds like a waste of space to me, but she's smitten. It's all 'my Beau this' and 'my Beau that'. At first I thought she was being a bit of a drama queen, but it turned out Beau's his actual name, can you believe? At least Candice says it is. He's a musician. A struggling one, but a musician all the same. I bet he's really called Keith or something.

She's coming back over now with two glasses of ersatz-champagne balanced in one hand and a plate of buffet fodder in the other.

'Here you go, Jenny. A couple of salmon and cucumber on brown, a Scotch egg, and a few of those little tomatoes you like.' She flicks a napkin over my lap, then perches on the arm of my chair and takes a sip of her drink. 'A hundred years old, eh? What's it like being a centurion?'

'I've no idea, love. I've never been a Roman soldier.'

'You what?'

'I'm a *centenarian*.'

'Oh, right. Well, anyway, I just can't imagine living that long.'

The lights have been turned up and the music is now playing at an acceptable supermarket level.

'By the time you're my age, Candice, it won't be that unusual. I can't imagine it'll warrant a card from the monarch, whoever he is. How old are you now?'

'I'll be twenty-three this year.'

'So, you were born in what, ninety-six?'

She leans in and gives me a playful shoulder charge. 'Yes, wow! Nowt wrong with your brain, is there? You're dead clever, you. I wish I were that good at maths.'

You'd think I'd just performed a series of quadratic equations instead of simply subtracting twenty-three from two thousand and nineteen. I sometimes despair of the youth of today.

I feel the vibration of her phone at the same time she does. She stands up and fishes it out of her pocket, frowning as she stares at the illuminated screen. She taps out a message, her thumbs a blur of black nail varnish.

'I told him I was staying late,' she sighs. 'Honestly, he's so forgetful sometimes.' She shows me a photograph of a grown man pulling a sulky face, his bottom lip protruding like a spoilt child's. Tendrils of jet-black hair curl over his bandanna and, behind his lilac-tinted sunglasses I can see he's wearing eyeliner. Never trust a man who wears sunglasses indoors, and as for eyeliner? Well, I expect you can imagine how I feel about that.

'That's Beau, is it?'

She strokes the photo with her forefinger, smiling at the image. 'Isn't he gorgeous? He's taken a selfie to show me how sad he is that I'm not at home with him. He's not had anything to eat apparently, poor thing.'

'Lost the use of his legs, has he?'

'What? No, of course he hasn't. It's just I usually get the tea on.' She thrusts the phone back into her pocket. 'I'll fetch him a little doggy bag from the buffet.'

She takes another sip of her fizzy wine and surreptitiously glances at her watch. 'I feel bad now,' she says. 'I should've reminded him this morning, but he was still asleep when I left and I didn't want to wake him.' She drums her fingers on her thigh.

'Candice, you go home if you want to. No need to stay on my account.'

She pats my arm. 'Absolutely not. This is your special night and I'm not going anywhere until I've seen you into bed.'

'I don't want to get you into any trouble, love.'

She frowns. 'Trouble? There's no trouble. Beau's not like that. As long as he knows where I am, he doesn't mind me going out once in a while.'

'That's good of him,' I say, but the sarcasm seems to go over her head.

I suddenly can't be bothered any more. The little paper plate on my knee's not up to the task. It's too flaccid, and a couple of cherry tomatoes have rolled onto the floor. 'I think I'd like to turn in now, Candice.'

'What!' She jumps up, knocking my glass off the coffee table. 'Oh bugger,' she says, bending down to retrieve it. 'Well, at least it's not broken. I'll fetch you another and then we can have the toast. You can't go to bed before we do the cake.'

She claps her hands and manages to get everybody's attention. 'Okay, listen up now, peeps. Jenny needs her beauty sleep, so we're going to cut the cake and sing "Happy Birthday".'

As Candice lights the candles, somebody makes the inevitable gag about having the fire brigade on standby. There aren't a hundred candles – that would be ridiculous – but there are at least fifty, spread over the four tiers.

Frank suddenly appears at my side, offering his elbow. 'May I?'

He smells divine; he always does. I shuffle to the edge of my seat and brace myself. With one hand planted on the arm of the chair and Frank hefting me by my elbow, I manage to stand on the first attempt. He pulls my walking frame towards me and doesn't let go of me until he's sure I'm safe. The cake is over on the other side of the room, and I'm worried the candles will have burned down before I reach it. Candice hasn't planned this very well. As I lumber across towards it, a tuneless rendition of 'Happy Birthday' is sung at an agonisingly slow pace. To a round of applause, I manage to find enough breath to blow out the few candles that haven't burned down to the icing. I feel Frank's arm around my shoulders as he gives me a squeeze and a kiss on the cheek. 'Happy birthday, Jenny.'

'Speech,' shouts Candice, cupping her hands round her mouth.

The room falls silent with expectation and I suddenly feel choked. Most of the people here are virtual strangers, cajoled into attending the birthday party of an old woman who's outlived everybody who ever mattered to her. In my mind's eye, the years roll back. It's like looking at one of those old newsreels with stuttering black and white images, people moving faster than they did in real life.

Back in my room, I sit on the edge of my bed as Candice kneels on the floor and rolls down my tights. She notices my swollen feet and absently massages them. I don't know what they pay her in here, but it's not enough.

'Did you have a nice time, Jenny?'

'I did, love,' I say with sincerity. 'It's a long time since anybody did something like that for me.'

She stands up and tosses my tights into the linen basket. 'Do you need any more help getting into your nightie?' Without waiting for my answer, she unfastens the zip on the back of my dress. 'There, I'll leave you to it. Be back shortly with your cocoa.'

I appreciate the gesture. She's done the difficult bits for me – the tights and the zip – and now she's left me to get on with it. It's important to instil self-worth and a level of independence even for someone my age. I still have my dignity. I'll forgive her for the lipstick incident earlier.

I'm sitting up in my single bed by the time she returns, udder cream still dewy on my skin. I reach out for the mug with both hands. I'm not really a shaky person, especially considering my age, but I'm not taking any chances. Neither is Candice. She's only filled the mug to three quarters. I stare at her face, marvelling at the freshness even at this time of day. Her eyebrows alone are something to behold. They're the most important feature of the face, so she tells me.

She wanders over to my dressing table and picks up a framed photo. 'Who's this beauty?' she asks.

I dug out the photograph this morning. Thought it would be nice to remember I used to be able to turn heads. 'It's me, you daft article. Can't you tell?'

She holds the picture up next to my face and blows out an appreciative breath. 'Absolutely stunning, Jenny. You must've been fighting them off in your day.'

Modesty prevents me from going overboard, but she's not far off the mark. I've often wondered if my life would have turned out differently if I'd looked like the back end of a bus.

She returns the photo to the dressing table and her eyes settle on the polished wood of my jewellery box. 'I haven't seen this before either.' Her fingers fumble with the catch and she lifts the lid. There's a fine line between nosiness and interest.

'Fetch it over here, love.'

She carries the box across to my bed and settles herself on the duvet. 'It's gorgeous, Jenny.'

I'm glad she appreciates the craftsmanship that went into making this box, but it's what lies within that makes it truly special. Not jewellery, but a lifetime of memories.

Uninvited, she sticks her hand in and pulls out a wooden carving of a girl, her arms outstretched, encircling an empty space. I stiffen as she turns it over in her hands.

'Looks like there's something missing from it.'

I take a sip of my cocoa. 'There is.'

I don't elaborate as Candice has another root round and pulls out a pebble, a pink marbled pebble picked up off a faraway beach a lifetime ago. I hold out my hand and she drops it into my palm. The familiar contours are comforting, even though my heart aches at holding it again. I promised to treasure it, and I have for many years. I still do.

Candice is rummaging through letters, photos and old newspaper cuttings yellowed with age. She pulls out a two-column clipping, one that has only resided in the box for a few months. The paper is still white and the ink has not lost its sharpness. The headline jumps out at me, and even though I've seen it countless times before, it never loses its impact. I close my eyes for a moment. There's just one word: *Slaughtered!*

She peers at the article, her eyes narrowing. 'What's all this?' she asks.

I take the clipping from her, fold it in half, then take a breath. 'I need to ask a favour of you, Candice.'

'Sure,' she says, breezily. 'What can I do for you?'

She sounds as though she's expecting me to ask her to pop out for a loaf, but she'll soon realise it's more than that. Much more.

'There's something I need to do, and I can't do it by myself.

I need someone I can trust to help me. By the time I've told you my story, though, I hope you'll understand just how important it is that I make this journey.'

'Journey? What journey?'

'It's the last chance I'll have to lay the past to rest.' I take her hands in mine, squeezing them until my knuckles turn white. 'Please say you'll come with me, Candice.'

2

Jenny Tanner gripped the little boy's pudgy hand. It felt like a ball of dough in her own cool palm. She offered him a reassuring smile. 'Can you try not to look so sad, our Louis? You'll put folk off.'

As the sun spilled in through the skylights, dozens of other evacuees milled around the community hall, some crying, some pushing and shoving, some gazing open-mouthed at the sight of the trestle table laid out with slabs of fruit cake and cups of tepid milk. The feverish atmosphere only added to Louis's apprehension.

Jenny nodded towards the table. 'You want some?'

He pouted and shook his head. 'Not hungry.'

'You must be! You haven't eaten for over three hours.'

'Feel sick. I wanna go 'ome.'

Jenny sighed. 'Remember what you promised Mummy? You told her you'd be a brave lad, didn't you, hmm? You even crossed your heart,' she added solemnly.

She regarded his tear-streaked face, the smattering of freckles across his nose, his ears, a furious red colour, sticking out just a little too much. Their tearful departure a few hours earlier had been so traumatic, Jenny was convinced poor little

Louis would be scarred for the rest of his life. Their mother had done an admirable job of keeping the mask in place, even though it was obvious to Jenny that all she wanted to do was give way to the tears and let her face crumple. She had hugged her son so tight his cheeks had turned crimson and he was forced to beg for freedom. He had had another paddy when he found out he was only allowed to bring one toy. The obvious candidate was Mrs Nesbitt, the one-eyed teddy he slept with each night, rubbing the bear's ear under his nose until he drifted off. Peter, the stuffed rabbit Jenny had knitted him when he was born, had been the first casualty of the war, and Louis had made a wholly disproportionate fuss at having to leave him behind.

'I only ask one thing of you, Jenny,' their mother had said. 'Stay together. At all costs, stay together.'

Jenny's stoicism had almost wavered then. 'But what if—'

'No, no.' Her mother had cut her off. 'I won't hear of it.' She'd clamped her hands over her ears and shaken her head.

When the train had pulled into the station, Louis had clung to his mother's leg and she'd had to limp along the platform, dragging the dead weight of him behind her. Jenny boarded the train first and held out her arms to the boy as their mother peeled him off and offered him up to his sister.

Jenny knew how hard it had been for their mother to let them go. Connie Tanner had stubbornly resisted the first wave of evacuations seven months earlier, but with Hitler's army gaining ground with each passing month, the so-called Phoney War had come to an end, and she had finally agreed that her children would be safer in the countryside.

She felt Louis tugging her sleeve. 'What now, Lou?' she asked distractedly, eyeing the billeting officer with his officious clipboard.

Louis pointed to his shorts, a damp patch between his legs darkening the fabric.

'Oh Louis, why didn't you say you needed the lav?'

'I don't know where it is.'

'We could've asked.' She bit back her impatience. 'Give me your case. We'll have to get you changed. Nobody's going to want a little boy who wets his flamin' pants.' She aimed for a breezy tone but fell short by some distance.

She beckoned to a sturdy woman in a WVS uniform, her buttons straining against her ample bosom. Her mother's words rang in her ears. *Be polite, talk proper, don't let them think they're better than you.* 'Excuse me, we've . . . er . . . had a little accident.' She tilted her head at Louis.

'Oh bless him.' The woman crouched in front of him and held out her hands. 'Come with me, bach, and bring your case. We'll have you clean and dry in no time.'

'Give Mrs Nesbitt to me.' Jenny held out her hand and Louis reluctantly let go of his teddy.

Watching them go, she slumped gratefully into the nearest chair and pressed Mrs Nesbitt to her face. The bear smelled of home; of the liver and onions her mother was so fond of cooking even though they both hated it. Crushed by tiredness, she dug her fingers into her scalp, massaging away the beginnings of a headache. Goodness only knew what a state she must look after the two trains and a bus ride it had taken them to get here from Manchester. With a determined effort, she stood up and limped over to the

15

trestle table, her cane thumping on the wooden floor. 'Is there any of that fruit cake going? Erm . . . please.'

A purple-faced woman in a floral housecoat slid two pieces onto a green china plate. 'It's bara brith, home-made it is.'

Jenny frowned and brought the plate up to her nose. 'Smells like fruit cake to me.'

The woman pursed her lips. 'It's bara brith, and you'd better get used to it.'

They had only been told they were going to Wales after their first train journey. It was another country, where they spoke a different language. Her mother would have kittens when she found out. Jenny had gazed in wonder at the road signs and the unpronounceable village names full of knotty consonants she'd never be able to get her tongue round. From Llandudno Junction, the coach had followed the bends of the river until they had arrived in the little market town of Penlan, deep in the Conwy valley, the verdant hillsides dotted with sheep, a distinctly agricultural smell hanging in the air.

'Here we are then,' announced the WVS woman, returning with Louis in tow. 'All clean and dry.' She pushed him towards Jenny. 'You be good for your mammy now.'

'Oh no,' said Jenny, pulling him onto her knee. 'I'm not his mother, I'm his sister.'

'His sister?'

'That's right. I've evacuated with him because it's not safe for me in Manchester either.' She took a shallow breath. 'It's my lungs and my leg, you see.'

The woman nodded, although clearly she didn't see.

'Polio,' Jenny confirmed. 'When I was twelve.'

'Oh dear, well that's . . . that's unfortunate.' Blushing, the woman turned and bustled off.

Jenny folded her arms and leaned back in the chair, her head resting on the wall behind. She dared to close her eyes and almost at once felt the pull of sleep. She could hear the low bubble of voices as children were selected by host families and led out of the hall and into the unknown. She felt someone squeeze her shoulder. 'Excuse me.'

She sat up and blinked. 'Yes?'

The billeting officer pointed to an elderly couple who were standing by the table sipping cups of tea. 'They would like to offer this young chap a billet.'

'Louis?'

'That's right.' He held out his hand to Louis, who sat cross-legged on the floor at Jenny's feet. 'Come with me then, young man.'

As Jenny stood, her cane toppled to the floor. 'Oh no, I'm sorry, he can't go without me.'

Louis clung to her leg, squashing his face into the folds of her skirt.

'They only have room for one of you, I'm afraid. I promise you he'll be well cared for. They've had children of their own, so they're no strangers to little ones.'

'Listen to me, either I go with him or else he doesn't go. We're to stay together.'

The billeting officer tried to stifle his impatience. 'No, dear, you listen to me. The people of this community have been kind enough to extend a welcome to you and all these other city kids, and throwing that back in their faces is not conducive to good relations.'

'Please,' she implored. 'Look at him, he's distraught, he wouldn't survive without me.' She reached out and touched the man's arm. 'There must be somebody who'll take us.'

He looked at his list, running his finger down a column. 'Mmm . . . The Evans family are down to take two, but they've requested two strong lads to help out on the farm. Neither you nor your brother fall into that category,' he sniffed.

Jenny looked around the hall. Indeed, most of the older lads had already gone, leaving only a forlorn group of young waifs, clutching their boxed-up gas masks and oversized cases, bewilderment written into their expressions.

She stared hard at the man before bending down to speak to Louis. 'Will you go with them, Lou?'

He clutched a handful of her skirt. 'No, Jenny, please. I want to stay with you.'

She swallowed down her annoyance at the billeting officer's intransigence. She would've liked to tell him where he could shove his clipboard, but decided that appealing to his better nature would be more productive. 'Look, he's a sensitive lad and I promised our mother we'd stay together. Surely there's something you can do.'

He tapped his pen on his chin. 'Wait here.'

Louis peeled himself away from Jenny, his eyes swollen with tears. He stuck his thumb into his mouth and twirled a piece of his hair in his fingers. Jenny felt the first flutter of exasperation. Why did he always have to be such a baby? She sank into a chair and closed her eyes, unable to fight the crushing tiredness any longer.

*

18

She woke to the clatter of china being cleared away and chairs being scraped along the wooden floorboards. She rubbed the stiffness from her neck and eased a dozing Louis off her knee and onto the floor, settling him onto her coat. The chatter of apprehensive schoolchildren had gone and she tuned in to the billeting officer, who was having a rather fraught conversation with a young man who'd just burst through the doors, all of a fluster. 'Am I too late?' she heard him ask.

'Pick of the crop's gone for sure, Lorcan lad. Where've you been?'

Jenny watched as Lorcan dug his hands into his pockets. 'Mam's ill with the flu. Tad's tending to a calving problem. I've only just finished the milking.'

The billeting officer nodded in Jenny's direction. 'I've saved you the scraps,' he chuckled.

She shifted under the young man's incredulous gaze.

'Those two?' he said.

'Brother and sister; she's twenty-one, he's nearly five, although he acts like a toddler.' The billeting officer winked at Lorcan. 'She's quite a looker, wouldn't you say?'

'Sorry, Llew, I can't take them.'

'You'll have to. You're on my list to billet two children, and those are the only two left. Jennifer May Tanner and Louis Francis Tanner.' He struck a line through both names.

'But she . . . she's not even a child. Why's she even here?'

Llew shielded his mouth with his palm and lowered his voice. 'She's crippled, got a gammy leg, I believe. Uses a cane.'

'Llew, you've got to help me. Mam'll go mad. We need boys for the farm, see? We've had to turn over five acres of pasture

19

to spuds and beets. Come the harvest, we'll need all the help we can get.'

'This isn't a cattle auction, Lorcan. You can't be choosy. You should have got here earlier if you were going to be so picky.' Llew clamped his clipboard to his chest. 'They're all yours. Tell your mam I said hello. I hope she's feeling better soon.'

Lorcan wandered over to Jenny, offering an apologetic smile. 'Hello there,' he said. 'Sorry about all that.'

Louis stirred; his thumb fell from his mouth and left a trail of slime glistening on his chin.

'Jenny Tanner,' she said, offering her hand. 'And this sleepy one here is my brother Louis.'

Lorcan hesitated, wiping his hand down his trousers, although it looked like it would take a lot more than that to remove the day's grime. 'Lorcan,' he said. 'Lorcan Evans. Follow me.'

'Both of us, you mean?'

He seemed to wrestle with his decision, clearly in a state of flux. 'Yes, both of you.'

Outside, a sharp shower had dampened down the trees and hedgerows, but low in the sky the sun was out, and a warm breeze ruffled the luminous green leaves. The whole day smelled laundry-clean, and Jenny took a head-clearing breath. Lorcan had taken both cases and slung their gas masks over his shoulder. 'Is it far?' she asked.

'About a mile,' he replied.

She brandished her cane. 'Erm, I don't want to sound ungrateful, but I'm just too tired to walk that far. It's been a long day.'

'There's no need. The other Jenny'll do all the work.'

'The other Jenny?'

Lorcan stopped beside a donkey waiting patiently by the side of the road. He pulled on its long furry ears. 'Most donkeys are called Jenny.' He threw the cases into the cart and held out his hand. 'Do you need any help?'

Jenny looked at the steps, wondering how she could haul herself aboard without making a fool of herself.

'Hold on,' said Lorcan. He disappeared round the back of the hall and came back with a wooden fruit box. He upended it and set it down next to the cart. 'Is that better?'

With the aid of his hand, she climbed the two steps up into the cart.

'Ta,' she said settling herself on the hard wooden seat.

Lorcan turned to Louis. 'Shall I lift you in?'

Louis nodded and held his arms aloft.

'For goodness' sake, Louis,' said Jenny. 'You can climb in by yourself.'

Lorcan swept him up and plonked him down next to her. 'It's no trouble. He's only got little legs.'

Jenny smiled. 'You're very sweet, but this mollycoddling will have to stop soon enough.' She tapped Louis under his chin. 'Won't it, hmm?'

The donkey's sides heaved as it jounced along impossibly narrow lanes, the hawthorn hedge so thick the thorny branches scratched at their arms. At the end of what was now little more than a rough track, Lorcan jumped down and opened a gate. A wooden sign, crudely painted with the name *Fferm Mynydd* hung at an angle, and Jenny tilted her head to read it.

The farmhouse itself was exactly how a five-year-old might draw a cottage: oblong, with three square windows along the top, a window in the bottom left-hand corner, another in the right. A stone porch, with a stable door, separated the two. There was even a crooked chimney emitting a long curl of smoke. The stone had been whitewashed, probably some time ago judging by its greyish hue, and the window frames were painted a rather bold shade of green.

'Welcome,' said Lorcan, offering his hand to Jenny. 'Welcome to Mynydd Farm.'

Jenny frowned. 'Say that again.'

'Mun-ith. *Mun* as in *bun*, *ith* as in *dither*. It means "mountain". He gestured towards the gorse-clad hill rising up behind the farmhouse.

'Mun-ith,' she tried. 'Have I got that right?'

'Close enough,' he replied, lifting Louis out of the cart.

A black and white dog lay on the doorstep. At the sound of their voices, it lifted its head and cocked one ear before bounding over, tongue flapping. Louis hid behind Jenny.

'Hello, boy,' said Lorcan, ruffling the dog's ears. 'This here is Brindle. Do you want to stroke him, Louis?'

Louis shook his head, still cowering behind his sister.

'For the love of God, our Louis,' said Jenny. 'He won't bite.' She looked to Lorcan for confirmation. 'Will he?'

'Of course he won't. He's as daft as anything.'

'Lorcan, you're back.' An older man appeared from one of the barns, his brown overalls stained with what seemed to be blood. He removed his elbow-length rubber gloves as he approached. 'What's this?' He looked from Jenny to Louis, his face attempting a smile but not quite managing it.

22

'Tad, this is Jenny and her brother Louis, from Manchester. This is my father, Bryn Evans.'

Be polite, remember your manners. 'Pleased to meet you,' said Jenny, offering her hand but then quickly withdrawing it when she saw that the rubber gloves had not prevented his hands from becoming covered with whatever fluid streaked his overalls. There was a metallic tang about him.

'I thought you were coming back with two boys, Lorcan. These two don't look like they'll be much help round here.' Bryn pointed at Louis. 'He looks like a stiff wind would blow him over.'

Jenny threw a protective arm around her brother's shoulder. 'He can hear you, you know.' Her mother's face flashed up. *Be respectful.* She lowered her voice and spoke as calmly as she could. 'This isn't exactly a picnic for us either, Mr Evans. Do you think we wanted to leave our home and our mother behind? Have you any idea how traumatic that is for a little lad like this one 'ere?'

Lorcan stepped in, his hands spread in a calming gesture. 'It'll be all right, Tad. They've had a long journey. Let's just make them welcome, and I'm sure everything will seem better tomorrow.'

Bryn shook his head, a knowing smile finally reaching his lips. 'You never could resist a pretty one, could you, Lorcan?'

To Jenny's great annoyance, she blushed.

The bedroom had been given a thorough airing pending their arrival. The metal-framed twin beds took up most of the space, with a gap between just wide enough for a cabinet. The floorboards were bare, save for a sheepskin rug that

Jenny decided must've looked a lot better when it was still attached to its original owner. In the corner was a rocking chair with a faded gingham cushion. Louis scrambled onto the chair and began to rock backwards and forwards, clinging onto the arms. For the first time that day, a trace of a smile appeared on his lips. Jenny had to crouch to look out of the low window. The craggy moonlit mountain obscured the wider view, but she had to admit it was better than the view of the bins in the back alleys of Manchester she was used to. She pulled the frayed curtain across, rubbing the thin material between her fingers. She wondered if she could get her hands on some scraps of fabric and run up a new pair. Mrs Evans would surely appreciate that.

'Right, Louis, let's get you washed and ready for bed. Which one do you want?'

'Can't I share with you?'

'I'll be right here next to you. You've really got to learn to sleep on your own. Mummy indulged you far too much if you ask me.' She pulled his hand. 'Come on, before this water gets cold.'

She dunked the rough flannel in the bowl of warm water Lorcan had provided and rubbed it round the back of Louis's grubby neck.

'Ow, that hurts.'

She ignored his protest. 'Swish your hands in the bowl, Louis, give them a good wash.'

Once he was in bed, she tucked the bedclothes in tight, pinning him down as though this would prevent his escape. Then she held her hands behind her back. 'I've got a surprise for you. Which hand do you want?'

Louis tried to sit up.

'Oh no you don't, you need to stay lying down or else you're not getting it.'

He frowned as he concentrated on his choice, his eyes darting left and right.

'Quick, Louis, which hand? It's not that hard.'

'Left.'

'Ta-da!' The knitted rabbit hung limply in her left hand.

'Peter!'

'Sneaked him into my case, didn't I?' She tucked the rabbit under Louis's arm next to his teddy and kissed his forehead. 'Now go to sleep.'

In spite of his exhaustion, it took Louis almost an hour to settle. Jenny rubbed his back in ever-decreasing circles until, hardly daring to breathe, she picked up her cane and backed out of the room.

Downstairs, Lorcan sat by the stove, absently stroking the dog's head, which was resting in his lap. His dark hair had been swept off his face in an apparent attempt to tame the curls and his complexion bore testament to the amount of time he must spend outdoors.

Jenny tapped her cane on the stone floor. 'Am I all right to come in?'

The dog lifted its head and shuffled off to lie down in front of the hearth. Lorcan rose from his chair. 'Yes, please have this one, it's comfier.'

She sat down on the chair, so devoid of stuffing it almost swallowed her whole. 'Where're your mum and dad then?'

25

'Mam's still poorly in bed and Tad's gone up already. Milking starts at five thirty.'

'Five thirty in the morning?' Jenny asked, her eyes widening at the thought of Bryn Evans having to be up and about at such an ungodly hour.

Lorcan pulled up a stout wooden chair. 'Best time of the day it is.' He winked. 'You'll soon see.'

She crossed her legs and the dressing gown she had thrown over her nightdress fell open slightly. She noticed Lorcan look before averting his eyes and making a desperate attempt to show he hadn't noticed. 'Erm . . . Louis asleep, is he?'

Jenny wrapped the dressing gown tighter and uncrossed her legs. 'You can ask me about it . . . if you want.'

Lorcan scratched behind his ear and ran his hands through his hair, a gesture she would come to learn meant he was feeling uncomfortable. 'What happened?' he ventured.

She spoke matter-of-factly. She was used to it now, could hardly remember a time before. 'Caught polio when I was twelve. Left me very weak down the left-hand side, especially my leg, which as you can see is not quite as thick as the other one. Had a leg brace as a kid but now I get about with this.' She indicated the cane propped up by the chair. 'It affected my lungs too. I was in hospital for three months. Then I goes and gets bronchitis when I was fourteen, which really didn't help, but I'm still here, battling on.'

'That's so . . .' Lorcan searched for the word. 'I mean, that's . . . well, it's . . .' He gave up. 'So you decided to evacuate because of your health?'

Jenny sighed. 'That was partly it, but also because of Louis.

Mum didn't think he'd survive on his own. Well, you've seen what he's like. He's such a baby sometimes.'

'Must be daunting for him, though. Coming to a place so far away from home, a foreign country almost.' Lorcan laughed, his eyes glinting in the light of the fire. 'He'll be all right though. I'll make sure of it. And Mam and Tad, they'll love him too. I know they wanted two strong boys, but we'll manage.'

'Yeah, I suppose kids are adaptable,' she agreed. 'It's my mother I worry about. She's on her own now since Daddy died. Everything falls on her, the running of the house, earning a living for all of us. She's a wages clerk in a factory. I help out of course, but my work's on and off like, and now with this war on and me out here, I doubt there'll be much demand for my services.'

'Oh, what services?' Lorcan asked.

'Dressmaking. People bring me a pattern and some fabric and I make the clothes up for them on my Singer. I also do alterations, mending, that sort of stuff. It suits me, I can work from home and it's not too physically demanding.'

'There might be more work for you than you think. People are going to have to look after the clothes they've got.'

A gust of wind hollered down the chimney, the other-worldly sound making Jenny shiver and glance over her shoulder. Lorcan reached for the poker and prodded at the logs. 'Your father's dead, you say?'

She closed her eyes, trying to remember her father as a living, breathing person, instead of a lifeless corpse, dressed in his best suit, nestled inside a coffin that seemed too small for him. Barely a day had passed when she hadn't regretted her decision to go to that funeral home. 'Heart attack,' she confirmed. 'Died when I was seventeen. Louis was just a baby. He has no memories of him.' She massaged the top of her cane. 'Poor little sod. He could've done with a father figure to toughen him up. Mother's spoiled him rotten.'

Lorcan looked at her, his glacier-blue eyes narrowed in sympathy. His voice was low, barely audible. 'I can't imagine not having Tad.'

'What about brothers or sisters?'

He shook his head. 'No, it's just me.'

'How old are you?'

'Twenty-two.'

'Old enough to be called up, then.'

'Farming's a reserved occupation. I'd like to enlist, but Mam's dead against it and I'm not sure I could put her through it, to be honest.' He gave a resigned shrug. 'No, I'm needed here so I'll just have to be content with that.'

'You're still contributing, though. We all need to eat.'

'Aye, you're right, I suppose.'

Jenny smiled and drummed her fingers on the arm of the chair, gazing around the kitchen with its low wooden beams and uneven stone floor. The dresser in the corner sported three shelves of blue and white crockery depicting Chinese-looking temples, and a row of copper pans hung from a ceiling rack. She took another surreptitious glance at Lorcan as he bent to stoke the fire. There were definitely worse places they could have ended up.

3

The house was in darkness when Candice arrived home. She shook out her rain-blasted umbrella and eased her key into the lock, cursing as the plastic bag got caught round the door handle. 'Damn,' she whispered as she wrestled it free. A pile of pizza delivery leaflets and brown window envelopes cluttered the communal hall, which as usual stank of mildewed carpet. She would never get used to that smell. She fought her way past the two bikes leaning against the wall, just beside the notice asking people not to leave their bikes in the hall.

A sleepy voice wafted down the stairs. 'Candice, is that you?'

'Yes, Beau. Sorry, did I wake you?'

She bounded up the stairs and found him in bed, propped up on the pillows, his hands clasped around the back of his head.

'Why're you in bed anyway? It's only eleven thirty. Not like you to turn in before one.'

'Dunno.' He shrugged. 'It was boring without you. Why've you been so long?'

She sat on the bed and took out a package. 'I told you it was Jenny's hundredth birthday party. We needed all the

29

guests we could muster because she's no family. I had to stay, and then when I put her to bed she wanted to talk, and she can't half rabbit when she gets going. Any road, I've brought you a couple of tatty pies and a sausage roll.'

He folded his arms and shook his head. 'I'm not hungry any more. I've gone past it.'

'There's stuff in the fridge. You could have got yourself something.'

'Not my department, though, is it? Cooking's your job. Do I ever ask you to empty the bins?'

'What's that got to do with anything? If I came across a bin that was overflowing and you weren't here to empty it, then I'd just get on with it.'

'Fine,' he said huffily. 'I'm too tired for an argument. Have it your way.'

She settled herself next to him, her fingers tracing the outline of the angel tattoo across his chest. She ignored the stench of weed coming off his hair. 'I'm sorry, Beau.'

He turned to face her, his words floating out on a sigh. 'No, I'm sorry. I'm being pathetic. I just miss you so much when you're not here. I hate to think of you partying without me.'

'Partying?' She laughed. 'Believe me, I'd rather have been here with you.'

'Yeah, I suppose the Final Curtain Care Home isn't exactly a hotbed of iniquity.'

'Stop calling it that, Beau. You know damn well it's Green Meadows Senior Living.'

He stayed quiet, his fingers twisting the sheet. 'I don't like you having to work so hard. I feel like I'm not pulling my weight.'

'Of course you are. It's not your fault your line of work's so unpredictable. In any case, you got three hundred quid for that wedding the other week, and when word starts to spread, there'll be more. You're still waiting to hear about the regular Thursday-night slot at that bar in Fallowfield too, don't forget. If that comes off, then we'll be laughing. Together with my wage, we might be able to afford to buy somewhere one day.' She snuggled into his chest. 'Imagine that, eh? An actual place of our own.'

She closed her eyes, the rhythmic rise and fall of Beau's chest allowing her mind to wander. 'I've never lived in a house that wasn't owned by somebody else. Never really had a place to call home.'

'Right, that's it,' Beau said firmly. He flung the duvet off and sat on the edge of the bed, his fingers meshed in his hair. 'I'm gonna get a proper job. It's just not right you having to carry the load.'

She eased herself onto her knees, massaging his shoulders as she spoke. 'Give over. You'll do no such thing. I'm not having you giving up on your dreams. You're an extremely talented singer-songwriter. You're the whole package. You've got the voice, the looks, the charisma. I'm not going to let you waste all that. You'll get your big break one day.' She kissed the back of his neck. 'You should go on one of them talent shows on the telly. You're way better than some of the rubbish they get on there.'

He pulled her onto his knee. 'What did I do to deserve you, eh?' He kissed her mouth, his familiar tobacco-scented breath strangely comforting. 'Now, why don't you fix me something proper to eat.' He held up the bag of buffet

31

remnants, his expression one of disgust. 'Instead of this shit.'

He was in a bad mood now anyway. Might as well get it over with. 'You're going to have to fend for yourself for a week. I'm going away.'

'What? When? Away where?' There was a hint of panic in his voice.

'Jenny wants me to go with her to Italy. It's something she has to do. I'm not exactly sure what yet, but once I've heard the whole story, she assures me I'll understand. It's for an anniversary, a memorial or something. It's not until May, so you've plenty of time to get used to the idea.'

'You're leaving me?'

'It's only a week.'

'You're leaving me on my own for a whole week?'

She patted him playfully on his arm. 'You'll be fine, silly.' She leaned in to kiss his cheek, but he turned his head away.

'Beau?'

He tugged at the sheet, rolled over and faced the window. 'I don't want you to go, Candice, and I'm hoping it's not too much to ask for my feelings to be taken into consideration.' He reached out and switched off the bedside lamp. 'Hopefully by morning you'll have come to your senses.'

4

The glittery stars have clogged up the vacuum cleaner just like I knew they would. The number balloons have lost their plumpness, the silver foil now wrinkled and barely fit for purpose. It comes to us all.

I'm sitting with Frank in the conservatory, both alone with our thoughts as we stare at the withered snowdrops next to the newly blossomed daffodils. The sun's streaming in now, but over yonder, the sky's the colour of a particularly nasty bruise. I had a bad night after talking to Candice. I'm not sure dwelling on the past is all that good for me, but sometimes you have to face up to it and do what's right, no matter how painful. I've put a big red ring around the date of the anniversary on the calendar. It's something to aim for. At a hundred years old, I don't make any long-term plans obviously, but if I can survive for the next couple of months and do what I need to do, then I can die in peace.

I sneak a look at Frank. His eyes are closed, his hands clasped under his chin, supporting his head. He's as dapper as usual. I don't think I've ever seen him without his paisley cravat. Apart from the time he dribbled his mulligatawny down it. Now, there's somebody who shakes, bless him – St Vitus's Dance my mother would have called it – but life in here would be a lot less cheery without him. He's always got an amusing tale to tell. As a raconteur, he could give that Stephen Fry a run for his money. And what he doesn't know about musicals isn't worth knowing. He's very quiet today, though. I reach over and touch his arm. 'What's up, chuck?'

He lifts his head and attempts a smile, although his brain forgets to tell his eyes. With a juddering hand he takes out his hanky and makes a ham-fisted attempt to dab his cheeks.

'Frank, love. Whatever's the matter?'

'Sorry,' he sniffs. 'I had no desire to bring the mood down, what with the balloons still up.'

And suddenly I remember. I feel like the most selfish person in the world. 'It's a year today, isn't it?'

He nods and presses the handkerchief to his mouth.

'I'm so sorry, Frank.'

Really, what can you say to someone who's lost the love of their life? There's an awful lot of claptrap bandied about these days, none of it useful. 'You'll always miss him. You're meant to.'

When he speaks again, his voice is rough, as though he's gargling with gravel. 'I count myself lucky, Jenny. We had nearly sixty years together and made it to the final chapter.'

I squeeze his hand. 'It would've been nice to know what was in the epilogue, though. It's never enough, is it, Frank?'

He snorts out a half-hearted laugh before his voice cracks again. 'I just miss him so much. I don't know how I've survived a year without him.'

'It's important to keep talking about him. Keep his memory alive in your heart, remember the good times. Come on, tell me more about him. Where did you two meet?'

34

He turns in his chair to face me, and I see his features are suddenly animated. 'I replied to his advertisement in the local paper.'

I raise my eyebrows and he laughs out loud.

'Not that kind of advertisement. This was 1960 and homosexuality was against the law. No, he was a French polisher and I needed something polishing.' There's a cheeky glint in his eyes now.

'Dare I ask what?'

'I'd just started my own cabinet-making and furniture-restoring business and a customer had brought in a treasured table that had a deep scorch mark I was unable to remove. Ernest came with his bag of cloths, oils and lubricants, donned a pair of white cotton gloves and proceeded to caress that wood as though he cared about nothing else in this world. The sheen on it by the time he'd finished, well . . .' Frank places his hand across his heart. 'I knew I was in the company of an artist. I was immediately smitten.'

'I imagine it must've been difficult, though, given the times.'

'I can't deny that, but we loved each other and that was all that mattered.'

'There you are!'

We both turn as Candice enters the room and interrupts our little chat. I forget to close my mouth as I stare at her. 'What happened to you?'

Instinctively her hand flies to her cropped chestnut hair. Yesterday it was down to her waist; now it barely reaches her chin.

'Why? Don't you like it?'

'It's . . . it's different. But why? You had such lovely long tresses.'

She looks at her reflection in the conservatory glass and attempts to fluff up what's left of it. 'It was Beau's idea. He even gave me the money for it. He cut a picture out of a magazine. He thinks it's more edgy. Much more suited to someone who works in the beauty industry.'

'But you work in a residential care home, Candice. Wiping up after old people. We're not fussed about the edginess of your hair.'

'Ah, well you see, Beau's agreed that I can take an eyebrow course, and then I'll be able to have clients at home, you know, in my spare time. When I've saved up enough, I'll be able to do Beauty Therapy Level Two and get a job in a proper salon.' She wrinkles her nose at me. 'You really don't like it?'

I exchange a look with Frank, who thus far hasn't been able to tear his gaze away from what I can only describe as a hatchet job. 'As long as you like it, Candice, that's all that matters.'

'Beau loves it. I've just come straight from the hairdresser's, so he's only seen a selfie, but he sent me back a heart-eyes emoji. Look.'

Don't get me wrong, I'm no Luddite. It might even surprise you to learn I can use the internet, but I've no idea what it is I'm supposed to be looking at here.

What on earth is a heart-eyes emoji?

She thrusts the phone back into her tabard pocket. 'Right, I'm off to fetch the tea trolley. Do you two want yours in here?'

Frank presses himself out of his chair. 'No thank you, Candice. I feel the need to take the air.'

'Shall I come with you?' I ask.

'No, no, I'm grand, Jenny, thanks all the same.'

We both watch as he leaves the conservatory, his gait still strong and purposeful. There are many reasons people come to Green Meadows and we all need varying amounts of care. Even at my age, I'm not the most labour-intensive resident they've got, but Frank moved here for the company. Some folks like to stay in their own homes after losing their loved ones, but he couldn't cope with it. He kept seeing Ernest at every turn, and the memories were so vivid it was like he was still alive. Two toothbrushes in the pot beside the sink, Ernest's slippers resting on the hearthrug, his overcoat hanging in the hall, flecks of dandruff still speckling the collar. The house was like a shrine to him, a shrine Frank couldn't bring himself to dismantle and then continue living there without him.

'Jenny? Jenny?'

I've allowed my thoughts to wander again, and now Candice is shaking my shoulder, her perfect eyebrows raised in concern. 'Yes.'

'I said, I'm due on a break in half an hour. I'll bring your tea then and we can carry on with your story.'

She's such a sweet girl. She must have better things to do than listen to me ramble on, but it's important she knows everything before we embark on our trip to Italy. I just hope she can handle it.

5

It took a few moments for her head to clear, to banish the fug of sleep that seemed to have robbed her of her faculties. She felt the bed bounce, followed by warm breath in her ear. 'Jenny, wake up. I need the toilet.'

Without lifting her head, she turned to look at Louis's face beside her on the pillow, the close proximity of his stale breath causing her to look away again.

'Can't you hold it?' She pulled the alarm clock close to her face. 'Aargh, Louis, it's only five o'clock.'

His hand was clamped around his crotch. 'I need to go now.'

'You'll have to use the pot under the bed. I'm not traipsing down to the bottom of the garden in the middle of the night.'

Back home in Manchester, they were fortunate enough to have an inside toilet. At least it could be argued that they had an inside toilet. It was situated in a lean-to on the side of the kitchen, and it was so cold in there that in winter the water sometimes froze and they had to take a broom handle to it before they could go. But here, there were no such luxuries, and last night she and Louis had had to make their way along a crazy-paved path with the aid of an oil lamp. There was no flush and no toilet paper, just a bucket of water and a rusty nail holding squares of cut-up newspaper. The smell of ammonia had caused their eyes to water, and Louis had been decidedly unimpressed. It had been something else for him to cry about.

When she woke again an hour later, Louis had crawled into bed beside her and manoeuvred himself under her arm so that the weight of his head had cut off the blood supply to her fingers. She opened and closed her palm to dispel the resulting pins and needles. 'Louis, can you just sit up a minute.'

He rubbed his eyes and blinked in the half-light. 'Can we go home today?'

She stroked his face, choosing her words carefully. 'Oh, my dear sweet Louis. You know we can't go home just yet. It might not be safe with the bombs an' all. We're better off here in the quiet countryside. You'll like it once you get to know everybody. And it's so pretty, isn't it? Look.' She drew back the curtain and pointed at the mountain looming over the garden. 'Look at that. Isn't it beautiful?' She cocked her head and listened carefully. 'I can hear running water.' She eased herself onto her knees and craned her neck to look more closely. 'Oh, would you believe it? There's a flippin' waterfall, Louis. How about that, eh?' She stared at the sparkling funnel of water plummeting off the mountain and into a dark green mossy pool beneath.

Louis stuck his thumb into his mouth and curled up in the warm space where Jenny had been lying. She rested her elbows on the wide stone windowsill, mesmerised by the glittering water. She ducked down when she saw Lorcan approach, dressed only in a long shirt. Allowing herself a peep, she watched as he stuck his hands under the flow, sloshing the water onto his face. Then he gripped the hem of his shirt and in one fluid movement pulled the garment over his head. Embarrassed by his nakedness, she was still unable to look away, and instead continued to watch as he stood under the waterfall with his back to her, his tanned arms in sharp contrast to his pale torso. He turned around then and looked directly up at her window. She caught only a hint of his amused smile before she ducked down once more, the tympanic rhythm of her heartbeat resounding in her ear, her cheeks crimson with shame.

He was seated at the breakfast table, carving thick slices of bread, as they entered the kitchen. Jenny could hardly meet his eye. 'Mornin', Lorcan.'

'Morning. Did you sleep well?'

She nodded. 'Yes thank you, we did.' She squeezed Louis's hand. 'Didn't we, Louis?'

He stayed silent. 'Manners, Louis,' she whispered.

'Yes thank you,' he managed, his voice muffled by the teddy bear clamped under his nose.

'Well, sit down, the pair of you, there's tea in the pot. Mam'll be down in a minute. She's feeling much better today and is keen to meet you. Tad's just cleaning up after the milking, so we'll wait and then we can all have breakfast together.' The dog, Brindle, sat by his side, his hopeful, adoring eyes never leaving his young master's face. Lorcan tossed a cube of cheese into the air and the grateful creature jumped up and snapped his jaws around it.

Louis giggled. 'He caught it.'

'Of course he caught it. He's clever, see,' said Lorcan. 'Very intelligent, border collies are, they can—' He stopped as the door opened. 'Mam, you're here.' He gestured towards Jenny and Louis. 'Come and say hello.'

Mrs Evans was a petite woman, with an air of compact neatness about her. Her blue eyes were ringed with tiredness, but her mouth afforded the two interlopers a generous smile.

Jenny held out her hand, adopting a formal tone. 'I'm pleased to meet you, Mrs Evans. Thank you for having us.' She hardly recognised her own voice. Her mother would be so proud.

'You're both very welcome. I'm sure it can't be easy for you.' The woman knelt down so she was level with Louis's face. 'And what's your name, little man?'

Louis spoke into his teddy bear, his reply barely audible. 'Louis Francis Tanner.'

She pulled his arm away from his mouth and took hold of the teddy. 'And what's his name, then?'

'Mrs Nesbitt,' whispered Louis. 'She's a girl bear. Jenny's going to make her a little skirt so you can tell.'

'Mrs Nesbitt, is it? Well, there's lovely. Did you choose the name?'

Louis nodded. 'And I've brought my rabbit. He's called Peter.' It was the most he'd said to a stranger since leaving home.

'You're fond of Beatrix Potter then, are you?'

Louis wrinkled his nose. 'Who?'

Mrs Evans straightened up, laughing. '*Who?* he says.' She ruffled his hair. 'Come on then, let's get some breakfast inside you and then you can start on your chores.'

'Oh, we're keen to help, Mrs Evans,' Jenny interjected. 'We'll do whatever we can, I promise. We'll try not to be a burden. I know we're not quite what you were expecting when you agreed to take two evacuees, but we're grateful just the same.'

The woman waved her away. 'We'll manage, Jenny. And less of the Mrs Evans. My name's Delyth – you can call me Del.' She turned to Louis. 'And you little man, can call me Mammy Del, okay?'

Louis looked unsure. 'You're not my mummy. I want my real mummy.' His chin dimpled and he took a shuddering breath.

'Louis!' said Jenny. 'Don't be so rude. I'm really sorry, Mrs Evans. He doesn't mean it.'

'I do mean it.' Louis stamped his foot on the floor. 'I want to go home.'

She gritted her teeth. 'Well you can't,' she hissed, fighting with every fibre to control her temper.

Lorcan placed a hand on Louis's shoulder. 'I could really use a strong boy like you to help me collect the eggs. Do you think you could do that? You can carry the basket for me.'

'Go on, Louis,' Jenny urged. 'Go with Lorcan, then you can see the hens.'

Louis nodded in defeat and slipped his hand into Lorcan's.

'Thank you,' she mouthed.

Lorcan winked as he shrugged on his jacket. 'Any time.'

After breakfast, Jenny insisted on clearing away and washing up the pots. Lorcan and his father had taken Louis off to bottle-feed the orphaned lambs. Delyth sat in the armchair close to the range as she waited for the pan of water to boil. 'Lorcan tells me you're quite the seamstress.'

'Yes, I'm a dressmaker. My mother taught me to sew at an early age. I used to make bookmarks, embroider handkerchiefs and tablecloths, that kind of thing. Then I progressed to making clothes.' She smoothed down the folds of her skirt. 'I made this.'

Delyth nodded her approval. 'You're incredibly talented. It's lovely.'

'I could make you something, Mrs Evans . . . I mean Del. If you could get hold of some fabric and a sewing machine, I could make you a nice dress.'

'I already have a good dress, Jenny. One good dress is all I need. For chapel on Sundays. No need to waste time or money on getting another one.'

'Oh, all right then. Well let me know if you change your mind.'

She poured the boiling water into the sink and added the suds, agitating the water with a wooden spoon to form a pillow of bubbles. She could feel Delyth's eyes on her as she scrubbed the plates clean.

'Are you in any pain?'

'No, no pain now. I can do most things, but I get tired more easily than your average twenty-one-year-old. And I have a weak chest, a combination of the polio and a bout of ill-timed bronchitis. It was touch and go at one point and the prognosis wasn't good, but thankfully I'm still here.' She turned and smiled, her hands still immersed in the water. 'I have to keep going for Mummy's sake, and for Louis's too. She was truly devastated when my father died. Obviously you'd expect her to be upset, but her grief was unlike anything I'd ever seen. She took to her bed for months and left me to fend for our Louis. He was only a baby, and I hadn't quite turned seventeen and still had all my own health problems.'

'That must have been difficult,' Delyth empathised. 'You must be one strong young lady to cope with all that. How's your mammy now?'

Jenny dried her hands on her apron and thought about her mother. The long silences that could stretch on for days, the hastily hidden half-bottles of whisky she'd find behind cushions. There were good days too, though, plenty of them. Her mother's relapses into grief had lessened over the past four years. She excelled at her office job in the factory, which came with a decent wage, and was determined to make a comfortable life for her two children. She smothered Louis, babied him almost to the point of suffocation, trying to give him the love and protection of two parents but in doing so not allowing him to grow up, or experience the rough-and-tumble life of any other boy his age. Consequently, he was timid, shy and frightened of his own shadow. It was no wonder she had resisted the first wave of evacuations so vehemently. Nobody could protect her children as well as Connie Tanner could.

'She's much better now, thank you,' Jenny said. 'Not happy about having to send us away, obviously, but she knows it's for the best and hopefully it won't be for too long.' She folded up the tea towel. 'We'll write to her this morning. Let her know we're safe and have been welcomed into a lovely family.'

Delyth nodded. 'That should put her mind at rest. I can't imagine having to send my Lorcan away. I thank God he's in a reserved occupation. I couldn't bear to think of him fighting in some foreign country.'

'He's a credit to you, Mrs Evans. So thoughtful, and he's a natural with our Louis.'

'Thank you. I agree with you, but of course I'm biased.' She stood up and turned to leave, pausing at the door to give Jenny a queer look. It seemed an age before she spoke again, and when she did, there was a note of steel in her voice that had not been present before. 'Try not to break his heart, will you?'

6

She dumped the bag of groceries on the kitchen counter, fished half a dozen used tea bags out of the plug hole and tossed them in the bin.

'Hiya, babe.' Beau's arms encircled her waist as he kissed the back of her neck.

'Would it kill you to put the tea bags in the bin, Beau?'

'Ah, don't have a go as soon as you walk through the door. I've been working flat out on new material today.'

'Oh, really? And you couldn't have found five minutes to run the vac round?'

Ignoring her question, he held her at arm's length and cocked his head. 'Let's have a proper look then.' He rubbed the ends of her hair between his fingers. 'It's not bad. A bit too short maybe.'

She instinctively tugged at her hair. 'What? This was your idea. Chin-length you said you wanted.'

'It's fine, stop whining.' He peered into the bag of groceries. 'I'll leave you to get the tea and then I'll tell you all about my great idea.' He kissed the tip of her nose. 'Fetch us a can of Special Brew whilst you're at it.'

'Beau, can't you at least get your own drink.' She gestured

around the kitchen at the unpacked bags and stacks of dirty dishes. 'I've got my hands full here.'

'Oh, okay then.' He took a can from on top of the fridge, pulled the ring and took a long guzzle. 'Sorry, I didn't realise it was so much trouble.'

After their meal, she lay on the sofa with her legs outstretched, her bare feet resting in Beau's lap.

'What do you want to watch then?' he asked.

She didn't care what they watched. She could happily just stare at him all evening. He was wearing his usual skinny black jeans, ripped at the knee, his old Jack Daniel's T-shirt and a single strand of metallic beads. Unkempt, dishevelled and a tiny bit grubby, but utterly irresistible.

'Never mind the television. Why don't you tell me about this great idea you've had?'

'Okay,' he drawled. 'If you insist.'

He pushed her legs away, stood up and fished a piece of paper out of his back pocket. He held it aloft, so high that she couldn't make out what it was.

She tried to reach it. 'Give it 'ere then.'

He snatched it away. 'No, I'm going to give you a chance to explain first. I'll give you a clue. It's a receipt.'

She felt a flush of heat in her ears. 'A receipt? What for?'

'Seriously, you can't remember making a frivolous purchase?'

'Frivolous purchase?' she echoed. 'Erm, no. I . . . I haven't bought anything for myself in ages. I can't think . . .'

'So the lipstick was for me then?'

'Lipstick? But I haven't . . .' She sighed with relief as she remembered. 'Oh, that one. That was a present for Jenny.'

'Jenny?'

'You know, from Green Meadows. The one who turned a hundred yesterday. I told you, you never listen.'

She picked up her magazine, idly flicking through the pages, indicating that the conversation was over even though her gut told her it was far from it.

'Are you for real, Candice? You spent seventeen pounds fifty on an effing lipstick for a centurion?'

'She's a *centenarian*. A centurion is summat to do with the Romans.' She returned to the magazine, staring at the blank space where the picture of the ravishing model used to be; the one with the short hair that perfectly complemented her elfin features instead of making her look like a pre-pubescent schoolboy. She could feel her throat tightening as tears threatened.

Beau sat down beside her, his tone gentle as he stroked her cheek. 'What *are* you like, eh? You're such a soft touch. It's one of the many things I love about you, but we can't afford it if we're both going to reach our potential.' He held up the receipt again. 'Things like this are damaging to our ambitions. You want that beauty course, don't you?'

'You know I do.'

'Then it's a good job I've got the perfect solution.'

'Please tell me it doesn't involve buying a lottery ticket.'

He reached down the side of the sofa and brought out a red hard-backed book. 'This . . . this is the answer.'

She sat up a little straighter. 'What's that?'

'It's a ledger.'

'Come again?'

He shuffled towards her and opened the pages. 'See all these columns here, this is where we record our transactions.'

'Transactions?'

'Yes, expenditure and that. This column here is where we write down exactly what we've spent our money on.'

She pushed the ledger away. 'Seems like a lot of faffing about to me.'

'Candice, you don't have to worry about it if you don't want to. Let me take charge.' He waved the receipt in her face. 'We both know how hopeless you are with money. We'll never save anything if you keep on with this reckless spending.'

'Reckless spending? For God's sake, Beau, it was one lipstick and it wasn't even for me. I can't remember the last time I bought anything for myself. You might like to lounge around in the same pair of jeans and T-shirt for days on end, but I wouldn't mind the occasional new top every now and then.' She folded her arms and turned away from him. A few seconds of silence passed before she felt him nuzzling her neck.

'Babe, you know it makes sense.' He traced his finger along her collarbone. 'Come on, don't be like this. I'm the muggins who's going to be doing all the work. All you need to do is give me a receipt for everything you spend. We can then work out where there are savings to be made. It'll just make us think about where our money's going. Hmm?' He nudged her shoulder. 'What do you say? Shall we give it a whirl? It's entirely up to you, babe, we won't if you don't want to.'

He obviously took her silence to mean she wasn't convinced. 'Okay, you're right. It's a terrible idea. Who cares if you have to work at the Final Curtain for the rest of your natural? Here's me thinking you wanted to better yourself, but if you're happy taking care of other folks' bodily functions for the minimum wage, then I'll say no more about it.' He moved to

49

the end of the sofa, picked up the remote and aimed it at the television.

She sneaked a look at his profile. His high cheekbones and ridiculously long eyelashes were wasted on him. Wasted on any man for that matter. He was right, though. It was going to take a determined effort for them both to achieve their dreams.

'All right then, we'll give it a go.'

He pressed the mute button. 'Only if you're sure, babe. I don't want to force you into anything.'

'I'm sure.' She smiled. 'I'm sorry, I know you're only trying to help. What do I have to do?'

'Nothing. I'll do all the boring nitty-gritty stuff. I'll try to fit it in with everything else I've got going on. All you need to do is give me the receipt every time you spend anything. That way we'll see exactly where our money's going and where we can make savings.'

She snuggled against his chest, grateful that he was taking things so seriously. 'Thanks, Beau.'

'I doubt there'll be any spare cash to squander on a trip to Italy, though,' he continued. 'But this way we'll be able to save enough for us both to go away together one day.'

'Oh no, it's fine, Jenny's paying for everything.'

She noticed his lips stiffen. 'Is she now?'

She wasn't in the mood for another one of his sulks about the trip. She knew he would never give his blessing, but she'd promised Jenny she'd go with her and she had no intention of breaking that promise. Beau would just have to get used to the idea.

7

You get to do a lot of sitting around at my age. Let's face it, I'm not the most agile person in here. Upstairs, I'm still as sharp as a tack, though. I was once fluent in three languages, so maybe that's helped to keep the old grey matter from turning to sludge. I like to be occupied, keep my brain ticking over with Sudoku or crosswords, that sort of thing. I used to enjoy playing bridge and poker, but holding the cards became difficult. There's many a time I've dropped my hand, revealing everything I've got to my delighted opponents.

'Come on, Frank,' I say. 'You've been staring at them tiles for half your life.'

He's feeling a bit more himself since last week. So much so that he was up for a game of Scrabble, but he's taking so long over his go that I'm sure his mind's still elsewhere.

'We should set a time limit,' I tell him. 'I don't know how long I've got. It's all right for you, you're only a youngster. I might pop my clogs before this game's over.'

He allows me a gracious smile. 'You're good for a few years yet. A hundred is the new eighty.' The big red ring on my calendar flashes up in my mind. God, I hope he's right.

He finishes placing his tiles on the board. 'There you are.

I make that . . . let's see . . . dum-de-dum-de-dum . . .'

He's pretending to work it out but he knows damn well what it adds up to.

'Thirty-eight, plus the fifty for going out, so that's eighty-eight.'

'Well done, Frank,' I say through gritted teeth. There's no way I can win now. It's good to see the smile back on his face, though.

'Ernest was an absolute demon at Scrabble. I could rarely beat him. He really was a formidable opponent.'

I raise my eyebrows. 'Unlike me, you mean?'

There's a strange look in his eye that I can't quite interpret. 'You're formidable in so many other ways, Jenny.'

Candice breezes in and takes a seat at the table. Her hair has been forced into a stubby ponytail and she smells of chip fat. She sniffs the crook of her arm. 'Phwoar, I'm going to have to change my clothes. Mrs Culpepper paid me extra to give the extractor hood a good going-over, and then I got stuck into the fridge.' She examines her fingers. 'I've broken two nails in the process, but it's worth it for this.' She pulls a roll of notes out of her tabard pocket and lowers her voice. 'Thirty quid in cash.'

'That's lovely, Candice,' I say. 'Make sure you treat yourself to something nice.'

'Oh God, no. I'm giving it to Beau. He's started an official fund so I can save up for Beauty Therapy Level Two.' Her face takes on a dreamy look, one that makes me want to shake her, to be honest. 'He's so thoughtful.'

I have a horrible niggling feeling, but she seems so happy I'm forced to keep my opinions to myself. After all, I've never even met the bloke. 'Has he got any more concerts in the pipeline then?'

She laughs. 'Concerts? He's hardly Ed Sheeran, Jenny. No, not yet, but he's still waiting on the nod for a regular slot at a bar in Fallowfield.'

'I see, well let's hope something comes of it.' I fold the Scrabble board in half, trapping the tiles to make it easier to funnel them into the cloth bag.

'Did you win?' asks Candice.

'Did I 'eck as like.' I toss my head in Frank's direction. 'This one here had the Q, the X and the Z. I can't compete with luck like that.' I wink at him to show I'm not really a sore loser.

Candice holds out the tile bag for me as I tip them in. Her phone buzzes in her pocket and she gives a furtive glance towards the door. Mrs Culpepper doesn't like the staff to have their mobile phones on whilst they're on duty. I can see her fingers are itching to check who it is.

'Go on, have a look,' I say. 'I won't snitch.'

She gives me a grateful smile and takes out the phone. After a few seconds, her hand flies to her mouth and she all but manages to stifle a squeal.

'Good news?' I ask.

'It's Beau,' she says, nodding furiously. 'He's got that regular slot I was just telling you about. Thursday nights at the Lemon Tree, payment in cash.'

It comes as no surprise to me that Beau wouldn't be contributing to the economy. No pesky taxes for him.

'Did you hear that, Frank? Her boyfriend's got a regular . . . erm . . . gig at the Lemon Tree. We'll have to go along.'

Candice seems to find this hilarious. 'It's not your type of place, Jenny, but I'll take a video with me phone if you like and you can see for yourself how talented he is.'

She shoves the phone back into her pocket as Mrs Culpepper appears in the doorway. 'Dinner is served,' she announces in her posh, unidentifiable accent.

The meal was excellent. They always are in here. Simeon, the head chef, is such a character he really should have his own reality show. Most of the time he's in his chef's checked trousers and white gravy-splattered tunic, but when he does appear in his civvies, he'll think nothing of teaming red trousers with a – brace yourself – mustard jacket! I've seen him wear a straw boater with a gold and green striped waistcoat and spotted bow tie, just to walk to work. He has a rather cavalier approach to hand-washing, but nobody in here has died of food poisoning yet, as far as I know. He always comes out of the kitchen to check we've enjoyed our meals. I think he likes fishing for compliments, to be honest, and I always oblige. His French apple tart would not look out of place in a Paris patisserie. It's hard to tell how old he is because he's overweight in the way chefs often are and his puffy face bears no wrinkles. I'd guess at around forty.

This evening, he squats down beside my table, his knees cracking. 'How was everything tonight, my angel?' He's also an outrageous flirt.

'Simeon, that apple tart of yours is gastronomic perfection.'

He flicks me under my chin, his face only inches from mine. 'Your opinion on my tart means the world to me.' He clamps his palm to his chest. 'Thank you.' I actually think he means it.

'It was wonderful, Simon,' agrees Frank. 'Exceptionally light and buttery.'

'How many times? It's Sim-*e*-on, not Simon.'

I know Frank gets his name wrong on purpose. He finds it funny when Simeon throws his arms in the air and huffs and puffs as though that missing 'e' is the most important thing in the world. I suppose it is to him. If your surname's Sidebottom, you need a slightly more exotic first name.

I usually like to take a nap after my evening meal. Just twenty minutes or so to bridge the gap before bedtime. The sun's early March rays are streaming through the conservatory glass, giving the impression that it'll be hot outside. Candice fans herself with the *Radio Times*.

'Do you fancy a little stroll, Jenny? It'll be good to get some fresh air. Make you sleep better.'

The gardens do look quite resplendent, I have to admit, and Candice does spend a lot of time indoors. I think the fresh air will benefit her more than it'll benefit me. I nod my agreement. 'All right, Candice, but can you get my chair, and a blanket for my knees. It won't be as warm as it looks.'

I hope I've already established that there's absolutely nothing wrong with my brain, but let me remind you that I am one hundred years old, suffered from polio as a child and now have arthritic joints. Evening strolls are not something to be entered into lightly. I'm so relieved Candice has agreed to come with me to Italy. I think it's caused some friction between her and that boyfriend of hers and I'm sorry about that, but he needs to grow up a bit. Everything's in place now anyway. Flights, hotel, driver, it's all sorted. All I have to do now is stay alive.

Candice huffs a bit as she pushes my chair to the edge of the circular pond, startling the heron, which takes flight, a goldfish flapping in its beak. She applies the brake and sits down on the bench beside me, gnawing at the skin around her thumb.

'Is there something on your mind, pet?' I ask.

She turns to face me, fussing with the crocheted rug over my lap. 'How can you tell when you're really in love?'

I am genuinely thrown by this left-field question. 'Don't you know, Candice?'

She wrinkles her nose. 'I guess so, but it's so confusing sometimes.'

'You're telling me,' I reply with a barely audible snort. 'Love can be confusing. I can't argue with that.' If only she knew.

8

1940

The end of their first week at Mynydd Farm was marked by what Jenny's mother would call a proper Sunday lunch. Jenny had politely declined to attend chapel with Delyth, receiving only a slightly judgemental frown in return.

'I'll stay here and cook the lunch if you like,' said Jenny.

Delyth had changed into her only good dress and Jenny nodded her approval at the transformation. 'You look right bonny in that clobber. It really shows off your waist, and I love the little collar.'

'Yes, well, we can all make the effort once a week to praise the good Lord.' Delyth wriggled her hands into a pair of white cotton gloves. 'You sure you won't change your mind and come with me?'

'Not today, if it's all the same.'

'Very well. I'll see you later then.'

She'd started peeling the spuds when Lorcan rushed in, all wild-eyed and flustered. 'I'm afraid I've traumatised the lad. Is he here?' His arm dangled by his side, his fingers gripping the legs of a lifeless chicken. He slammed it down on the draining board and Jenny stared at the bird's broken neck.

'You mean our Louis? No, I haven't seen him.' She pointed at the chicken. 'Did . . . did you do this?'

'Yes, of course.'

'You broke its neck?'

'Well we don't tickle them to death, Jenny.'

She put down the peeler and untied her apron. 'Where is he now?'

'I don't know. He ran off, but don't worry, he can't have gone far.'

She pushed past him and hurried into the yard. 'Lou, Lou, where are you?'

Lorcan followed, echoing her. 'Louis, come out now.'

'Louis,' cried Jenny, her voice tinged with dread. 'This isn't funny any more. Come on out from wherever you are.' Aware that she sounded stern and cross, she softened her tone. 'Come on now, you little tinker.' She began patrolling the outbuildings, peering over stable doors, prodding at the mounds of hay with her cane and limping in and out of the stalls in the shippen. Breathless with fear, she grabbed Lorcan's arm. 'He . . . he's gone.' She swept her hands through her hair. The sudden exertion had made her lungs ache, and she struggled to inhale. 'Do . . . do you think he . . . he left the farm?'

'He might've, Jenny, but don't worry, he won't come to any harm even if he has.'

'You don't know that. Anything could 'appen to him. He's not yet five. He doesn't know his way around.' She clutched at her chest and sat down on the low wall surrounding the garden. 'Where's your tad?'

Lorcan nodded towards the mountain. 'Up there, checking

58

on the lambs.' He placed his hand on her shoulder. 'Are you feeling all right, Jenny?'

She dismissed his concern with a flick of her hand. 'Don't worry about me. Just fetch the donkey and we'll take the cart. If he's left the farm then he's probably gone down into Penlan.'

He shook his head. 'She's lame, we'll have to go on foot.'

As Jenny stood, her cane toppled to the ground. She kicked at it savagely. 'Damn and blast it.'

Silently Lorcan bent to retrieve it, and placed it in her hands. 'We'll find him, Jenny, trust me.' He took hold of her elbow. 'Lean on me for extra support now. It's downhill all the way into town. There you are, you can do it, see?'

She hooked her arm through his. 'I hate being so pathetic, Lorcan. It's not me. I'm a strong lass.' She tapped the side of her head. 'In here, I'm indestructible, I can do anything, but this . . .' She indicated her cane. 'It marks me out as some kind of invalid, and I hate that. I hate it.'

With Lorcan practically propelling her down the narrow lane, they reached the centre of Penlan in just over twenty minutes. Her lungs felt as though someone had taken a cheese grater to them. The cobbled main square was deserted, the shops closed, and the only sound came from the water trickling into a fountain. 'Let's try the community hall,' said Lorcan.

They crossed over the humpbacked stone bridge, Jenny trying not to think about the swirling black water below and how it could carry off a small child without so much as a by-your-leave.

'God, if anything's happened to him, I'll never forgive myself. I promised Mum I'd look after him. Louis, Louis!' Her throat felt raw, as though all the screaming had shredded her vocal cords. She stood on tiptoe and peered through the window of the community hall. 'Nothing. It's all locked up. He's not here.'

Lorcan stood with his hands on his hips, the first stirrings of doubt registering on his brow.

'Where to next?' Jenny gasped.

'Let's try the park.'

He sprinted back over the bridge, Jenny hobbling after him with a determination she hadn't thought she was capable of. Fear was a ruthless driver. She caught up with him at the iron railings.

'He's over there, look,' Lorcan said. 'On that bench.'

She squinted in the direction of his finger. 'Oh, thank the Lord.' She opened the gate and they began to walk towards Louis. 'Who's that with him? There's someone next to him, talking to him. Oh my God, he's got an ice cream. Where did he get that from? Louis, Louis, come here, you little . . .'

The relief of a moment ago was already morphing into anger. The stranger had his arm across the back of the bench, his body turned in to Louis's as he watched him lick the ice cream. 'It's good, yes?' she heard him ask, and watched in disbelief as Louis actually smiled and nodded his agreement.

As she drew level, she vented her anger at the man. 'Oi, you, what do you think you're doing?' She grabbed Louis by the arm and pulled him up. The ice cream fell off the cone and splattered onto the grass.

'Aww, Jenny, now look what you've done.'

Jenny glared at him. 'Stop whining, Louis.' She turned to

60

Lorcan. 'We need to call the police. This is a classic case of abduction, this is.'

The stranger looked alarmed as he spread his palms in a calming gesture. 'Oh no, there'll be no need for that, *cara*.' He stood up and offered his hand. 'Domenico Bernardi, but please call me Nico.'

Everybody round here sounded different to Jenny, but Nico's accent was nothing like the musical tones the Evans family spoke in; it was much more exotic. He was still holding her hand, his black eyes locked on hers as she gazed at his breathtakingly handsome face. She felt all her anger vanish and she simply couldn't look away. It was as though she'd been hypnotised or put under the most magical spell, as the rest of the world disappeared.

Lorcan's sigh brought her back to earth. 'It's all right, Jenny. I know him. Bernardi's Gelateria in town. You've probably seen it, the one with the red, white and green canopy.'

She turned at the sound of his voice. She had forgotten he was there.

Nico finally released her hand and nodded at Louis. 'I found this little chap wandering about on his own. Oh, the tears.' He placed his palm on his own chest. 'It nearly broke my heart, so what was I to do? I opened up my shop specially and gave him the magic gelato. And now he's all better.' He ran an affectionate hand over Louis's head.

'Sorry, Jenny. Don't be mad,' said Louis, kicking at the grass. He glanced up at Lorcan and jabbed his finger towards him. '*He* killed Joyce.'

'Joyce?' said Jenny.

'My favourite chicken. Lorcan killed her.'

What sort of a name was that for a chicken? She shook her head, refocusing on the important bit. 'You shouldn't have run off, Louis. Anything could have happened to you.'

'Like what?'

'Well, I don't know . . . anything.' Now wasn't the time to run through all the doom-laden scenarios with a traumatised little boy who had just witnessed the slaughter of his favourite bird.

Lorcan crouched down in front of him. 'We don't name the chickens, Louis,' he said gently. 'They're not pets, they're food.'

'I was going to bring him back, honestly,' interrupted Nico. 'He couldn't remember the name of the farm, but when he told me Lorcan had killed his chicken, I knew where he came from. He's been telling me all about how his *mamma* sent him away so he could be safe and be sure no bombs fell on his head.'

'Thank you, Nico,' said Jenny. She stared at the ground, worried that her flushed cheeks would give her away. 'I'm really grateful, we both are. I can't bear to think what might've happened if you hadn't found him.' She indicated the river. 'All that water there . . . He can't swim, you know. If he'd fallen in . . .'

Nico shushed her. 'Hey, hey, that didn't happen. Do not distress yourself with these . . . these imaginings.'

'We need to go now, Jenny,' said Lorcan, taking hold of Louis's hand. 'We've still got the lunch to get ready.'

She nodded and took Louis's other hand. 'Bye, Nico.'

'*Ciao*. Hope to see you again soon. Please come for gelato. I have a small batch of vanilla ready. I will save a scoop just for you, Jennifer.'

The way he said her full name made her skin tingle. 'Please, it's Jenny.'

Nico shook his head in exaggerated fashion. 'But Jenny is just for those stubborn biblical beasts. You are much more beautiful than a donkey. May I call you Jennifer?'

9

Bryn Evans was in the kitchen, the lifeless chicken on a wooden slab on the table in front of him. The pile of golden feathers contrasted with its pasty, pimply skin. Jenny covered Louis's eyes. 'Why don't you go and see if you can find the kittens, Louis?'

He wriggled out from under her hand and stared at Joyce, wide-eyed and curious. He took a step closer and tentatively prodded the pale flesh. 'Won't she be cold now?'

Bryn picked up the meat cleaver and held it over the chicken's head. 'She's going in the oven, sonny. That'll warm her up.' He chuckled, but it was more matter-of-fact than mean. 'We'll make a farmer of you yet, boyo.' With a resounding thwack, he brought the cleaver down and Joyce's head fell to the floor.

After supper, with Louis tucked up in bed, Lorcan and Jenny took a stroll out to the waterfall behind the house. The bright moonlight illuminated the path, turning the mountain mono-chrome. Jenny stared up at the little white blobs on the slopes. 'How on earth do those lambs cling on?'

'They don't always. I've seen a fair few bobbing in the water below the waterfall.'

She thumped his arm. 'Stop it, don't tease me.'

'It's true. I'm not kidding you, Jenny. It's horrible listening to their mams calling for them, I can tell you. Can melt the hardest of hearts. Even Tad's.'

'It makes my legs turn to jelly just thinking about it. I'm not good with heights. I remember when I came home from hospital after the polio, my father arranged for a special outing, a trip to Blackpool. He was that excited, I think he'd arranged it more for himself than for me. Anyway, we went to the Tower and he paid an extra sixpence each for us both to go up to the top in the lift. Well, when we got there, I couldn't step out and onto the viewing platform. My legs just wouldn't cooperate. I blamed it on the polio, but the truth was, I was absolutely terrified. I was quite literally frozen with fear.'

'Oh dear,' laughed Lorcan. 'I suppose we all have our phobias. I'm not that fond of mice, to be honest. A bit of a drawback for a farmer.'

They came to a wooden bench beside a cluster of faded daffodils and sat down. Jenny picked off a crusty petal, rolling it between her fingers. 'What's Nico like, then?'

He drew his eyebrows together. 'Why do you ask?'

'Erm . . . well . . .'

How could she tell him that since their fleeting encounter a few hours before, she had been unable to get Nico out of her mind? She couldn't explain it. Perhaps there was no rational explanation. When his eyes had met hers, she'd felt something click. As though everything that had gone before had been leading up to that moment. It was like slotting in the final piece of a jigsaw, a satisfaction that her life was now complete. It sounded ridiculous even to her own ears.

'He came over from Italy with his family a few years back.' Lorcan's voice jolted her back to the present. 'Runs their café and ice cream business.'

She leaned in and nudged him playfully. 'Am I sensing some history between the pair of you?'

He scuffed the dirt with his feet. 'No, not really. It's just that he's so . . . Well, he's charming, isn't he, and the local girls can't seem to get enough of him. He has the looks of a film star and he runs an ice cream parlour. How can us simple farmers compete with that, eh?' He gave a short laugh, but there was no humour in it.

Jenny sneaked a look at him as he gazed wistfully at the mountain, his shoulders sagging in the resigned manner of somebody who knew they'd already been beaten before the race had begun.

After a moment, he slapped his palms on his thighs. 'Anyway, I'm not sure Bernardi's will be in business much longer. They're only making limited amounts of ice cream since the sugar rationing came in. It's a luxury we can do without whilst there's a war on.'

'Perhaps he'll go back to Italy then.' She was surprised by how much she wanted this not to be the case.

'It's possible, but the local girls have been donating part of their sugar rations to him. Anything to keep him and his ice cream here. Can you believe it? He could persuade a drowning man to give up his life belt, that one.'

Jenny laughed. 'He certainly had a way about him. Good job he was there, though. When I think about what might have happened . . . Louis was really close to the river, you know.'

'Don't think about it then,' said Lorcan. He reached into the pocket of his jacket. 'Here, this'll take your mind off it. Mam's drawn up a list of jobs for you and Louis.'

Jenny took the two bits of paper. 'Oh dear, she's put Louis in charge of Ivor and Megan. He's terrified of them goats. I can't blame him either. The way Ivor sharpens his horns on the walls of the pigsty. And his eyes, they're the eyes of the devil himself.'

'Ivor's harmless, and he's good for keeping the grass and what have you down. He eats everything in his path. Louis just has to move their tethers around and check they have enough water. Mam'll reduce his workload once he starts school.'

Jenny folded up the scraps of paper and tucked them into her waistband. 'I said we wouldn't be a burden and I meant it.' She gazed up at the dark sky, where the first stars were just beginning to pinprick the black velvet. 'In fact, I think this place could be the making of our Louis.'

She shivered against the evening chill, pulling her shawl tight across her chest. Lorcan shrugged off his jacket. 'Here, have this.'

She leaned forward so he could arrange the jacket around her body. He turned up the collar, his face only inches from hers, his warm breath on her cold cheeks. She caught the smell of his hair, the household soap he'd used on it that morning still lingering amongst the curls. 'Thank you, Lorcan.'

She glanced up at the farmhouse, not a chink of light escaping the blackout. The darkness was tangible, almost suffocating. Somewhere on the mountain, a lamb called for its mother, the plaintive cry reverberating through the valley. She thought of Nico and the feel of his hand in hers, the kindness in his eyes and the care he had shown for her darling Louis. As her warm breath met the frigid air, she smiled through the fog. 'I'm glad you picked us, Lorcan.'

10

A few days passed before Jenny was able to escape the farm again and have some time to herself. Laundry had been number one on her list of chores and had proved particularly labour-intensive. She was used to washing clothes by hand, but the garments at Mynydd Farm were so heavy, caked with muck and soil and God only knew what else. And the smell. She had had to turn her head and bury her nose in her sleeve as she ran them up and down the washboard. She'd proved to be less than adept at wringing them out, too. Delyth's hands were so strong that the clothes barely needed putting through the mangle after she'd finished with them.

The clear mountain air and spring sunshine had put some colour into her cheeks and her breathing was becoming less laboured by the day. She hooked the wicker basket over her arm and called out to Louis. 'I'm going into town. Are you coming?'

He ambled out of the barn, mud smeared across his face, a small knife in his hand.

'What're you doing with that knife? Give it here, you'll have somebody's eye out.'

Lorcan trailed behind him. 'He's all right, Jenny. I'm teaching him.'

Louis held up a rough chunk of wood. 'I'm learning how to wickle.'

'It's whittle, Louis,' corrected Lorcan.

'Well whittle over here then,' said Jenny. 'We're going out.'

Louis hid the knife behind his back and shook his head. 'I want to stay with Lorcan.'

Lorcan shrugged. 'He'll be fine here with me.'

'Lorcan's made loads of things, Jenny. I'll make something for you when I get good at it. I'll make you a hedgehog or a toytoise and then when I'm really good, I'll make you a table.'

She smiled at his boyish enthusiasm. He had never had a father or even a big brother to indulge him in such innocent pastimes.

'I'm surprised you've got time, Lorcan.'

'I make time. I promised my grandaddy I'd finish the chess set he was working on before he died.'

'I'm helping make the prawns,' said Louis.

Lorcan winked at her. 'Pawns, Louis, pawns.'

Jenny stared at them both, Lorcan's hand draped casually over Louis's shoulder. 'Thank you, Lorcan. It's really kind of you.'

'It's no trouble. It's not as if I've got a little brother of my own to pass my skills on to. And I've got a short while before we go up the lane to fetch the cows for milking. Louis is coming with me. I'm putting him in charge of Brindle.'

Louis beamed. 'I can whistle for him. Listen.' He pursed his lips and blew out a silent breath. Over by the barn, the untroubled Brindle continued to nap in the sunshine. Louis frowned and tried again, the sound this time a hollow whoosh. Brindle had the decency to open one eye and give a lazy thump of his tail, but it was going to take more than that to call him to heel. 'I could do it before,' the little boy insisted.

Lorcan patted his head. 'Keep practising, Louis, you'll get it soon enough.'

'If you're sure he won't be a nuisance and get in the way, then I'll go on my own.'

'A nuisance?' said Lorcan, feigning horror. 'Never! He's my right-hand man now.'

She took it easy navigating the narrow lane down into the town, marvelling at the burgeoning countryside, the smell of the unfurling hedges, tiny birds darting in and out, chunks of sheep's wool pinched in their beaks ready to line their nests. By the time she arrived at the stone bridge that crossed the river, she was only slightly out of breath, but she paused for a moment, tilting her head towards the sunshine. Although there was still a chill in the April air, the sun's rays were strong enough to penetrate the high cloud and warm her cheeks.

She thought of her mother back home amongst the dreary grey ginnels of Manchester, anxiously scanning the skies for enemy planes with their deadly cargo. She closed her eyes and muttered a silent prayer. She couldn't shake off the guilt she felt that she and Louis were safe whilst their mother might be forced to endure terrifying night raids that would send her scurrying to the shelter. It didn't seem right to her. Why should the children be spared whilst the adults had to fend for themselves? Would the air-raid shelters even be capable of withstanding a direct hit? The ARP wardens had warned of fatal mustard gas attacks. Although the unflappable Connie Tanner had dismissed these stories as scaremongering, a ruse to get people to wear their gas masks, Jenny's imagination ran away with her. *You can't smell it, but it eats you alive from the inside out*, they said. She wondered whether her mother even cared about her own safety, still entrenched as she was in a pit of grief over the death of her husband.

She was deep in thought, staring down at the cobbles as she gingerly picked her way along the pavement, when she heard a cry of '*Ciao, bella!*' and looked across the street. Nico was standing under the canopy of his shop, his white shirtsleeves rolled up, a knee-length black apron tied around his waist. 'Over here, Jennifer.' He gesticulated. 'Why do you look so sad?'

He pulled out a chair for her and took the one opposite for himself. Two empty coffee cups and a used ashtray sat on the table between them.

'How is your little brother?' he asked, spreading his hands wide.

'He's grand, thank you,' she replied, trying to quell the ridiculous onset of nerves.

Nico turned his mouth down in an exaggerated clown fashion. 'Then what is the matter? You look like you lost a shilling and found sixpence.'

'I was just thinking about my mother at home. You know, worried about the bombs and everything, wondering if she'll be all right.'

'You look like you need gelato. I still have some vanilla left. It's not so sweet, but I'm sure it will put a smile back on your face. What do you say?'

She was hardly going to say no. 'Go on then, ta.'

'*Eccellente.* I'll just be a minute.' He scooped up the used cups and disappeared into the shop.

'Here you are,' he said, returning and placing a small glass of ice cream on the table. 'This will take all your sadness away, Jennifer.'

Just the way he said her name made her want to swoon. She really must pull herself together. 'I doubt that, but thanks anyway.'

'Why not?' He shrugged. 'It worked for your brother.'

She dug the spoon into the cup and shovelled in a large blob.

Nico threw his arms in the air and took the spoon off her. 'No, no, not like that,' he tutted. 'Here, let me show you.' He dipped the spoon into the glass and brought out a marble-sized lump. Closing his eyes, he turned the teaspoon over and ran it along the length of his tongue, coating it with the white ice cream, which he then rolled around his mouth as though it were a fine wine.

He opened his eyes and stared at her, his magnetic gaze making it difficult for her to look away. 'See?' he said, breaking into a broad smile. 'It is a sensuous experience. It is not to be rushed.' He brought out another scoop and held the spoon to her lips. 'Your turn.'

She obediently opened her mouth, dismissing all thoughts of the perils of spoon-sharing. 'Very nice,' she agreed.

'Ha,' he guffawed, rocking back in his chair. 'Nice? You can do better than that, Jennifer. It practically dances on your tongue, tantalising your taste buds until it slides down your throat, leaving you begging for more.'

He held up another spoonful. 'Come on now. Tell me what you really think.' An amused smile played on his lips, his dark eyes narrowing with delight.

73

She could feel her heart galloping in a way that she wasn't used to. Heat began to rise from her toes until she could feel the flush of it across her chest and neck. She swallowed the ice cream, then blotted her lips with a napkin. 'Luscious, smooth and ever so slightly sinful,' she pronounced.

Reaching across the table, he covered her hand with his own. 'And what about the gelato?' He winked.

A disembodied voice hollered his name. 'Nico!'

He jumped and withdrew his hand, his face instantly colouring.

'*Sì, Mamma?*'

The voice continued to shout in Italian from inside the café.

'I'm with a customer, Mamma,' he called back with a roll of his eyes and an apologetic smile. 'She wants to know what is taking so long.'

An older woman appeared then, her tiny stature at odds with her booming voice. She stood with her arms akimbo, a tea towel slung over one shoulder, her silver hair scraped back into a bun. She whipped the tea towel across the back of Nico's head, then switched seamlessly to English. 'You can't be sitting around all day chatting. The machine needs cleaning out and then you have to take a mop to the floor. I've never seen anything like it, anybody would think that—'

Nico raised his hands in a calming gesture. 'I will, Mamma, I will. First let me introduce you to Jennifer. She's staying up at Mundy Farm.'

'Mun-ith,' Jenny corrected. She held out her hand to the older woman. 'Pleased to meet you.'

'Ah, Delyth told me about her evacuees. My name's

74

Valentina, but everybody calls me Lena.' She turned to her son. 'Don't be too long now, Nico.' She bustled back into the shop. 'Enzo! Enzo! Where are you? There is work to be done.'

'She seems nice,' said Jenny.

Nico rubbed his ear theatrically. 'She is. She could start a conversation with a brick wall and end up with a friend for life, but she only has one volume, I'm afraid.'

'What about your father? Where's he?'

'Around somewhere. Skulking out the back smoking his pipe probably, enjoying the peace until Mamma catches up with him.'

'Is it just the three of you, then?'

Nico nodded.

'And how long have you lived here?'

'Ten years now. I came when I was twelve. It's good. I'm happy here.' He laid his fingers on the back of her hand, the lightness of his touch disarming. 'Especially now.'

She'd often wondered whether she would know when she was in love. She needn't have worried, because right there, in that moment, she had the answer.

11

The heat in the shippen was almost unbearable. Although the early May morning was far from warm at this hour, the cows' breath and body heat combined to make conditions feel stifling. Jenny moved the milking stool along to the next stall, took out a rag and gave the cow's udders a quick clean. If there was any muck in the milk, then it might be rejected by the dairy and Bryn would be none too pleased.

She squeezed hard, her hands pulling down on alternate udders until the cow yielded her milk. The supply exhausted, she delved into a pot of unguent and scooped up a blob to massage into the cow's chapped udders. She felt Lorcan's hand on her shoulder. 'Are you all right, Jenny? It's not too much for you, I hope.'

She held out her hand to him and he heaved her off the stool. 'I'm fine, Lorcan, stop fussing.' She offered a smile to take the sting out of her words.

In the five weeks since they'd arrived at Mynydd Farm, Jenny's health had improved beyond measure. She could catch her breath more easily, her leg felt stronger and her complexion had taken on a rosy glow that previously could only have been achieved with the help of rouge.

He tucked a stray strand of hair behind her ear, a gesture that could have been interpreted as intimate had he let his hand linger. Instead he looked furtively over his shoulder. 'Look, there's a dance tonight at the community hall.'

'Well, have a good time then.' She smiled.

He ignored her teasing. 'I . . . well, the thing is . . .' He twisted his cap in his hands. 'I was wondering if you'd like to . . . um . . . come with me.'

She looked at his expectant face, the almost pleading expression in his eyes. It would be brutal to turn him down. It was only a dance, not her hand in marriage, and disappointingly, she'd had no other offers. 'I'd like that.' She nodded. 'Look out, your dad's coming.' She returned to the milking stool and positioned the pail under the next cow.

'Have you two not finished yet?' said Bryn. 'Milk'll be sour by the time we get it to the dairy at this rate.'

'We're nearly done, Tad. Jenny's been a huge help.'

He smacked the nearest cow on her hindquarters. 'Righto then. Let's get this herd back to the fields and we'll have a birthday breakfast for the lad.'

'Oh, my poor little Louis!' Jenny gasped. 'He'll think I've forgotten his birthday.' She picked up her cane and almost ran out of the shippen.

Delyth was stirring a pot of oats when Jenny burst into the kitchen. 'Goodness me, Jenny, what's all the rush?'

'Where's our Louis?'

She nodded skywards. 'Upstairs, searching under his bed for presents.'

'He'll be lucky.'

Lorcan came into the kitchen and shrugged off his overalls. He rummaged in the drawer of the Welsh dresser and brought out a package wrapped in brown paper, a piece of frayed string holding everything together.

'It's for Louis,' he said, just as the lad appeared in the doorway.

'For me?' Louis grabbed the present with both hands.

'What do you say, Louis?'

He beamed at Lorcan. 'Thank you.'

Jenny shook her head as she watched him tear at the paper, his tongue sticking out in concentration. 'Careful now, you don't want to drop it.'

He ripped off the wrapping and held up the dome-shaped carving, running his fingers over the smooth wood. 'It's an owl,' he said, pressing it to his chest.

'Can I see, Louis?' The detail was astounding, the feathers so exquisitely carved she expected them to feel soft in her hands. 'It's beautiful, Lorcan. Did you make this?'

Lorcan nodded. 'I learned at the feet of a master.' He looked at his mother, whose face was a mixture of pride and sadness.

'Lorcan and my father were incredibly close,' she said. 'Not only did they share a name, but also a love for the simple things in life. My father taught him the basics, but Lorcan possesses a natural talent Daddy merely honed.'

Jenny looked at the owl again before passing it back to Louis. 'He'll treasure it forever, Lorcan. It'll always remind him of his days here.'

Delyth handed him another parcel. 'This one's from me and Tad.'

Louis peeled off the paper and turned the oblong box over in his hand. 'What is it?'

'It's for your pencils,' she said, taking the box and sliding off the lid. 'See? You can take it to school with you on Monday.'

Louis wrinkled his nose. 'I don't want to go to school.'

Jenny intervened, her tone firm but gentle. 'We've been through all this, Louis. You've got to go. You're not on holiday here, you know. You'll love it when you get there.'

'But I'm needed here. I've got to feed the chickens and look after Ivor and Megan and Jenny the donkey.'

'Nice try,' said Jenny. 'But you're going to school.'

They all turned towards the door as Bryn barged in, his face red and his bushy greying hair clinging to the sweat on his forehead. 'That's everything sluiced down in the yard. Where's the birthday boy then?'

Still slightly afraid of Bryn and his booming voice, Louis shyly raised his hand.

Bryn scooped him up and squeezed him tightly. 'Happy birthday, lad.' He let Louis drop to the floor before slipping his arm around Delyth's waist. 'I'm starving, woman, and I can't smell any bacon frying.'

Delyth laughed. 'There's one more thing before breakfast.' She sat down and patted her knee. 'Come here, Louis.'

He scrambled onto her lap and snuggled into her chest. Jenny smiled at the obvious affection between them.

'This came for you.'

He took the telegram and pressed it to his nose. 'Can you read it, Mammy Del?'

'I certainly can. It says: "HAPPY BIRTHDAY LOUIS STOP I MISS YOU STOP LOVE MUMMY".'

79

Louis wrinkled his nose. 'What does she want me to stop?'

Delyth laughed. 'Nothing, bach. The telegram machine doesn't do full stops so we have to write out the word instead.'

'Oh, I see,' he said, although he clearly didn't. 'Can we have breakfast now?'

Jenny took the telegram and slipped it into her pocket. She'd read it again later with Louis and make time to share some memories of their mother. Louis was fond of Del, but Connie must not be forgotten.

Taking advantage of the warm sunshine, Jenny sat on the garden bench under the shade of the lime tree. She prised the lid off Delyth's sewing tin and threaded a needle. Chickens scratched and clucked about her feet and two blackbirds high in the tree above sang to each other. Here in the peace and solitude of the remote Welsh farm it was difficult to imagine that there was actually a war on. She wondered if their stay would turn out to be short-lived, and was surprised by the disappointment she felt at the thought.

She looked up when she heard the sound of a bell. Someone was coming up the track pushing a bicycle with a ridiculously large basket on the front, a cap pulled low over his eyes. She didn't recognise him until he spoke.

'*Ciao, bella*,' Nico said, removing the cap and using it to mop his brow. 'That hill is a killer when you're riding this thing.' He nodded at the cumbersome bike. 'It has only three gears and I think the chain needs oiling.'

'Hello, Nico,' she breathed. 'What brings you here?' Her mouth had dried up and she longed for a sip of water. He was dressed in a T-shirt with no sleeves, affording her a tantalising a glimpse of his olive skin, which was now covered in a sheen of sweat. She stared at the contours of his muscles and the dark hair covering his forearms. His chest heaved as he took in several deep breaths.

He propped the bike against the tree and flopped down next to her on the bench. 'What are you doing, Jennifer?'

She laid down her sewing, trying to still her shaking hands. 'I'm just mending this dress for Delyth. It has a tear here, see?'

'You are so clever.' He leaned back, spreading both his arms along the back of the bench. 'Thirsty work, that bike ride.'

'Is that your way of saying you'd like a drink?'

'Ah, *bella*, I thought you'd never ask.'

'Delyth's made some lemonade. It's a bit tart because she didn't have enough sugar.'

'But she had the lemons?' he asked in surprise. 'I thought Hitler was determined we should all die of scurvy.'

'I think she'd had them since the last war. They were like bullets.'

'I will try the lemonade then, tart or not.' He jumped up. 'But first I must give you something.'

He unbuckled the straps on the basket and lifted the lid. Using both hands he pulled out a large box wrapped in newspaper, which he set down carefully on the bench. 'It's for Louis. For his birthday.'

'For Louis? How did you know?'

He tapped the side of his nose. 'It is my job to know these things.'

Under the paper was a small wooden crate packed with ice, a cake nestling in the middle.

'The ice cream cake is my speciality.' Nico kissed his fingers. 'I made it especially for you.'

She gave him a sideways look. 'You mean especially for our Louis.'

He only missed half a beat. 'Of course, I meant especially for your little brother.'

'He's out in the fields with Lorcan.'

'Then let's get this into the kitchen. We don't want him returning to a pool of melted ice cream.'

Jenny followed him into the farmhouse. 'Stick it under the milk cooler. That should help.'

She took two jam jars from the cupboard and poured out the lemonade, handing one to Nico.

'Kind of you to get the best china out for me.' He winked, taking a sip and squeezing his eyes closed as he tasted the sharp drink. 'Very good,' he managed, sucking in his cheeks. 'Although a little more sugar would not go missing.'

'Amiss,' she corrected. 'There's a war on, in case you hadn't noticed.'

'Sure, although it is not my war. Il Duce has the good sense to stay out of it.'

'Mussolini's a complete buffoon, from what I've heard.'

He frowned. '*Buffo*? You're saying he is a clown?'

'Well, as I said, it's what I've heard, but let's not get bogged down with all that now. Drink up, I've got work to do.'

He glanced towards the door, lowering his voice. 'Tonight, Jennifer, I would like to take you to the dance. Would you make me very happy by saying yes?'

'At the community hall, you mean?'

'*Sì*, that is the one. Please say you'll come.'

She gazed down at her jam jar, swirling the contents then running her finger around the rim. She longed to accept but she couldn't do that to Lorcan. She'd given him her word and she'd not go back on it even though every cell was screaming at her to say yes to Nico.

'Jennifer?'

She looked up, registering his incredulous gaze, as though he could hardly believe she was taking so long to answer such a straightforward question. 'I'm already going, Nico.'

'Well that is good then. I'll—'

'Lorcan has already asked me to go with him.'

Nico froze, his expressive hands halted in mid-air, his mouth agape.

'He asked me earlier and I said yes.'

'You're going to the dance with Lorcan?' he said, as though this was just too ridiculous to contemplate.

She nodded. 'Yes, I am.'

He pressed his fingers into his eyes and inhaled sharply. 'I am so stupid. It is all my fault. Oh, why did I wait?' He held out his hand. 'Look at you, as if you wouldn't already have a date for the dance.'

'I can't go back on my word, Nico.'

'I wouldn't hear of it.' He touched her arm. 'You must go with Lorcan.'

He retrieved his bike and swung his leg over the saddle. 'I just hope he knows how lucky he is.'

She had almost forgotten how good it felt to stare into the mirror and see a perfectly coiffured hairstyle instead of the loose curls that fell about her shoulders. She hardly recognised herself. She'd brought with her a stubby eyebrow pencil and a flaky block of mascara, and Delyth had given her a pot of her home-made rouge, which consisted of the end of a lipstick melted into some cold cream. She sucked in her cheeks and rubbed some along her cheekbones, turning her face left then right to admire the effect. She leaned closer to the mirror and applied the pillar-box-red lipstick that had once belonged to her mother, shaping her lips into the hunter's bow favoured by Joan Crawford and her ilk. Then she sat back and looked at herself, nodding. Not everybody could carry off this look.

As she applied a thin smear of petroleum jelly over the lipstick, she heard a knock on the door. 'Come in.'

Delyth bobbed her head round. 'My oh my, Jenny, there's beautiful if ever I saw it.' She took a step into the room as Jenny stood and smoothed down her brown and white polka-dot dress.

'Did you make that?'

'Yes, I did. It's one of my favourites. I've made it for lots of my customers.'

Delyth rubbed the fabric between her fingers. 'You're so clever, bach. I can just about manage to sew a button on.'

'I'll make one for you if you like.'

'Oh no. I've already told you, I've got a dress. Where on earth would I wear something like that? Anyway, I thought you might like a splash of this.' She handed Jenny a dark blue glass perfume bottle.

'Thanks, that's really kind of you.'

'Well, I've had it for years. Can't even remember what's inside,' she laughed. 'Might take your skin off, that's if it hasn't evaporated altogether.'

Jenny removed the stopper and took a sniff, her eyes watering. 'It's still quite . . . erm . . . potent.' She dotted some behind her ears. 'That should keep the flies away.'

'Lorcan's ready downstairs. Are you coming?'

Jenny picked up her cane and nodded towards the door. 'Lead on, I'm right behind you.'

Lorcan had undergone a similar transformation. Gone were his overalls, his unruly curly hair and his grime-suffused face. Instead, he wore a bulky brown suit, only one size too big for him, the trousers held up with a pair of black braces. His hair had been tamed with the aid of some Brylcreem, and there was no trace of the agricultural smells that normally followed him around.

He stood open-mouthed as she came into the kitchen. 'Jenny, you look wonderful, so pretty.'

'You too,' she replied. 'Well, not pretty, but you know what I mean.'

He offered her his elbow. 'Shall we?'

She slipped her arm through his. 'I think we should.'

The community hall had been transformed from functional to gorgeously indulgent. Ropes of frivolous Union Jack bunting were strung along the walls, and each table sported a vase of velvety pansies in purple, yellow and mauve. The kitchen, which usually served the Women's Institute teas, was decked out with bottles of spirits and cheap glasses, and in the corner, an unwieldy gramophone churned out the latest dance tunes.

Lorcan slipped his arm around Jenny's waist and guided her to a table. 'What would you like to drink?'

She turned towards the hatch, surveying the array of bottles. She wasn't used to alcohol. With her leg, it wasn't a good idea to add anything destabilising into the equation.

'I'll just have something soft, please.'

'Really? Are you sure?'

'Honestly. I need to be careful. I'll perhaps have a proper drink later.'

He returned a few moments later with an elderflower cordial for her and a bottle of beer for himself. 'Cheers,' he said, clinking the bottle against her glass.

She gazed around the room. A few couples had already taken to the dance floor, limbs entwined as they moved in time to the music. Lorcan reached across the table and took hold of her hand. 'Do you want to?'

She propped her cane against the chair. 'Dance, you mean? I'd love to, but you might have to hold me up.'

He held her at a respectful distance, his back stiff and his arms straight as he glided her around the room in an approximation of a waltz. His hand felt surprisingly soft in hers, probably due to all the udder cream. That and the lanolin. Farmers who worked with sheep always had soft hands, Del had told her. She smiled to herself, relaxing her body and giving him the confidence to draw her a little closer.

'You're a good dancer,' she said when they'd taken their seats again.

'Give over. I'm just a shuffler. I've no idea what I'm doing.'

'Well you could've fooled me.'

The door opened and a shaft of early-evening sunlight slanted over the floorboards, illuminating an excited cluster of girls in their sticky-out skirts and gravy-browned legs who had gathered round the entrance. It was a few moments before he emerged from the throng, nodding to each girl, kissing some on the hand, the epitome of red-blooded Italian virility. His double-breasted blue suit fitted him perfectly, the white pin stripes elongating his figure. His blue-black hair shone like a raven's head and he'd left a barely visible smattering of stubble on his face. He took a long drag on his cigarette, his eyes narrowing as the nicotine hit the spot. Jenny could feel her heart racing and the sweat moistening her neck.

'What's the matter, Jenny?' asked Lorcan.

She bowed her head and fiddled with the vase of pansies. 'Nothing.'

'*Buonasera*, Jennifer,' said Nico, striding over. '*Ciao*, Lorcan.'

Lorcan swivelled in his chair and returned the greeting with a curt nod.

Nico held out both his hands. 'You look sensational, Jennifer.' He clamped a hand on Lorcan's shoulder. 'I hope you know how fortunate you are, Lorcan.'

Lorcan gave an irritable shrug. 'Bugger off, Nico.'

'Ha, charming.' He half bowed as he backed away. 'Save a dance for me, Jennifer.'

'Lorcan,' Jenny hissed. 'Did you have to be so rude?'

She watched as Nico pulled a giggling girl to her feet and took her in his arms. She felt her face flush as she tried to ignore the tidal wave of jealousy that threatened to engulf her.

12

2019

My eyes are closed, even though sleep could not be further away. Candice gently shakes my shoulder. 'Jenny? Jenny, are you still with us?'

I force myself to look at her. 'I've not thought about that night in an awfully long time, Candice.'

'God,' she says, in wide-eyed wonder. 'Nico sounds *so* irresistible. And exotic,' she adds with a glint in her eye. 'A bit like my Beau.'

I shake my head. That pillock sounds nothing like Nico.

'From the second he walked into that hall, Candice, the atmosphere shifted, crackling like the air before a thunderstorm. He had this effortlessly magnetic aura about him.'

'And he clearly adored you, Jenny.'

'*Colpo di fulmine*, the Italians call it. A lightning strike. Love at first sight.'

'How poetic,' she gushes.

'I suppose I have to take some of the blame for what happened next, because we were both culpable to a degree. I'll accept ten per cent of it – there's nobody to argue now.'

'What did happen?' she asks eagerly. 'I bet there was a punch-up between him and Lorcan.'

I pat her arm to silence her. 'Let me tell the story, Candice.'
'Sorry, go on.'

'Nico had kept his distance all evening, but I'd seen him
looking my way numerous times, his dark eyes crinkling as he
peered at me through the haze of blue smoke. I could feel
my lungs protesting and knew I had to get some fresh air. I
looked around for Lorcan and saw him talking to somebody
about some prize heifer or other. I signalled that I was going
outside, and he mouthed that he would be out in a minute.'
I sneak a look at Candice and am pleased to see she's still
enthralled. 'I don't know how anybody can talk about heifers,
prize or otherwise, for so long, but I waited for a good fifteen
minutes. I was rubbing my arms in an effort to ward off the
descending chill when I heard footsteps. I know you're prob
ably ahead of me here, Candice, so I'll skip to it and tell you
it was Nico.'

Her mouth forms a perfect O, even though she must have
been expecting it.

'He handed me a drink, a port and lemon as I recall. I
thought it would be churlish to refuse and I'll never forget
how that first swallow burned my throat. I wasn't used to it
then, so it only took a few sips for the liquor to go to my
head – not that that's an excuse, mind; I was still in control.
He ground out his cigarette under his foot, then removed his
jacket and slipped it round my shoulders. I didn't ask him to
do it. He just instinctively knew, I suppose, and took charge.
The sky was clear and without the cloud cover there was more
than a nip in the air. He stood in front of me, so close that
our breath mingled in front of our faces. I can only think I
must've been in some sort of catatonic state, because even

though I knew it wasn't a good idea for so many reasons, I was powerless to resist.'

'Did you?' asks Candice, sliding to the edge of the bench in anticipation.

I shake my head. 'Without a word, Nico slipped his hand around the back of my neck and worked his fingers into my hair.'

Candice blows out a short breath. 'Woo. What happened then?'

I close my eyes around the memory, long-forgotten feelings beginning to surface. 'He kissed me, Candice.' I pause to gather myself. 'And as his lips met mine, my head screamed *no, no, no*, but my heart never wanted the perfect moment to end.'

'That's so romantic,' sighs Candice. 'Two guys fighting over you, eh? After seeing that photo of you, I can well believe it an' all.' She nudges my arm. 'Carry on then, don't keep me in suspense.'

13

She could have stopped him the second he leaned in, but the intoxicating smell of his woody cologne, the unfamiliar smokiness on his breath and the feel of his warm hand on the back of her neck rendered her incapable of any meaningful protest. She had never been kissed that way before.

At the sound of footsteps scuffing along the path, he pulled away, fixed his gaze on hers and dragged his finger along her jawbone before disappearing into the night without another word.

'Jenny?' Lorcan called.

She took a few calming breaths, running her finger round her lips to remove any tell tale smudges. 'Here, Lorcan,' she breathed, her casual tone forced.

'There you are,' he said. 'Where've you been?'

She immediately felt the need to defend herself. 'Here. I've just been here, obviously.'

'Oh, right. It's just that there's a bench at the front. I assumed you'd be sitting on that.'

'A bench? No, I came round the back. I wanted to . . . um . . . hear the river.'

'The river?'

'Yes, the river.' She absently pulled the lapels of Nico's jacket together and sipped the port and lemon.

Lorcan took hold of the glass and sniffed the contents, his brow corrugating as he tried to work everything out. 'I thought you didn't want any alcohol – and whose is the jacket?'

She knew there was no point in lying. She let her shoulders drop. 'Nico was out here having a fag; he saw that I was cold and lent me his jacket.' She kept her tone light. 'He gave me a sip of his drink, saying it would warm me up, and then he went back inside.'

'Without his drink or his jacket?'

She lifted her chin. 'He's a gentleman.'

'Mmm . . . I doubt that,' he mumbled. 'Eye for the main chance, that one.'

'Do you think we can go in now? I need to return the jacket.' The scent of his cologne still lingered on the collar.

Lorcan's expression hardened. 'If you want to.'

The dance floor was now full of couples pressed together, swaying in time to the tinny music.

'I can't see him, can you, Lorcan?'

'Perhaps he's gone.' He brightened. 'Come on, let's have this last dance.' He held out his hand and she had no choice but to take it. She shrugged off Nico's jacket and laid it over a chair. Lorcan pulled her close this time, his arm wrapped confidently around her waist, his mouth only inches from her ear. 'Have you enjoyed yourself, Jenny?'

She thought about Nico, about the kiss, about the way he had wholly possessed her, for just one brief moment. 'I have, Lorcan, thank you.'

He smiled and tightened his grip, his fingers interlacing with hers. 'Good.'

Back at Mynydd Farm, in spite of the late hour, she lay on her bed staring at the damp patch on the ceiling. Louis had finally agreed to move into his own little room and she relished the new-found peace and privacy her bedroom now provided. Nico's jacket hung on the outside of the wardrobe. She hadn't been able to find him, and after asking around, she'd learned he'd left the community hall in a hurry, wearing an angst-ridden expression.

She propped herself up when she heard the tap on the door. 'Who is it?' she whispered.

'It's me,' said Lorcan. 'I've brought you a mug of cocoa.'

'Come in then.' She swung her legs off the bed and perched on the edge.

'Thought you might need warming up after our walk home.'

'How thoughtful.' She took the mug and blew on the foam before taking a sip. 'Lovely, thank you.'

He sat down next to her, their thighs touching. She shuffled away a little, enough to make her feel more comfortable but not so much that he'd be hurt.

'I really like you, Jenny.' He examined his fingernails, his words laced with sadness.

'And I really like you, Lorcan.'

He took a deep sigh. 'Yes, but not in the same way.'

Stalling for time, she took another sip of cocoa. 'We've only known each other, what . . . five weeks.' Had it really only been that long?

He attempted a small laugh. 'If I don't move quickly, you'll be snapped up by someone else.'

She flicked him playfully on the arm. 'Don't be so daft.' She paused, glancing at the jacket on the wardrobe. 'Who's going to snap me up?'

He stood to leave. 'Oh, I think you know who, Jenny.' He hesitated in the doorway. 'Goodnight.'

14

2019

Arriving home from work that evening, Candice fished the crumpled receipts from her pocket and smoothed them out on the kitchen counter. Beau would be pleased at the savings she'd made by switching to a budget supermarket. She glanced at the clock on the wall, frowning as she stirred the pot on the stove. It wasn't like him to go out without telling her where he was going or what time he would be back. He knew she was due to finish at Green Meadows around seven and that she'd be back in time to make a special meal to celebrate the good news about his regular booking at the Lemon Tree. Listening to Jenny's story had only made her half an hour late, and she'd sent him a quick text to explain.

It was gone nine before he appeared in the doorway, a half-drunk bottle of champagne in one hand, a polystyrene takeaway carton in the other.

'Where've you been, Beau?' She kept her voice level, careful to ensure there was no trace of an accusatory tone.

He slapped the heel of his hand into his forehead. 'God, babe, I'm so sorry. I forgot you were going to cook something. When you said you were running late, I assumed you'd changed your mind.' He tossed the takeaway carton in the general direction of the bin, but it missed, and bits of shredded lettuce scattered on the floor. 'I've had a kebab, but don't worry, I can still force down some of what you've made.'

'Force down? That's good of you.'

He put down the bottle of champagne and pulled her towards him. He smelled of Paco Rabanne with a hint of cigarette smoke and an almost undetectable whiff of stale sweat. 'Come on, don't be like that.' He lifted the lid on the pot and took a dramatic sniff. 'Mmm . . . smells delicious. What is it?' He nuzzled into her neck, making her giggle in spite of herself. She could never be mad at him for long.

'It's a three-bean casserole. Pinto beans, haricot beans and kidney beans.'

He laughed and tickled her ribs. 'Good one, Candice. What is it really?'

'What do you mean? It's *really* a three-bean casserole.'

He peered into the pot as though his eyes had deceived him. 'Where's the flamin' meat?'

'It's vegetarian, Beau. There's no meat. It's better for you and costs a lot less.' She picked up the supermarket receipt. 'Look how much I saved. I thought you'd be pleased.'

He stared at the ceiling and inhaled deeply. A muscle in his jaw pulsed as he clenched his teeth. 'Okay,' he said eventually. 'I don't think you've quite understood this economising thing.' He glanced around the kitchen, his eyes settling on the four cans of lager on top of the fridge.

'What the fuck are those? Where's my Special Brew?'

'That's the supermarket's own brand. Everybody knows it's the same stuff inside but it's half the price.'

'Candice, you are so naïve sometimes. I can't drink that

camel's piss.' He ran his finger down the receipt. 'So that means you've actually wasted two pounds seventy-five.' He looked at the cans with renewed disgust.

'Well, I've bought own-brand everything now. Washing-up liquid, shampoo and even caged eggs because the free-range are too dear.'

'Them things don't matter, Candice. As long as we don't compromise on the essentials.' He took hold of her chin. 'Do you understand the difference? Next time get me my Special Brew, okay?'

She nodded and turned her attention back to the casserole. 'Do you want some or not?'

'Obviously not,' he scoffed. 'I'm not eating that crap.' He patted the sofa. 'Come and sit here and tell me why you were so late home.'

'I've already told you. I was talking to Jenny – well, listening to her actually – and I didn't realise the time.'

He tapped his chin and stared at her. 'This the one who thinks she's taking you away?'

She chose to ignore the comment. She wasn't in the mood for an argument about her forthcoming trip to Italy.

'Yes, the lady who turned a hundred last week.'

He threw his head back, laughing. 'Bloody hell, Candice. You're a genius.'

'What're you on about?'

'Does she suspect?'

'Suspect what?'

'That you only sit around listening to her waffle so that she'll write you into her will?'

She thumped him on his arm. 'Beau, that's a terrible thing

to say. Nothing could be further from my mind. You're so cynical sometimes.'

He stayed quiet, and Candice could almost hear the cogs grinding. 'A hundred years old, though, and no family? No sense in it all going to the cats' home.'

'All what, Beau? I've no idea how much money Jenny has. She's in residential care for a start, and that doesn't come cheap.'

'She likes you, though. Would you say you're close?'

'Yes, I suppose we do have a bond. She's a lovely lady, very spirited and way too switched on not to see straight through me.'

'Does she have anything worth nicking, then? Just to tide us over, like?'

She gave him a hard stare. 'If you think I would . . .' She stopped when she saw him grinning. 'Is this a wind-up, Beau?'

'Of course it is, babe. I know you wouldn't do anything so unscrupulous.' He stood and slung his leather jacket over his shoulder. 'Right, I'm off to get my Special Brew.' He stopped at the doorway and gave her a backward glance. 'Think about it though, eh?'

15

I think Candice will make a more than competent beauty therapist. She has the looks, aside from the 'edgy' hair she's sporting at the moment, and she has a lovely way about her as well. She's genuinely interested in other people, especially me for some unfathomable reason.

'It's been a few days since we last had a chance for a proper chat,' she says. 'I'm dying to know what happened after the dance, after Nico kissed you.'

She gently combs my wet hair and I close my eyes, remembering with high-definition clarity the events of almost eighty years ago. 'I wasn't looking for love exactly, but that's what happens when you let your guard down, Candice. Two come along at once.'

She stops combing, squeezes something from a tube into her palms, then digs her fingers into my scalp as she massages in some cream or other, which she assures me will make my hair soft and shiny. I don't like to tell her that the shininess of my hair is the least of my worries.

'Mmm . . . this smells wonderful,' she enthuses, dipping her nose towards my head. 'Frangipani and orange blossom. Sorry, carry on.'

I gaze up at the ceiling, trying to order my recollections. 'I remember I couldn't sleep, so I lay on my bed running through Lorcan and Nico's respective good points. Both were handsome in their own way. Lorcan had those ice-blue eyes, unruly dark hair and a little-boy smile. He was also thoughtful, caring and a natural with our Louis, who doted on him.'

'Ah, bless.' Candice says, wiping her hands on a towel.

'Nico was so charming, though, and he oozed confidence, which only made him more desirable.'

'I'd have thought Lorcan was a much safer bet.'

This irritates me more than it should, probably because I know she's right.

'Did Louis like Nico?' she continues, oblivious to my sour expression.

'Of course he did. Probably because he brought him ice cream. Kids are fickle like that.'

She nods sagely, as though she has a wealth of experience with kids. I expect she does, living with that spoilt brat Beau.

'I'd felt comfortable and safe in Lorcan's arms as we shuffled around the dance floor, his warm breath in my ear, his fingers intertwined with mine.' I sigh at the memory. 'And it was nice, honestly, but it wasn't quite nice enough.'

Only the passage of time has made me realise it was more than enough.

'I know exactly what you mean, Jenny. You're right, something just has to click, doesn't it? When I first met my Beau, it was love at first sight too.'

My features remain passive as I stare at her in the mirror. 'Love at first sight can often be cured by taking a second look.'

She immediately takes offence and pulls at my hair a little

too hard. 'Don't be so mean. You said it was like that for you and Nico, so you of all people should know what I'm talking about.'

'Candice, it was only the other day that you asked me how you could tell when you were really in love.'

She only misses a beat. 'Did I? Well, you know how it is sometimes.'

Indeed I do. 'Where did you meet him?' I ask.

'At the petrol station where I used to work part-time. He came in for a packet of fags and a Twix. I saw him walking across the forecourt and he just looked so cool, with his leather jacket and a fag stuck to his bottom lip. I banged on the glass to tell him to put it out because it wasn't allowed, what with all the petrol fumes an' all. He ground it out with his shoe and mouthed an apology. When he came in, I couldn't take my eyes off him. He was so unlike anybody I'd met before. So confident, you might even say cocky. He paid for the fags and the Twix and then he opened the wrapper and offered me one. A stick of Twix, I mean, not a cigarette. Well, I'd not long since had me tea, so I wasn't hungry, but he insisted.' She places her hand across her chest, her eyes shining at the memory. 'And then he said, "I'll be back to pick you up later. What time do you finish?" Just like that. Can you believe it?'

I have no trouble at all believing it but choose not to say anything.

'We were living together a month later. Talk about whirl-wind.' She points to my head. 'I'll just give it a quick blast so you don't get a chill.' The whirring of the hairdryer fills the silence.

Ten minutes later, my hair is fluffed up and feels as soft as the feathers in a pillow. 'Thank you, Candice. That's just the job.' All this remembering the past, together with the scalp massage, has made me sleepy. I feel drugged as she helps me to my feet and into the wheelchair.

'Where to now?'

'I think I'll have a little lie-down, love.'

She wrinkles her nose. 'But that'll flatten the back of your hair.'

Oh, to be young again and care about such things. 'Take me to the conservatory lounge, then. I'll have a nap in there in the sunshine.'

She pushes me out into the corridor, one wheel making an irritating squeak, which becomes even more irritating as we gather pace. 'It's Beau's first gig at the Lemon Tree tonight,' she says. 'I'm so excited.'

'Yes, you must be,' I reply. 'And the money will help too, I expect.'

She parks the wheelchair and gives me a queer look. 'He does try, you know. It's not his fault he can't get more gigs.'

'Whose fault is it then?'

She seems hurt and I realise I've pushed it too far. I take hold of her hand. 'I'm sorry, love. I didn't mean to upset you. I just hate to see you having to work so hard while he's . . . doing whatever it is he does.'

'I don't mind. I love it here. And in any case, I know it's not forever. My ambition is to have my own salon one day.'

I run my thumb over her chapped knuckles. 'When did you last have a holiday, Candice?'

'A holiday?' she asks, as though she has no concept of what this might be.

'Some time off,' I clarify. 'It's a couple of months before we embark on our trip to Italy. I think you could use a break before then.'

She snatches her hand away. 'I don't need time off, Jenny. I'm fine.' She takes the chair opposite me and massages her temples.

'Candice?'

She lifts her head. 'What?'

'Is there something you're not telling me?'

'Like what?'

'I don't know. You just seem tired and a little . . . irritable. Has Beau come round to the idea of you going away yet?'

She wrinkles her nose. 'Well, you know how it is. He's sad about it because he'll miss me so much. We've hardly been apart since the day we met, so it will be hard.' She stands and brushes herself down. 'Right, Mrs Culpepper will have my head on a stick if I don't make a start on laying the tables for tea.'

'Have you lost weight, Candice?'

She instinctively squeezes her waist. 'What? No. Although Beau did say the other day that he thought I could do with losing a few pounds. He calls me his little Chubster.' She giggles, but I can tell it stings.

'Little Chubster?'

'It's just a pet name. He doesn't mean it as an insult or owt.'

I'm not quite sure how it's possible to dislike somebody you've never even met. 'Don't listen to him, Candice. You're perfect the way you are.'

She gives me a doubtful smile before scuttling off. This trip to Italy will be cathartic for me, but I'm determined that Candice will have a little fun too. It's the least she deserves.

16

Candice battled her way along the pavement using her umbrella as a shield instead of for its intended purpose. Seriously, was there any weather worse than horizontal hailstones? The bus had been late, meaning she'd had to run down Mauldeth Road, leaving her shiny-faced and breathless as she arrived at the Lemon Tree. She shook out the umbrella as she approached the entrance. A doorman stood with his meaty arms folded.

'Can I get past, please?' she asked.

'Ticket.'

'What? Since when? It's a bar, I don't need a ticket, surely?' She could hear low-level music coming from inside, tinny-sounding dance tracks accompanied by flashing lights. 'Look, my boyfriend's playing here tonight. You're not telling me I need a ticket to see him, are you?'

He produced a clipboard and ran his finger down a list.

'What's your name?'

'Candice Barnes.'

To his credit, he checked the list twice before tossing the clipboard onto the desk. 'Nope, sorry, your name's not on the list. That's a tenner, please.'

'Are you sure?' She could feel her nose begin to fizz.

'I haven't got a spare tenner and my boyfriend didn't mention anything about having to pay.'

He moved out of the way and pulled her over the threshold, pointing to the small stage in the corner of the room. 'Is that him there? The one carrying on like he's Jon Bon Jovi?'

Candice stared at Beau. He had his foot up on a chair as he chatted to two giggling girls, one of whom apparently thought it was appropriate to stroke his bicep.

'Yes, that's him,' she said tightly.

The doorman gave her a sympathetic look. 'Go on then, but don't tell everybody.'

She pushed her way to the front, apologising to some big oaf who barged into her and sloshed his lager down her sleeve. 'Beau, I'm here,' she called, waving.

He looked over the heads of the two girls and gave an almost imperceptible shake of his head, his eyes unblinking as he stared at her.

It was difficult to understand what he meant, but as she took another step forward, he removed his foot from the chair, took the elbow of the inappropriately demonstrative girl and turned his back on Candice.

She pressed her hand to her mouth, suddenly feeling like a gatecrasher who'd blagged her way in. She felt a hand in the small of her back. 'Come on, love, I'll get you a drink.'

She turned to see the bouncer smiling, his kindly expression at odds with his bulk.

He clicked his fingers at the barman. 'Whatever the lady wants,' he said, guiding Candice towards a vacant bar stool. 'Put it on my tab.'

'Thank you,' she muttered. 'A glass of Sauvignon, please.'

'I'll have to get back to the door.' He glanced in Beau's direction, shaking his head. 'You have my sympathy, sweetheart.'

She'd barely touched her drink before Beau arrived by her side, his face flushed and his shirt open to the navel, revealing his angel tattoo.

'You missed the first set,' he said accusingly. 'Where've you been?'

'I've been at work, and never mind giving *me* the third degree, who were those two?' She nodded towards the girls, who were now giggling in the corner, foreheads together as they clutched their lurid cocktails.

'Fans, Candice, fans. And it doesn't look good when my girlfriend comes tottering over.' He called to the barman. 'Pint, please, mate.'

She picked up her glass and took a fortifying gulp. 'Oh, well excuse me. I'm sorry if I'm cramping your style.'

'There's nothing in it, Candice. Fans like to think their heroes are single, that's all. It'll put them off if they think I have a girlfriend.'

'I'm hardly Yoko Ono, Beau, and you're definitely no John Lennon.'

He managed a laugh. 'You're so funny, Candice.' He kissed her on the cheek. 'You know you're the only girl for me.' He eyed her glass. 'That's a large one, babe. Did you really need all that? What about our economising?'

She was about to tell him that the doorman had bought it but instinctively knew this wasn't a good idea. She stepped around the question, shuffling to the edge of her stool. 'Tell me about your set, then. How did it go?'

He took a long draw on his pint, leaving a line of froth on his top lip. 'They loved me, Candice.' He took a step back and spread his arms wide, gazing down at his skinny frame. 'I mean, obviously, how could they resist this?'

She hadn't noticed his trousers until then. 'Where did they come from? Are they real leather?'

He tutted at the ceiling. 'Are they real leather? Of course they are. I'm a rock star. I can hardly go on stage in polyester.'

'But—'

He silenced her with a finger to her lips. 'I know what you're going to say, babe, but trust me, this is an investment. Don't worry, I've budgeted for it, and in any case, they only cost about the same as your eyebrow course.'

'Oh, well that's brilliant. Can I go ahead and book it, then?'

He lifted a piece of her hair and twirled it in his fingers, his nose wrinkling. 'You look a bit dishevelled, if you don't mind me saying so.'

She brushed his hand away. 'Yes, I do mind you saying so. I've come straight from work. The bus was late and I had to run the last half-mile in a bloody hailstorm.'

'All right, Candice, calm down. Jeez . . . I was only saying.'

'Well don't.' She swivelled on her stool, turning away from him as she picked up her drink. She felt him run his finger down her spine and shuddered involuntarily.

'Candice?'

'What?'

'Aw, come on, don't be like that. I'm due on stage again soon and I won't be able to concentrate if you're mad at me.' He lifted her hair and blew gently onto the back of her neck.

'Careful, Beau. I wouldn't want your two *fans* over there to get jealous.' She turned to face him again. 'Next week, then?'

'What about it?'

'Can I book the eyebrow course for next week?'

He patted his front pockets. 'No can do, I'm afraid. Money's a bit tight.'

'Like your trousers,' she muttered.

He kissed her forehead. 'Oh, you do make me laugh, Candice. Look, leave it with me and I promise to sort it. Couple of weeks tops, okay?' He finished the rest of his pint in one long gulp. 'I'd better go and get myself sorted. Don't want to keep the punters waiting.' He pressed his lips to hers. 'Love you.'

She watched him weave his way back to the stage and sling his guitar strap over his head. He fiddled with the tuning pegs, probably more for dramatic effect than any useful purpose. With a quick swivel of his head, he flicked his hair out of his eyes. There was a ripple of applause as he leaned towards the microphone. 'Gee, thanks, you guys.' For some unfathomable reason he'd adopted an American accent, even though he originally hailed from Basingstoke.

'He's not bad, actually.'

Candice turned to see the bouncer leaning against the bar. 'Yes, indeed. He's exceptionally talented.'

'Hmm . . . that's as maybe. He's still a bit of a prat, though.' He pointed at her half-empty glass and shouted to the barman, 'Stick another one in there, please, Gaz.'

She covered the glass with her palm. 'Oh no, not for me. You've been too kind already.'

'Nonsense,' he dismissed. 'Gaz, pour this girl a drink.'

17

I'm sitting in my favourite spot in the conservatory overlooking the garden. Frank is by my side, snoring softly, even though it's not yet lunchtime and he hasn't long since got out of bed. There are few pleasures that come with getting old, but just sitting in quiet contemplation with your best friend by your side is one of them. I cover his hand with my own and he gently stirs and shifts position. I can see Simeon out in the garden, snipping herbs for lunch. That's how posh it is in here. There's not much there at this time of year, though. The mint and parsley are yet to flourish, but I can see that Simeon's clutching a bunch of woody rosemary. Makes sense: I know from the menu that it's lamb for lunch. I'm thankful every single day that I chose this place to spend my final few years. Some of the homes I looked at, well, you wouldn't want to board your dog there. It'd make your toes curl if I told you how much it was costing, but I've done my sums and reckon my money will last another five years. If I do manage to survive that long, I expect I'll be past caring where I live.

Candice should be here very soon and I'm excited to see her. She's such a sweet girl, and although I'll be pleased for her, I'm dreading the day she leaves and pursues her dreams.

I shake that thought from my head. There's a while to go before that happens, and we have our trip to Italy coming up. I'm literally counting off the days and that big red circle on my calendar is getting ever closer. I'm fighting fit, I know I am, but every sniffle, every ache, every weird heart palpitation reminds me that time's running out. I've lived for a hundred years. A couple more months isn't too much to ask, is it?

I can hear raised voices in the corridor. Mrs Culpepper's trademark shrill tone has gone up an octave. 'Do you value your employment here, Miss Barnes?' I hear her say. I jab at the button that will tilt my chair and help me to my feet. The motor kicks in and the low humming it makes is enough to wake Frank. 'What's going on?' he asks.

The chair spits me out and I reach for my walking frame. 'I don't know yet, but I intend to find out.' My aged bones and muscles protest as I try to move quickly. I make a determined fist of it, though, and manage quite a speedy shuffle.

In the corridor, Candice is standing in front of Mrs Culpepper, her head bowed as she fiddles with the toggles on her coat. 'I'm sorry, Mrs Culpepper. It won't happen again.'

Mrs Culpepper seems to soften. 'Make sure it doesn't, Candice. We have standards here, you know, and tardiness will not be tolerated.' With a quick nod to me, she turns and bustles off down the corridor. Candice sticks her tongue out at her retreating figure.

'What did you do, Candice?'

'Oh, hello, Jenny,' she says. 'I didn't see you there.' She gives a helpless shrug. 'Late, wasn't I? I didn't do it on purpose. I got my days muddled up and didn't realise I should've started at eight this morning.'

She looks terrible. Pale face, dark rings under her eyes, hair scraped back off her face with an Alice band, revealing a large spot over her left eyebrow.

I hold out my hand. 'Come to my room, will you? I need help with something.'

She bites down on her bottom lip. 'Mrs Culpepper wants me to start on the tables.'

'They can wait. Take me to my room, please.'

I take charge and insist she sits down. She ignores the armchairs by the window and with a nervous glance towards the door sits down on my bed. She immediately chews at the skin around her thumbnail.

'Stop that, Candice.'

She withdraws her hand and smooths out my already flawless duvet cover instead.

'Okay, then. Let's have it,' I say, thrusting a mug of tea in her hands. It's been a while since I've entertained a guest in my room, and it feels good to do something as simple as make a brew for someone who's obviously upset. A proper brew too, made with boiling water in a pre-warmed teapot. I fear it's a lost art.

I lower myself into an armchair. 'I'm waiting.'

She blows on her tea before taking a sip. 'It's Beau.'

I resist an eye roll. I might've known.

'What's he done now?'

'Don't say it like that, Jenny. It was all a misunderstanding.'

I take in her bedraggled appearance with renewed horror. 'Has he hit you?'

'What? No! How could you even think that? Beau would never raise a hand to me.'

I purse my lips and raise my eyebrows. It's an expression I hope she'll interpret as one of disbelief without me having to actually admit it.

'We had words after we got back from the Lemon Tree, that's all.'

'Go on.'

She gives a dramatic sigh. 'It was all my fault.'

'I doubt that, but please continue.'

She rubs her forehead vigorously. 'Aargh, I'm never drinking again.'

'Again, I doubt that.'

She slumps back and rests her head on my pillow, staring at the ceiling. I notice a fat tear slide down the side of her face, but say nothing.

'I hadn't had much to eat, that was the trouble. Simeon made me a chip barm before I left here, but it wasn't enough to soak up all the alcohol Adrian bought me.'

'Adrian?'

'The bouncer at the Lemon Tree. He took pity on me and decided it was his job to buy me drinks while Beau was on stage. I tried to refuse but he wouldn't take no for an answer and it'd been ages since I'd been to a bar and had some proper fun. Beau was brilliant, he had the audience bouncing, and when he was done with his second set they actually shouted for an encore.'

She lifts her head to look at me. 'I honestly thought in that moment all our financial problems would be over. He'd get the regular slot, then word would spread and he'd be playing to bigger venues, perhaps performing his own stuff, writing for other bands even.'

There's a solid lump of dread in the pit of my stomach. 'What happened?'

She swings her legs off the bed and sits up. 'I was on my third glass of wine, and they were big ones, so I'd had the best part of a bottle.' She pinches the bridge of her nose as she inhales. 'Adrian was sitting on the stool next to me and we were facing each other. He told me a joke about something or other just as I was taking a sip of my wine. I laughed so much that I spat my wine out just like they do in cartoons. Some landed on his thigh and I automatically leaned forward and wiped my hand along his trousers.' She groans and holds her head in her hands. 'At this point, Beau appeared.' She shakes her head. 'Well you can imagine how that looked to him.'

'But surely you explained the situation?'

'I tried to, but he was livid. He ignored my explanation and just took a swipe at Adrian.'

'He punched a bouncer?' From the picture I've seen of Beau, he couldn't knock the skin off a rice pudding.

'He tried, but Adrian was too quick for him. He's ex-army, you know. He grabbed Beau's wrist and had his arm up round his back before Beau could blink.'

I try to resist a smile, because I can see how distraught Candice is. Silly little sod she's got herself shacked up with.

'Anyway, needless to say, that's the end of Beau's career at the Lemon Tree and it's all my fault. I can't do the eyebrow course now and heaven knows how long it'll be before we have enough money for me to do Beauty Therapy Level Two. I've ruined everything.'

'I'm sorry, Candice, but I fail to see how any of this is your fault. It was unfortunate, I'll grant you that, but you're not responsible for Beau's loss of control.'

'He doesn't see it that way.'

'Why am I not surprised?' I mutter, not quite under my breath.

'We had a massive barney when we got home. Neighbours were even banging on the ceiling.'

'And he didn't hit you?'

She hesitates too long. 'No, I've already told you. There was a bit of . . . um . . . shoving, that's all.'

'Shoving?'

'It was nothing.' She stands up abruptly. 'Now I'll have to go or Mrs C will be on the warpath again. I can't afford to lose this job an' all.'

Several hours pass before I have a chance to speak to Candice again. She helped out with the lunch, filling our glasses and scraping our plates when we'd finished. I could tell she was deliberately avoiding eye contact with me or anybody else. Mrs Culpepper stood in the corner of the dining room, her hands clasped behind her back, her beady eye missing nothing.

I'm sitting at the jigsaw in the day room when Candice finally appears. Over my shoulder she picks up a puzzle piece and edges it into place.

'I've been looking for that one for ages,' I exclaim. 'Thank you, Candice.'

'At least I'm good for something,' she sighs.

'Stop that. Self-pity's not an attractive trait, love.'

She picks up another piece of the jigsaw, absently turning it over in her fingers before slouching down in the chair next to me. 'I've got some time if you want to talk. I need to know what happened to your *love triangle*.' She frames the last two words with air quotes and seems to find it amusing. I swallow my annoyance at her casual mocking of my love life, because she doesn't know what she's saying. I've opened Pandora's box now, and it's too late to put the lid back on.

18

Cocooned in the Welsh countryside, in the protective embrace of a loving family, it was easy to forget there was a war on. Rationing barely took its toll. There was a glut of milk, butter and chicken, and they were even permitted to keep a pig for their own consumption. Jenny and Louis ate better here than they had in Manchester, thriving on the abundance of fresh home-grown vegetables, the affordable offal their mother was fond of cooking already a distant memory.

Jenny wandered into the kitchen to find Delyth with her elbows on the table, massaging her temples with her fingers. 'He's getting closer, Jenny.'

'Who's getter closer to what?' she asked, plonking down the basket of eggs.

'Hitler, that's who.'

'What's he done now?'

'Invaded Holland and Belgium, hasn't he?' Delyth jabbed at the table with her finger. 'Mark my words, it'll be us next.'

Jenny shook her head. 'No, no, Del, that won't happen.'

'That's probably what the Dutch and the Belgians thought.' Delyth stared at her through dimmed eyes. 'Where will it all end, bach?'

Jenny gazed out of the window at the sunshine shafting through the trees. Ivor the goat had climbed onto the garden wall, craning his neck to reach the low-hanging branches. She turned to Del but was only able to offer a weak smile. She had no answer.

Nico stood outside his shop, winding the canopy over the tables to shield them from the May sunshine.

'Morning, Nico,' Jenny said. 'Terrible news, isn't it?'

Almost a week had gone by since the dance, and the opportunity to slip into town had not presented itself. She decided to keep it casual and make no mention of the kiss, even though it had consumed her every waking thought since.

He took a step towards her, both arms outstretched, pending an embrace. She laid his jacket across them. He looked at it as though he'd never seen it before. 'Oh, right, I wondered where this had gone. Thank you. Come, come.' He pulled out a chair. 'Sit down and tell me all about this terrible news you have.'

'Erm . . . surely you've heard? The German invasion of Holland and Belgium?'

'Oh, that,' he said dismissively. 'I thought you had something important to tell me.'

'You don't think that's important?'

'I am Italian. This war is not mine. I try to keep my distance.' He reached across the table until his fingers touched hers. 'I feared you would never come.'

'I've been busy. There's so much to do at the farm, and Del can be a right tyrant when she wants to be.'

'I haven't been able to get you out of my mind, Jennifer.

I am almost insane with it. I wanted to come to the farm to see you, to explain my feelings, but I was afraid it would make things difficult, you know, with Lorcan.' He clutched his stomach. 'In here, I feel sick, I cannot eat. What is wrong with me?'

'Ha, I knew it!' Lena appeared in the doorway, a knowing smile on her lips. 'My son, he is in love.' She threw her arms in the air, Italian-style. 'All week he has been moping like a puppy, picking at his food, gazing off into the distance when he has work to do.' She flicked Nico's ear. 'I'm right, aren't I, hmm?'

'Mamma, you are embarrassing Jennifer.'

'No I'm not, I'm embarrassing you.' She flicked her head skywards and disappeared into the shop.

'I'm sorry about that,' said Nico.

She hardly dared hope. 'Is it true?'

He took both her hands in his. 'Jennifer, I don't have these feelings ever before so I don't know what it is, but I do know that when I am not with you, I cannot think about anything but when I will next see you. It has been driving me crazy. I want to take you out, I want to cherish you, I want to—'

Smiling, she put her finger to his lips. 'What did you have in mind?'

'Really? You will allow me to take you out?'

'Nico!' his mother hollered from inside the shop. 'Just get on with it. You have work to do.'

'Tomorrow,' he said. 'We shall go to the seaside. I will pack a picnic lunch.'

Jenny nodded slowly. 'That sounds perfect.'

*

She didn't want to keep it from Lorcan, but neither did she want to make an announcement either. That would mean making a bigger deal of it than it actually was. He was in the stable, picking the stones out of the hoof of the carthorse, talking away to the beast as though it understood every word.

'Can I help you with anything?' she asked, holding her hand under the horse's whiskery muzzle.

Lorcan straightened up, rubbing his back like someone three times his age. 'You can fill up his water if you like.'

'Are you all right, Lorcan?'

'Just slept funny, I think, nothing to worry about.'

'Lorcan, I—'

'Jenny! Lorcan!' Louis clattered into the stable, his satchel flying behind him. '*Un, dau, tri, pedwar, pump!*'

Lorcan cracked a smile. 'Well, there's clever.'

'What are you two on about?'

'I can count to five in Welsh,' beamed Louis.

'He's like a little sponge, I tell you,' said Lorcan, oozing pride.

Jenny gazed in wonder at her brother. He'd been terrified of starting school, but already, at the end of his first week, all his fears had evaporated. He delved into his satchel. 'I've got homework.' He held up a dog-eared exercise book. 'My teacher gave me some special words to learn because I live on a farm.'

Lorcan looked at the book. '*Ceffyl, buwch, dafad, asyn, gafr.*'

Jenny smiled. She loved to hear him speaking Welsh. Even though the family were careful to stick to English when she was around, she sometimes overheard them talking to each other in their ancient native tongue.

'Horse, cow, sheep, donkey, goat,' said Lorcan. 'You'll learn those in no time, a clever lad like you.'

'I hope so, because I can't understand what all the other kids are saying. There's only me and Donald from back home who can speak English, apart from the teacher.'

'I didn't learn to speak it myself until I was eight years old. Don't worry, I'll help you with your Welsh. Mammy Del and Tad will help you too. You'll be speaking it like a native before you know it.'

Jenny bent down and peered at Louis's face. She reached up her sleeve for a handkerchief, blotting it on her tongue. 'Come here, you little rascal. What've you got round your mouth?'

Louis licked his lips. 'Ice cream. Nico gave it to me when I came out of school.'

Lorcan turned away and picked up the horse's foot, scraping with the hoof pick a little more savagely than before.

'Well I hope you said thank you.'

Louis nodded. 'I did. He had a little bag of cakes, biscuit things they were. Said they were for your picnic tomorrow. Can I come?'

Jenny opened her mouth, but struggled to find the words. 'Erm . . . well, I'm not sure . . .'

'You can stay here with me, Louis. Looks like it's going to be warm, so I'll teach you to swim in the pool under the fountain if you like.' Lorcan stared at Jenny, his cerulean eyes clouded with defeat. 'If that's all right with you.' He tossed the hoof pick into a bucket and walked out.

Later, Jenny tucked Louis into bed and kissed his forehead. 'Night, Lou, sweet dreams.'

He snuggled into his pillow, Mrs Nesbitt tucked under his chin. 'Jenny, you've made Lorcan sad.'

She sat back down on the bed. 'What're you talking about?'

Louis shuffled into a sitting position, his eyes wide. 'He's sad because you didn't ask him to go on the picnic tomorrow.'

'Did he say that to you?'

He wrinkled his nose, his tone serious. 'No, but I can tell.'

'It's not that kind of picnic, Louis. It's just for me and Nico because we're . . . um . . . special friends.'

'But Lorcan is a special friend too, isn't he? He's my bestest friend,' he added sagely.

'You like Nico too, though, don't you?'

'Yes. He gives me ice cream.'

'And what if he didn't give you ice cream? Would you still like him then?'

Louis shrugged. 'Dunno, maybe.'

She pressed him back onto the pillow. 'Time to sleep now, Lou.'

'But I'm not tired,' he pouted. 'Can I do my homework in bed?'

She opened her mouth in mock-horror. 'Where has my little Louis gone? The boy who didn't want to start school, who said it was a waste of time and he wasn't going to go and nobody could make him?'

He pointed at his own chest, frowning. 'I'm here.'

'I know you're here,' she said, laughing. 'I meant . . . Oh, never mind.' She passed him his homework book and a pencil. 'Just ten minutes and then you have to go to sleep.'

She watched from the doorway as he wrote out the Welsh

words, his tongue protruding in concentration. 'Love you, Louis.'

He didn't bother to look up, just nodded and waved her away. 'I know.'

Outside in the mild evening air, the smell of woodsmoke mingled with the hawthorn blossom. Jenny pulled down a branch and sniffed the cluster of white flowers, wrinkling her nose in disgust.

'Smell like death, don't they?' said Lorcan, appearing with a struggling lamb tucked under his arm. He ran his hand over the creature's head. 'There, there, little one, calm down now. I've got you.' He produced a bottle of milk from his pocket and stuck it into the eager lamb's mouth, then sat on the wall, fighting to keep hold of the bottle as the animal tugged at the teat.

Jenny tickled the lamb's head. 'Another orphan?'

Lorcan nodded. 'Aye, I thought I'd found her a foster mam, but she's taken umbrage and won't let it anywhere near her.'

'Poor little thing.'

He shrugged. 'She'll be all right, I'll make sure of it. Perhaps Louis could take charge of her.' He pulled on the lamb's ear. 'I remember my first pet lamb. I did such a fine job of nurturing her, she followed me everywhere, and when I left the farm for any reason, she'd wait by the gate bleating after me until I disappeared out of sight. Drove Mam mad. Of course I made the mistake of naming her. Gwendolene, I called her. Made it difficult when she eventually went to market.' He ran a hand through his mop of curls. 'On second thoughts, perhaps it's better if Louis steers clear. You know how attached he gets to the animals.'

123

He fell silent, the only sounds a blackbird high in the tree above and the sucking noises of the greedy little lamb.

'So,' he said eventually. 'You're off on a picnic tomorrow, are you?'

'Yes, that's right. It was good of our Louis to mention it.'

'It's not a secret, is it?'

'No, but I wasn't sure how you'd feel about it.'

The lamb had drained the bottle but continued to grab at the teat with her teeth, engaging Lorcan in a tug-of-war. He wrenched it out of her mouth. 'It's got nothing to do with me, Jenny. You can picnic with whoever you want.' He scooped up the lamb and walked off.

19

2019

Candice runs her fingers over the cottage pictured in the jigsaw. 'Is this what the house in Wales looked like?'

I peer at the thatched roof and cream stone walls covered in burgeoning wisteria. 'Not really, love. This kind of house only exists on jigsaws and boxes of chocolates.' I catch her look of disappointment. 'Mynydd Farm had a charm all of its own, but what made it special was the people who dwelled within its whitewashed walls.'

'You were fond of them, weren't you? I can tell. The Evans family, I mean. They weren't your blood relations and yet you speak of them as though they were. I wish I had that.'

I suddenly feel incredibly selfish and self-centred. 'You've listened to me prattling on long enough, Candice. Why don't you tell me about your family?'

She scoffs so loudly that old Myrtle on the sofa nearby snaps awake, dislodging her false teeth in the process.

'What, what was that? Who's there?' she asks, before dropping off again, her teeth resting in her lap.

'I've never had a family, Jenny, not one worth speaking about anyway. When I was seven, my pathetic excuse for a mother dropped me off at a babysitter's and never came back.'

'That's awful, Candice. You poor little mite. Did she have her reasons?'

'You could say that. She was found dead in a squat several days later. Heroin overdose.'

I'm not sure what's more shocking, the circumstances of her mother's demise or the casual way in which Candice tells me.

'Oh, you poor little darling.' I hesitate before asking my next question, because I instinctively know the answer is not going to lift my mood.

'Was your father on the scene?'

'Don't make me laugh. Sharon wasn't particularly fussy when it came to bed partners. I've no idea who he is and neither had she.'

'You were only seven, though. What happened to you then?'

'Shunted around from one council-run care home to another.' She picks at her nail varnish. 'There were a few foster families along the way, but they didn't work out. I was always told it was my fault; that I was a difficult child.'

'Sounds as though you didn't have much of a role model.'

She nods slowly. 'I never felt I belonged to anybody. There wasn't a single person in the whole world who loved me. Can you imagine that? I don't ever remember Sharon telling me she loved me either. I wasn't even allowed to call her Mummy. I did once, and this is the permanent reminder.' She leans in to give me a closer look at a small scar dangerously close to the edge of her eye. 'She lashed out and caught me with this sovereign ring thing she used to wear.'

'That's terrible, Candice. I'm so sorry.'

126

'Oh, she didn't do it on purpose. It wasn't premeditated or owt; she just did it instinctively.'

I refrain from pointing out that a mother's instinct should be to protect and nurture.

'It was the only time she hit me, and I made sure I always called her Sharon after that.' She slaps her hands on her thighs, indicating that she's done with talking about her miserable past. 'That's why I'm so happy with Beau. At last I've got someone who actually cares about me.'

I try to remain impassive, but evidently fail.

'Don't look like that, Jenny. Beau's good for me.'

I don't feel like getting into a difficult conversation about Beau, so decide to leave it for now and change the subject. 'Do you want to hear about the picnic?'

She looks around. 'I didn't know there was going to be a picnic.'

'There isn't. I meant my picnic with Nico.'

She sneaks a look at her watch. 'Go on then, I'd like that.'

I close my eyes, allowing the memory to unfurl. 'Even as I sit here now, I'm amazed at how clearly I remember that day. I don't wish to come over all soppy, Candice, but it was quite simply perfect. Perhaps if I was a writer or a poet I'd be able to create a better picture, but I'll just stick to the facts. I don't have time for much else.' I keep my eyes closed as though I'm under hypnosis. 'The day was warm and I was wearing a daffodil-yellow cotton dress I'd run up myself. Nico wore a white shirt and had rolled up his sleeves to reveal his tanned arms. He carried a wicker picnic basket with a red and white checked cloth over the top.' I pause and squeeze my eyes tighter still. That sounds like too much of a cliché. Maybe my memory isn't all it's cracked up to be after all.

'Jenny, are you all right?' Candice brings me back to the present.

'I'm grand, thank you. I'm sorry to disappoint you, Candice, but nothing happened on that picnic. Nothing untoward, anyway. There was no ripping off of each other's clothes, no rolling around on the rug.'

The colour has risen in her cheeks. 'Thank God for that.'

'There wasn't even a kiss. We just talked and talked. He wanted to know everything about me, and made me feel like the most special, interesting person in the world. We must've been out for hours, because neither of us noticed the darkening sky or the drop in temperature. When we got back to the farm, Nico picked up my hand and held it to his mouth, his eyes never leaving mine.'

'That's so sweet,' says Candice, and I swear she has tears in her eyes.

'I'm ashamed to say it now, but in that exquisite moment, I never wanted the war to end.'

'That's beautiful, Jenny.' She clamps her palm to her chest.

I lower my voice almost to a whisper. 'But then something terrible happened, and that's when everything changed.'

20

1940

The walk into Penlan, which had once seemed insurmountable, Jenny now covered with ease. There was no stopping to catch her breath and no need to take a break on the bench when she got there. She still used her cane, but even this was becoming more of a hindrance at times. In the month since the picnic, she and Nico had only managed snatched moments together, and the thought of seeing him again propelled her forward as effectively as a cattle prod. The time they spent with one another seemed to be dictated by Del and her never-ending list of chores. Jenny sometimes wondered if she did it on purpose.

She knew something wasn't right the minute she arrived in the cobbled square. A cluster of women stood outside Bernardi's Gelateria, arms folded and lips pursed, nodding knowingly at each other.

'What's going on?' Jenny asked the assembled throng.

'Been a spot of bother,' said one.

'Well, you can hardly blame people,' added another.

Jenny stared at the broken window, then at the shattered glass sprinkling the pavement.

'Excuse me,' she said, shoving the two women out of the

way. The sign on the shop door had been turned to read *Closed*, and she banged her fist against the glass. 'Nico, it's me, let me in.' She looked back at the crowing women. 'Bugger off, the lot of you.'

'Not until he comes out and explains himself.'

'Who?'

'That fascist, that's who.' The woman's expression was one of disgust, as though she'd bitten into a ripe juicy apple and found a maggot. 'I always knew there was something fishy about him.'

'Fascist?' Jenny frowned. 'What are you on about? Nico . . . Nico, open this bloody door.'

He appeared then, unshaven, his eyelids heavy with tiredness. He seemed reluctant to meet her gaze. 'Jenny, what do you want?' He wedged his foot in the door.

'I want to know what this is all about.' She pushed against the glass. 'Let me in, will you?'

Nico looked over her head to where the women stood resolutely, their faces hardened in judgement. Then he removed his foot and eased the door open just enough for her to squeeze through.

'Thank you. Now will you tell me what the hell is going on?'

'I assume you have not heard then?'

'Heard what?'

He dropped his shoulders in defeat. 'It had been coming, I think. I really hoped it would not come to this, but Mussolini, yesterday evening he declared war on Britain and France.'

'What? No,' she whispered. 'What was he thinking?' She

gave a determined shake of her head. 'No, that cannot be right. There must be some mistake.'

Nico exhaled so forcefully she felt the whoosh of his breath on her face. 'There is no mistake.'

'Come here.' She pulled him close, resting her head on his chest as he wrapped his arms around her.

'So,' she said eventually. 'What's all this got to do with the broken window?'

His jaw tightened a little as he took her hand. 'Come with me.'

He led her into the darkened back room, the heavy curtains blocking out all the light. 'Mamma, Papà, Jenny is here.'

Lena and Enzo were sitting at the table, Lena with a handkerchief pressed to her face. They were both staring at the large stone sitting between them.

Nico picked it up and held it out to Jenny. 'This came through the window.'

'You mean somebody threw it?'

Lena sobbed into her handkerchief. 'We live here for ten years. How can they do this to us?'

Enzo squeezed his wife's shoulder, then looked at Jenny. 'They did not even have the courage to sign it.'

Jenny pinched the bridge of her nose. 'I'm sorry. I don't know what you're talking about. Sign what?'

Nico pulled a piece of paper from his back pocket. 'This note, it was wrapped around the stone.'

She read the message scrawled across the paper: *EYETIES GO HOME. OUR ENEMIES ARE NOT WELCOME HERE.* The writer had used capital letters and appeared to have pressed down hard with the pen, revealing the anger behind the spiteful words.

She looked at him helplessly. 'But you *are* home. What does this mean? What the hell is an Eyetie?' She could feel the anger beginning to colour her cheeks. 'How dare someone do this?' She placed a hand on Lena's shoulder. 'I'm really sorry. I'm ashamed that the people of this town think it's all right to treat you this way. They're just a bunch of idiotic, small-minded, ignorant . . .' She grabbed the note and brushed past Nico.

The tight-lipped throng was still standing outside the shop. 'Right, come on then, which one of you wrote this?' She held up the piece of paper.

There was a general muttering as they nudged each other, but nobody answered.

She raised her voice. 'I asked you a question. If you feel so strongly about this, at least have the courage to own up to it.'

A woman shouldered her way to the front. 'What's going on?'

'Del,' Jenny gasped, the relief causing her words to tumble out. 'Somebody threw a stone through the window. A stone with a wicked note attached.' She swept her arm around the square. 'But not one of these cowards is willing to admit it was them.'

Del read the note as she bundled Jenny back inside the shop. 'I came as soon as I heard the news on the wireless. Where're Lena and Enzo?'

'In the back. They're proper shaken up.'

'I'm not surprised.'

She took her place at the table, taking hold of Lena and Enzo's hands. 'I'm so sorry. You don't deserve this.'

'We are the enemy now,' said Nico. 'It does not matter that

132

we have made this place our home, built up our business here. We are Italian and now we are at war with Britain.'

'But that's ridiculous,' said Jenny, her voice full of fury. 'Nothing's changed, you're still our friends. I will not have you driven out like this.'

Enzo struggled to his feet, evidence of his advancing years proven with each cracking bone. 'I'm going to take a broom to that glass outside, and then we're going to open the café as usual. Come on, Lena.' He heaved his wife up by her elbow. 'Domenico, can you please find someone to fix the broken window?'

Nico dug his fingers into his hair. Deep grooves seemed to have appeared in his forehead overnight. 'How is this right, Jennifer? My parents, they do not deserve this treatment. They have been a part of this community for a decade.'

'It will all blow over, don't worry.' Jenny gestured around the square. 'These people know you are not the enemy really. They've just had a shock. They'll be lining up for ice cream before you know it.'

'No, Jennifer, no more ice cream. There's not enough sugar. I don't think we can carry on any more.'

She shook her head. 'Don't be so defeatist. This gelateria is the lifeblood of the square.'

'Not much of a gelateria without the gelato.'

'Branch out then, use your imagination. You can get through this, we all can. Nothing's the same now there's a war on. We've all had to make sacrifices.'

He managed a smile. 'Oh, you are right, my sweet Jennifer. What would I do without you?'

The shuffling of feet caused them both to look up at the two policemen standing close by.

Nico stood and opened his arms. 'Ah, PC Morgan and Sergeant Williams, I believe. Am I glad to see you.' He pointed at the window. 'As you can see, we have had a small incident.' He pulled out a couple of chairs. 'Please sit down. Can I get you a drink, on the house, naturally?'

The younger of the two officers, PC Morgan, shook his head. 'This is not a social visit, Mr Bernardi.'

Nico laughed and clamped a hand on his shoulder. 'What is this *Mister* Bernardi business? We were at school together, Richard. Now, I don't want you wasting your time trying to find out who did this. I won't bring charges, because I understand that people act differently in wartime. I am willing to overlook this damage so that we can all get along peacefully just as we have been doing for the last ten years.'

PC Morgan looked down at his boots and then at his superior officer. 'We're not here about the window.'

'Oh,' said Nico, gripping the back of a chair. 'Then how can I help you?'

Sergeant Williams stepped forward, sweat moistening his broken-veined cheeks. 'Domenico Bernardi, you are under arrest.'

Nico guffawed, the genuine mirth erasing his newly acquired worry lines. 'Did you hear that, Jennifer? They have come to arrest me.'

'I heard them, Nico,' she said, a tiny nugget of fear burrowing deep inside her chest. 'I'm just not sure why you find that funny.'

'Well, there has to be some mistake. Why would they arrest

me? I haven't done anything wrong.' He turned to PC Morgan. 'Richard, tell her I haven't done anything wrong.'

'You haven't, Nico, but the orders have come from the top.'

'From Mr Churchill,' added Sergeant Williams. 'To quote, we have to "collar the lot".'

'Collar the lot?' Nico shrugged. 'What does that mean?'

Jenny clung to his arm with both hands. 'You're not taking him anywhere.'

Sergeant Williams adopted his best policeman's voice. 'The orders are clear. We have to arrest every male Italian resident in Britain. It's a defence measure, you see. You're all enemy aliens now.'

'Enemy aliens?' Jenny fought to keep her voice level. 'Don't be ridiculous. I've never heard anything so absurd in—'

Sergeant Williams interrupted. 'Where is your father, Mr Bernardi?'

'Oh no, surely not?' said Nico. 'He's practically an old man. I will come with you peacefully, but I beg of you not to take Papà.'

'We're just carrying out orders, Nico,' said PC Morgan. '*Every* male Italian is what Mr Churchill wants.'

'Well Mr Churchill can go whistle,' said Jenny.

Nico pulled her close. 'I will go with them. We will sort it out. Please can you look after Mamma and Papà?'

'But how long will that take?'

Nico looked at the two policemen. 'Well?'

'You just need to come to the station and we'll take it from there. Now please go and get your father. You need to pack a bag each, some clothes, your shaving things.'

'Shaving things?' said Jenny. 'Surely you're not keeping him long enough to grow a beard.'

Sergeant Williams turned to his colleague, a weary smile on his face. 'We'll die of old age at this rate.'

Jenny stared after Nico as he hurried back into the shop, overwhelming feelings of fury and helplessness driving her to sit down and cover her face with her trembling hands. She took a sip of her coffee, spitting it back into the cup when she realised it was stone cold. She looked at the younger policeman. 'Please – Richard, is it? Please don't take him away. I'm begging you.' She tugged at his sleeve. 'And Enzo, you can't take *him*. He's no threat.'

Sergeant Williams interrupted. 'The Enemy Alien Tribunal will be the judge of that, if you don't mind. Mr Bernardi senior will be interviewed to assess his threat level, just like everybody else.'

'It's okay, Jennifer,' said Nico, who'd emerged carrying a battered suitcase. 'I will cooperate. The sooner we get this sorted, the sooner we can carry on with our life.' He pulled her to her feet and held her face in his hands. 'And what a life it promises to be.' He looked fiercely into her eyes. 'I love you, Jennifer.'

She wavered on the spot, clutching at his elbows for support. 'I love you too, Nico.'

He pulled her into a tender embrace. 'I've been in love with you since the second I saw you.' He placed his lips softly to her ear. '*Colpo di fulmine.*'

He drew away, and called to his father, who was standing in the doorway. 'Come on, Papà!'

Lena clung to her husband's arm. Her features seemed

to have collapsed. 'I wait up for you, Enzo, you hear me? I wait up for you. Forever, until you come home.'

Sergeant Williams fished in his back pocket and addressed Nico. 'Put your hands behind your back, please.'

'Handcuffs? Aw, come on now. Is that really necessary? This whole thing is a . . .' Nico drummed at his temple, 'a farce, that is the word. A complete farce. Tell him, Richard.'

PC Morgan turned to his superior. 'Sir? Do you think we can leave the handcuffs? After all, they've said they'll come willingly. I don't think they'll give us any trouble.'

Sergeant Williams withdrew his truncheon and slapped it against his palm. 'They'd better not.'

Jenny linked her arm through Lena's as they watched the two men walk away, a police officer on either flank.

'I'll see you soon!' she shouted. 'Try not to worry. They'll have this mess sorted out in no time.'

A stillness lay over Mynydd Farm on her return, an eerie quiet that seemed to reflect the seriousness of what she had just witnessed in town. That two innocent men could be forcibly removed from their home in handcuffs whilst jeering neighbours looked on was inconceivable to her; the feeling of utter despair had sucked the fight out of her. She had left Del tending to the distraught Lena, who simply couldn't comprehend why they had snatched away her dear, gentle husband.

She trudged across the paddock, the long grass hindering her progress, as she made her way over to her namesake. The donkey looked up and twitched her ears in greeting as she approached. 'Hello, girl,' said Jenny, holding out her palm. 'Everything's so simple in donkey world, isn't it?' The

137

donkey nuzzled in her pocket, her velvety lips seeking out the pieces of carrot Jenny usually brought. 'There's nothing in there today, I'm afraid,' she cooed, absently pulling on the creature's tufty mane. She bowed her head and rested it on the donkey's neck. 'I love him so much and he said he loved me,' she managed through her tears. 'Nico said he loved me.' Her deep, guttural sobs were muffled by the animal's soft fur.

She lifted her head at the sound of feet dragging through the long pasture. 'Lorcan! How long have you been there?' She wiped her face with her sleeve, embarrassed by her tears.

His expression was difficult to read. Two vertical lines were stencilled between his eyebrows, but his eyes held a lightness that seemed at odds with his questioning expression. He dragged the long blade of grass he had been chewing from between his teeth. 'Not long. Why?'

She could feel the heat singeing her cheeks. 'Did you hear . . .?'

He took a long stride forward. 'About Nico getting arrested? Yes, I did.'

'No, I meant . . .'

'Bad news for him. I wonder what's going to happen now.' He draped his arm across the donkey's hind quarters, shaking his head. 'You think you know someone, and then this.' He tutted and shrugged his shoulders. 'I think we've all had a lucky escape.'

'What on earth are you talking about? Nico and Enzo are no threat to us. It's just a precaution. Common sense goes out of the window during wartime; people overreact to everything, including Mr Churchill.'

Lorcan raised his eyebrows. 'No smoke without fire.'

'You're enjoying this, aren't you?'

He bent down and plucked another blade of grass, nibbling on it thoughtfully. When he spoke again, she had to strain to hear his tremulous voice. 'You really have no idea, do you?'

'No idea about what?' She frowned.

He reached out and took hold of her wrist, his thumb caressing the pale skin underneath. 'I love you, Jenny.' He pointed at his chest as if to emphasise his declaration. 'Me. *I* love you.'

Her involuntary laugh disguised her shock. 'Give over, Lorcan. What a daft thing to say.' She pushed him playfully on his shoulder. 'Honestly, you are such a tease.'

His expression remained impassive, his features frozen. 'I mean it, Jenny. From the moment I first saw you—'

She held up her hand to stop him. Nico had said the same thing. *Since the second I saw you . . .*

'When . . . I mean, how . . .' She shook her head. 'Why have you never said anything before?'

'If you pick the blossom, then you must do without the fruit.'

'I've no idea what that means.'

'It means I didn't want to rush things. You don't get the chicken by smashing open the egg, as my grandaddy used to say. You have to be patient and wait for it to hatch.'

'Do you have to speak in riddles?' She bit her lip, not trusting herself to say anything else.

'You must have known I was falling for you,' he continued. 'I've tried to tell you before, but *he* always seemed to get in the way. It was me who took you to the dance that night, but it was *him* you couldn't take your eyes off.'

'Now you're just being stupid.'

'Am I?'

'Yes, you are.'

'So you didn't kiss him that night, then?'

She hesitated too long to give a convincing lie. And really, what was the point? She rubbed at her forehead, giving herself more time to formulate an answer. 'Yes, we kissed. I'm sorry, Lorcan.'

He bunched both his fists, his voice quivering. 'I knew it. Bloody Eyeties, they're all the same.'

'What . . . what did you just call him?'

He frowned. 'Nothing.'

'Yes you did, you called him an Eyetie.'

'So?'

She took a step backwards, suddenly craving some distance between them. 'It was you,' she whispered. 'You threw that stone at Nico's window.'

21

Candice rubs her hands up and down her arms and gives a dramatic shiver. 'Ooh, I've got goosebumps, I have. What a traitor!'

I straighten out my spine as best I can. I'm stiff from sitting at the jigsaw table for so long. 'He always denied it, and I was desperate to believe him. I hated the idea that somebody who was normally so kind and considerate could be that spiteful.' I stretch my arms above my head. 'Candice, love, I'm tired now. Would you mind taking me back to my room?'

She stands and positions my walking frame next to me. 'Do you want to walk with this, or shall I get the wheelchair?'

I think about my suite at the end of the corridor, the green carpet stretching ahead like a ribbon of freshly mowed grass. I hate giving in to my old age, but sometimes we must accept what we can and cannot do. 'Can you get the chair, please?'

'Of course, just wait here, I'll bob along and get it now.'

'I think I'll have a little nap before tea,' I say when she returns. 'Frank fancies a game of crib later and I'll need my wits about me or else he'll fleece me for everything I've got. He's acquired a giant set of playing cards to make it easier for me to hold them, bless him.'

141

She settles me into the chair and pops down the foot rests. 'You're more than a match for anyone, Jenny. I wouldn't like to take you on in any challenge.'

'What, not even the hundred-yard dash?'

'Well, okay, I'd probably beat you at that,' she concedes. 'But anything using your brain, well, I wouldn't stand a chance.' She releases the brake and manoeuvres me out of the day room. 'I've really messed up this time. Beau's never going to forgive me for losing him his Lemon Tree gig.'

'He'll get over it, love. He's a grown man. These things happen.' I'm glad I have my back to her when I ask my next question. 'Are you afraid of Beau, Candice?'

She gives a snort of laughter, but it sounds forced. 'Afraid? Don't be daft. Why would I be afraid of him?' She stops as she waits for the electronic door to open, then pushes me through. 'No, I'm not afraid of him. I love him. He's my world.'

I can't quite put my finger on what it is, but I'm sure she's hiding something. 'You're a good girl, Candice. You deserve the best.'

'Beau *is* the best. Stop fretting.'

We arrive at my bedroom door and she turns around and pushes it open with her back, dragging me over the threshold. 'Here we are then. You've got about an hour before tea. Do you want it in here?'

In all the years I've been here, I can count on one hand the number of times I've eaten my evening meal alone in my room. 'Certainly not, Candice. I can still manage to put my face on and join the others in the dining room. I may only be one chest infection away from meeting my maker, but I'm not quite dead yet.'

She laughs as she hefts me out of the chair and guides me to my bed. 'I hope I'm as feisty as you when I'm a hundred.'

'Feisty or cantankerous?'

'Hmm . . .' she says, adjusting my pillows. 'You said it.'

She glances at her own reflection in my dressing table mirror. 'Look at the state of me.' She tips her head upside down and ruffles her hair. When she stands up, she looks like she's had her fingers in the plug socket.

'Do you want to borrow my brush, Candice?'

'I think it's going to take more than that, Jenny. I honestly don't know what Beau sees in me sometimes. He could have anybody he wants, and yet—'

'Enough of that!' I shout, my patience deserting me. I stop short of wagging my finger at her. 'Enough of that nonsense. You're a lovely-looking girl, a right bonny lass if ever I saw one, but more important than that, you're beautiful on the inside. You have such a kind heart, and if anything, he's the lucky one.' I end my little outburst with a determined nod of my head.

She continues to stare at her reflection, turning her head from left to right. 'Do you really think so? Beau says I could make more of myself if only—'

'Candice! I'm sick of hearing what Beau says. You're perfect just the way you are.'

She tears her gaze away from the mirror and looks at me instead. 'Believe me, Jenny, I'm far from perfect.' She squeezes my hand and offers me a watery smile. 'I'll be back to collect you later for tea. You have a nice rest now.'

I'm far too agitated to rest. That bloody Beau has an uncanny ability to vex me no end. God forbid I ever get my hands on him. My heart rate has accelerated way beyond what is good for me. I need to calm down. My eyes settle on my memory box, and I suddenly know what I have to do.

I carry the box back over to my bed and with a shuddering breath lift the lid. I'm all fingers and thumbs as I root to the bottom of the box, a fleeting moment of panic gripping me when I can't find what I'm looking for. My sigh of relief must be audible out in the corridor as I snatch up the photo and press it to my chest. My heart aches and tears blur my vision as I study the picture. Her wide, trusting eyes stare back at me as she hugs her dolly to her chest, oblivious to the tragedy that is to come. 'My darling girl,' I whisper. 'My beautiful, brave girl.' With trembling lips, I kiss her face. 'Sleep tight, Eva. God bless.'

I feel calmer now. I am going to do what's right. I glance at the red ring on the calendar, eight weeks away. I *am* going to make it.

Candice dithered on the pavement, looking left and right before casting a final furtive glance over her shoulder. She wasn't comfortable with it, but Beau had left her no choice. Naturally, she hadn't told him about the visit, and if it proved to be unfruitful, there would be no reason to ever mention it and he'd be none the wiser. He had been in a foul mood all week. She could understand his disappointment about losing the gig at the Lemon Tree, but a week-long sulk really was a disproportionate reaction, in her opinion.

There were a few early-doors drinkers huddled around the tiny brass-topped tables, picking at bags of crisps and nuts. The place had a different vibe at this time of day. There was no loud music or flashing lights, and in one corner an elderly gentleman was sitting reading a newspaper, a black Labrador at his feet. She approached the bar and scanned the array of drinks behind it.

The barmaid looked up from her magazine. 'Yes, love?'

'Um . . . just a lime and soda, please.'

'Ice?' She reached above her head and pulled down a tumbler.

'Erm, yes please. Is . . . is the manager in?'

The barmaid hosed the soda water into the glass. 'If you mean Mike, he's not due in for another couple of hours.'

Candice took a sip of her drink. Damn, she should have made sure he was here before ordering.

'Can I give him a message?'

'Well, I was just wondering . . .'

'Hello again. Didn't expect to see you back here.'

She turned to see Adrian standing with his arms folded, his pecs straining against his white T-shirt. He didn't look half as threatening now he wasn't dressed all in black, but nevertheless, she could well see the folly in Beau's attempt to land one on him. The guy was solid muscle.

'How're you?' he asked, sounding as though he actually cared about her answer.

'Fine,' she lied. 'I just came to see if . . . if there was any chance that . . .'

'That we'd consider hiring that skinny runt of a boyfriend of yours again?'

She didn't even try to defend Beau. 'He's an idiot, I know that, but he's really sorry and promises it won't happen again.'

'Sent you to do his dirty work, did he?'

'Oh God, no. He'd go mad if he knew I was here, especially talking to you.'

'Jealous type, is he?'

She managed a laugh. 'You noticed?'

Adrian leaned on the bar and regarded her carefully. She recognised the manly scent of his black peppercorn body wash. 'Been giving you a hard time, has he?'

She averted her gaze and picked up her glass, shaking it to

loosen the ice cubes before taking a sip. 'Not really,' she said eventually. 'He's just been a bit . . . quiet, that's all. I feel sorry for him. He tries so hard and he was made up when he got this slot, and then I had to go and ruin it all.'

'I think you'll find *he* ruined it all when he tried to lamp me.'

She prodded at the ice cubes with her straw. 'Does it matter who's to blame?'

'He wasn't bad, as it goes,' conceded Adrian. 'A few people have been asking when he'll be back.'

'Really? Oh, it would be brilliant if he could come back. On a trial basis again, obviously. But I promise you he'll behave. I'll make sure of it.' She reached out to touch his arm, then retracted her hand quickly. 'Please, Adrian. Can you have a word?'

'Beau, Beau!' she shouted, bounding up the stairs. She fumbled with her key in the lock, the excitement causing her to drop it on the floorboards. 'You'll never guess what?' She managed to get the door open. 'Beau, where are you?'

She dumped her bag on the kitchen counter and headed for the bedroom. The unmade bed was empty, save for a greasy takeaway pizza box lying where she usually did. 'Urgh, that's disgusting,' she muttered, picking it up. A couple of olives fell onto her pillow. 'For God's sake . . . Beau, where are you?'

She had tried to ring him with the good news, but he'd failed to answer and had ignored her subsequent text messages. He hadn't spoken a word to her over the last week. No matter how many times she apologised, he could hardly bear to look at her. Now she slumped down on the sofa and stared at the coffee table, littered with scribbled notes in his handwriting. She picked up the nearest one.

To the ends of the earth I'd go for you
To the end of time I'll never stop loving you
But you make it so hard, I can hardly continue
Like an anchor you drag me down with you (rpt)

She could feel her anger simmering below the surface. Was he comparing her to an anchor? 'Oh Beau, you're as pathetic as your crappy lyrics.' She screwed up the paper and threw it across the room. 'But even though you make it impossible sometimes, I do love you.' She picked up her phone and dialled him again, but predictably it went straight to voicemail. She clicked the red button. There was no point in leaving another message for him to ignore.

She woke up feeling disorientated, her neck stiff and her mouth furred up and uncooperative. A rogue spring from their ancient sofa was digging into her hip. She reached out blindly for the glass on the coffee table and half sat when she couldn't find it.

'This what you're looking for?'

She rubbed her eyes. 'Beau, is that you?'

She heard him move across the room and flick the light switch. She covered her eyes with her arm. 'Aargh, too bright, please turn it off. Ooh, me head's throbbing.'

'I asked you a question.'

She blinked several times as she waited for her eyes to become accustomed to the sudden brightness. Beau stood over her, holding the empty wine bottle.

'Where've you been, Beau? I've been worried.'

He tipped the bottle upside down theatrically. 'Yeah, it looks like it.'

She shuffled to the end of the sofa. 'Why didn't you answer my calls?'

'Candice, I'll be the one asking the questions. What's going on?'

'What time is it?'

'Half ten.' He placed the bottle on the table and folded his arms. 'I came to pick you up from work, to take you out for a bite to eat. I know I've been a childish prick this last week, so I wanted to do something nice for you.'

She couldn't control the sudden rush of heat to her neck. 'You . . . you came to Green Meadows?' Even in her wine-fogged stupor, she realised what this meant.

'Yes, I did, and guess what?'

She struggled to her feet and faced him, swaying gently as she placed her hands on his arms. 'Beau, I was going to tell you. Let me explain.'

He remained unmoved. 'I'd like that.'

She gestured to the sofa. 'Let's sit down, or can I get you a cup of tea?' She made for the kitchen but he grabbed her wrist. 'Ow, you're hurting me.'

He released his grip. 'Forget the effing tea then and just tell me where you went.'

'To the Lemon Tree,' she shouted, suddenly eager to get it

over with. 'I went to the bloody Lemon Tree to see if they would have you back. I wasn't hiding anything from you, I just didn't want to get your hopes up.'

He stared at her, his jaw clenching as he inhaled a deep breath. 'You . . . you went to see if they would have me back? Without even finding out if that was what I wanted?' His voice had taken on an ominous tone. 'You went to beg on my behalf? Have you any idea how emasculating that is?'

'Sorry, Beau. I didn't think . . .'

'No, you never do, that's your trouble.'

'But . . . but . . .' she babbled. 'It's good news. Adrian said you can go back. Apparently people have been asking after you. You were a big hit, they loved you. You can go again next Thursday and—'

'Adrian?'

'Yes, he rang his boss whilst I waited and squared it with—'

'Adrian? Mr bloody Universe, you mean? You went back to see the guy who was all over you?'

'He wasn't all over me, and stop putting words in my mouth, Beau. I didn't go back to see him, he just happened to be there, that's all.'

'How convenient. Had a laugh at my expense, did you?'

'It wasn't like that, honestly.' She collapsed back onto the sofa. 'I don't know why I bother. You're an ungrateful prat sometimes.' She rubbed her wrist pointedly, looking him in the eye. 'I'm parched. Can you fetch me a glass of water, please?'

'Hmm, what do you expect when you guzzle a bottle of red wine? Did you keep the receipt, by the way?' He turned towards the sink and filled a glass from the tap, handing it to her. 'Well?'

She dug into the pocket of her jeans and offered him the crumpled scrap of paper.

'Five quid?' He laughed. 'No wonder you've got a banging headache.'

She rested her head on the back of the sofa and closed her eyes. 'I know I shouldn't have bought it, but I thought we could have a little celebration. It was the cheapest one in the supermarket, special offer.' She felt him flop into the seat beside her, and opened her eyes. 'I'm sorry, Beau. I've messed up – again.'

He traced his finger down her cheek. 'You're so sweet, Candice. You're always thinking of somebody else. What're we going to do with you, eh?'

He pulled her under his arm and kissed the top of her head. 'I think it might be better if I gave you an allowance. It seems that just providing the receipts for everything isn't working.'

'Pocket money, you mean? You're going to give me pocket money?'

He interlaced his fingers with hers. 'Don't be silly, it's not pocket money. It's been going on for generations. Used to be called housekeeping.'

'I don't know, Beau. It seems a bit drastic. I'm not that bad with money, am I?'

'Well, it's up to you, babe. We can carry on as we are or you can let me take care of everything and then we'll save up much quicker for all the things we need.'

'But my wages are paid into my own account.'

'Yes, I've been meaning to mention that.' He drew her hand up to his lips and kissed it. 'I think we should open a joint account and have both our wages paid into that. Much better to have all our money in one place, where I . . . we . . . can keep an eye on it.'

'Hmm, I'm not sure . . .'

'And now I've got my slot back at the Lemon Tree, I'll let you book your eyebrow course.'

She sat up to face him. 'Really, Beau. Do you mean it? It's a hundred and eighty pounds. Are you sure we can afford it?'

'You leave that to me. Come on, time for bed.' He heaved her up off the sofa, grabbing her round the waist as her legs buckled, pulling her into a tight embrace against his own body. 'It's all right, Candice. I've got you.' He pressed his lips to her ear. 'And I'll never let you go.'

23

I've really missed Candice these past ten days or so. The place hasn't been the same without her and I've had to put up with an agency girl tending to my needs and not taking the slightest bit of interest in anything I have to say. It's as though I'm too old to have an opinion on anything and what I think doesn't matter as I'll be dead soon anyway. It's certainly made me appreciate Candice.

March has now slipped into April. After the usual white rabbits shenanigans, I found myself getting a little choked up wondering how many more months I would see, how many more times I would get to say those words. There's less than six weeks to go before our trip to Italy, and I'm determined to be on that plane. I have to be. There're things I have to do.

Candice is back today, though, and I have a surprise for her. Well, it's not a complete surprise, because I had to ask her for the measurements, but I've run her up a pair of curtains for her flat. I still have my old Singer sewing machine, and for somebody with my dressmaking skills it was hardly a challenge but I'm pleased that I can still see well enough to sew in a straight line and my fingers are just about dextrous enough to feed the fabric under the presser foot without causing major injury. Obviously, threading the needle was beyond my capabilities and Frank was no use either, what with his propensity to shake, but Mrs Culpepper stepped in and did the job.

I'm doing all right really, I suppose. In fact, I'm going to an aerobics class this afternoon. Don't laugh, I'm not kidding. Granted, I won't get out of my chair, but there'll be plenty of toe-tapping, leg extensions and overhead clapping, all set to music. It can be quite exhausting, but it keeps the blood flowing and staves off death for another day.

I can see Candice now coming up the driveway. There's definitely a bounciness to her gait and immediately my spirits lift. She looks radiant; there's colour in her cheeks and her hair has grown a little bit. I think she must've had it in rollers or something. There's a definite kink to it.

I'm beaming at her as she comes into the day room. Frank waves a hand in greeting, but it's me she makes a beeline for.

'Candice, love. It's good to have you back.' I reach up to clutch her freezing hand. 'Is it cold out there, petal?'

'A bit nippy, yeah,' she says bending to give me a kiss on my cheek. 'How've you been without me?'

'We've all missed you. Have you had a nice break?'

She reaches into her shoulder bag and pulls out a piece of paper. 'Ta-da!'

'What have you got there?'

'Have a look.' She thrusts the paper under my nose.

It's a diploma in Brow Lamination and Tinting. 'You did it,' I say, with genuine pride. 'Well done, Candice. I'm so pleased for you.'

'Can you believe it? I'm now qualified to see clients at home.

At least I will be when I've got my public liability insurance sorted out. We've cleared out the box room. Beau's got rid of all his clutter – old football programmes he's never going to read again, some sheet music and what have you, boxes of vinyl records that weren't worth anything and in any case he'd nothing to play them on. He was really good about it. We could've filled a skip with the clobber he was hoarding.'

'That's marvellous, Candice.' Her enthusiasm is infectious. 'And how is everything going at the Lemon Tree?'

'Oh, fantastic. They love him down there. He's only done two evenings since I last saw you, but he's really settled in, and you'll never guess what?'

'You'd better tell me then.'

'He's got another seventy-three followers on Instagram.'

I'm not quite sure what this means, but by the way her eyes are shining, I can only assume it's a positive thing.

'Everything's looking up for the pair of you then?'

'I'll say it is, Jenny. Once I start seeing clients at home, I'll be able to save up for Beauty Therapy Level Two and get a job in a salon.'

'Well,' I say, patting the back of her hand. 'We'll certainly miss you in here.'

'It won't be for ages yet. You can't get rid of me that easily.'

It's a relief to hear, but I don't say anything. The last thing Candice needs is me guilt-tripping her into staying and not fulfilling her ambitions. With any luck, she'll last me out.

'Come with me to my room,' I say. 'I could do with stretching my legs. No need for the chair; I'll manage with the frame, I think.'

*

155

She's thrilled with the curtains, genuinely delighted and completely in awe of me for making them.

'You're just so clever, Jenny. I don't know how you do it.'

'Curtains are a doddle, Candice. Anybody could run up a pair.'

'I couldn't. I wouldn't have a clue where to start.'

Perhaps she's right. We all have our strengths. And our weaknesses.

'And look here,' I say, reaching for a brochure. 'Page nineteen, that's our hotel in Italy.'

She studies the picture, her mouth open in wonder. 'My God,' she says. 'It's beautiful. Are you sure you can afford to go to all this expense?'

I refrain from telling her I can't afford not to. 'You let me worry about that, Candice.'

'Right then, I'd better crack on. Smells like Simeon has done his speciality for lunch. Make sure you leave me some.'

The smell of simmering apples and cinnamon wafts around the day room, the warm, buttery fumes reminiscent of a distant time and a different kitchen. My throat tightens and I fumble up my sleeve for my handkerchief.

'Jenny?' Frank says, his voice full of concern. He doesn't miss a trick, that one.

'I'm fine, Frank, you just concentrate on your crossword.'

He doesn't listen, he never does. In a flash he's by my side.

'Heavens above, Frank, you can't half shift when you want to.'

'What's the matter, Jenny?'

'Nothing, I've already told you I'm fine. Why don't you listen?'

I'm annoyed at myself for using such a sharp tone with my best friend. 'Oh, I'm sorry, Frank, just ignore me. I've been doing a lot of reminiscing recently and I'm tired . . . really tired.'

'You're allowed to be at your age. Come and have a sit with me on the sofa.'

I don't protest as he guides me out of the chair and over to the sofa overlooking the garden. He sits down next to me, puts his arm around my shoulders and pulls me close. Even at my age, it feels good to be in the arms of a man again. I expect it's a long while since Frank held a woman too. Maybe he never has. Perhaps he's always known women weren't for him.

'There, that's better, isn't it, Jenny? You lean on me now, I've got you.' I can smell his sandalwood cologne and the shoe polish he uses religiously every single day, and my heart swells with love for him. 'Your Ernest was a lucky fella, Frank.'

It takes him a while to answer and I'm worried I've upset him. 'No,' he says eventually. 'I was the lucky one.'

I close my eyes and snuggle into his chest. We must look like an old married couple to someone who knows no better.

'I'm going on a road trip, Frank.' I haven't told him about Italy yet because I know he'll try and persuade me not to go. He'll only say it'll be too much for me at my age.

He turns to me, just the one eyebrow raised. I can never understand how he does that. 'Road trip?' he says, tilting his head like an inquisitive puppy.

'I think that's what the young 'uns call it. I want to go back, Frank. One last time, I want to go back to Italy. In fact, I have to.'

'It's a long way. Do you think you're up to it?'

Here we go, I knew it.

'It may well be the death of me, but it's a chance I'm willing to take.'

'Why now?'

'Time's hardly on my side.' I manage a laugh. 'Seriously, though, it's seventy-five years since . . .' my throat closes up, 'since it happened. There's to be a commemoration. There was an article about it in *The Times* a couple of months back.'

He shakes his head, his eyes downcast. 'Yes, I remember you showing it to me. Shall I come with you?'

I smile at him with renewed affection. 'I appreciate the offer, but Candice is taking me. It'll be good for her too. If anybody deserves a break, she does.'

24

Beau was lying with his head on the pillow, arms behind his head, a skinny joint pinched between his lips. 'I'm really going to miss you, Candice.'

She stopped folding the washing and regarded his naked frame, only a crumpled sheet covering his modesty. She fanned her palm in front of her face. 'Do you have to smoke that in here, Beau?'

He took an exaggerated drag, his eyes narrowing. 'I said . . . I'm really going to miss you.'

'Well I'm going to miss you too, obviously, but it's only a week and you've got plenty here to keep you busy.'

'It should be me taking you to Italy, not some bloody interfering old biddy who's just using you because she has nobody else to go with.' He dropped the smouldering joint into his coffee mug. 'Italy is for lovers, babe.'

'Believe me, I'd much rather be going with you, Beau. I should be spending my first trip abroad with the guy I love.' She pulled a dress from the wardrobe and held it against her body as she studied her reflection in the mirror.

'Do you?' he asked.

She turned to face him. 'Do I what?'

'Love me.'

She threw the dress onto a nearby chair. 'You know I do,' she sighed.

He patted the space next to him. 'Leave all that then and come back to bed.'

'It's only five o'clock. I'm not tired.'

He grabbed hold of her wrist. 'Who said anything about sleeping?'

She pulled her hand away, laughing. 'You're insatiable, you are.'

'It's your fault for being so irresistible.'

She glanced at her reflection in the full-length mirror, her lacy underwear flattering her figure. 'Really? Do you fancy me now then?'

'Candice, I've always fancied you, you silly cow.'

'But when you said I could do with losing a few pounds, I thought . . .'

'I only suggested that because I knew it was what *you* wanted. I knew you'd be happier if you lost the bulge around your tummy and those love handles.' He held out his hand. 'And I was right, wasn't I? You look amazing, you can't deny that. Since you gave up the booze and all those oniony snacks you were so fond of, you've transformed yourself. And think of the money we've saved.'

'I haven't given up the booze. Just cut down, that's all. You make it sound as though I was an alcoholic with a fetish for Monster Munch.'

'Get away with you. You're just being over-sensitive as usual. You know, I can't believe you sometimes. You were always moaning your clothes were too tight and you looked fat in photographs.'

'Was I?' She frowned.

He softened his tone, injecting just a hint of humour. 'I worry about you, Candice. You've a shocking memory. I've lost count of the number of times you asked me if I thought you looked fat in something.'

She sat down next to him on the bed, smiling. 'I'm sure it wasn't that many.'

He ran his finger along her collarbone and down between her breasts. 'Come on, forget about all that now.' In one swift move he grabbed her hips and lifted her over his body so that she straddled him. 'You're beautiful, Candice. You're beautiful and you're all mine.'

She leaned down and kissed him on the lips. 'Better make it quick then, or else we'll be late.'

The day room had been prepared with two semicircles of chairs set out to afford the best view of the makeshift stage. Simeon had created some rather elaborate canapés; not for the first time, Candice thought he was wasted working in a residential home.

Beau removed his guitar from its case, slung the strap over his shoulder and began to tune the instrument. 'I can't believe you talked me into this, Candice. I must want my head feeling.'

'Don't be like that, Beau. They're going to love it, and I really want you to meet Jenny.'

He continued as if she hadn't spoken. 'I'm not even getting paid for it. When did I become such a soft touch?' He strummed his fingers against the strings, the sound echoing in the empty room. 'And look at the state of me. I'm supposed to be a rock star. I look like a geriatric Val Doonican.'

161

Candice had suggested he ditch the leather pants and ripped T-shirt and persuaded him to wear his dark jeans and a plain white cotton shirt. He had acquiesced to a point but had drawn the line at doing up his buttons, meaning his angel tattoo was still partially visible.

'I've no idea who Val Whatshisname is, but you look gorgeous.'

'Candice,' boomed Simeon, entering the room holding aloft a silver platter. 'I thought I heard voices.' He set down the platter, gave her shoulders a squeeze and kissed her on the cheek. 'Good to see you, kiddo.'

'Hi, Simeon.' She indicated Beau. 'This is my boyfriend.'

Simeon held out his hand. 'Pleased to meet you. I'm Simeon.'

Beau didn't look up. 'All right, mate.'

Simeon glanced at Candice, his eyebrows raised. 'Right, I'd . . . um . . . better crack on.'

'Is he always like that?' Beau asked once Simeon was out of earshot.

'Yes, he is,' she laughed. 'He does have a bit of a quirky dress sense. Not everyone can carry off red trousers with a mustard jacket, and I shouldn't think they'd want to. And the green bow tie is a step too far in my opinion, but he—'

'I wasn't talking about his crappy clothes. I meant is he always so bloody pervy? He was practically drooling over you.'

'For God's sake, Beau, Simeon's a colleague, that's all. He doesn't mean anything by it. He's married with three kids an' all.'

'That's the drawback, I suppose,' pouted Beau. 'Now you've got this knockout figure, men just can't keep their hands off you. Perhaps you should start piggin' out again. I miss my little Chubster.'

She took a step towards him and removed the guitar, laying it down on the chair. 'How many times, Beau? There's only you. There'll only ever be you. When will you realise that?'

He managed a smile. 'It's the downside of having a stunning girlfriend, I suppose.' He reached up to touch her face. 'Don't ever leave me, Candice.'

She clamped his hand to her cheek. 'Never.'

25

Candice has gone to a lot of trouble to organise this little musical evening for us. I can't say I'm really looking forward to it, what with Beau Devine as the headline act. I'm still aghast that that's his real name. Candice is convinced he was born to be a rock star. With a name like that, he was hardly going to end up as a banker or a scaffolder, but I think 'rock star' is pushing it a bit. I believe he's toning down his act for us, though. Not many heavy rock fans in here. I've decided to give him a chance for Candice's sake, even though I've pre-judged him and I'm rarely wrong about these things. People forget I've had a lifetime's experience of men.

There's a knock on the door and I heave myself to my feet. Frank's standing there, elbow crooked in anticipation. 'May I?' he smiles.

'You certainly may,' I reply, linking my arm through his. 'It's not often I have such a hot date come to call for me.'

He laughs readily and leans in towards me, his generous dousing of cologne making my eyes water.

There's a general hum of conversation as the room fills up and we settle down next to each other on the two comfiest seats at the front, thoughtfully reserved for us by Candice. A few feet away is a little wooden platform masquerading as a stage and a microphone on a thin silver pole. It's more Darby and Joan than Bridgewater Hall, but it'll do for us lot. From 'backstage', Candice sticks her head round the door and gives me a thumbs-up. She looks luminous, positively blooming, and for one awful moment I consider she might be pregnant. God, I hope not.

'What's up?' asks Frank.

'What? Nothing, why?'

'You just have a frown on your face, that's all.'

'Nowt I can do about that, Frank. When you get to my age, it's all just wrinkles we have no control over.'

There's no time for his response as Candice walks out and claps her hands. She bows her head to the microphone. 'Now then, settle down. I'd like you to give a warm Green Meadows welcome to our first act, Ellie Spencer. Ellie has been writing her own songs for several years now, quite a feat considering she's only eighteen.' She glances down at her card. 'She has a four-octave vocal range and her voice has been compared to that of Mariah Carey.'

From the back, Mrs Culpepper says a little too loudly, 'By whom? People who've never heard Mariah Carey?'

Candice is tight-lipped and wisely chooses to ignore the unnecessary barbed comment from her employer. 'Please put your hands together for Ellie Spencer.'

Now, I'm tone deaf myself, but even I can tell that Ellie Spencer is quite a talent. I've no idea what a four-octave vocal range is, but she definitely sounds all right to me. She's a bonny lass, with a sizeable chest that no doubt houses a pair of lungs that enable her to hit the glass-shattering high notes. She sings a couple of her own songs, then a couple of more familiar ones, and we give her a thunderous round of applause, and those that can, a standing ovation.

It's Beau's turn now, and he certainly has a hard act to follow. After Candice's blushing introduction, I catch my first glimpse of him as he struts onto the stage. He raises one hand in the air to acknowledge the muted clapping. 'Thank you,' he says, adjusting his guitar strap. 'It's lovely to be here, thank you for having me. I hope you enjoy what I have to offer.'

I'm momentarily stunned. He seems like a thoroughly decent young man. He's dressed conservatively, although I can see he has some sort of tattoo under his shirt. From the huge wings, I would guess at an eagle. He's not wearing any eyeliner and he's dispensed with the sunglasses. He has a small, hooped earring in one ear, but I can cope with that.

Frank nudges me. 'Blimey, not what I was expecting at all.'

'Nor me.' I frown.

I can see Candice by the side of the stage. She's gazing at Beau as though he's the only other person in the room. He catches her looking and gives her a wink and a smile that looks like genuine affection. It's such a tender, private moment I'm forced to look away, doubting myself. What if I'm wrong about him?

I assume these are not the songs he usually plays, because I know most of the words, and even though I wouldn't inflict my limited vocal abilities on anyone else, some of the others are singing along. Frank is swaying and tapping out the rhythm on the arm of his chair. He raises his eyebrows and nods in my direction. 'He's pretty good, eh?'

'He is,' I say grudgingly.

He finishes with a jaunty version of 'When I'm Sixty-Four', seemingly oblivious to the fact that his audience would give their eye teeth to be sixty-four again. Then he takes a bow as Candice rushes onto the stage, her face a beacon of beaming pride.

We all put our hands together and someone at the back manages to produce a whistle through their false teeth.

'Thank you,' says Beau, taking another bow. 'Thank you for having me.'

Candice leans into the microphone. 'I hope you all enjoyed that. You've heard me raving about how good he is, and now that you've seen it for yourselves, you know I wasn't kidding.' She turns and kisses his cheek. 'Thank you, Beau.'

After the lights have gone up, Simeon moves between us with platters of crab puffs and tiny beef-filled Yorkshire puddings. I take one of the latter and momentarily wonder if it's a two-bite job or whether to shove the whole thing in at once. I decide to take the plunge, but haven't bargained for the whoosh of horseradish, which causes my nose to fizz.

'Jenny,' says Candice as I whip out my hanky. 'I'd like you to meet Beau.'

He sticks out his hand. 'Good to meet you at last, Jenny. Candice is always talking about you.' His palm is moist and clammy and it's all I can do to resist rubbing my hand along the arm of my chair.

'Is she now? I can't imagine that's a particularly interesting conversation.'

'Oh, I just switch off. She's always wittering on about something.'

Candice thumps him on the arm. 'He's only joking, Jenny.'

'Are you looking forward to your trip?' Beau asks as he squeezes Candice's hand. 'I know she is. She was that excited when I said she could go.'

I immediately bristle, and can't help myself. 'It was good of you to grant her permission.'

He makes a noise something between a scoff and a laugh. 'Um . . . I'm not sure it was like that.' He turns to Candice. 'Was it, babe? You didn't feel like you had to have my permission to go, did you?'

'Course not,' says Candice, although her voice is high and hollow. 'Anyway, don't you have to be off?' She turns to me, her face flushed. 'He's doing a late-night set at the Lemon Tree. Makes sense as I'm here all night anyway.'

Beau presses his lips to hers. 'I'll see you in the morning, babe.'

He takes my hand again and looks me directly in the eye. 'It was nice to meet you, Jenny.' And he squeezes my hand just a little too hard.

I decide to wait in the day room until Candice has finished seeing to the others. I'm far too agitated to sleep anyway. Frank has left me with a balloon of brandy, which he assures me will help me drift off. I take a sip of the fiery liquid, but I'm not a fan. I'll ask Candice to pop it into a mug of warm milk instead. The chairs have been cleared away and the only light comes from a standard lamp in the corner, which creates a soporific glow.

Candice gently pushes the door open and creeps into the room.

'It's all right, Candice. I'm still awake.'

'Oh, lovely,' she says breezily. 'Can I get you anything else before you turn in?'

'Some warm milk, please, but that can wait. Come and take the weight off for a while.'

She settles down on the chair next to me, kicks off her shoes and tucks her legs beneath her. 'Well?'

'Well what?'

'What did you think of Beau?'

I swill the brandy round the glass, contemplating how to give an honest but inoffensive answer. 'Well, I'm not sure I'm the best one to judge. There's hyenas on the Serengeti that can carry a tune better than I can, but he sounds like a competent singer, as you said.'

'And?'

I was really hoping she wouldn't pick at this thread. I want to tell her he's an arrogant, controlling manipulator with a very high opinion of himself but she's perched with her hand under her chin, her eyes shining in anticipation. 'He's . . . um . . . charming,' I finally manage.

'Isn't he just?' she says. She closes her eyes and the smile on her lips suggests she's thinking how lucky she is.

'Candice,' I venture with some trepidation. 'Beau knows I'm paying for the trip, doesn't he?'

'Course he does. We couldn't afford it otherwise.'

'Then . . . um . . . I'm just wondering why you had to ask him for permission to go.'

Her head snaps up and she glares at me. 'I knew you'd bring this up, Jenny. I didn't *have* to ask for his permission. That came out all wrong. We talked about it and I asked if he minded if I went. It's what couples do, in case you've forgotten.'

I'm momentarily stunned. Candice has never spoken to me like this before. 'I'm sorry, love, I didn't mean to upset you.'

'You don't like him, do you?'

I don't wish to incur her wrath, but I'm not going to lie either. 'I don't know him, Candice.'

'You wouldn't be so mean if you knew his background.'

Oh, here it is. She's going to make all kinds of excuses for him. 'Do you want to tell me?'

'He's an orphan.'

'An orphan?'

'Yes,' she says determinedly. 'His parents were killed in a plane crash nearly three years ago.'

'A plane crash?' I realise I'm sounding like a particularly dense parrot.

'Yes, a light aircraft in Malaysia.'

'Well, I'm sorry to hear that.'

'It was a special holiday to celebrate their anniversary, and they took a trip into the rainforest jungle type thing. The engine failed and killed both of them and the pilot as well.'

I have an image of a smouldering plane, broken in half, buried amongst the trees. 'That's awful, Candice. Poor Beau.' I genuinely mean it.

'He doesn't have any brothers or sisters, so he's only got me now, you see, and as I only have him, we need each other.'

I keep my tone level. 'You should really only be with somebody because you want to be, not because you need to be.'

'I do want to be.'

'How long have you known him?'

She hesitates a little too long and her answer only comes out as a whisper. 'Seven months.'

'Is that all?' I say, genuinely shocked. 'You didn't waste much time before moving in together.'

'A month.' She shrugs.

The brandy balloon is now warm in my hands and I risk a tentative swig. She looks crestfallen, and I decide to tread more carefully. 'You can't rush into these things, Candice.' I reach for her hand, clasping it between mine. 'There's nobody who knows that better than I do.'

26

She stood outside the police station, a rolled-up sheaf of papers clutched in her fist. She'd left her cane behind, not wishing it to be a reminder that she might be slightly less able than her peers. Especially today, it was crucial not to display any signs of weakness. She swatted at the irritating cloud of midges buzzing around her head and adjusted the angle of her straw hat before striding up the three stone steps and through the heavy door, bracing herself for the confrontation. There was nobody behind the desk. She banged her palm on the brass bell several times.

'All right, calm down,' came the disembodied voice from the back. 'I'm on my break here.'

Sergeant Williams appeared, rubbing his eyes. 'Oh, it's you. What can I do for you?'

Jenny slammed the roll of papers on the desk. Sergeant Williams glanced down but didn't touch them. 'And what, pray, is this?'

'It's a petition.'

'A petition?'

'That's right. A petition demanding the release of Enzo and Domenico Bernardi. It's been signed by everybody in town . . . well, almost everybody. Obviously there's still a small number of petty-minded, ignorant people who know no better, but they're in the minority, thankfully. It's outrageous what you're doing to the Bernardi family, and the people of Penlan demand that they be released forthwith.' She took a deep breath and balled her fists to prevent her hands from shaking.

Sergeant Williams narrowed his eyes but said nothing. He picked up the bundle of papers and met her eyes with a penetrating stare before turning away and dropping it into the metal bin.

'What are you doing? You can't do that. Get them out at once.'

He leaned so far over the desk that she could smell the Camp coffee essence on his breath. 'Listen to me. I don't know who you think you are, or indeed who you think *I* am.' He cast his arm around the station. 'This is my jurisdiction. You think I can swan up to Mr Churchill brandishing your little pile of papers, demanding the release of prisoners of war?'

Tears of frustration threatened, but she would not give him the satisfaction. 'They're enemy aliens, not prisoners of war.'

'It makes no difference, there's nothing I can do.' He wiggled his fingers. 'Now run along, there's a good girl, and stop wasting valuable police time, or else I'll have to charge you.'

'Oh, you think you're so clever, don't you? You won't get away with this. That petition is a properly orchestrated demonstration of the way people around here feel. You can't just ignore it.' She prodded the desk with her finger. 'You haven't heard the last of this.'

173

Sergeant Williams was already flicking through his newspaper. 'I asked you to leave.'

The day was warm and sticky and she could feel the sweat moistening the back of her neck. She removed her straw hat and fanned herself with it as she crossed the square and sat down next to Lena under the shade of the canopy. 'I tried, Lena, I really did, but bloody Sergeant Williams was useless.'

Lena poured her a glass of ginger beer. 'I appreciate your efforts, Jenny. Is so kind of you. And just seeing all those names, well, it really gladden my heart. It make me realise that perhaps we are loved in this town after all.'

'You are,' Jenny emphasised. 'By most people, anyway. There'll always be a few nasty bigots, but they're not worth worrying about.'

In spite of the unappetising brown froth floating on the surface, she took a polite sip of the ginger beer, peering over the top of her glass at the older woman. The last three weeks had ravaged Lena almost beyond recognition. Her hair was now completely white and her face seemed to sag under the weight of excess skin. Jenny patted the back of her hand. 'You'll get through this, Lena. I promise we'll all be here for you, so don't you . . . Lena?'

Lena had stopped listening and now rose slowly from her chair, staring past Jenny. She clutched at the gold cross around her neck and brought it to her lips. '*E un miracolo.*' She dropped to her knees, seemingly oblivious to the hard cobbles. '*Santa Maria, madre di Dio.*'

Jenny took hold of her elbow, helping her stand again. 'Lena?'

174

Lena nodded across the square, a smile lifting her features. '*Mio Enzo*. He come back.'

Jenny followed her gaze to where Enzo stood, his arms outstretched.

Lena gathered up her long skirt and ran towards him, tripping over the kerb in her haste. She recovered her balance and fell into the arms of her husband as he dropped his case and scooped her up.

'Enzo, Enzo, what have they done to you?'

'I am fine, *mia cara*, do not worry. They have treated me well.'

She clasped his face between her hands, covering it in kisses. 'I've been so worried, Enzo, I haven't eaten, I haven't slept, I—'

'Shush, shush, I'm home now.'

Jenny had kept a respectful distance but now stepped forward, unable to refrain from asking the question Lena hadn't yet asked.

'And Nico?'

Enzo took hold of his wife's hand, shaking his head. 'No, he's fine but cannot be released yet.' He pointed to his own chest. 'Me, I am old, they do not consider me to be a threat, but Nico, he is young, feisty, and perhaps they think he cause trouble.'

'Where is he?' asked Lena, her voice quavering. 'What have they done to him?'

'I already tell you, Lena. He is quite well but he's to be . . . um . . . sent away.'

Jenny gasped. 'Sent away where?'

'He's been taken to Liverpool docks, but I don't know where he will go from there.'

'No!' shrieked Lena. 'Not my boy, not Nico! He would not hurt anybody. This whole thing is ridiculous.'

Enzo slipped his hand into his pocket and brought out a crumpled piece of paper, offering it to Jenny. 'He asked me to give you this. I had to hide it in my shoe so that the censors could not get at it.'

Blushing slightly, she brought the paper to her nose, searching for a tangible reminder of Nico, but instead it smelled of sweaty feet. She pocketed the note. 'Thank you, Enzo. I'll read it later.'

'Now,' said Enzo, 'I need my wife to make me coffee, and none of that chicory rubbish. I assume my private supply is not yet exhausted.'

'Of course,' Lena laughed. 'I keep it specially for you.'

Jenny watched as they linked arms and walked back to the sanctuary of their café. She could hear Lena badgering her husband for more details about her son. Her happiness would not be complete until he too was back in the fold.

The farmyard appeared deserted. In the heat of the afternoon, humans and animals alike had sought shade, and even the chickens were slumped in their dustbowl. Jenny tiptoed into the barn, closing the door quietly behind her. A large rat scurried across her path, but she paid it no attention and instead focused on Nico's words as she sat down on a bale of straw.

My darling Jennifer,

I fear I am writing to you from hell itself. We've been herded into a disused cotton mill, where the conditions are unsanitary and overcrowded. There is a terrible stench from the latrines, rats everywhere and not enough food. The atmosphere is one of hopelessness, injustice and despair. But it is not these things which make this place hell. Oh no, I am in hell because you are not here. Every night, I pray that tomorrow is the day I will see you again. Your face is in my mind and your name is on my lips each night as I try to sleep and each morning when I awake after a fitful night dreaming about when we can be together. I think about nothing but when I will see you again. I cannot eat, which makes me popular with my fellow internees as I often give them my share. Papà has been told he can go, and I am happy for him and Mamma.

I wish I had better news for you, *mia cara*. I'm told I'm being transferred as a Category A alien and will be incarcerated for the foreseeable future. I do not know how long that means. Nobody knows. Some people have been taken to the Isle of Man, which is not too far away, so maybe this is what they plan to do with me.

Wherever I go, it may be difficult for me to write, so I hope this letter will sustain you until we meet again.

I love you, my beautiful Jennifer.

Yours, Nico xx

She smoothed out the letter and cradled it to her chest, marvelling at the emotions it had stirred in her. To be truthful, they hardly knew each other, and yet he'd laid bare his feelings for her, his passion raw and unconstrained. How she wished she could run to him right there and then. To reassure him that she felt the same way. It was meant to be. *Colpo di fulmine.*

She folded the letter and tucked it into her pocket just as the barn door creaked open. She shielded her eyes from the sudden bright shaft of sunlight.

'There you are,' said Lorcan. 'I've been looking for you.'

'Well, now you've found me.'

'What's up? Have you been crying?'

'I'm fine,' she sniffed. 'Enzo's back.'

'Really? Well, that's great news.' He hesitated a second too long. 'And Nico?'

She shook her head. 'He's been given a different classification. He's going to be shipped somewhere, probably the Isle of Man.'

'For how long?' Was she mistaken, or could he not keep the glee out of his voice?

She flicked straw off her skirt. 'Nobody seems to know what the hell is going on any more. This whole war just seems so pointless. Such a waste of innocent lives.'

Lorcan's voice was quiet but sincere. 'It wasn't me, Jenny. I promise you it wasn't.'

'What wasn't you?'

'I didn't throw that stone at Nico's window. I may not be his greatest fan, but I hope you know me better than that.'

She felt the letter nestled in her pocket and nodded quietly. 'I believe you, Lorcan.' She rose from the bale of straw until their eyes were level. 'I have to.'

27

2019

She always enjoyed the walk home after a night shift. Five thirty in the morning was a blissful time of the day most people never got to witness. A time for thinking, reflecting and clearing the head. She waved a greeting to the milkman as he hauled a crate from the back of his van, wishing she could stop buying supermarket milk and support the local dairy instead. Beau was right, though: they couldn't afford to be that ethical whilst trying to save money. She knew he'd be fast asleep in bed by now, and quickened her pace at the thought of crawling in beside him.

She crept into the bedroom, gently peeled back the duvet and snuggled up against his naked body. The smell of sweat and beer was strangely comforting. She kissed the back of his neck as she folded her body around his.

He stirred but didn't turn around, his voice slurred with sleep. 'Your feet are flamin' freezing, Candice. Get 'em off me.' He shrugged her off and pulled the duvet tight under his chin.

'How was the Lemon Tree?' she whispered.

'Go to sleep, Candice. We'll deal with it in the morning.'

She propped herself up on her elbow. 'Deal with what?'

'The situation,' he mumbled. 'Now just leave it.'

'What situation?' she insisted. 'You can't just say that and then expect me to go to sleep.'

He turned over to face her. 'What've you been saying about me?'

'What . . . Nothing, why? I mean, who to?'

'Your workmates . . . and that old bint you look after.'

'Jenny?' Even though she knew she'd done nothing wrong, her stomach tightened. 'I haven't said anything, nothing bad anyway.'

'And that other guy. The fat one that looks like he's been dragged backwards through TK Maxx. I've seen better dressed rough sleepers.'

'Simeon, you mean? I can't remember ever talking to him about you. Where has all this come from?'

'I saw the way he looked at me, as though he thought you could do better. He obviously fancies you and you did nothing to discourage him, I noticed.'

Candice sat up, rubbing her face. 'Beau, I really don't know where to start with all this. I told you, Simeon's happily married with three kids. And as for Jenny, she said you were . . . um . . . charming.'

'Oh, come off it, Candice. She hated me on sight.'

'Nobody hates somebody they've only just met.'

'Agreed. Unless they've had their mind poisoned.'

She flung off the duvet and sat on the edge of the bed, massaging her temples. 'You're being ridiculous, Beau. You're bloody paranoid, you are. I haven't said anything bad about you to Jenny. Quite the opposite, in fact. I'm always telling her how happy you make me.'

'I don't think you should be going to Italy with her.'

She swung round to face him. 'But I thought you'd come round to the idea. I can't go back on my word. If I don't go, she won't be able to go either. She's a hundred years old, she can't travel on her own.'

'Then she'll have to find some other mug to take her.'

'Beau,' she reasoned. 'Please, I can't tell her you won't let me go . . .'

'Just tell her you've changed your mind then.'

'Changed my mind? Why would I do that? It's not as if it's going to cost us anything, and Mrs Culpepper has given me the time off.'

Beau stared blankly at the ceiling before trying a different tack, that of a whiny toddler. 'But I'll miss you, Candice. You know I don't like being on my own. I can't help it. It stirs up all kinds of feelings, like when . . . you know . . . when I lost my parents.'

'It's not the same, Beau. I'll be back before you know it.'

'That's what my parents said. I never saw them again.'

'But they died on one of them little planes. I'm going on a big jet thing. They don't tend to fall out of the sky.' She snuggled into his neck, running her fingers over his chest. 'I can't imagine how hard it must've been for you, Beau. When I lost my mum, I was too young to understand the impact it would have, and in any case, she was hardly a candidate for Mother of the Year.' She felt the beat of his heart beneath her fingers. 'But we still have to live our lives. *We* didn't die.'

He clamped his hand over hers. 'I couldn't bear it if I lost you as well.'

'You won't, I promise.'

'I don't know, you seem to care more about that old woman than you do about me. I suppose I was just hoping you'd take my feelings into account and put me first for a change.' He reached for his cigarettes and fumbled for his lighter. 'I mean, it's not much to ask.'

'Do you have to smoke in bed, Beau?'

He blew out a cigarette-infused breath. 'Stop changing the subject. Do you love me?'

'Aargh, not this again. You know I do.'

'Then why did I ask?'

'Because you need constant reassurance and I think that comes from losing both your parents at the same time. You feel they abandoned you, no matter how irrational that sounds, so you constantly seek confirmation from those closest to you. It's all part of the grieving process. You're at the depression stage, and it's manifesting itself as insecurity.'

'Christ, Candice, you do talk bollocks sometimes.'

'Well,' she shrugged, 'that's my theory and I think it makes sense. Now can you put that fag out and let's try and get some sleep before the sun comes up.'

28

Candice is looking a little grey around the edges this evening, but she attempts a cheery greeting. 'Have you had a good day, Jenny?'

She tries, bless her, but really one day is much the same as another in here. 'Not too bad, thank you, love. You look tired, though. Didn't you manage to sleep after you got home this morning?'

She's back to the annoying habit I know she's tried to stop. She nibbles at the skin around her thumb, wincing as she bites a piece off. 'Not really. Beau wasn't feeling great when I got back, so we spent some time talking.'

'Oh dear, that's a shame. Has he eaten something that's not agreed with him – or has he got the man flu?'

She shakes her head. 'Nothing like that. That would be a lot simpler. No, he's still grieving for his parents, and this trip of ours has brought back bad memories.'

'How so?' I frown, genuinely puzzled.

'Well, you know. They went on holiday and never came back.'

'And he thinks lightning's going to strike twice?'

'Yeah, kind of. He knows it's irrational, but that's what grief does to you. It distorts reality. He knows deep down that the chances of me dying the same way are extremely remote, but nevertheless it's causing him a lot of anxiety.'

I have to bite my tongue in order to give a measured response, even though my instinct is to scoff. 'Let me guess. He's asked you not to go.'

I can see by her reaction that I'm right, but it gives me no pleasure.

'Oh Candice, love. The last thing I want is to cause any problems between the two of you. If it'll make things easier, tell him you won't go.' Inside, I'm fuming that Beau has resorted to emotional blackmail, but nothing that weasel does surprises me. 'I'll go on my own.'

It's a ridiculous notion, of course, and Candice knows it. 'I wouldn't put it past you to try, Jenny, but there's no way that's happening. I gave you my word. I'm going with you and that's that.'

Relief threatens to overwhelm me. She can be very assertive when she wants to be, and she doesn't strike me as the type of girl who's going to be pushed around, but we can never really know what goes on behind closed doors, can we?

'Is Beau your first boyfriend, Candice?'

She gives me a questioning look, as though she suspects my motive for asking is not just curiosity. She's right.

'I've had a few . . . um . . . you know . . . one-night stands and that, and there was someone who I once thought was special but he just turned out to be using me.'

'Oh?'

She shakes her head. 'I don't want to go into all that now. Let's just say that growing up in care, some people take advantage of vulnerable kids.'

184

'You weren't abused, were you, love?'

Her thumb instinctively goes to her mouth, but she stops herself biting it and chews her lip instead. 'It didn't seem like abuse at the time, but looking back, yeah, I suppose it could be described as that. It was certainly an abuse of power.'

'Well, you should do something. I mean—'

She holds up her hand. 'There's no point, it's all in the past, and I said I don't want to talk about it. I'm fine. So the short answer is yes, Beau is my first serious boyfriend. Why d'you ask, anyway?'

'Just making conversation.' I shrug, but I know she's not that daft.

'Come on,' she insists. 'If you've got something to say then I'd rather you just came out with it. It's obvious you don't like him, and he picked up on that, by the way.'

'I . . . um . . . well, I just wonder if he's a bit controlling. I mean don't you think he stifles you a little bit?'

She grits her teeth and I fear I've pushed it too far. I can see she's fighting to control her temper. 'No, I don't, Jenny. And I'm not being funny or owt, but I can't see what it's got to do with you anyway. I know you're only looking out for me, but I've managed on my own for most of my life and I really don't need you sticking your nose in, thank you.'

There's a click of stilettos in the doorway. Mrs Culpepper is standing there, arms folded, her face thunderous. 'Candice, my office, please. Now.'

A couple of hours pass before I see Candice again. I'm not in the most sociable of moods, so I've retired to my room. There's a hesitant knock at the door.

'Come in,' I say, straightening up in my chair.

Candice pops her head round. 'I've come to apologise,' she whispers.

'Whatever for?'

'The way I spoke to you before. I was a bit . . . erm . . . sharp.'

'Mrs Culpepper give you a hard time, did she?'

'Yes.' She nods. 'You could say that. She gave me a warning.'

'Oh Candice. Come in and sit down for a bit. I'll sort it with her. You've done nothing wrong. It was all my fault. I shouldn't have pushed you like that, but it's only because I'm so fond of you.'

She comes into the room and takes hold of both my hands. 'I know you are, and you're special to me too, Jenny.'

I rub my thumbs across the back of her hands. 'Sometimes when you love someone a great deal, you make all kinds of excuses for their behaviour.'

'But—'

I silence her with a finger to her lips. 'I have no doubt at all that you do love him, but can you honestly say that you're completely happy?'

'Yes,' she says, turning away. 'I don't know why you're being like this.'

'Because you have nobody else to look out for you.'

'I've told you, I don't need anybody else!' she shouts.

'Shush, you'll have Mrs Culpepper on the warpath again if you carry on like that.'

She slumps into a chair and folds her arms. 'I'm perfectly fine, stop worrying. You've got Beau all wrong, please believe me.'

Her phone buzzes in her tabard pocket and she looks at me, keeping her arms folded. We both know it's him.

A few seconds pass before it buzzes again. I can tell it's killing her not to take a look.

'Why don't you see what he wants?'

'It might not be him. You're always jumping to conclusions.' She takes the phone out of her pocket, squints at the message, then fires one back. Her crimson cheeks give her away.

'Everything all right?'

'Of course.'

Her tone has changed from indignation to defiance, but I can tell she's lying. Everything looks far from all right. What I wouldn't give to get my hands on that phone.

'Well, that's a relief then, I'm glad you're okay.' I pause for effect. 'I know what it's like to feel conflicted. Not knowing which way to jump or whether you're better off staying where you are. Better the devil you know and all that.'

She lifts her head to meet my gaze. 'I'm not with you.'

'Sometimes circumstances can push you in the wrong direction and you end up making bad decisions. Sometimes decisions are taken out of your hands and fate intervenes.' She clearly has no idea what I'm talking about, and I'm not sure she cares, but I press on. 'When I heard Nico was being sent away, I was devastated. Our relationship had barely got going but I knew that I was in love with him and he'd made it very clear he loved me. I was fond of Lorcan, but not in the same way. With him I was comfortable, happy in his company even, but he was just so normal and a little bit boring, I suppose.' I give a snort. 'Never underestimate normal and boring, Candice.'

187

'Beau's certainly neither of those things,' she says. 'Quite the opposite; he's exciting, unpredictable, dangerous even.' To my amazement, her eyes are positively shining.

'And I can see how attractive those traits can be at first. But is that what you want for the rest of your life?'

'Yes.' She nods determinedly. 'I love him and I know he'd do anything for me, for us, for our relationship. Look how he took control of our money. If he hadn't done that, I wouldn't have been able to save enough to take the eyebrow course.'

I rub my fingers over my chin in a classic thinking pose, but don't say anything.

'It's not like you to be quiet, Jenny.' Her smile says she clearly thinks she's won the argument.

'There's one word in what you just said that worries me.'

She tuts towards the ceiling and mutters under her breath. 'I might've known. Come on then, let's hear it.'

'Control. You said he'd taken control of your money.'

'So? Did you also not get that I was grateful to him.'

I steeple my hands and bring them to my lips, taking a deep breath before continuing. 'It's like when a drop of water seeps through the roof of a cave. It's hardly noticeable at first and seems harmless, but over time, it's there for everyone to see.'

'What is?' she sighs, clearly impatient.

'A massive stalactite. Everybody can see it. It can't be ignored.'

Her expression suggests she thinks I'm crazy. 'What are you on about?'

'Then one day it becomes so heavy that it snaps off. And if you happen to be standing underneath . . .' I lift my eyebrows. 'Well, you can imagine.'

I can tell she's mad at me now, because she stands up so suddenly her phone tumbles to the floor. Obviously I'm not quick enough to retrieve it before she does, and she stuffs it back into her pocket. 'I'm going now, Jenny. I'll be back to tuck you in later. I'm here all night again.'

With that, she stomps out of the room, leaving me alone with only memories for company.

29

1940

The sun hovered just above the horizon, turning the sky pink with the promise of another warm and cloudless day. The town square was just coming alive as people opened up their businesses, determined to carry on as normally as the war allowed. Jenny glanced across at Bernardi's Gelateria, but the shutters were still down, the chairs stacked under the canopy. In the four days since Enzo had returned, there had been no further news of Nico.

She entered the newsagent's to find Nerys with her elbows on the counter, her head resting in her hands as she scanned the newspaper. 'Morning, Nerys.'

Visibly startled, the flustered woman folded the paper and shoved it under the counter. 'Morning, Jenny.'

Jenny eyed her suspiciously. 'What's wrong?'

'Nothing, I don't know what you mean.'

'Yes you do. You have a sheepish . . . no, a guilty look on your face. And your neck has gone all red. That's a dead giveaway. What are you hiding?'

Nerys reached under the counter. 'Not much gets past you, does it?' she sighed. 'I didn't want to be the bearer of bad news.'

'A bit of a problem seeing as you're the newsagent, wouldn't you say?' Jenny reached for the paper. 'What bad news anyway?'

Nerys turned the *Daily Telegraph* round so Jenny could read the headline.

ARANDORA STAR SUNK BY U-BOAT.

The first stirrings of dread lodged in her stomach as she read on.

1,500 ITALIAN AND NAZI INTERNEES IN PANIC. FIGHT FOR LIFEBOATS HAMPERS RESCUE.

In a daze, she grabbed the paper and stumbled out of the shop.

Nerys called after her retreating figure. 'I'll put it on your slate, shall I?'

Jenny banged on the Bernardis' front door, her knuckles bearing the brunt of her impatient effort. 'Enzo, Lena, wake up.'

She took a couple of steps back and shouted in the direction of their bedroom two floors above. 'Enzo, Lena, you need to get down here now.'

She could hear Enzo struggling to open the sash window. 'What's all this noise at this time in the morning?' he called.

'Enzo, thank God. Please come down and let me in.'

She waited for what seemed an eternity for him to find his dressing gown and descend two flights of stairs, Lena huffing in his wake. She tried to control her impatience as he struggled with the bolts on the front door, until finally they were face to face.

'What is this all about?' he asked, rubbing his eyes.

Jenny prodded the newspaper. 'Look at this. A ship has

been torpedoed. A ship carrying Italians to Canada.' She struggled to take a breath. 'I'm worried Nico could've have been on board.' She ran her hands through her hair. 'Hundreds of them have died.'

Lena grabbed the paper. 'No, no, this cannot be true. Why would they do that to innocent people?' She turned to her husband. 'Enzo, they cannot do that, can they?'

He shook his head. 'I don't know, Lena. It's a war, people don't always follow the rules.'

Lena handed the paper back to Jenny. 'Read it to me, please. Every word, don't leave anything out.'

Jenny cleared her throat, her mouth suddenly dry, her tongue uncooperative. She swallowed hard before continuing. 'A panic among one thousand five hundred German and Italian internees being taken to Canada in the fifteen-thousand-five-hundred-ton Leyland liner *Arandora Star* heavily increased the death toll when the vessel was torpedoed and sunk by a German submarine three hundred miles off the west coast of Ireland. About one thousand scantily clad survivors were landed at a Scottish west coast port yesterday from a British ship.' She stopped, her heart pounding in her ears. 'I need a drink of water, Lena.'

Lena scuttled off, returning seconds later with the tepid glass. 'Survivors?' She clutched at Enzo's elbow. 'Did you hear that, Enzo? There are survivors.'

'Carry on, please, Jenny,' Enzo urged. 'What else does it say?'

She looked at the paper again, trying to find where she'd left off. 'Erm . . . the liner was not in convoy at the time she was sunk. The owners state that a considerable proportion of

192

the crew were saved. The greater part of the drowned internees appear to have been . . .' She stopped and pressed her hand to her mouth, as though not saying the words would prevent them from being true.

Lena moved closer. 'Jenny, tell us . . . please.'

She took Lena's hand. 'The greater part of the drowned internees appear to have been Italian.'

'No!' Lena's scream was chillingly primeval. Her limp body slid to the floor, her face buried in the hem of her nightdress. 'Not my Nico,' she wailed. 'Please not him. Enzo, do something.'

Enzo turned to Jenny, dry-eyed, his features frozen in shock. He could only manage a hoarse whisper. 'I need to know if my son was on that ship.'

Sergeant Williams looked up as Jenny burst through the door of the constabulary once again, his expression immediately hardening. 'I thought I told you—'

'It's nothing to do with the petition.' She slammed the newspaper down on the duty desk. 'Look at that.'

He took his time to read the headlines before blowing out a long, slow breath. 'That's tragic that is, I tell you.'

Enzo puffed his way up the steps and through the door, standing breathlessly next to Jenny. 'Can you help us, Sergeant?'

'Well now, I'm not sure what you expect me to do. I'm really sorry and all, but . . . I don't know, what about the Italian embassy?'

'Can we use your phone then?' Jenny asked. 'Please.'

The sergeant pushed the telephone across the desk. 'I suppose so.' He pointed at Enzo. 'Now that he's been released, I'm sure it won't be construed as helping the enemy.'

'Pathetic,' Jenny muttered under her breath as she dialled the operator.

She handed the receiver to Enzo. 'Here, you'll have to talk to them. I'm not family and I don't speak Italian.'

Enzo nodded, taking the receiver in his shaking hand as he waited for the connection.

After a short conversation, he hung up. 'The Italian embassy closed down. There is nobody left to help us.'

'What do we do now, Sergeant Williams?' asked Jenny.

The policeman shook his head. 'How the hell should I know?'

A full week passed before the official news finally reached Penlan. Lorcan was in the yard, a hay bale slung across his shoulders.

'Lorcan!' shouted Enzo. 'Where is Jenny?'

'In the kitchen,' he replied, dropping the bale. 'Why? What's the matter?'

His breathing ragged, Enzo took out his handkerchief to wipe the sweat from his brow. 'That hill, it nearly kill me.'

'Are you all right, Enzo? Come over here, have a sit-down on the bench.'

'No, I need to speak to Jenny.'

'Fine, as you wish. I'll go and get her.'

Jenny appeared then, her footsteps faltering.

'Any news?'

Enzo dug into his pocket and pulled out a letter. His voice wavered. 'This. It come this morning.'

She took it and read aloud the words that had no doubt shattered countless families.

'It is with deep regret that the Secretary of State directs me to inform you that since a certain D. Bernardi No. 456098 appears on the lists as sailing on the *Arandora Star* on the thirtieth of June 1940 and has not been subsequently recorded on the embarkation lists of internees who have left this country for Canada or Australia, or among those detained in internment camps in this country, he must be presumed missing and probably lost.'

'I'm so sorry, Enzo,' Lorcan said. 'That's tragic.'

'But it doesn't mean he's dead, does it?' insisted Jenny. 'He's only missing. It only says he's *probably* lost. We mustn't lose hope, Enzo.' She clutched at his arm. 'If we lose that, we've got nothing.'

30

She lay huddled under the eiderdown in the foetal position, Nico's letter clutched in her fingers. How was it possible that the world still turned when he was missing? Somehow five months had slipped by since that terrible day when the news had arrived by telegram. She tortured herself with images of him drowning, imagining his panic as the frigid Atlantic Ocean filled his lungs until all the fight was squeezed out of him and he sank to his watery grave. She didn't know it was possible to miss somebody so much. Their fledgling romance had barely begun, and now their future had been snatched away. The memories they would have made, the children they would have had, none of it would happen now.

She could hear Lorcan arguing with Louis downstairs about when he should go to bed. She tucked Nico's letter under her pillow and reluctantly heaved herself up.

Louis was standing in front of the fire, his arms folded in defiance. 'I want to stay up to see Father Christmas.' He pointed at Lorcan. 'But he won't let me.'

Jenny kissed the top of his head. 'Lorcan's right, Lou. You need to get to bed. Father Christmas doesn't come to children who are still awake, everybody knows that. You don't want to be the only little boy in Penlan who doesn't get any presents.'

Lorcan agreed. 'You need to listen to your sister, Louis.' He pointed to Bryn's old sock nailed to the beam over the fireplace. 'If you want to find anything in there in the morning, I'd go to bed.'

Louis nodded towards the fire. 'But won't he get burned when he comes down the chimley?'

Jenny pulled him onto her knee, revelling in the scent of his freshly washed hair. 'Ah, my little Lou-Lou. It's chim-*ney*,' she emphasised. 'You always have to find something to worry about, don't you?'

'We'll make sure the fire is out in plenty of time,' said Lorcan. 'Now come and give me a hug, and then be off with you.'

'And keep the noise down,' warned Jenny. 'Mammy Del and Tad are in bed already. Cows still need milking on Christmas Day.'

'Eggnog?' asked Lorcan, once Louis had gone. 'It's not Christmas Eve without it.'

'Aye, go on then. Do you want me to do it?'

He placed his hand on her shoulder. 'No, let me. It's always been my job to make the Christmas Eve eggnog.'

She laid her head against the back of the chair, her face tilted up to the beams. Lacing her fingers across her stomach, she closed her eyes. She didn't think she would ever get over the agony of losing Nico. It just wasn't possible to fix a broken heart. Like a shattered crystal vase, the pieces could be glued back together but it would never function the same again.

There would always be the fine cracks where the water seeped out. She constantly replayed their last meeting in her mind, agonising over whether she had conveyed her feelings for him adequately enough. She couldn't bear the thought of him not knowing how she felt.

'Penny for them,' said Lorcan a few minutes later, as he handed her the frothy eggnog. She blew into the mug before taking a sip of the warm cinnamon-infused drink. 'Oh, I . . . um . . . I was just thinking about Lena and Enzo, that's all. Terrible how they were all but forced to go back to Italy. It must be agony for them not knowing what happened to their son.'

He laid his hand gently on hers. 'Nico's dead, Jenny.'

She stared into her mug, unable to meet his pitying gaze. 'I know,' she whispered.

He patted her knee. 'Let's see what's on the wireless. Maybe a play or some carols. Get us in the festive mood.' He fiddled with the knobs as he spoke. 'This war has already caused no end of tragedy, and who knows how much more we will have to suffer before it's over, but I'm grateful because it brought you and Louis here. I can't imagine never having met you.'

Poor Lorcan. The pain of unrequited love. She was fond of him, no doubt. But she knew what love felt like now, and this wasn't it. It never could be.

The newsreader was coming to the end of his recap, his clipped nasal tones interrupting her thoughts. '. . . after suffering a second night of heavy bombing. The town in the north-west of England was bombarded with almost two hundred tons of high explosives, with heavy loss of life and catastrophic damage to buildings.'

Jenny sat up, eggnog splashing down the front of her skirt.

'Did he say a town in the north-west of England?' She grabbed at Lorcan's sleeve. 'You don't think that could be Manchester, do you?'

'I . . . I've no idea, Jenny.'

She scrambled to her feet and grabbed her coat off the hook. 'I need to go into town and place a call to my mother.'

He glanced at the clock on the mantelpiece. 'It's too late now. I'm sure it'll be fine. Isn't Manchester a city, anyway?'

'I suppose so,' she conceded. 'Bloody censorship rules. Why can't they just be honest with us?'

She picked up the Christmas card their mother had sent and pressed it to her nose. She had long forgotten what her mother smelled like, and disappointingly, the card offered up no reminders.

'She'll be all right,' said Lorcan gently. 'I know she will. Please try not to worry, and don't say anything to Louis.'

A week later, the news was confirmed by the dreaded telegram. Instead of dispatching the telegram boy on his bike, the post-mistress had delivered it herself, her expression confirming Jenny's worst fears. She hadn't even needed to read it. Connie Tanner had spent Christmas buried under the rubble of their smouldering terraced house. She had been right to send her children away after all.

31

Candice had spent most of the night in between rounds checking her phone for further messages from Beau. There had been none. She had repeatedly texted him, could see he had read the messages but was ignoring her. No, worse than that, he was torturing her. He had somehow discovered that her red lace thong was missing, assumed this meant she must be wearing it for work and had got it into his head she must be having an affair. She quickened her pace as she rounded the corner and then ran down the street to their front door. She was later than usual because there had been a bit of a kerfuffle during the night with one of the residents, an elderly gentleman, getting confused and climbing into bed with another resident, who was not best pleased at finding a man in her bed after an absence of forty years. It had taken Candice a long time to calm her down and explain it was all just an innocent mistake.

Beau was out of bed and sitting on the settee with a fag and a mug of tea the colour of rust.

'Morning,' she ventured. 'How are you?'

He narrowed his eyes. 'What sort of a question is that? How do you think I am?'

'Why haven't you answered any of my messages?'

'Couldn't be arsed, Candice, to be honest. I wasn't all that interested in your pathetic excuses.'

She dumped her bag on the sofa, removed her coat and began to unbutton her trousers. She pulled them down to her ankles and stared at Beau. 'There.'

He gave a cursory look. 'Proves nothing. You could've changed them.'

'Beau,' she said, flopping down next to him, 'why would I go to work in a skimpy red lace thong, eh? It's not even that comfortable.'

'Where is it then, Candice? Explain that.'

'I don't know. I'll have to have a look. What were you doing rummaging around in my underwear drawer anyway?'

He ignored the question and instead took hold of her hand and led her into the bedroom. He nodded towards the drawer. 'Go on then, find it. I'll wait.'

She opened the drawer and fished through a tangle of knickers, tights and bras.

'It's not here,' she breathed. 'That's weird.'

'Weird? It's not weird, Candice. I know damn well you wore that thong for work, and I know why.'

She sighed, suddenly weary and desperate for sleep. 'You're wrong, Beau.'

'I don't think so,' he scoffed. 'You've been sleeping with someone behind my back.'

'At Green Meadows? Hmm . . . now let me see.' She tapped her chin with her fingers. 'Our oldest male resident is ninety-three and can barely stand up, let alone get anything else up. Our youngest resident is only seventy, though, so he's a possible candidate, and then there's Frank, but don't let the fact that he's gay get in the way of your barmy accusations.'

'I wasn't talking about the residents, you stupid cow.'

'You mean the staff?'

'Yes, exactly.'

'Simeon by any chance?'

'You admit it then.'

She dug her fingers into her hair. 'Aargh, you're being ridiculous, Beau. Why are you like this?' She sat down on the bed. 'Why can't you get it into your thick head that I love you, I will forever only love you and I'm not having an affair with Simeon or anybody else?'

He sat down next her, taking hold of her hand. 'I really want to believe you, babe, but it makes no sense. That red lace thong is missing and you can't tell me where it is. What am I supposed to think, eh?'

'You're not supposed to think the worst of me.' She touched his cheek, his stubble rough beneath her fingers. 'There has to be trust, Beau. If there's no trust, then what's the point? It's the foundation of every relationship, it underpins everything.'

'I have to trust my gut feeling, Candice. And my gut tells me you're having an affair.'

'Well, your gut is flamin' wrong.'

He held out his hand. 'You won't mind showing me your phone then.'

'Wh . . . what? No, why?'

'What are you hiding? Give it to me.'

'For God's sake, I'm not hiding anything.' She rummaged in her pocket and slapped the phone down on his outstretched palm. 'There,' she snapped. 'Knock yourself out.'

She watched as he tapped in her passcode and began scrolling through her messages. 'Mmm . . . you could have deleted them, or maybe you have another phone I don't know about.'

'Oh yeah, right, because you give me enough money to be able to go and buy another one.'

'He could have bought it for you.'

She bowed her head, her voice weary with exasperation. 'He? He? There is no he.' She jabbed at her own temple. 'This is all just in your head, Beau.'

She stiffened as she felt his hand on the back of her neck. 'Have I ever been violent towards you, Candice?'

'No, of course not. You think I'd stick around if you were?'

He gently stroked under her hair before sliding his hand inside her blouse and kissing the top of her shoulders. 'I love you, babe. But if I ever find out you've been unfaithful, I will kill you.'

She turned to face him, the blood rushing in her ears. 'Are you threatening me?'

His expression darkened; his mouth pulled into a tight line. Then he threw his head back and laughed. 'Your face! You know I'd never lay a finger on you, Candice.' He clamped her head between his palms and squashed his lips to hers. 'I adore you.'

32

There's one of those pubs just over the road from Green Meadows, one where they give fancy names to bog-standard dishes just so they can charge you a few bob extra. Gastro pub, I think the term is. Frank likes to go, though. Says it makes him feel as though he's still part of society. I can take it or leave it myself; after all, there's no finer chef round these parts than our Simeon.

It's unseasonably warm for a spring evening, so we've walked the two hundred yards or so and I feel rather sprightly. We decide to sit in the beer garden, and I have to say, it's quite splendid, with its cobbled courtyard and topiary hedges cut into the shape of fat birds. Frank guides me to a two-seater under a wisteria-clad pergola and places a pastel rug across my knees. 'Righto, flower,' he says. 'What can I get you?'

'Just a small G and T please, a plain one, nothing fancy.'

He returns with the drinks and settles himself next to me as he raises his glass to chink against my own. '*Cin cin*,' he says before taking a sip.

I prod at my own drink with the straw. Clearly the instruction 'nothing fancy' was either not relayed to the barmaid or else Frank chose to ignore me.

'What's the matter now?' he asks. If I'm honest, there's a hint of impatience in his voice.

'There's a slice of dried-up orange in my drink.'

'I know there is. It's the latest thing.'

'Blimey, Frank,' I say, fishing out the offending fruit. 'When did things get to be so complicated? Gin and orange my mother used to drink back in the day. Not fresh orange, mind, oh no, orange cordial, can you believe? Used to sneak a sip when she wasn't looking.' My eyes mist over as long-suppressed memories emerge. 'Couldn't stomach one now, though.' I twist the stem of my glass in my fingers, staring at the ice cubes tinkling together. 'Last time I tasted gin and orange was at my mother's funeral.' I take a deep breath. 'Never again. Terrible day that was.'

Frank tilts his head. 'I can imagine. I—'

I shake my head vigorously to stop him. 'No, Frank, you don't understand. I mean it was truly awful.' My hands have started to tremble, but if he notices, he doesn't say anything. 'January 1941 it was. She died at Christmas but there was a backlog, what with there being a war on. Me and our Louis travelled home to Manchester for it. Bryn, Delyth and Lorcan all came with us, bless 'em. I mean, they'd never even met my mother, but they wanted to be there for us. There weren't many people there, just the neighbours and a few of her work colleagues. Louis gripped my hand for the whole service, and then at the burial he wrapped his arms around my legs so I could hardly walk. He was only a few months short of his sixth birthday, the poor lamb.'

Frank's voice is quiet, barely a whisper. 'How terrible.'

'It was.' I nod. 'For as long as I have breath in my body, I

205

will never forget climbing those stairs to break the news of her death to him. With every step, I knew I was closer to shattering his world. He was such a sensitive kid, a habitual worrier and frightened of everything. He barely uttered a word when I told him. He didn't believe me, although why he thought I'd lie about a thing like that is anybody's guess. He didn't even cry, just tucked his teddy bear under his chin and snuggled back under his blanket.'

'Aye, well, kids have a funny way of dealing with things,' says Frank. 'Have you seen that tub of heather over there? Buzzing with bees it is.'

I ignore his blatant attempt to change the subject. I know he doesn't want me to get upset, but I need to talk about it. 'All through the funeral service, even though he was clingy, he was dry-eyed. It was only at the graveside, when we threw in a handful of soil, that he let go of my leg and suddenly wailed, "My mummy, my mummy!"' I turn to look at Frank. His expression is difficult to read. 'I have never heard a more heart-rending scream of pain either before or since. Del reached out to pull him towards her, but she wasn't quick enough, and he . . .' my throat aches and I'm forced to swallow hard, 'he jumped down onto the coffin.'

Frank picks up his pint and takes a sip. His hand is shaking more than ever. 'The poor little chap.'

'Everybody just froze for a second as Louis scraped at the coffin with his bare hands, sobbing inconsolably. Lorcan was the first to react. He jumped down too and held him up to Del, who clutched him to her chest, her own tears falling onto his head. I don't think I've ever witnessed such immeasurable suffering.'

Frank seems genuinely moved by my tale, and it's a while before he speaks again. 'You've never really talked about your brother before.' He pauses. 'Why is that, if you don't mind me asking?'

I do mind, I mind very much, but it's a fair question, I suppose. 'We . . . um . . . we became estranged. It's a long story for another day, Frank. I can't go into all that now.'

Of all the terrible memories I have, that one is right up there with the worst of them.

I adjust my focus and let my eyes wander over to the other side of the beer garden. Now, my eyesight's not as good as it used to be, I'll grant you that, but if I'm not mistaken, Beau is sitting on the low garden wall, engrossed in his phone.

I nudge Frank. 'Well bugger me. Look over there. It's Candice's boyfriend. She didn't tell me they were coming here.'

'Does she have to report her movements to you?' Frank says. He seems to have a right mood on him now.

'Obviously not,' I say, a little too icily. 'I just thought it might've come up, that's all. It's her day off today, so perhaps it was a spur-of-the-moment thing.'

Beau looks up from his phone and seems to stare directly at me before lifting his hand in greeting. I go to wave back, but it's not me he's looking at. It's a rather striking redhead, in an emerald-green satin dress that swishes just above her knees. I put my hand down, suddenly feeling rather foolish. As if Beau would acknowledge me. He's probably forgotten who I am. She hands him a pint of what I assume is lager and sits down next to him, their thighs almost touching. He says something and she dips her head towards his shoulder, laughing.

My back is stiff and inside I'm seething. 'Look at that cheating rat, Frank,' I hiss. 'Have you seen him, cavorting with another girl behind Candice's back?'

Frank follows my gaze. 'I'd hardly call it cavorting. They just seem to be having a drink together. Nothing wrong with that.'

'Nothing wrong with that? Are you out of your mind? I'll tell you what, I bet Candice doesn't know.'

'And don't you go telling her either,' he warns. 'It's got nothing to do with you and there's probably a perfectly innocent explanation. Candice'll only see it as you sticking the knife in Beau. She knows you don't like him. Don't make it any worse.'

'I'm just looking out for her, Frank,' I reply sulkily. 'She's got nobody else.'

I pick up the menu and dip my head behind it.

'I think he's looking over,' I say after a minute. 'Do you think he's seen us?'

'Does it matter if he has?' I can tell Frank is becoming a little spiky.

'I don't want him to be forewarned that he's been caught red-handed. It'll just give him more time to think up an excuse.'

Frank slams down his pint a little too hard. 'Jenny, will you just leave it. It's got nothing to do with you.'

I know he's right, of course. I also know I'm going to ignore him and follow my own instincts.

Candice breezes in the next morning, her step so light and carefree she's almost floating. 'Morning,' she gushes. 'Did you miss me yesterday?'

'We always miss you when you're not here, love.' I take my teaspoon and bash the top of my boiled egg, not wishing to meet her eye.

'I have good news,' she says, taking the chair opposite. I risk a look at Frank next to me, but he says nothing. He doesn't need to. His eyes tell me all I need to know. Keep shtum or else.

'What good news?'

'I've got another job.' She leans back, her eyes shining.

My stomach lurches. 'You mean you're leaving?' I feel sick at the thought of it.

'Not straight away, no.'

'How's all this come about?'

'Well, you know those flyers Beau got done for me, advertising my eyebrow business?'

I nod, even though this is the first I've heard of any flyers.

'Turns out Fliss, the owner of that beauty salon down Stretford Road, says I can use her premises to see clients in return for a cut of what I charge. It means I'll be able to get masses more customers and yet still be flexible enough to work here for the time being. I'll be able to save loads more cash towards Beauty Therapy Level Two.' Her face is frozen in delight as she seeks my congratulations.

'That's great news,' I manage, stabbing a soldier of toast into my egg. 'I'm pleased for you, Candice.'

'It's all thanks to Beau, actually.' She lowers her voice. 'He hates me working nights here, so he took it upon himself to find me more work in the beauty industry. He knows that's what I really want to do. Apparently Fliss goes into the Lemon Tree, and she was looking at one of the flyers and they got talking and that was that. Beau sorted it all out. I've got to meet her myself yet, just to check that we like each other, but I can't see any reason why we wouldn't get on.'

I steal another look at Frank, who raises his eyebrows and gives an almost imperceptible shake of his head.

I turn my back on him. 'Where was Beau last night?'

This brings Candice up short. She opens her mouth, but no words are forthcoming. Eventually she finds her voice. 'Erm, working, why?'

'We saw him in the pub over the road. He was with another girl. I'm so sorry, Candice.'

Frank gives an audible groan. 'Jenny, what did I tell you?'

'Another girl? What do you mean?' asks Candice. Her effervescence of a few moments ago has fizzled out.

'He was having a drink with this redhead and they looked pretty close to me.'

Frank butts in. 'They didn't, Candice. They were just having a drink, nothing more than that.'

'Redhead, you say?' Her shoulders sag with relief. 'Well, that's Fliss, I expect. I know he saw her last night. I assumed it was at the Lemon Tree, but they could have gone somewhere else.' She stands up. 'Yes, that'll be it; as Frank says, nothing to worry about.' She's obviously flustered, though, and knocks over a glass of orange juice in her haste to leave.

Frank dabs at the table with his napkin. 'Happy now, Jenny?'

I do feel a little foolish, but I have no regrets. I know I'm right about Beau.

33

She hadn't told Beau she was coming. Not because she wanted to catch him out, but because she wanted to surprise him. At least that was what she told herself. Their paths had barely crossed this week with one thing and another, and she was desperate to spend time with him even if it was just as a member of his audience.

'Hello again.'

She swivelled round on the bar stool. 'Oh, hi, Adrian. How are you?'

'Yeah, not bad as it goes. Yourself?'

She glanced nervously at the stage. Beau was due out any minute. 'Okay, yeah.'

He nodded at her almost-empty glass. 'Fancy another?'

'Oh well, you know.' She wrinkled her nose and attempted a laugh. 'I'd better not. Not after all the kerfuffle it caused last time.'

He shook his head. 'What are you doing with a prat like him, eh?'

There really was no answer to that. 'Can we just leave it, please?'

Adrian stood his ground. 'Are you really okay?'

'Yes,' she replied, her patience wearing thin. 'Why does everybody think it's okay to interfere in my life? I'm fine.'

He held his palms aloft. 'All right, if you say so.' He backed away. 'You know where to find me if you need anything.'

'Such as?' She frowned.

'I've no idea. Just anything . . . any time, okay?'

'I'm fine,' she reiterated through gritted teeth.

At the end of his set, Beau held his guitar over his head, an emulsion of sweat on his forehead, his chest heaving as though he'd just completed an Ironman. He took an exaggerated bow. 'Thank you, thank you,' he said to the audience. A few people were on their feet, some whistling, some shouting for more. 'Thank you,' he breathed again. 'I'd like to slow it down a little now, for all you lovebirds out there.'

Candice suppressed a smile. Lovebirds? Since when had Beau started talking like that?

He fiddled with the tuning pegs, then placed one foot on the chair and rested the guitar on his knee. 'This is one of my own compositions. I hope you like it.'

He nodded to a guy dressed all in black with headphones around his neck. The lights were dimmed even further. Beau strummed his guitar, closing his eyes to the soft melody, his voice thick with emotion. He held out his hand to a swaying girl at a table close by, inviting her to join him on stage. She looked at her two companions before pointing to her own chest. 'Me?' she gushed. He nodded and took hold of her hand, pulling her on stage.

She gazed adoringly at him as he sang to her as though she

was the only other person in the room. Feeling like an intruder, Candice was forced to look away.

'Thinks he's Barry Manilow, that one,' Adrian observed, folding his arms across his chest. 'I wouldn't put up with it if I were you.'

'It's all part of the act,' Candice replied in a forced casual tone. 'Means nothing.'

He nodded slowly. 'If you say so.'

She picked up her handbag and shrugged on her jacket. 'I do.' She turned to leave. 'Just one more thing. Please don't tell him I was here.'

It was gone two in the morning by the time Beau crawled in. His breath smelled of some sort of alcohol she couldn't identify, and his clothes reeked of smoke.

She could hear him creeping around the bedroom.

'It's all right, I'm awake,' she said stiffly.

He flopped on the bed beside her and kissed her cheek. 'Oh, sorry, babe. Did I wake you?'

'Not really. I haven't been able to get off.'

'That's good news for me then,' he said, straddling her and bending to kiss her neck.

She turned away. 'Not now, Beau.'

He stopped and cocked his head. Reaching for his face, she could just make out his features in the gloom. 'I'm tired, that's all. Do you mind?'

He climbed off the bed and pulled his shirt over his head before tossing it on the floor. 'Okay, fine.'

'How was the Lemon Tree?'

'Yeah, it was good. Usual crowd, got quite a following in there now as it happens.'

'Was Fliss there?'

'Who?'

'Fliss, the girl you met from the beauty salon.'

'Um, no. Why do you ask?'

'No reason.' Her attempt to sound breezy failed spectacularly. She paused, struggling to keep her tone light. 'What does she look like?'

'Fliss? I dunno. All right, I suppose. You're meeting her tomorrow, so you can see for yourself.'

'Where did you go with her last night then?'

'What's with the third degree, Candice?' He threw his boxers on top of the discarded shirt. 'Don't you trust me? She's about forty, for God's sake. You've no reason to be jealous.'

'Oh my God,' she scoffed as she struggled into a sitting position. She clicked on the bedside lamp, squinting at him. 'Me, jealous? That's rich coming from you.'

He leaned in close, laughing in her face. 'Now you know how it feels. Not very nice, is it?'

'But I haven't done anything wrong,' she insisted. 'Whereas you, you've been carrying on behind my back.'

'What are you on about, you daft bat?'

'I know you were seeing someone else last night.'

'Yes, I told you. I met Fliss in a coffee shop on Stretford Road. I did it for you, remember, although I don't know why I bother. You're such an ungrateful cow.'

'But after that you went to that posh pub near work with another girl. I know you did. You were spotted.' Inwardly she chastised herself for sounding so hysterical. She noticed his

214

jaw tighten as he exhaled a deep breath through his nose. 'Spotted by who?'

She hesitated. 'Erm . . . no one.'

'Come on, out with it. Who's been grassing me up?'

'Well, it was Jenny, if you must know.'

'Surprise, surprise,' he said, dropping onto the bed. 'And you had the nerve to lecture me about trust.'

'You're not denying it then.'

He traced the leafy pattern of the duvet with his finger. 'Yeah, I probably should've told you, babe, but Marsha's just an old friend, that's all.' He brought her hand to his lips, but she snatched it away.

'You can do better than that, Beau. What's really going on?'

'Okay, okay,' he conceded. 'Old girlfriend, then. We were an item once, many moons ago. I happened to bump into her in Tesco, we got chatting and she asked if I'd like to go for an early-doors drink. You know, for old times' sake and all that. She's off to Australia next week for the foreseeable. I spent most of the time telling her about you, as it happens.'

'How come you've never mentioned her before?'

'Why would I do that? She's history. We went out for a while, it was good, and then we went our separate ways. End of.'

She could feel her cheeks burning with embarrassment. Damn Jenny. Beau was right, she was an interfering old bag sometimes.

'Besides,' he continued, 'I wouldn't have needed to be anywhere near Tesco if you'd done your job right.'

'My job?'

'Yes, you forgot the washing capsule things and you know

I wanted you to do my best white shirt. I need it for the weekend.' He pulled the duvet over his head. 'Now you'll have to get up early and do it before work. Night, babe.'

Sleep had never been further away, and even though it wasn't quite light, she decided to get up and put the white shirt in the machine. The cheap coffee she made herself was bitter and yet tasteless all at the same time. She reached for the good stuff they kept at the back of the cupboard. Beau had allowed her to splash out as long as they only had it once a week. That way it would last longer and be more of a treat, allowing them to appreciate the extra expense. She prised the lid off and peered into the almost-empty jar. Clearly the once-a-week rule didn't apply to him.

She heaved herself out of the chair when she heard the machine beep at the end of its cycle. Popping open the door, she stared in disbelief at the shirt inside, the first fingers of panic clutching at her heart. 'No, no, no,' she whispered, pulling it out and turning it over as though her eyes were deceiving her. 'What in the name of . . .?' She felt inside the machine and tugged out the offending item. Her red lace thong.

She dumped the pale pink shirt into the washing basket and paced the kitchen, chewing the skin round her thumbnail as she pondered what to do. One of those colour-run-removal sachets might do the trick, but the shops weren't open yet. At the sound of the toilet flushing, she shoved the shirt back into the machine and closed the door.

Beau appeared in the doorway, his eyes half closed. 'You woke me up with that washing machine, babe. I'm knackered. Any chance of a brew?'

'Erm . . . yeah, sure. Kettle's not long since boiled.' She kept her tone light. 'You'll . . . erm . . . never guess what I found?'

He clicked his lighter to the end of his cigarette. 'What did you find?'

'My red lace thong!' She hooked the underwear on the end of her finger. 'See.'

He squinted through a cloud of smoke. 'Where was it?'

'In the machine.' She laughed. 'I must've missed it when I emptied it last time.'

'Right, mystery solved then.'

Her hands shook as she carried Beau's mug to the table. She knew she shouldn't be scared to tell him about the shirt. These things happened; he would understand, surely. 'Beau,' she began. 'I've done something stupid. Not deliberately – it was an accident – but . . . well, the thing is, the thong was still in the machine when I washed your white shirt, and now it's come out . . .' She faltered when she saw his mouth drop. 'It's come out all pink.'

He took a sip of his coffee before replying. 'Pink?'

She nodded. 'I'm really sorry.'

'You're telling me my best white shirt is now pink?' he clarified.

Her voice was barely audible. 'Sorry.'

He took hold of her hand and she resisted the urge to snatch it away. 'Why do you look so scared, babe?'

'I . . . I'm not. It's just that I feel so stupid.'

He pulled her down onto his lap. 'It was an accident,' he emphasised. 'Don't beat yourself up about it. You can buy me a new one and we'll forget all about it.'

Relief surged through her veins. 'Are you sure you're not mad?'

He bounced her up and down as though she was a toddler. 'Of course I'm not, silly. Jeez, what do you think I am? I'll just take the money out of the beauty course fund and we'll forget it ever happened.'

'Oh, right,' she said, the disappointment evident in her voice.

'Wait, hang on a sec,' he said, turning her face towards him. 'You're not expecting *me* to pay for another one, are you? It wasn't me who was the careless sod.'

'No, you're right. It's all my fault. No reason why you should have to suffer just because I'm an idiot. How much was it anyway?'

'Oh, I dunno. Ninety, I think.'

'Ninety? Ninety quid for a shirt?'

'Yes, Candice. Ninety quid for a shirt. *You* might be able to get away with wearing a bloody tabard for work, but I can't. I have my image to maintain.' He picked up a piece of her hair, twirling it in his fingers. 'Any chance you could make me some breakfast? I'm starving.'

34

Bad news this morning. With only six weeks to go until Italy, the doctor has been and said my blood pressure is up and my pulse rate is a little irregular. I feel as fit as a flea, so I'm sure it's nothing to worry about, but then he spotted the travel brochure and asked me who was going on holiday. I thought about telling a fib, but came clean in the end. He shook his head and frowned at me in a rather stern way, but I stood my ground. There is nobody on this earth who can stop me from getting on that plane.

There's always something to do at Green Meadows. Today is baking club, one of the more popular pastimes. Simeon swans around like Paul Hollywood, passing judgement on our efforts. His kitchen now resembles the carnage you might see after a particularly robust earth tremor, and I can tell he's getting rather tetchy about it.

He drags his finger through the dusting of flour coating my work station. 'Jenny, would it kill you to wipe up as you go along?'

'It might.' I nod. 'I'm a hundred years old, it's not going to take much to see me off.'

He tuts at the ceiling. 'You'll probably outlive me at this

rate.' He plants his hands on his hips and surveys the disaster zone. 'Okay,' he commands. 'Bring your bakes up to the table.'

I look at Frank, who is studiously sprinkling his Welsh cakes with a generous layer of sugar, his tongue sticking out in concentration. 'Frank, would you mind taking up my offering?' I've made a lemon polenta cake and it looks rather splendid, even though I say so myself.

He duly obliges and carries both our plates to the display table, which is bedecked with a red and white gingham cloth.

Simeon sweeps his gaze along the row of cakes, nodding his approval until he gets to Myrtle's date and ginger slab. *Slab* being the operative word. It has sunk in the middle and appears to have the density and appeal of a house brick.

'I'll try one of yours,' I say to Frank.

He smiles as he hands me a serviette with one of his creations nestling in the folds. 'Enjoy.'

I take a bite, and as I feel the sugar stick to my lips and smell the mixed spice, I am transported back to Del's kitchen. She always seemed to have a griddle on the go and warm Welsh cakes were Louis's favourite, liberally spread with butter, obviously.

'Delicious, Frank. Truly.'

I'm not sure why, but he can't meet my eye. 'Thank you, Jenny.'

Mrs Culpepper comes in and claps her hands as though she's addressing a classroom of unruly kids. 'Come, come, now. Let's get this lot into the day room so Simeon can start on the real cooking.'

In the day room, we sit with our cups of tea in our laps, our stomachs full of cake and all of us fighting to keep our eyes open. I put my cup and saucer on the side table, close my eyes and succumb. Afternoon naps are the preserve of the elderly, toddlers and university students.

I'm not sure how long I'm out for, but when I do wake, the afternoon tea detritus has been cleared away and Candice is sitting in the window staring out at the bird table.

'Hello, Candice.'

She doesn't turn around, and I'm worried she's still mad at me for telling her about Beau going to the pub with another girl.

'Candice,' I say a little louder.

She looks at me then, and I'm so shocked by her appearance that I forget to close my mouth. 'Whatever's the matter, love?'

'Nothing. Why?' She rubs her hands vigorously over her face, which does at least put some colour in her cheeks.

'You look so . . . so . . .' She looks absolutely dreadful, but I can't bring myself to say it. 'You look so tired.' Her face is blotchy, her eyes have purple crescents beneath them and her hair is flat and greasy.

She gives a dramatic yawn. 'I didn't sleep well last night, and I was up early this morning to wash Beau's . . .' She stops, perhaps realising that an interrogation is about to follow.

'Wash Beau's what?' I hope I'm not going to regret asking this question.

'Beau's best white shirt.' She sighs. 'It's a long story, but I've ruined it. It came out all pink.'

'Hmm . . . And I guess he wasn't best pleased.'

She shakes her head. 'He was really good about it actually, but I've got to buy him a new one. Well, the money has got to come out of the beauty course fund.'

My heart aches for her. She looks so beaten and ground

221

down that I swear if Beau walked into this room right now, I wouldn't be responsible for my actions.

'Why don't you let me pay for it?'

'Oh no,' she says. 'I couldn't let you do that. Beau would go mad if he knew you'd bought his shirt.'

'I wasn't talking about the shirt, Candice. I'll pay for your beauty course.'

I've been thinking about this for a while. Not only can I afford it, but it also removes an element of Beau's control over Candice. He's forever using it as leverage against her. It'll take that power away from him. It's the right thing to do, even though once she qualifies, she'll no longer have to work at Green Meadows. That thought is unbearable, and I push it to the back of my mind.

Her eyes immediately mist over and she reaches for my hand. 'You'd do that for me?'

'There are no pockets in shrouds, as they say.'

'But . . . but . . . you're already paying for me to go to Italy. I couldn't—'

I shush her with a wave of my hand. 'Give over, Candice. I'll hear no more about it.'

She needs a distraction. I twist the gold band on my finger and change the subject. 'I haven't told you about my wedding yet.'

She shuffles to the edge of her seat, resting her chin on her palm. Her eyes still shining, she actually manages to sound enthusiastic. 'Ooh, go on then.'

35

1942

The sound of thundering feet on the stairs was enough to wake her even before he barged open the door and leapt onto her bed. The ancient springs squeaked as he bounced up and down on the mattress. 'Jenny, Jenny, wake up.'

'Louis,' she replied, her voice still thick with sleep. 'Never mind me. You've woken the dead with all that racket.'

He tugged on her arm. 'Come on, Jenny, it's time to get up.'

She stretched her arms over her head, coaxing out the stiffness. 'What time is it?'

'Half six.'

'Is it really that time already? What's the weather looking like?'

'Mammy Del says it's going to be perfect wedding weather.'

She tickled his ribs, making him wriggle, then patted the space beside her. 'Come and sit here a minute, Louis. I want to talk to you.'

'But I need to get ready,' he protested. 'I've got to get me suit on, and Mammy has made me a butter knowle. I'm not sure what it is, but it sounds tasty and I'm starving.'

'It's a flower, you daft article,' she laughed. 'You wear it on your suit to show that you're an important part of the wedding.'

'I am,' he beamed. 'The most important part.'

'Indeed you are. Even more important than the bride and groom, I'd say.' She smoothed down his unruly hair and pulled him into her arms. 'I want you to know that you'll always be the most special little man in my life.'

He nodded solemnly. 'I know, Jenny.'

'We've been through a lot, me and you but we survived because we stuck together.'

Almost two and a half years had passed since they'd said that final tearful farewell on the chaotic railway platform, but she could still remember her mother's impassioned plea: *At all costs, stay together.*

Louis pondered her words, a thoughtful frown on his face. 'It's a good job she did send us away, because we'd be dead otherwise.'

'But it was so hard for her, Lou. It broke her heart.' She kissed his forehead. 'And we'll never forget her, will we, eh?'

'Never,' he said, scrambling off the bed. 'Now get up, Jenny. There's still lots of chores to do even on your wedding day.'

She could hear Del stacking the crockery downstairs in the kitchen. The best willow pattern plates, which were normally just for show, had been taken off the dresser the day before and given a thorough soaping. Jenny gazed at her wedding dress hanging on the outside of the wardrobe, a creation she herself had designed and modified from Del's own dress. The delicate veil was dotted with tiny rosebuds and was so sheer you could read the newspaper through it. She had always imagined she would wear her own mother's veil on her wedding day, but that had gone up in smoke along with everything else their mother had held dear.

This Christmas would see the second anniversary of Connie's death, and today Jenny felt her loss more keenly than ever before. Having to stay strong for Louis had meant her own grieving process had had to be put on hold. Although he'd initially been devastated, he had proved to be the more resilient of the two of them. He spoke about Connie now and then but only in passing, and Jenny worried he could barely remember her. They hadn't got a single photo to keep her memory alive. She would always be grateful to the Evans family, especially Del, who loved Louis as though he were her own flesh and blood. Jenny owed her everything.

The hesitant tap on the door brought her back to the present. 'Who is it?'

'It's me.'

She pulled the eiderdown over her head. 'No, it's bad luck, go away.'

'Please, I need to see you. I need to check you haven't changed your mind.'

She smiled at his teasing. 'Come in then, but only for a minute. I've got to start getting ready.'

He settled himself on the edge of her bed and pulled the covers off her face. Gazing into her eyes, he brushed a strand of hair from her cheek. 'I love you, Jenny.'

She paused, testing the words out in her head first. 'And I love you too, Lorcan.'

He cocked his head, a half-smile on his lips, his voice full of hope. 'Do you really?' He smelled of warm milk and cow dung.

'Really,' she said emphatically. 'Why else would I have agreed to marry you, eh?' She thumped him on the arm. 'Now go on with you, I've got to make myself beautiful.'

'Hold on a minute, I have to give you something first.'

He reached behind his back and held out a package wrapped in brown paper and secured with a length of chunky pink wool.

She fingered the bow, tugging gently to release it. 'What's this?'

'Open it,' he beamed.

She peeled off the paper and stared at the hand-crafted box.

'I made it for you, Jenny,' he said, eagerly. 'It's a jewellery box and one day I'm going to fill it with all the beautiful pieces you deserve.'

She ran her fingers over the highly polished rosewood, as smooth as a slab of marble. A narrow inlaid border made from seashells framed the initial *J* carved out in relief.

'Lorcan, it's exquisite. It must have taken you forever.'

'You're worth it.' He opened the box to reveal a red velvet interior with a cream satin-lined lid. 'There's a little drawer underneath too,' he enthused. 'For all your treasures.'

'Thank you, Lorcan.' She swallowed the unexpected tears. 'It's really special.'

He jumped up and kissed the top of her head. 'And so are you.'

She clutched the jewellery box to her chest as he closed the door. His happiness was all-consuming. She could detect it in

226

his eyes, feel it in the tenderness of his touch as he brushed her hair away from her face. All this lovely boy had ever wanted was to love and cherish her. Nico was gone forever. It could have been something magical, but it wasn't to be. Even after more than two years she still thought about him every day. He had stirred something in her that Lorcan had never quite been able to manage. But Lorcan was a good man, dependable, loyal and devoted to her. She should count herself lucky. She would grow to love him in time, she was sure of it. Love should be the final goal of a marriage, not a prerequisite.

The others had left for the chapel, leaving Jenny alone at the kitchen table, a steadying tot of whisky in her hands. The kitchen seemed hollow, as though its beating heart had been ripped out. Her eyes swept across the table, marvelling at the biblical-scale miracle the Evans family had managed to pull off. There were fish-paste finger sandwiches, hard-boiled eggs from their own chickens, and a gloriously rich rabbit and game stew thanks to Lorcan and Louis, who had spent the previous week out in the fields shooting anything that moved. Neighbours had pooled their food coupons, and the resulting wedding cake now took pride of place in the centre of the table. Admittedly, a decorative cover of white cardboard masqueraded as icing, but beggars couldn't be choosers.

She could see Louis outside, giving the donkey a final brush as he adjusted the sprig of flowers he'd tucked into her head-band. His cast-off suit and serious expression made him look much older than his seven years. He appeared at the kitchen door, his hands behind his back. 'I've got something for you,' he ventured. 'A present. I made it.'

She smiled at his eager face, his ears reddening. 'Bless you, Louis.'

She held the carving in her hands, turning it over as she marvelled at the smoothly honed and polished wood. Lorcan was obviously a good teacher. 'You've never made this, our Louis?'

'I did,' he beamed.

'Is this me and you?'

He nodded, taking the carving off her. 'The big one is you and the little one is me.'

Through her tears, she studied the two figures. The larger one had her head bowed and her arms outstretched but joined together at the hands so that they formed a circle into which the smaller figure slotted and nestled against her skirt.

'It's . . . it's . . . absolutely . . . I don't know what to say. You're so clever.'

'It's like a jigsaw, but not a flat one. These two pieces can be pulled apart, see, but they'll always stick back together. Just like us two.' He demonstrated, holding the little boy carving aloft and leaving the girl with her arms empty.

She took the carving back and slotted it together again. 'I'll treasure it forever, Lou-Lou.' She held out her hand. 'Come here.' She hoisted him onto her knee, her tone serious. 'I know you're giving me away, but it doesn't mean I'm actually going anywhere.'

'I know. That's why I made the carving. You can pull us apart but we'll always find our way back to each other where we belong.'

She pulled him close to her chest, squeezing him hard. 'I love you, Louis.' This time she meant every word of what she said.

He wriggled free. 'I can't breathe, Jenny.'

She blotted her face with her handkerchief. 'How do I look?'

Louis tilted his head, studying her blotchy face. 'Mmm . . . you've looked better.'

She laughed as she headed for the stairs. 'Just give me five minutes to fix things, and then we'll be off.'

She remembered the first journey they'd taken in the donkey cart. Fresh from the evacuation hall, Louis clinging to her legs, snivelling all the way back to the farm and then refusing to jump down by himself. She looked at him now, sitting in the driving seat, his hands expertly working the reins, his voice strong and confident.

He guided the donkey to a gentle halt outside the chapel. The slight breeze carried the organ music round the churchyard. She brought her bouquet up to her nose and inhaled the fruity warm smell of the honeysuckle. Del had grown the peach and cream-coloured shrub around the front door of Mynydd Farm because it was said to ward off evil spirits. It was also a sign of fidelity and would make the perfect bouquet, she said. The message had been received loud and clear.

Louis gathered up her veil as she stepped off the cart, leaving her cane behind. She relied on it less and less these days and was determined it would be left out of the wedding pictures. A shortage of film meant they were only permitted to take two photographs of their special day, and she wanted them to be perfect.

Louis busied himself tying up the donkey, patting her neck and telling her to be a good girl. He produced a carrot from his pocket by way of a bribe. Wiping his hands down his trousers, he turned to Jenny. 'Ready?'

She took a breath and nodded. 'I think so, Louis.' She crooked her elbow. 'Here, take my arm.'

They stood side by side, contemplating the tree-lined path leading to the entrance to the chapel. It was fashioned out of ancient moss-covered gravestones and in wet weather proved rather hazardous underfoot. But today, the September sun shone through the trees, lighting their way as effectively as a street lamp. The pipe organ began a shaky rendition of Mendelssohn's Wedding March.

'Come on then, Louis. Let's not keep them waiting any longer.'

She brought the veil over her face and took a hesitant step forward. A step further towards the man who loved her unconditionally, the man who would do anything for her.

As they reached the church door, she felt the shift in atmosphere. From within came murmurs of excitement, a clearing of throats and feet shuffling on the gritty floor. 'She's here,' somebody whispered.

She looked down at Louis and smiled. 'Ready?'

He nodded vigorously, his wide smile confirming he was more than ready.

Gripping her bouquet, she inhaled a calming breath. There was no turning back now. 'I'm doing this for us, Lou, for our future.' She smiled at his eager face. 'There'll always be a home for us here now.'

'Will Lorcan be my proper brother then?'

She gave it some thought, well aware she was stalling for time. 'Technically he'll be your brother-in-law, I suppose, but it doesn't matter what you call him. He loves us both and he'll take care of us for the rest of our lives.'

'I'd like that,' he said. 'Now come on, they're all waiting.'

'Jennifer.'

She froze at the sound of the once-familiar voice.

'Jennifer,' he said again. 'Jennifer, it's me.'

Slowly she turned around, the blood rushing in her ears. It couldn't be.

A slender figure stumbled towards her, his cap clutched in his hands. 'Jennifer. It's me, Nico. I came back . . . just like I promised.'

36

'Jenny, Jenny, come ON! Everybody's waiting.'

She shifted her gaze away from Nico and stared at her little brother, who stood with his hands on his hips, his expression pleading.

'It's my job to get you in there on time and now everybody's going to think it's my fault, but it isn't my fault, it's his.' With as much venom as he could muster, he pointed at Nico.

'Louis, please,' she begged, her breathless words sounding hollow to her own ears. 'I can't go in there now.'

'You have to.' He jerked his thumb towards the chapel. 'Lorcan's waiting for you and you promised you would marry him.'

'I know I did, Lou-Lou. Give me a moment. Everything's changed now.'

Nico touched his shoulder, but Louis shook him off. 'Louis,' he tried. 'I did not come here to do this. Jennifer has made her decision to marry Lorcan and I respect that, but I had to come and see her for myself. Not to talk her out of it but to see that she was happy and to give her my blessing. I want her to marry the man she loves.'

Jenny covered her face with her hands, shaking her head. 'I don't love him, though,' she breathed.

'What did you say?' Lorcan was silhouetted in the church doorway, his expression darkening as he stepped into the sunlight.

'Lorcan,' Jenny began. 'I'm so, so sorry . . .'

Lorcan pushed up the sleeves of his suit as he strode towards them. 'Is that . . . is that you, Nico?'

Nico held his palms up. 'Yes, but I come in peace, I never wanted any of this.'

'I thought you were dead. Where've you been all this time – and why show up today, of all days?' He lurched towards Nico, grabbing his lapel, breathing into his face. 'Go away. You're not welcome here. Get lost.' He shoved him so hard he stumbled backwards and landed on the grass, then stood over him. 'Go on. Get out of here.'

Louis stared from one man to the other, his eyes widening at the unfolding drama. 'Jenny won't go into the church, Lorcan. Tell her,' he implored. 'Tell her she's got to marry you.'

Lorcan unclenched his fists, his rage dissipating only to be replaced by disbelief. 'Jenny? Is it true? You don't love me?'

Words were redundant. The tears sliding down her cheeks said it all. She merely nodded and stared at the ground.

'Why?' he said incredulously. 'Because of *him*?' He spat out the last word.

'I'm so sorry, Lorcan,' she said again. 'Believe me, you'll never know how sorry I am. As long as I live, I'll always regret the hurt this has caused you, but it would be wrong to marry you when I'm in love with someone else.'

He brought his palms together as though in prayer. 'Please, please, Jenny. Don't do this to me. You love me, you said so.'

'I do love you, Lorcan, in my own way.' She paused, the pain in his eyes making it difficult for her to carry on. 'But it's not enough and it never will be.'

He collapsed onto his knees. 'No! How could you do this to me, Jenny? I can't believe you could be so cruel.' He looked up, his face twisted with grief. 'It was supposed to be the happiest day of my life . . . of both our lives.'

She crouched down beside him, laying her arm across his shoulders. 'It wouldn't be right to marry you. I was wrong to think it could work.'

He shrugged her off, staring at the ground as a teardrop plopped off the tip of his nose. 'I can't believe it,' he whispered. 'This was supposed to be the beginning of something magical.' He took hold of her hand. 'Please,' he implored. 'Please don't do this to me. You will grow to love me in time. I know you will.'

'Come on, Jennifer,' Nico said. 'I think perhaps we should go now. Let things settle down.'

Lorcan struggled to his feet, bunching his fists. 'Oh, that's right, run away, typical Eyetie.'

'All right,' Nico said calmly. 'I'm going to forgive you for that because I can see you are upset.' His tone was measured as he pointed his finger in Lorcan's face. 'But if you disrespect me or my fellow countrymen again, I promise you, you will regret it.'

'Are you threatening me?' Lorcan raised his fist, halting it in mid-air as Louis screamed.

'Stop it, stop it now.' He turned to his sister. 'This is all your fault. I hate you. I never want to see you again.' He fled towards the chapel, almost tripping in his haste to get away.

Lorcan stared at Jenny. 'I'll go after him. I can't bear to be anywhere near you at the moment.' He made a fist and clamped it to his chest. 'You may as well have ripped my heart out.' He stared after Louis's retreating figure. 'And there's no telling whether that little lad will ever forgive you.'

37

I can see Candice is having trouble comprehending my actions. I sometimes find it hard to believe myself what I did.

'But why did you agree to marry someone you didn't love?'

'I wanted security for our Louis, and I did love Lorcan in a way. But there was no spark, no rush of blood when he entered a room, no shivers when his fingers found mine. He was good-hearted and dependable, though, and he loved me far more than I deserved. He would do anything for us and I knew that if I married him, we'd be cared for and secure for the rest of our lives. I know that sounds selfish now.' I wait for her to disagree, but she's still baffled by my actions and doesn't seem ready to take my side just yet.

'So you thought you'd settle for second best?'

Her tone is accusatory and yet bewildered at the same time.

'I thought I would learn to love him, but it was like squeezing my feet into shoes that were a size too small. I could just about manage it and the shoes would look and feel good for a time, but by the end of the day my feet were sore and begging for release. Loving someone shouldn't feel that hard.'

She ponders this. 'I suppose you're right.'

'I knew the second I saw Nico in that churchyard that I wasn't going to go through with my wedding to Lorcan. Nico was a changed person. He seemed vulnerable and worn down. He'd been detained for two years in a camp in Australia even though he'd done nothing wrong. He had no idea that we'd all been told he was missing, presumed drowned. Once he was released, he came back to Penlan, only to find that Lena and Enzo had returned to Italy. He'd written to me several times, but the letters never arrived.'

Candice shakes her head but says nothing, so I press on, trying to justify myself to her even though I'm not sure why I need to. 'When I fell into Nico's arms, he squeezed me so tightly that I knew I was safe and back where I belonged. Back in a place I was always meant to be. Nico was my happy ever-after, not Lorcan.'

Candice blows out a gentle breath as realisation dawns. 'Has this got anything to do with why you're going to Italy?'

I take hold of her hand, smooth and unblemished next to my gnarled, liver-spotted one. If only it were possible to live as long as I have without getting old. 'This'll be the last trip I ever make, Candice. I've put it off for long enough, but there are some things I need to reconcile if I'm to die in peace.'

'I get the feeling it's more than just a little holiday.'

I pat her hand. 'Much more, Candice. Much more.'

38

'Wow, you look amazing, babe. You sure you're only going off to work?'

She turned away from the mirror and looked at Beau sprawled on the bed, his naked body tangled up in the duvet, his eyeliner smudged beneath his eyes. 'You know I am; stop trying to pick a fight.'

'I'm only joking, Candice. Jeez, you're so sensitive.'

She ignored his remark. 'I'd like to go on the bus if you don't mind. I don't want to arrive for my first day all sweaty and out of breath.'

He opened his bedside drawer and pulled out his wallet. 'Sure, babe. How much do you need?'

'Erm, a tenner should do it. I'll have to get myself some lunch too.'

'Lunch? Christ, Candice, we're supposed to be saving. Not sure you should be splashing out on lunch.'

She finished applying her lipstick, taking her time to answer. 'I need to eat, and it's hardly splashing out. I'll probably just get some Cup-a-Soups and a packet of Hobnobs. Should see me through the week.' She held her arms out. 'How do I look?'

He regarded her through narrowed eyes. 'Like a proper beauty therapist. That uniforms suits you.'

They'd spent ages online going through salon wear before settling on a dusky-pink asymmetrical tunic with navy piping. She would have preferred to make the selection without Beau breathing down her neck, ruling out anything too revealing or too expensive, but at least he was happy with the choice. It was an end-of-line too and a bargain at only fifteen quid, which especially pleased him.

'Here,' he said, holding out a ten-pound note. 'Are you sure that's enough? You don't need to buy anything else?'

'Really? Do you mean it, because I could do with a new pair of shoes. Look.' She removed her black slip-on pumps and showed him the holes in both heels. 'Don't look very professional, do they? I'd really like to get some more if that's okay with you. They're not expensive ones.'

He took hold of one shoe and prodded at the hole with his finger. 'You've been walking round in these, have you? Don't your feet get wet in the rain?'

'Well, yes, but I thought—'

'Why didn't you say something before?' He laid the shoe down on the bed and took hold of both her hands. 'It's your money too, don't forget. I only look after it because you're so bad with it, but this . . .' he picked up the shoe again, 'this breaks my heart, babe.'

'I'm sorry, Beau.'

'Sorry? What are you sorry for?'

'I . . . um . . . I don't know really.'

He squeezed her hands harder. 'Candice, you need to toughen up. Assert yourself a bit more. If you need more money, just ask for it. I don't want people thinking I keep you in poverty.'

'Perhaps I could have my bank card back, then I won't need to ask.'

He released his grip on her hands and touched her cheek instead. 'Steady on, I don't think we're quite there yet, babe. We don't want to spoil all the progress we've made.' His accompanying smile was only just the right side of patronising.

'I'm fine now, Beau, honestly. You worry too much.'

'Hmm, perhaps,' he said, leaping off the bed. 'But once a spendthrift, always a spendthrift.'

The salon looked deserted, and she wondered if she had made a mistake with the day. Then, as she peered through the door, Fliss emerged from behind a curtain, a cigarette wedged between her lips as she carried a tray of nail polish. Candice tapped on the glass.

Fliss set down the tray, stubbed out the cigarette and fanned the air around her before coming to open the door.

'Ooh, caught me having a crafty fag. Come on in, love.' She beckoned Candice over the threshold, her countless bracelets jangling like wind chimes in a storm.

'Don't worry on my account,' Candice said. 'I'm used to it.'

'Against the law, though, int it? Never mind that I own the place and should be able to do whatever I like, the law says you can't smoke in the workplace.' Fliss flicked her head towards the back door. 'There's a place you can go out there if you need your fix.'

'It's all right, I don't smoke, ta.'

'Oh, right, well you're probably wise not to.' She gazed

down at her own fingers, rubbing away at the yellow stain. 'Wish I'd never started, but here we are. Can't turn back the clock, can we? Now,' she pointed a long acrylic nail towards a chair at the back of the shop, 'that's yours. Make yourself at home and don't hesitate to ask if you need anything. I was in your shoes once, you know, just starting out in the beauty business, and look at me now with me own salon. Mind you, my Derek thinks I should sell up and move to Fuengirola with him. He's a good bit older than me and he's got a bob or two.' She coughed into her hand. 'Ooh, I'm parched. Stick the kettle on, love. He's done all right for himself. Not that that's why I'm with 'im, you understand. In any case, he likes to be seen with a beautiful blonde on his arm.'

'I see,' said Candice, filling the kettle from the sink.

'And when he couldn't find any takers in the beautiful blonde department, he had to make do with yours truly.' Fliss gave a throaty laugh.

She was actually a striking woman. It was no wonder she had caught Beau's eye. She might be on the wrong side of forty, and Candice had seen less make-up on a pantomime dame, but there was a magnetic quality about her that was endearing.

'It's really good of you to give me a chance like this.'

Fliss dismissed her with a wave of her hand. 'It's mutually beneficial, cocker. I've got enough on my plate with the nails, the fake tans, the facials and what have you. No, you crack on, love. It's all good. What time's your first appointment?'

'I've got one at nine thirty and another at twelve.'

'Is that it?'

'Well, it's early days, and in any case I've to be back at Green Meadows later.'

'That's the old folks' home you work in?'

Candice nodded. 'It's a residential care home actually. It's very posh and I like it there, but it's shift work and Beau's not keen on me being out all night.'

Fliss nodded her agreement. 'I can imagine. He's besotted with you, isn't he?'

Candice couldn't hide her surprise. 'Is he?'

'Oh God, yes. He didn't stop talking about you the night I met him in the . . . um . . .' She clicked her fingers in the air. 'Oh Lord, my memory . . .'

'The Lemon Tree,' Candice supplied.

'That's the one. I thought it was quite sweet. I mean, there was loads of girls in there who were all over him. Must be hard to resist for a red-blooded guy like Beau.' She gave another coarse laugh. 'You're a lucky girl, Candice. Gorgeous *and* loyal. That's quite a rare combination in the music industry.'

'Yes,' mused Candice. 'I suppose it is. What . . . erm . . . what did he say?'

Fliss frowned through the smoke haze. 'About what?'

'About me. You said he never stopped talking about me.'

She shook her head. 'I didn't take notes, love. I can't remember specifically, but I remember thinking how much he must love you.'

It was all she needed to hear. She made a mental note to tell Jenny she was wrong.

39

We're sitting under the wooden gazebo, the knotty, twisted vines of the wisteria just beginning to show signs of blossoming. Candice is proving to be an attentive listener, and I'm so relieved she's invested in my story. The worst part is yet to come, of course. However, our trip is now only three weeks away, and I'm still managing to put one foot in front of the other. I think I'm going to make it.

Candice pours me another glass of Prosecco. Didn't I tell you it was posh in here? It's not even a special occasion, unless you count celebrating the fact that we're all still alive. Frank is close by, a straw boater pulled low over his eyes as he sups his pint and balances the crossword on his knee. My mind wanders, but my eyes focus on the blackbird tugging an unfortunate worm out of the turf.

'So, you married Nico then?' Candice asks finally. I'm annoyed that she wants to skip ahead. Perhaps she senses my time's nearly up and doesn't want me to shuffle off before I get to the end.

Still, no point in prolonging the suspense, I suppose. This isn't an episode of *EastEnders*. 'Yes, I did, Candice. I married Nico.'

'Oh heck, poor Lorcan.' She pats her heart with her hand. 'And poor little Louis.'

'I imagine it must've been hard for all of them,' Frank chimes in.

Good God, who rattled his cage? I'm momentarily taken aback. I'd no idea he was paying us any attention.

I've told Frank bits of my story in the nine months or so I've known him. Nine months? Good grief, is that all? I feel as though I've known him all my life. We all have a great deal of time on our hands in here. Plenty of opportunity to just talk and reflect on the past. After all, none of us has much future to think about.

'I thought about Louis constantly in the immediate aftermath of what happened,' I say. 'I've wrestled with my conscience so much over the years, agonised over the decision I made until it nearly drove me insane. It is to my eternal regret that he got caught up in it all.'

Wordlessly Candice passes me a serviette, and I dab my eyes. She shuffles to the edge of her seat. 'Bless him. What happened then? With the wedding, I mean.'

It still makes me groan out loud when I think about it. 'I wanted to go into the chapel and tell everybody the wedding was off. I may be many things, but a coward is not one of them. I thought I owed them all an explanation, but Lorcan wouldn't hear of it. Louis sided with him, and they both stood with their arms outstretched, preventing me from going inside. I wanted to hang on to what little dignity I had left, so when Nico took my hand and pulled me away, I meekly followed him.'

I reach for my Prosecco glass and drain the contents in one

go. The bubbles fizz up my nose and the serviette is called into action again.

'We went to the square, to the gelateria, but it was all boarded up. Obviously, with the war still on, nobody was looking to purchase a business, especially one that relied so heavily on rationed commodities.' I nod at the bottle of Prosecco and Candice takes the hint and refills my glass. 'We managed to find a room for the night in the next town. The news had spread like measles, and people in Penlan were not exactly sympathetic towards us.'

Candice nods her agreement. 'I can imagine. The Evans family were such a big part of that community, and everybody loved Lorcan, didn't they?'

She makes it sound as though she was there. She's obviously been taking it all in.

'The hotel room was so dreary. I remember everything was brown. Brown carpet, brown walls, brown curtains, even the eiderdown was brown. There was no colour, no joy; it seemed to reflect the seriousness of the situation. It wasn't a room we could be happy in.'

'I bet you felt you didn't deserve happiness.' Candice has taken on the air of an agony aunt, a slightly judgemental one.

'The room only had one double bed,' I continue, smiling inwardly as her eyes widen.

Frank stands up suddenly – well, as suddenly as an octogenarian can manage. 'Uh-oh, time for me to go, I think. I'll leave you two ladies to talk about the particulars.'

I shake my head at his retreating figure. 'Nico was the perfect gentleman. He insisted I take the bed and he slept in the armchair by my side.' I manage a small laugh. 'It wasn't how I expected to spend my wedding night.'

'You had no regrets, though?' She seems desperate to hear that I made the right decision.

'I knew Nico was the man I was meant to be with. But as I said, I had plenty of regrets about the hurt I'd caused, not just to Lorcan, but to Del and Bryn too. And as for Louis, well . . .' I gaze up at the clear sky. Two planes have crossed paths and their vapour trails make a huge cross directly above our heads. 'That was my biggest regret of all.'

40

Jenny stared up at the farmhouse, recalling the first time she'd laid eyes on it. Back then she had regarded it as a sanctuary that would keep them safe for the duration of the war. Now it seemed like a formidable fortress she had no permission to enter.

Ivor and Megan lifted their heads and stared at her with their sinister yellow eyes. Composing herself, she lifted the knocker and rapped three times. Nico had wanted to come with her, but she'd insisted this was something she needed to do by herself. She wiped her hands down her skirt and swallowed hard. It would be difficult, but she was no coward.

She was about to rap again when the door was opened a crack. Delyth stuck her head through. 'What do you want?' She didn't bother to hide her animosity.

Jenny's rehearsed words evaporated on her lips. 'I . . . I . . . um, I've come for my stuff and to collect our Louis.'

Delyth eased herself through the gap in the door before closing it behind her. 'You've got a nerve, I'll give you that.' She was clearly in no mood to make things easy.

'Look, you'll never know how sorry I am, but can we please keep it civil. There's a small boy involved here and I don't want to upset him.'

'Ha,' Delyth guffawed. 'It's a bit late for that, don't you think? He's utterly heartbroken. He's cried himself to sleep for the past three nights.'

'Oh . . . oh, the poor thing.' Jenny took a step forward. 'Well, I'm here now, so if I could just come in and pack up our stuff . . .'

Delyth ignored her. 'What did I tell you when you first arrived here?'

Jenny shook her head. 'I'm not following you.'

'I told you not to break my son's heart.' Delyth flicked a tear away. 'My Lorcan is the sweetest, gentlest soul ever to walk this earth, but you treated him like something you'd found on the bottom of your shoe.'

'No, I didn't. I—'

'Oh please. Don't try to defend yourself. I'm not interested in your pathetic excuses. You don't deserve him. He's better off without you.' She jabbed a finger into Jenny's chest. 'And one day, he'll find true love, you mark my words. There's somebody out there who'll love him the way he deserves to be loved, and when he meets that person, he'll wonder what the hell he ever saw in a trollop like you.'

Although Jenny hadn't been expecting a red carpet, Delyth's venomous words hurt and she felt tears stinging her eyes.

'That's right,' Delyth said. 'Turn on the waterworks. Make it all about you.'

'Please, Del. I know I've hurt many people. Believe me, it would've been a lot easier to go through with the wedding, but is that really what you would've wanted? Is it what Lorcan would've wanted? For me to marry him out of pity or a sense of duty?'

Delyth looked at the ground, her voice just a whisper. 'It's agony seeing him in so much pain.' She glanced up. 'Should you ever be lucky enough to be blessed with a son, I want you to remember this moment.' She paused and wiped her eyes again. 'Perhaps then you'll understand.'

Jenny nodded. 'I can't keep apologising, Del. If I could just come in and pack our things—'

'*Our* things?' Del interrupted. 'I don't think so. Louis isn't going anywhere.'

'Don't be ridiculous, of course he is. He's my brother. He's coming with me.'

'He doesn't want to.'

Jenny frowned. 'He doesn't want to?' Her contrition of a few moments ago morphed into anger. 'You've poisoned him against me, haven't you?'

Delyth laughed. 'No, bach. You did that all by yourself.'

Jenny shouted at the upstairs window. 'Lorcan, are you there? You need to come down and talk some sense into your mother.'

Delyth folded her arms. 'He's not here. He's up on the mountain with Bryn.'

'When will he be back?'

She shrugged. 'He'll be hours probably, and in any case, he doesn't want to see you either.'

'He told you that, did he?'

'In no uncertain terms.'

'Right, I'm sick of this. Where's Louis?'

'I don't think you're listening to me.' Delyth spoke slowly, as though talking to an imbecile. 'Louis . . . isn't . . . going . . . anywhere.'

'For God's sake, Del. You're being unreasonable.'

'That's rich coming from you.'

Jenny rubbed her temples, trying to erase the beginnings of a headache. 'I need to talk to him. You can't deny me that, surely?'

Louis lay on the bed staring at the ceiling, Mrs Nesbitt clamped to his chest.

'Lou-Lou,' she whispered. 'It's me, can I come in?'

She hesitated on the threshold, awaiting his permission, but when none was forthcoming, she stepped into the room and sat down on the end of his bed. He turned onto his side and faced the wall.

'Louis,' she urged. 'Don't be like that, come on.' She rubbed his back but he shrugged her off. 'Louis, please. Just look at me.'

'Don't want to, go away.' He drew his legs into a foetal position and rubbed his teddy's ear under his nose. 'You never did make a skirt for Mrs Nesbitt and you promised you would. Why do you never keep your promises?'

This was more difficult than she had imagined, but she tried to keep calm. No sense in getting all aeriated with the little fella. 'I know you're upset, Louis. And I'm so, so sorry about that. You're the last person on this earth I'd wish to hurt.'

There was no response, but she ploughed on anyway. Things needed to be said, and perhaps it was better this way. 'Louis, I couldn't marry Lorcan when I didn't really love him, not in the way a wife is supposed to love her husband. When you're bigger and have a wife of your own, perhaps you'll understand.'

She heard him sniff as he buried his face in Mrs Nesbitt's fur. 'I know you're fond of Lorcan, and you couldn't have wished for a better brother. He's taught you so many things and you've flourished under his wing.' She gave a small laugh. 'Do you remember what you were like when you first arrived here, eh? Frightened of everything, and so timid. Now you're like a different boy, a proper little farmer, and I'm so proud of you.'

He remained silent, seemingly determined not to make this easy for her.

'Anyway, come along now. We need to get your stuff packed up.'

He rolled onto his back then and sat up, his red-veined eyes puffy. 'I'm not leaving the farm and you can't make me.' It was said with a quiet determination.

'You know I can't stay here now, Louis. We have to go.'

'I don't have to go. Mammy Del said she'll look after me forever.'

'I haven't got time to argue. Nico's waiting for us.'

She pulled his little suitcase from under the bed, opened his wardrobe and began to take down his clothes. He jumped off the bed and pushed her so hard she stumbled backwards, lost her footing and landed on her bottom, leaving her momentarily shocked into silence.

'Lou . . . Louis,' she said, heaving herself to her feet and abandoning the soft approach. 'Pick up that suitcase this minute and start packing.' She rubbed her right buttock, which had borne the brunt of her fall. 'You're acting like a spoilt brat and I'm not having it. Do you hear me?' She grabbed him by the arm, more roughly than she had intended, just as Del appeared in the doorway.

She moved towards Jenny. 'Take your hands off him at once.'

Louis ran to her and clung to her leg. 'Jenny hurt me, Mammy Del.'

Del smoothed his hair. 'Yes, well she's good at that, bach.'

'I'm sorry, Louis. I didn't mean—'

'Why don't you just get your things and go, Jenny?' Delyth nodded at Louis. 'He's made his feelings quite clear. He doesn't want anything to do with you, so I think it's best all round if you just disappear.' She waved her hand. 'Go on, swan off with your fancy man and leave us alone to get on with our lives.'

'No chance,' said Jenny. 'He's my brother and he belongs with me. For one thing, I promised my mother we'd stay together, and I don't intend to break that promise.' She held out her hand. 'Come on, Louis.'

He shook his head. 'I'm not going.' Then, much louder, 'I hate you.'

Delyth could not hide her smugness. 'I think that was pretty clear. Now, if there's nothing else, I'll leave you to pack. You can let yourself out when you're done.'

The packing hadn't taken long. She'd arrived here almost two and a half years ago with few possessions, and was leaving without many more. She lifted the jewellery box from her dressing table. Many, many hours of work had gone into it but she knew it had been a labour of love for Lorcan. She traced her finger around her initial before lifting the lid and feeling the soft velvet. He had promised to fill it with jewellery, but now that would never be. She pushed the box into her suitcase, pressed the catches into place and took one last look around the spartan room. Her eyes settled on Louis's wooden carving, her wedding present. She picked it up, her fingers caressing the smooth head of the little boy figure. Then she prised it out, leaving the girl's arms empty, and headed downstairs, clutching the two separate pieces in one hand, her suitcase in the other.

In the kitchen, Louis and Delyth were making up a batch of Welsh cakes, Louis standing on a stool, his features set into a scowl as he stirred the mixture. Jenny dropped her suitcase on the floor and held out the carving of the small boy to him. 'I think you should have this.' She placed it on the table. 'I'm taking my part, and one day, when you find it in your heart to forgive me, bring yours back to me and I'll slot it into place.' She laid a hand on his head. 'Where it belongs.'

Without another word, she picked up her case and headed out of the door for the last time.

41

Candice is sitting with her legs crossed, her palm supporting her chin. The frown on her face betrays her dismay. 'But how could you leave your little brother behind? He worshipped you.'

I need to put up a robust defence. I'm used to it. 'It was the hardest thing I've ever had to do in my entire life. I was inconsolable when I returned to Nico and told him what had happened, but he made me see that Wales was the best place for Louis. It wasn't fair to uproot him again and drag him across Europe. There was a war on, don't forget, and I'd have been taking him to an enemy country, as Italy was at that time.'

Candice leans back in her chair and folds her arms. She looks as tight as a bale of hay as she shakes her head slowly, her expression one of disbelief.

I take a shuddering breath, forcing myself to continue. 'Nico and I had a quick registry office wedding to facilitate our journey. I was now Italian by marriage, which did help, but the journey was long and tortuous and I was terrified for most of it. I was sure I was going to be arrested on suspicion of being some sort of spy. We sailed from Glasgow to Lisbon on a hospital ship, which constantly had to alter course to avoid mines and U-boats. I was so glad Louis hadn't come with us. Despite how much it hurt her, my mother had been brave enough to send us away so we'd be safe. Can you imagine if he'd then been blown up in mine-infested waters because of my selfishness?'

Candice nods, although I can't tell if she really understands the dangers. Not many youngsters can fully appreciate the horrors of war.

'From Lisbon we made our way to Italy by any means we could. Trains, trucks, we even did a couple of days by pack mule. It was arduous and very frightening, but I had the man I loved by my side and he made it all bearable.'

Candice is frowning, and I can almost hear the cogs whirring. 'That wooden carving . . .' she begins. 'The one in your room.'

'What about it?' I brace myself for the conversation to take another difficult turn.

'Well, it's not complete, is it? I mean, the little boy figure's still missing.'

I nod slowly. 'Not much gets past you, does it?'

'What happened to Louis's part then? Did he lose it?'

This is so difficult to talk about, I can't even meet her eye. 'I don't know, Candice. I don't know what happened to the carving because . . . because I never saw Louis again.'

'What?' She uncrosses her legs so quickly she loses her balance and nearly falls off the chair. 'What do you mean, you never saw him again? He was your brother.'

I can feel myself bristling, but I need to keep her onside. 'It wasn't for the want of trying, love. I wrote to him

255

countless times, and not one letter was answered. Not by him, at least. Delyth wasn't afraid to chuck her two penn'orth in, though. Told me to stop bothering her son. *Her son!* Can you believe that?'

'What did you do?' Candice asks.

'It was taken out of my hands. By September 1943, everywhere north of Rome was under German martial law. The Germans took control of the trains, the telephones and the postal system.'

'What about after the war, though? Surely you contacted him then?' Candice has a habit of making everything sound so simple.

'I did carry on writing, even though there was nothing left to say I hadn't already said a hundred times before. I told him I loved him, that I'd always love him, and that whenever he was ready he could join me in Italy, no matter how long that took. He was the only flesh and blood I had left and I couldn't give up on him, but I couldn't force him to join me either. I knew he was happy with Delyth and Bryn and I had absolutely no doubt that they'd take care of him. Del was a good woman, but I'd devastated her son by leaving him at the altar, so in her eyes I was the worst kind of human it was possible to imagine.'

I notice Candice is nodding along, seemingly agreeing with the sentiment.

'I'm not a bad person, Candice.'

She squeezes my hand. 'Nobody's saying you are.'

'Everything I did, I did for love.'

'Love for who, though?' Frank has returned, and I notice he's filled his glass again, so it might be the booze talking. I'll forgive his rather interrogative approach.

'I'm not going to apologise for marrying the man I loved, Frank. I begged Louis to join me, but he'd made it quite clear he didn't want to. I could hardly drag him away against his will.'

Oh, how I wish my old bones would allow me to stand up and flounce off. I shouldn't have to put up with this nonsense. I'm buggered if I'm being judged for my actions seventy-odd years ago by somebody who wasn't even there.

And it turned out I was right to leave him. It might have been the hardest decision I'd ever had to make, but it probably saved his life.

42

The second floor afforded the best view of the apricot sun as it emerged from behind a cloud and slipped into the sea. The horseshoe bay of Cinque Alberi was a natural haven for the coloured fishing boats that tilted idly on the swell. The air was thick with salt, a combination of the sea and a recent catch of anchovies.

Jenny used this part of the day as her thinking time, and the sun's dependable descent into the sea calmed her, reassured her that in spite of everything, the world still continued to turn. She squinted up at the tiny church at the top of the peninsula where she and Nico had had their marriage blessed. A year ago they had arrived in Italy as man and wife, but Lena had been adamant that in the eyes of God they were not married. Jenny had written to Louis countless times over the past year but had received nothing in return. She had no way of knowing if her letters had got through, and even if they had, whether Delyth would pass them on to him. She had paid a heavy price to be with the man she loved.

Her mother-in-law's voice bellowed up the stairs. 'Jenny, Jenny, come down here now.'

She closed her eyes, resenting the intrusion.

'I'll be right with you, Lena,' she sighed. 'Just give me a few more minutes, please.'

'No, no, you must come now. It is *molto importante*.'

Jenny twisted the wedding band on her finger. Ten months had crawled by since she had last seen her husband, and a part of her still resented the fact that Nico had put his country before her. She had given up her life in Wales, and by leaving Louis behind she'd betrayed the promise she had made to her mother. In return, Nico had left to join the Italian army the day after their blessing, and she'd made a home with Lena and Enzo in the tiny café on the harbourfront. She found it difficult to understand why Nico would even want to fight against Britain and her allies. He had lived happily in Wales for a decade and, whilst she acknowledged that he had been treated deplorably by the Enemy Alien Tribunal, she'd been heartbroken that he felt the need to avenge himself at the expense of their fledgling marriage.

She managed a smile at the group of women below. They'd formed a circle, their hands joined together, and were singing joyously, and although she couldn't understand all the words, it was obvious they were celebrating something.

'Jenny, what is keeping you, *bella*?' Lena hollered up the stairs again.

In spite of her urgent tone, Jenny ambled down the stairs, even pausing to run her finger along the wooden handrail to remove the traces of dust. She was used to Lena's excitable manner. Her mother-in-law could call her for breakfast and make it sound as though she'd prepared a banquet for royalty.

'What's all the kerfuffle about out there?' she asked.

A huge grin split Lena's face as she pinched Jenny's cheeks. 'They are celebrating. It is over.'

'What is?'

She tutted at the ceiling. 'The war, Jenny. The war is over. '*E*' *la pace, la pace incondizionata.*'

Jenny tried to hold onto her patience. Although her Italian was coming along, Lena was speaking too fast for her keep up. 'Lena, in English, please.'

'Oh . . . sorry. Erm . . . Marshal Badoglio, he come on the radio and he say there's been a . . . a . . .' she clicked her fingers in the air, 'an armistice. An armistice *incondizionato*. He say the Italians are not to go on fighting the Allies.'

'Well, what does that mean exactly?'

They had had their hopes raised before, just a month and a half ago, when Mussolini was toppled and twenty years of fascism seemed to have been confined to history. People had spilled out onto the streets then in spontaneous demonstrations of joy, but the war had still raged on. Perhaps cautious optimism was the best way forward.

'I don't know exactly what it means,' confessed Lena. 'But I think it must be good news, no? Everybody is happy. All Italian ships have been ordered to make their way to the nearest neutral port. We are not to carry on fighting.' Her eyes shone as she gripped Jenny's arms. 'Do you realise what this means? My son, your husband, he's coming home.'

Jenny sat on the harbour wall, her feet dangling just above the dappled water, and gazed at the horizon. Two days had passed since the armistice, and there had been no word from Nico. The King and Marshal Badoglio, together with much of the government, had fled Rome, leaving the country rudderless and vulnerable to the brutal heel of Nazi occupation. In spite of it all, though, she often mused how much Louis would love it here. There were plenty of jobs for young boys with nimble fingers: mending fishing nets and gutting the catch. Skinning rabbits and plucking chickens had become second nature to him, so pulling the insides out of a fish would be a doddle. She smiled as she imagined him running along the pebbled shoreline, skimming stones into the sea, his arms and legs as tanned as a coffee bean. She would go back for him one day, when this war really was over.

She watched a bare-footed little girl picking her way over the stones in the shallow surf, occasionally bending down to retrieve a particularly beautiful pebble and dropping it into her bucket. She recognised Eva then and waved a greeting, but the child was so entranced in her beachcombing she didn't notice. The hem of her dress had turned a darker shade of blue after its contact with the water. It would no doubt leave an ugly salt stain when it dried out later. Jenny thought about the bolt of peacock-coloured silk she had discovered in Lena's old blanket box. There would be just enough to make a beautiful dress for the little girl. Eva and her mother, Vanda, came into the café from time to time, and Jenny often slipped the child an extra piece of focaccia when her mother wasn't looking. A proud woman, Vanda was never comfortable accepting charity, but raising Eva all by herself often meant they struggled.

Eva looked up and noticed Jenny staring. She waved shyly, as though she'd been caught doing something she shouldn't, and Jenny beckoned her over.

'Can I see?' she asked, holding out her hand and switching to the basic Italian she had learned over the past year. 'Are all these for you?' She stuck her hand in the bucket and let the pebbles fall through her fingers.

The little girl shook her head, her long dark plaits swishing from side to side, then turned around as she heard Vanda call her name from further down the beach. Before she skipped off, she rummaged in her bucket and pulled out a pink marbled pebble, handing it to Jenny with a shy smile.

'For me? Why, *grazie mille*.' Jenny clutched it to her chest. 'I'll treasure it forever.'

She watched as Eva ran back to her mother. Vanda scooped up her daughter and held her tightly to her chest, covering her face in kisses. Jenny could hear Eva giggling as she struggled to get down and show her mother her precious haul. It was a simple but touching sight, and she was forced to look away. Yes, Louis would certainly love it here.

She stayed on the harbour wall, mesmerised by the waves lapping along the shoreline. A shadow crept over her, blocking out the sun's rays. She shivered and pulled her shawl tighter.

'Jennifer.'

She froze, the only movement coming from her thudding heart, then squinted up at the near-stranger. 'Nico?'

He nodded, offering both his hands and pulling her to her feet. 'Oh God, I've missed you,' he breathed.

She stared at his care-worn features, his dark skin ingrained with dirt or soil or God only knew what. His hair was shorter but still an inky black that matched his eyes. 'Nico,' she whispered, touching his face. 'Is it really you?' She pressed herself to his body, inhaling his unfamiliar scent. She could detect oil or grease and something reminiscent of burning leaves. 'I can't believe you're home.' She peeled away to take another look at him. 'Are you well? Have you been injured?'

'No,' he laughed. 'I am quite well.' He rubbed his eyes, leaving a smear of muck across his face. 'Just tired, that's all. I've been walking for thirty-six hours.' He took her face in his hands, lowering his lips towards hers. 'May I?'

She nodded slowly and closed her eyes. She felt the warmth of his breath first, and then his thumb grazed her cheek, until finally his lips met hers for an agonisingly fleeting moment before he kissed her again more deeply.

'Is . . . is it really over, Nico? The war, I mean. And how come they let you leave? Are you a deserter?' She looked around in panic. 'Will they come to arrest you?'

'You worry too much,' he laughed. 'It is true that the orders were to remain in barracks, but I'm not going to wait around for the Germans to take me prisoner. The roads are streaming with soldiers who just want to return home to their loved ones.'

'But disobeying an officer, isn't that—'

He silenced her with another kiss. 'There is much confusion, Jennifer, I cannot lie. Nobody knows what is going to happen, but I am home now and I promise I will never leave you again.'

She took the pebble out of her pocket and held it in her palm for him to see. 'Isn't it beautiful? Just look at the marbling.'

'Jenny, there's a beach full of stones down there.'

She shook her head. 'Not like this one. This one's special. A little girl gave it to me, and then, just like that, you appeared from nowhere.' She slipped it back into her pocket. 'I'm going to keep it with me always. It's going to be my lucky charm.'

43

2019

She peered through the curtain, giving it an impatient tug for good measure before craning her neck to see to the end of the street. 'Oh, where is it?' She took out her phone and glanced at the time again. 'I bloody knew this would happen.'

Beau lay on the sofa, his expression brooding. 'You know this is a sign, don't you?'

'A sign of what?'

'Are you thick, or what? A sign that you shouldn't go.'

She blew out an impatient breath. 'Not this again. I thought you were happy for me to go.'

Beau shrugged. 'Happy? Oh, I've never been happy about it. I suppose it's finally hit me, that's all. I was convinced you wouldn't go through with it, but it appears my feelings don't count.' He flicked some ash onto the carpet. 'As long as that bloody Jenny's happy.'

'You really are acting like a spoilt kid, Beau. It's only for a week. I've told you Jenny wants to return to Italy one last time. There's something she has to do and I'm not going to deny an old lady her last wish just because you'll have to make your own tea for once.'

'What's so important that she has to drag you along?'

'Something happened seventy-five years ago, apparently, something important to her. There's to be some kind of commemoration and she needs to go back to lay some ghosts to rest. That's all she's told me.'

He pinched the bridge of his nose, wincing dramatically. 'The memory's still so raw, Candice. You don't know what it's like. I watched my parents leave in a taxi for the airport and I barely even acknowledged they were going. I can't remember saying goodbye properly; I don't think I even looked up from my phone.' He paused. 'I never saw them again.'

She knelt down by the side of the sofa. 'Poor baby.' She smoothed her hand over his forehead. 'I promise you I will come back. It's not going to happen again. Do you hear me?'

He nodded. 'And you'll keep in touch?'

'Every day.' She smiled. 'Every hour of every day.'

At the sound of a car horn in the street below, she jumped up. 'Thank God for that. He's going to have to put his foot down, though.'

Beau heaved himself off the sofa, pulling her into his arms and squeezing hard. 'I'm going to miss you, babe. You've no idea how much you mean to me.' He released his grip, allowing her to breathe again. 'I love you, Candice.'

'And I love you too. Now, I've got to be going. Are you coming downstairs or what?'

'No, I don't want a scene on the pavement.'

She picked up her suitcase, hesitating at the door. 'You sure?'

He dismissed her with a flick of his hand. 'Please, Candice, just go.'

She hurried down the stairs as fast as the suitcase would

allow, flinging open the door at the bottom. A young man stood on the doorstep, poised to ring the bell. He looked unnervingly familiar.

'Oh, can I help you? Who're you looking for?' She waved to the taxi driver, who stood with the boot open ready to load her luggage.

'I'm looking for Beau Devine. I believe he lives here. Do you know him?'

She glanced up at the first-floor window. 'Erm . . . yes . . . yes, I do. He's my boyfriend. I'm Candice.'

'Oh, I see.' He pointed to her case. 'Are you off somewhere?'

'Yes . . . well, I'm going away but Beau's not coming with me. Look, I'm sorry, but I've gotta go. I'm running so late I'm worried I'm going to miss my flight.'

She started towards the taxi and then turned back. 'What did you say your name was?'

'I didn't, but it's Jay. Jay Devine. I'm Beau's brother.' He thrust a business card into her hand. 'Call me . . . please.'

44

I'm not sure if it's the fact we're so late for our flight, or because I'm in a courtesy wheelchair, but we are whizzed through security, bypassing the queue of irritable lesser mortals forced to make way for us. I've been awake since the early hours, a lump of dread in my stomach that only grew heavier as the hours crawled by. Candice was so late, I honestly thought she must have changed her mind. It wouldn't have mattered. There's nothing that could've stopped me from making this trip now.

My handbag is wedged on my knee, Eva's photograph and the pink pebble safely tucked into a zipped-up pocket. The porter-type bloke who has the job of pushing me must've been an Olympic sprinter in a former life. He hares us through the duty-free shop and I catch only a whiff of the latest scent as a bemused sales attendant attempts to spray a sample onto my wrist. Even Candice is having trouble keeping up. She seems distracted – I hope Beau hasn't been giving her a hard time again. He seems to suck the joy out of every situation, so it wouldn't surprise me.

The porter delivers us to the gate and helps me out of the chair and into a less comfy seat. 'All right, then,' he says, as he grips my hand with nicotine-stained fingers. 'Have a good holiday.' He enunciates every word as though I'm deaf or English isn't my first language.

I mimic his volume and tone. 'Thank you, we'll certainly try.'

Candice takes the seat next to me and stares into the distance.

'Candice?'

She gives a quick shake of her head. 'Sorry, miles away.'

'What's the matter, love? You've been in a funny mood since you picked me up. Has Beau been moaning about you coming away again? Honestly, I don't know how—'

'It's not that,' she interrupts, fishing in her pocket. 'Look.'

She hands me a business card for an interior design company I've never heard of: *Devine by Design.*

'What do I want with this?' I frown. 'Not much use to me, is it?'

'Look at the name.' She points. 'Jay Devine.'

'Ah, I see,' It takes a little while for the penny to drop these days. 'Any relation?'

She nods slowly, turning the card over in her fingers. 'Yes. He's Beau's brother.'

This brings me up with a start. 'Brother? But I thought he was an only child.'

She taps the card on her palm. 'So did I, Jenny. So did I.'

'How mysterious.' I bloody knew it! I've known all along that there was something fishy about him, but it gives me no pleasure at all to be proved right. 'What're you going to do?'

'I think I should call him.'

'And give him a chance to wriggle out of it? No, what you need to do is—'

She holds up her hand. 'I meant call this Jay Devine.'

An air-hostess-type person leans towards a microphone. 'Flight 2365 to Genoa is now ready for boarding through gate number twelve. Please have your passport and boarding cards ready.'

'It's too late now, love,' I say.

The announcement continues. 'We will be boarding those who require special assistance first.' She gestures towards me, smiling at this huge privilege that has come my way simply because I've been on this planet longer than anybody else in the queue.

I seize on the opportunity. 'Oh no, it's all right. You carry on. My friend here needs to make an urgent phone call.' I nudge Candice. 'Go on, hop over there, ring him, see what he wants.'

I watch as she taps out the number from the business card. She presses the phone to her ear and covers the other one with her hand in an effort to drown out the sound of an enthusiastic hen party who've obviously already had too much to drink. What is it about airports that make people think it's acceptable to drink even though it's barely nine o'clock in the morning? Still, it's nice to see people having a laugh. It's all harmless fun. As long as they're not sitting by me.

When Candice comes back, I swear to God I've seen more colour in a tub of lard. 'Whatever's the matter?' I ask. 'You've gone awfully pale.'

She sits down next to me, still staring at her phone, as though this conduit for bad news must've been mistaken. 'Jay . . . Jay's just told me that his father – his and Beau's father – has died and their mother would like Beau to attend

269

the funeral.' She looks at me, shaking her head. 'I can't believe it.'

It's hard to find the right words, because I doubt there are any. 'Oh love,' I manage. 'I'm so sorry.' Pathetic, I know, but it's the best I can come up with.

Everybody else has boarded, and now it's our turn. I need to be strong for Candice, and I stand on the first attempt, my simmering anger at Beau driving me on.

Once we're settled on the plane, Candice tells me more.

'Peter, that's Beau's father, died a couple of days ago. A heart attack, out of the blue. I couldn't take it all in, Jenny. I was just so shocked and Jay kept apologising for being the bearer of bad news. He wasn't able to tell Beau himself because he refused to answer the door and Jay didn't want to shout that kind of news through the letter box.'

'No, I should think not.' Inside, I'm raging but try not to show it. Candice needs a gentle touch right now.

'He was so glad I rang and said he would text me the details of the funeral so I could tell Beau. He thought it would be best coming from me.'

'It's unbelievable, Candice. What kind of a person wipes out their own parents like that?' I pause for her answer, but she doesn't have one. 'Why do you think Beau lied to you?'

'I've no idea. Jay said he had been estranged from the rest of the family for a couple of years now.'

It's clear that Beau's lie was all just part of the manipulation. Get Candice to feel sorry for him, make her more malleable, play the victim card whenever it suits him. I seethe quietly to myself when I think how he used it to try and persuade Candice not to come on this trip.

'To be honest, love, I did think there was something not right. I mean, how come he didn't inherit any money if his parents were both dead? You're always saying how short you both are. Did that not occur to you?'

She fans her boarding card in front of her face. 'I've never given it much thought. God, I'm so gullible.'

My heart breaks for her. She's such a sweet kid, she doesn't deserve this. 'What are you going to do now?' I ask.

'I need to give him a chance to explain. He must've had his reasons.'

I'd like to give her a bloody good shake, but I know she deserves better than that. 'Good idea, love, although I can't imagine what they were.'

She gives me a sideways glance. 'You're loving this, aren't you? Proves you were right all along.'

The pause I leave drags on until it's downright awkward. 'Look, Candice. It's no secret I don't like Beau,' I admit. 'You're way too good for him and I hate the way he manipulates you.'

'He does not.' She sounds quite indignant, and I know that if I force the issue, she'll push back too hard and end up siding with him.

I decide to focus on the practicalities and leave the emotional stuff for now. 'When's the funeral?'

'Oh, not for another two weeks.'

'Some breathing space then. Gives us a bit more time to think about what to do next. I'll help you, Candice. You're not on your own here. Oh, I know you don't think you need anybody else interfering in your life, but I'm here for you, so you'll have to get used to it.'

*

After spending the flight in companionable silence, each lost in our own thoughts, we exit the airport terminal and it feels like we've entered a sauna. I've forgotten just how hot the Italian summer can be. I'm glad to be in my own wheelchair again, which has miraculously survived its journey in the hold. Candice bends down and fans my face with her magazine. 'Blimey, Jenny, it's hot, int it?'

A dust cloud blows up in our faces as a taxi takes off a little too fast, its tyres scattering grit everywhere. An Italian chap caught in the carnage unleashes a torrent of expletives as he brushes his hand over his navy suit, cursing the inconsiderate driver. I smile to myself. Not much has changed.

Our driver appears out of nowhere, olive-skinned, narrow-waisted and smelling of citrus. His shirt is the whitest I have ever seen, his top button undone to allow us a glimpse of his gold chain. A rather tasteful one, I should add. Nothing like those vulgar chunky numbers favoured by rappers everywhere. He holds out his hand to Candice and she takes it shyly. '*Buon pomeriggio.*' He half bows before continuing. 'Welcome to Genoa. My name is Stefano Buccarelli and it will be my pleasure to take care of you.'

Although heavily accented, his English is perfect, and I'm pleased my request has been noted and delivered. My Italian is not what it was. I've hired him for the duration of our trip, so it's a relief to know the three of us will be able to communicate. Even though he still has hold of Candice's hand, I pipe up. 'I'm Jenny, and my friend here who appears to have been rendered dumb is Candice.'

He shifts his gaze to me. 'I am pleased to meet you both. Now, come, come. Let me help you.' He takes hold of the wheelchair and then stops to ponder. 'I think it's better if I take the cases, no?'

'Yes, of course,' interjects Candice. 'I'll push the chair. Please, it's fine. I can manage. I'm used to it.' She emits a silly little giggle and I frown at her.

'What?' she mouths, as Stefano sets off with a suitcase in each hand. 'He's gorgeous.'

It's only a little over half an hour to our destination, and I take the opportunity to rest my eyes, even though I'll miss out on the scenery: forested mountains on one side, the glittering Ligurian Sea on the other. As we drive, I allow my mind to wander back to when I called Cinque Alberi home.

In the beginning, Nico was by my side constantly, always physically connected to me, whether it be the light touch of his fingers on the back of my hand or his arm firmly around my shoulders, as though I were a treasured possession he had to guard with his life. It sounds suffocating when I think about it now, but it didn't feel like that at the time. We may have been in the middle of a war, but I felt safe, loved and cared for.

The small fishing village of Cinque Alberi is built around a horseshoe bay and has its toes in the Ligurian Sea and its shoulders in the vertiginous thyme-scented mountains behind. The houses along the bay are colourful buildings in vivacious shades of terracotta, pink, orange and yellow, the dark-green shutters the only thing they have in common. At one end of the bay, a peninsula juts into the sea, and on the top, the five pine trees that give the village its name stand next to the ancient church where Nico and I had our marriage blessed that cool November morning back in 1942.

I start to feel a bit queasy as the road twists and turns through the mountains on its way down to the sea. I open my eyes and crack the window a little. Candice is leaning forward, talking to Stefano. I can only see his eyes in the rear-view mirror, but I can tell he's smiling at her. On my right-hand side the sea comes into view and I take a deep breath. I've forgotten how this brilliant ribbon of blue suddenly appears out of nowhere.

'Ooh, look at that,' exclaims Candice. 'It's . . . well, it's breathtaking, int it?' She turns to look at me. 'Isn't it beautiful, Jenny?'

My throat feels tight and I find it difficult to speak. She'll have to be content with a nod of my head.

'Over there, see?' Stefano points to the peninsula curving round the bay. 'Those pine trees. It's where the village gets its name. Cinque Alberi, five trees.'

Candice repeats the name after him, as though she's learning Italian from a CD. 'Chin-kwa Alberry,' she says. It's not quite as exotic-sounding in her Manchester accent, but Stefano laughs. '*Sì*, Candice. You have got it. The trees, they are Italian stone pine, but we call them parasol pines because of their shape, like a—'

'Like an umbrella,' finishes Candice. 'Yes, I get it.'

'The village was named around the year one thousand, but nobody think about what will happen when the trees die. They only live around a hundred years, so these are not the original trees, but we have to keep planting because how can you have a village called Cinque Alberi without the five trees?'

Candice gives me a sideways look, and I can see she can't tell whether Stefano is joking or not.

'It's true,' I assure her. 'Stefano knows what he's talking about.'

'So, you are here on holiday then?' enquires Stefano.

Candice reaches for my hand before answering. 'We're here for the commemoration.'

I notice that he grips the steering wheel a little tighter and clenches his jaw. 'I see.'

At my first glimpse of the Hotel Villa Verde, something catches in my throat and throws me off guard. It wasn't here in the 1940s. Well, it was here but it was the private holiday home of a wealthy family from Genoa, until the Germans arrived, that is. Oh, there I go again. Meandering off the subject. *Focus Jenny, focus.* We'll get to that part all in good time. The hotel is embedded into the hillside at one end of the bay and has a panoramic window affording a view of the whole village. The lurid green-painted walls that gave the villa its name are now a more tasteful pastel pink, and the bougainvillea-clad terraces stand out against the lush vegetation. My palms are moist and I can feel tears stinging my eyes as the memories come flooding back. There is a hollowness in my stomach, as though my insides have been scraped out and all that's left is an empty husk. I squeeze the pebble tightly. I've made it this far, I can do this.

Candice and I are sitting out on the terrace by the pool, shaded by an umbrella from the heat of the late-afternoon sun. She's engrossed in her phone, her mouth a thin line of concentration.

'Have you rung him yet?' I venture.

She snaps a look at me, shaking her head. 'No, I've texted

to say we've arrived and sent him a picture of the bay. I've said I'll ring him in a bit, but I haven't really got the stomach for it.'

Right on cue, her phone starts to vibrate and she glances at the screen. 'Oh God, it's him.' She presses something with her thumb and the phone stops. 'I just can't face him at the minute, Jenny. I'm still too annoyed at him.'

'I agree, Candice. Let the bugger wait.'

She manages a smile. 'What am I going to do?'

I hope she's not expecting me to answer that one. 'See that house over there?' I say, changing the subject. She looks in the direction of my finger. 'The pink one with the line of washing strung between two windows,' I continue.

She squints. 'The one with the red canopy and tables outside?'

'That's the one. That was where I lived with Nico. And up there on the hillside, just below the five trees, is the tiny church where we were married in the eyes of God, according to Lena.'

'Really? Oh, I bet it was magical. Can we go and have a look?'

She sometimes forgets I'm a centenarian. There are over three hundred steps leading up to that church, uneven steps at that, carved out of the hillside itself. There's no other way to reach it than on foot.

'You'll have to count me out, love, but I want you to go.'

'Can't we get Stefano to drive us up?'

'There's no road up there. Just a rough track and then some killer steps.' I laugh at the memory. 'Imagine walking up there in all your wedding regalia.'

My wedding dress was simple, not really a wedding dress

at all, in fact. I'd had to alter an old frock Lena no longer wore, taking it in a couple of inches at the waist and adding a lace collar purloined from an old cream blouse she only wore to clean the house. My hat was an old-fashioned thing too, one of those cloche types, and was so tight it gave me a headache. Lena had worn it for her own wedding and insisted it was the pinnacle of fashion. She'd lent me her sable fur capelet for a touch of glamour, but I'd had to wear my stout brown shoes for the climb up the hill. The wedding party was small, just me and Nico, Lena and Enzo and Father Ascarelli. Thinking about it, he must've been about ninety years old himself, so heaven only knows how he managed to heave himself up those steps every day. That's the power of God, I suppose.

I reach into my bag and hand Candice a photo. 'There we are, look.'

She holds up the picture of me and Nico on our wedding day, standing on the edge of the hillside. It was his idea to stand so close to the edge, and I'm holding onto his arm for dear life, not daring to look down. My legs trembled as I willed Enzo to hurry up and take the bloody picture.

'Whoa,' says Candice, studying the photo. 'He *is* gorgeous. He looks like a young Marlon Brando. Those eyes, I mean wow, just wow. He looks like a lovely man.'

'Quite a catch then, you think?' I ask.

'Oh, yes, but look at you too. How did you fit all those curls under that hat?' She frowns as she studies my face. 'You look . . .' she thinks hard before settling on 'terrified.'

'I *was* terrified, Candice.' I point across the bay. 'We were standing on the edge of that cliff. Nico wanted the sea in the

277

background and thought it would make a dramatic photo.' I shudder as I remember my genuine fear, and how he seemed to find it funny.

She passes the photo back. 'What colour was your dress?'

'Sage green, and the hat was a sort of mossy green. The fur cape was a golden sable. It was beautiful, much silkier than mink. It belonged to Lena's mother way back when.'

I tuck the photo into the side pocket of my bag, next to the other one. One that was taken some years later in exactly the same spot. But this time there's just me. Me and a crude wooden cross.

45

Candice picked up her phone and took yet another picture of the sparkling bay beneath. They were sitting on the balcony, Jenny swaddled in one of the hotel's thick dressing gowns, her feet tucked into complimentary slippers.

'I feel like I'm in heaven,' sighed Candice. 'I've never been to a more beautiful place. And have you seen all them little toiletries in the bathroom? There's shampoo, conditioner, bath salts and even a teeny-tiny sewing kit.'

'You can take them home if you want, love.'

'Really? And the dressing gown and slippers too?'

Jenny laughed. 'Absolutely not.' She paused as Candice stared at her phone. 'Have you rung him yet?'

'No, I can't bear to spoil the mood. We've exchanged messages and I've kept it breezy, but I can't speak to him just yet. I've got the upper hand for once.'

'What time is it now, Candice?'

'Half past seven.'

'You'd better get your skates on then, love. Stefano's coming to take you for a drink down on the harbour. He'll be here at eight.'

Candice scrambled to her feet. 'What? How do you mean, a drink?'

'I'm not sure what's so hard to understand. I need an early night. It's been a long day. Now off you pop and get yourself ready.'

The cool shower felt good on her hot skin as she washed away all the grime that seemed to accumulate when travelling. She deliberated for far longer than she should about what to wear, eventually settling on a beige wrap-around dress decorated with navy polka dots. Whilst nowhere near the glossy length it once was, her hair had grown enough to accommodate a curling iron. She fixed the subtle waves with hairspray and applied the bold red lipstick Beau had asked her to stop wearing because in his opinion it made her look like a tart. He'd thrown away all the colours he disapproved of, but this one had been nestling inside the lining of her handbag. She chalked up a victory to herself as she pouted in the mirror, then glanced at the screen as her phone lit up with the first few words of his message. *Babe, where are u? I miss u. Please pick up.* Her thumb hovered over it for a second before she tossed the phone into a drawer and headed down to reception.

Stefano was already there, sitting on a sofa with his legs crossed, one arm stretched across the back, the other pressing his phone to his ear. He'd changed into white chinos and a black polo shirt and, astonishingly, no socks, even though he was wearing brogues. It must be an Italian thing. He waved as he saw her approach, then spoke into his phone. *'Devo andare. Ciao.'*

He greeted her with a polite handshake, then stepped back holding his arms out wide. '*Bellissima.*'

She caught the aromatic scent of his cologne, light and citrusy, like the mandarins she usually only associated with Christmas.

'Come, come,' he continued. 'Your grandmother insist I take you for a cocktail and we can watch the sunset.'

'Oh . . . um . . . Jenny's not my grandmother. She's my . . . well, she's a friend, and I'm really sorry she's so pushy. Honestly, it's fine, I'm sure you've got better things to do.'

'Well, she's paying for my time.' He placed his hand in the small of her back and indicated the door. 'But this one is, how you say? On the house.'

The sky had taken on a burnt orange hue as the sun dipped towards the sea, growing bigger and redder by the minute. Stefano secured them a table outside, overlooking the harbour, and held up his hand to a waiter. '*Due Negroni, per favore.*'

He turned to Candice. 'Forgive me if I order for you, but you have to try a Negroni.' He kissed his fingers. 'It is just about the most perfect cocktail. It is the colour of the sunset itself. You will love it.'

The waiter returned a few moments later with their drinks. Candice prodded at the slice of orange with her straw. 'What's in it?'

'Gin, Campari and sweet vermouth.' Stefano held his glass to hers. '*Salute.*'

'*Salute,*' she parroted. 'Cheers.'

She took a sip, feeling the hit of the alcohol instantly. 'Whoa. I'll be rockin' by the time I've finished this.'

His jaw was shadowed by stubble and his eyes were hidden behind Ray-Ban Aviators in which she could see her own reflection.

'Do you live here then, Stefano?'

He flicked his head towards the steep road leading out of the village. '*Sì*, up there on the right. I have my own business. Private hire, limos for weddings, that sort of thing. It's good.' He took another gulp of his drink, nodding towards the sun, only the top hemisphere now visible as it slid into the sea. 'And you can never tire of that view.'

Candice agreed. 'It really is amazing.'

'It's a simple life, but I love it. I work in Milano once and it was . . .' he shook his head, looking down at the table, 'it was too . . . I mean, the people, they were too busy rushing around. Nobody had the time to say hello, and I like to ease myself into my day, you know? Get up early, take a stroll, have a coffee. You can do that here. It's nice.'

'You sound like a middle-aged man,' Candice giggled. 'How old are you actually?'

'Twenty-nine.'

'A few years older than me, then.' She changed the subject. 'Jenny used to live here, you know.'

He sat up a little straighter and placed his elbows on the table. 'Really?'

She could feel his breath on her face. 'Yes, she married an Italian, came to live over here during the war. She really wanted to see it before . . . before she . . . um . . . well, you know.'

'You said she's here for the seventy-fifth anniversary of what happened.'

Candice nodded. 'Yes, she hasn't told me much about it, but she said it's something she felt she had to do before she dies. She's a hundred years old, you know.'

Stefano slumped back in his chair. 'No, never. I don't believe it.'

'She looks good, doesn't she? She's amazing.'

Stefano picked up his phone and aimed it at the setting sun. He showed the photo to Candice. 'I've taken this shot many times before, but it never disappoints.'

She looked at the photo showing her Negroni in the foreground, the thin dome of the orange sun behind and the sea reflecting the amber glow. 'Stunning. Can you send it to me, please? I've not brought my phone out with me.'

'Of course. What is your number?'

She reeled off the digits parrot-fashion. 'I think you might need to drop the zero and put something else in front. I'm not sure.'

'I know it,' he said, punching the numbers into his phone. 'All done.' He held his empty glass aloft. 'Now, are you ready for another?'

She fought to keep her hand steady as she tried to find the slot for the key card. It was gone eleven and Jenny would no doubt be fast asleep. The green light appeared and she heaved the door open, slipping straight into the bathroom. She regarded her face, flushed with alcohol, a smattering of newly appeared freckles across her nose. She changed into a hotel robe, crept into the bedroom past Jenny's sleeping form and retrieved her phone from the drawer. Twenty-seven missed calls from Beau. She shoved the phone into her pocket and edged out onto the balcony. After the coolness of the air-conditioned room, the warm breeze was comforting. Bolstered by the drink, she rang him.

He picked up immediately. 'Babe, where the fuck have you been? Why haven't you returned my calls? I'm out of my mind here.'

She spoke coolly. 'There was no need to worry. I texted you to say I'd arrived safely. That was all you needed you know.'

He was silent for a second. 'What's up, Candice? You sound weird.'

She leaned on the balcony railing. It was the moon's turn to put on a celestial show, lighting up the sea with a band of ghostly silver. 'I've been out for a drink, Beau. A cocktail, actually. It was lovely. Sooooo relaxing.'

'Are you pissed, Candice?'

'I might be,' she giggled.

She could hear the breath coming out of his nose, like a bull about to charge. 'So, you've been out on the lash whilst I've been sitting here worried sick?'

'Worried that I might be having some fun without you, you mean?'

He ignored her remark. 'I hope you're not going over the top with your spending. I know what you're like, Candice. Bloody clueless when it comes to money. I don't think you should—'

'Yeah, well I'm sick and tired of hearing what you think.'

She revelled in the shocked silence, fighting the urge to laugh even though the situation was far from amusing.

'What did you just say?'

Even the menacing tone was not enough to dampen her spirits. 'You heard me.'

'Candice, babe.' He gave a nervous laugh. 'What's got into you? I miss you so much and I don't like it when you ignore me. It makes me feel—'

She cut him off. 'I have a message for you.'

'What message?'

'What're you doing on the twenty-fourth of May?'

'How the hell do I know? What're you on about?'

'It's your father's funeral. Peter, isn't it? And your mother – Marcia, I believe her name is – said she would really like you to be there. Text your brother for the details. His name's Jay, by the way, but I expect you remember that.'

Without giving him a chance to respond, she ended the call, turned off the phone and shoved it into her pocket.

46

I feel thoroughly refreshed after a good night's sleep. I didn't even stir that much when Candice rolled in at God only knows what hour. I can see her now out on the balcony, her face tilted up to the sun as she inhales the invigorating sea air.

'Candice, love. Are you ready to go?'

She acknowledges me with a wave and comes back into the bedroom. 'I never want to leave this place, Jenny,' she sighs, flopping onto the bed. 'It's just magical. A place where you can leave your cares behind and relish the tranquil beauty.'

I smile to myself, not sure why she's suddenly talking like a travel agent. 'Get my frame, would you? I'm going without the chair this morning. The sun's put the marrow back in my bones and I'm not letting it go to waste.'

She links her arm through mine as we amble along the seafront. There's no sandy beach here, just a smooth pebble one, and it's all the better for it. Sandy beaches are overrated in my opinion. All that grit. It gets into crevices you didn't know you had. This beach has pebbles of all shapes, sizes and colours; greys, browns, creams and pinks jumbled up into one glorious glossy mess. I have to take a deep swallow as I think of Eva and the pink marbled pebble she gave to me that day, all those years ago.

'Are you all right, Jenny?'

Candice shakes me out of my reverie and I manage a bright reply. 'Course, I am, love.' I pat the back of her hand. 'Never better.'

It only takes about fifteen minutes for us to shuffle along to our destination. I have to bite down on my lip as I stand and stare at the once-familiar building. The occupants may be different, but the tiny café still feels homely and welcoming, the smell of freshly baked focaccia wafting through from the kitchen. There are half a dozen tables outside, each with a red-checked tablecloth held in place by some ingenious clips. We used to have to weigh the tablecloths down with pebbles off the beach. I have to steel myself as the memories come unbidden, memories of devastation and . . . the screams. Oh God, those screams. I close my eyes, grip my frame and take a steadying breath. Fortunately Candice doesn't seem to have noticed my distress.

'This one?' she asks, pointing to a table. 'Or would you prefer the shade?'

I gather myself. 'No, love, the sun's fine.' I pull my straw hat down to shield my eyes, but it's so good to feel the warmth on my body. 'Now, you have to try the focaccia, Candice. It's a speciality of the village.' I raise my hand to the young waitress and she approaches, pulling a pad out of her apron pocket. '*Sì?*'

'*Buongiorno. Potremmo avere due focaccia e due cappuccini per favore.*'

Candice is staring at me open-mouthed, and I must admit

287

I do feel a frisson of pride that I can remember some basic Italian, although in reality it's schoolgirl level these days.

The waitress returns with our order, and the minute she places the hot focaccia on the table, I'm transported back, as though I've boarded a time machine. I look at the bread with its dimpled crust filled with tiny pools of olive oil and its covering of salt crystals. I could make this with my eyes closed back in the day.

Candice leans down and sniffs it. 'Mmm, it smells delicious. My mouth's actually watering.'

I tear off a piece and hold it over my cup. 'It's traditional to dunk it in your coffee first.'

Candice pulls a face. 'Ew! That's disgusting. A digestive biscuit I could just about handle, but dunking bread in your coffee?' She shakes her head. 'Not for me, thanks.'

'Nor me.' I laugh. 'When in Rome and all that, but you have to draw the line somewhere.'

I tear off a small piece and pop it into my mouth, savouring the long-forgotten taste. 'Did you have a nice time with Stefano?' I ask as casually as I can manage. I'm sure she must think it's all a set-up, but honestly, it's not. I merely asked for a local driver-cum-guide who could speak excellent English and who could be on hand during our week's stay to ferry us around when needed. It's just a bonus that Stefano looks as though he could have modelled for Michelangelo.

She rubs her forehead. 'I did, thanks, but I think I had one too many Negronis. My head's bangin'.'

'Oh dear. Well, it's good to see you letting your hair down.'

She stirs a lump of brown sugar into her coffee. 'I rang Beau when I got back.'

Oh God. Just when we were having a nice time, she has to bring him up. 'And?'

'I told him I had a message for him. That his mother wanted him to attend his father's funeral and Jay would text him the details.'

'Lord above, Candice. What did he say?'

'No idea. I hung up and switched off my phone.'

So she does have a backbone after all. I should never have doubted her. 'What're you going to do now?'

She gazes out over the bay. 'Let him stew for a bit, I suppose.' She tries to sound casual, but the two deep ridges between her eyebrows betray her worry.

'For what it's worth, love, I think you're doing the right thing. Don't let him spoil your holiday.'

'And how are we this morning, ladies?' Stefano appears at our table, shifting his sunglasses to the top of his head and pulling up a chair. He nods to the waitress, who returns seconds later with a double espresso. '*Grazie mille, bella.*' He lifts the tiny cup and downs it in one go. 'Ah, that is better.' He rubs his hands together. 'Now, what is the plan?' He's wearing a lemon T-shirt today that's stretched across his chest, showing off his . . . pecs, I think the word is. His hair is as black and shiny as liquorice.

'Candice and I are taking a little stroll around the market, and this afternoon I would like it if you would accompany her on the hike to the top.'

'The top of where?' asks Candice.

Stefano and I share a knowing smile. I point to the five trees standing proudly on the peninsula, resplendent against the brilliant blue sky. 'Up there. I was telling you yesterday.'

'Oh yes,' she says, looking genuinely thrilled. 'I'd like that.' She places a hand on Stefano's forearm. 'If it's not too much trouble.'

I can see from his expression that trouble is the last thing he considers it to be. 'My pleasure, *bella.*'

47

'Will you be all right, Jenny? I'm not sure I like leaving you all alone like this.'

'Stop fussing, Candice. I told you, I'll be grand. It's lovely out there on the balcony and I'll be able to see you walking along the beachfront, and if I had a pair of binoculars, I'd even be able to see you on the top too.'

Candice adjusted her vest top in the mirror. 'You don't think this is too revealing, do you? Beau'd have a duck fit if he saw me out in it.'

'Well, Beau's not here, so let's not waste our time and energy thinking about what he would or wouldn't like.' Jenny smiled in appreciation of the outfit. 'I didn't realise you had such long legs, Candice. And they're so brown.'

'Out of a bottle,' Candice confessed. 'They normally look like corned beef.'

'And those shorts . . . well, I don't think I'd have the confidence to carry them off.'

Candice ran her finger under her eyes to remove traces of errant kohl. 'Not many hundred-year-olds could.'

Jenny laughed. 'I meant when I was your age. That's even if microscopic frayed denim shorts had been a thing back then.'

Candice turned away from the mirror. 'Too much?'

'Not at all. You look beautiful.'

She pulled on her white Converse. 'These are all I've got. Do you think I'll manage?'

'It's been a long while since I've been up there, love, but I expect they'll do. You go off and have the best day. You deserve it.'

The hike up to the top started off gently, and she was able to appreciate the orange and lemon trees burgeoning with unpicked fruit. The air was scented with a familiar smell she couldn't put her finger on.

She stopped and sniffed. 'What is that smell, Stefano?'

'Close your eyes,' he said.

'Why?' She smiled. 'What're you going to do?'

She could hear him rustling in the vegetation, and then came the overpowering smell of lavender as he held a sprig to her nose.

'I thought I recognised it,' she said, opening her eyes and taking the sprig off him.

'It helps if you block one of the senses. You could no longer see and so you had to concentrate on your sense of smell instead. It worked, no?'

'Well, you did shove it right under my nose, so . . .'

Stefano laughed. 'This is true.' He indicated the path ahead. 'Shall we?'

By the time they reached the top, Candice was out of breath and conscious of the dark stripe of sweat she was sure must be staining the back of her grey vest. She placed her hands on her hips for a breather. 'Phew. I'm knack . . . erm, I mean worn out.'

Stefano took hold of her hand. 'Come on, only a few more steps to go. We can sit in the church for a rest. It will be cool in there.'

He pulled her up the final few steps as though she were a reluctant toddler. 'You made it,' he said, letting go of her hand. 'Here we are.'

Candice gazed up at the tiny church. 'It's beautiful,' she breathed. 'Imagine getting married here.' She cast her hand around. 'Surrounded by the ocean.'

'Follow me,' instructed Stefano, retrieving a paper bag from his rucksack. 'We will go inside. I have special treat.'

They sat side by side on a hard wooden pew, ingrained with years of beeswax. 'Why are church pews always so uncomfortable?' Candice asked, rubbing her back.

'It is so you don't fall asleep during the sermon.' Stefano offered her the paper bag.

She peered inside. 'Ooh, cherries. Wow, I don't think I've ever tried fresh cherries before. The only ones I've had have been on the top of a Mr Kipling's cherry Bakewell.'

'These are spectacular, Candice. They will stain your lips with their sweet ruby juice and fill your heart with joy.'

'Who knew cherries had such super powers?' She popped one into her mouth. 'Is this church still used, then?'

'Every third Sunday of the month, that is all,' Stefano replied. 'But you can come and worship here whenever you want.'

'It's so peaceful. I can see why someone would drag themselves up here to pray. I bet it makes them feel closer to God.' She looked at him. 'I'm not that religious meself, but if praying helps people to get through the terrible things in life, then why begrudge them that comfort, eh?'

'*Esattamente.* To each their own.'

'It's such a romantic place to get married, though, don't you think?'

'It is indeed, although you can only marry here if you are a resident of Cinque Alberi.'

She picked another cherry out of the bag, twisting it free of its stalk. 'Jenny got married here, you know.'

Stefano raised his eyebrows. 'She did?'

'Yes, back in 1942, I think she said. She married an Italian, that's why she ended up living here.'

Stefano's interest was piqued. 'Do you know his name?'

'Yes, it was Nico, well, Domenico actually, and his surname was . . .' she pinched the bridge of her nose, 'um, it began with a B . . . Bernardi. That was it. Domenico Bernardi.'

He turned to face her. 'Are you sure?'

'Yes, why? Have you heard of him?'

He rose from the pew, screwing the empty paper bag into a tight ball. 'Everybody round here has heard of him,' he said eventually. He nodded towards the door. 'You'd better follow me.'

48

The weight of his hand on her shoulder startled her. 'What are you doing, Jennifer?' A week he'd been back, and she was still surprised whenever she heard his voice.

'Nico, you gave me such a fright, creeping up like that.' She covered the writing paper with a book, 'I'm just reading.'

He quietly removed the book and slammed it shut. 'No you're not. You're writing a letter. Why do you lie to me?' He picked up the paper. '*Darling Louis.*' He tore it in half. 'What is the point, Jennifer? It is killing you to keep writing and not getting anything back. I don't think you should write to him any more. Your life is here with me now.'

'I can't give up on him, Nico.'

'I don't see why not. He's obviously given up on you.'

'Don't say that.'

'The Germans are in charge now.' His fingers caressed the back of her neck. 'They won't allow private letters to get through. They've said this.'

'They might. There's no harm in trying.'

He crouched down beside her, taking both her hands in his. 'You love me, don't you?'

'You know I do.'

'Well then, it's time to let go of the past.'

'Louis will never just be part of my past, Nico. He's my flesh and blood. I love him.'

He squeezed her hands a little harder. 'I know you do, *mia cara.*'

'It's just that . . . I don't know . . . seeing Eva on the beach last week . . .'

'Who is Eva?'

'I told you. The little girl on the beach. The one with the plaits. Just before you came back, she gave me a pebble from her bucket and it made me think of our Louis. They're about the same age. He would love it here. Can't we—'

He pulled her to her feet. 'No, we can't. Come on, we've been apart for so long. It's you and me now, Jennifer. Just you and me.' He kissed her forehead, letting his hand wander to her belly. 'That is until we have a family of our own.'

Nico called out to his parents as he fiddled with the knobs on the radio. 'Mamma, Papà, come here now. There is going to be a broadcast by Il Duce.' Jenny sat opposite, her hands cradling a mug of warm milk. It had taken the Germans less than two months to discover the location of the country's most closely guarded prisoner of war. Mussolini was being held in a hotel high up in the Abruzzi mountains before German paratroopers rescued him and flew him to Hitler's headquarters in Germany. There was general confusion over what this meant for Italians.

The four of them huddled around the radio to hear Il Duce talk about his dramatic rescue and his plans to form a new Republican Fascist Party. Jenny's Italian was nowhere near good enough to keep up with him.

'What's he saying?' she asked.

Nico shook his head. 'He sounds broken. His speech is slurred, as though he's drunk.'

Enzo folded his arms on the table. 'I do not understand. I thought we were rid of him, and now this.' He flung his hands in the air. 'We're supposed to be free, we have surrendered, what is all this nonsense he is talking?'

Lena spoke, her voice unusually soft. 'Don't upset yourself, Enzo. This is no good for you. Everything will be all right. We won't let this man rule our lives again. We've come too far as a nation.'

'I wish I had your faith, my dear Lena, but I don't know . . . you can't trust these people.'

The weeks that followed were fraught with uncertainty. Enzo had been right to be worried. Italy was now officially part of the Allied forces, and, with the King and Badoglio hiding safely behind Allied lines in the south, had declared war against Germany. Mussolini, installed by the Führer as leader of the new Italian Social Republic, was calling up all fit young men to serve in its fighting force or else volunteer to work for the occupying Germans.

'It's an impossible choice, Nico,' Jenny said, as she hung onto his arm. 'You can't go away. It's not fair, and you promised you wouldn't leave me again.'

'I will not fight for or work with the Germans but I can't do nothing, Jennifer.'

Enzo cleared his throat and spread his hands on the table. 'There is another option.' He jerked his thumb over his shoulder. 'Up there, in the mountains, there are bands of men and women who are working for the Resistenza.' He looked Nico in the eye. 'You could join them.'

'Isn't that very dangerous?' asked Jenny. 'What if you were captured? Nico, I don't think you should do it.'

He removed her hand from his forearm. 'It will be my decision, *mia cara.*' He smiled and flicked her under her chin. 'And I don't take orders from my wife.'

His playful response had failed to take the sting out of his words, and she was momentarily stunned into silence. 'I . . . um . . . it wasn't an order; it was an opinion.'

Nico winked at his father. 'Are women allowed to have opinions, Papà?'

Enzo laughed and clinked his glass against his son's. 'Don't let your *mamma* hear you talking like that.'

Lena returned from the kitchen, perspiring from the heat of the oven. She placed a tureen of watery minestrone on the table. 'What are you talking about? What am I not meant to hear?'

Jenny jumped in first, determined to get her mother-in-law on her side. 'They think Nico should join the Resistenza.'

Lena removed the lid from the pot and momentarily disappeared behind the whoosh of steam. 'I think it is a good idea. In fact, I think we should all do what we can in the fight against the fascists and the Nazis and whoever else thinks Italians are unable to defend the country they love.'

Nico helped himself to a bowlful of soup and tore off a piece of hot focaccia, speaking with his mouth full. 'It is man's work, Mamma. No need for you to get your hands dirty.' He waved his bread in the air. 'You and Jennifer just stick to what you're good at.'

Lena glanced at Jenny, her mouth set in a stubborn line. 'Nico, when I say I'm going to get involved in the Resistenza, this is what I mean. You cannot stop me.'

Jenny lifted her chin. 'Well if Lena's getting involved, then so am I.'

Nico and Enzo looked at each other, but Lena continued. 'There is an old Italian proverb: "When women take up a cause, you can assume it has been won."' She squeezed her daughter-in-law's hand. 'You can count on Jenny and me.'

Later, after they had retired to their bedroom, Nico stood staring out of the window, perfectly still apart from the rise and fall of his chest. Jenny crept up behind him and circled her arms around his waist.

'Penny for them.'

His body was rigid as he continued to gaze at the horizon.

'Nico,' she tried again. 'What's the matter?'

'The tragedy is, I actually think you don't know.'

She twisted him to face her. 'Look at me, Nico. What are you talking about?'

'I'm talking about you embarrassing me like that in front of Mamma and Papà.'

She frowned. 'Embarrassing you? What on earth do you mean?'

'Do not play innocent, Jennifer. You know what I'm talking about. I forbid you to get involved with the partisans and yet you carry on as though I hadn't spoken. You made it look as though I have no control over my wife.'

She took a step backwards, her expression darkening. 'Control? No, you don't, Nico. You do not have control over me.' She raised her voice. 'I am my own person, not your puppet, and you don't forbid me to do anything.'

He grabbed her arms, squeezing tightly. 'Shush, stop shouting. Mamma and Papà will hear you.'

She shook him off. 'Don't you dare put your hands on me like that.'

He let his arms drop and turned to face the window again. 'I'm sorry, Jennifer. Forgive me, please. It's just that I love you so much and I couldn't bear anything to happen to you. It would kill me.'

She hesitated before placing her palm on his back. 'Come to bed, Nico. Let's forget about it.'

'I just want to keep you safe, that's all, and if that's a crime, then I'll plead guilty as charged.'

As he turned back to face her, she locked her eyes onto his and began to unbutton his shirt. He fumbled with the buttons on his fly, his breathing growing more urgent. Once he was naked, she gripped the hem of her nightdress and pulled it over her head. He stared at her body and smiled. 'You're so perfect.'

'Touch me,' she breathed.

She closed her eyes as she felt his hand on her breast, his exquisite touch so light she was forced to cry out as her legs trembled, threatening to give way. 'Please, Nico, I want you to . . . I . . . I need you to . . .' She was too embarrassed to say more, but words were redundant as he scooped her into his arms and carried her over to the bed.

49

Candice was sure she couldn't be this unfit. It had to be the heat and the altitude. 'Stefano,' she breathed as she bent double, her hands on her knees. 'Wait for me. I'm not a bloody mountain goat.'

He laughed as he watched her scramble up the narrow path above the church. 'You can do it, Candice, only a few more metres.'

She joined him at the top as he stood under the shade of one of the five pine trees. 'Phew! I'm glad that's over.'

He pulled a bottle of water from his rucksack and offered her a sip.

'Thanks,' she said, taking a slurp and, in the absence of a sleeve, wiping her mouth with the back of her hand. 'Right, what did you want to show me?'

He swept his arm around. 'Let us just take a minute to appreciate this incredible view.'

She placed her hands on her hips, feeling her heart rate slowly returning to normal as she gazed at the swirling sea hundreds of feet below. 'I'm running out of words to describe this place, Stefano. It's truly stunning.'

He held out his hand. 'Come with me now, and be careful.

Don't let go.' He guided her to the edge of the cliff and stopped beside a white headstone. 'There.'

She removed her sunglasses and stared at the carved inscription. *Domenico Bernardi. 8 Agosto 1918–12 Giugno 1946. Eroe della Resistenza. Riposare per sempre in pace.*

She instinctively took a step back from the edge. 'My God, that's Nico.' She nodded at the inscription. 'What does it say?'

'It says, "Hero of the resistance. Forever rest in peace."'

'What happened?'

Stefano took off his sunglasses and held them to his chest. 'It was terrible.' His voice was quiet as he gazed out to sea, shaking his head. 'He fell to his death.'

She had declined Stefano's invitation to stop for grilled sardines on the harbourfront, even though he insisted she would never taste anything so simple and yet so utterly divine in her entire life. *Just a squeeze of lemon juice and a twist of black pepper, it is all they need.* It was a difficult choice, because she would have liked nothing more than to spend another hour in his company, but she really needed to get back to Jenny, who'd been on her own all afternoon.

The young receptionist collared her on her way up to the bedroom. 'Erm . . . Miss Barnes, I have a message for you.'

Candice stopped. 'For me?'

'*Sì, sì*, here.' The girl handed her a piece of paper. 'He call many times.'

Too impatient to wait around for the lift, Candice sprinted up the two flights of stairs, her legs burning with the effort after all the exertions of the day.

'I'm back,' she cried as she entered the room. 'Jenny?'

There was no answer, but she could see the old lady lying on a sunlounger out on the balcony, an open magazine resting on her chest.

She slid back the door and gently touched the back of Jenny's hand. There was no response. She knelt down. 'Jenny? Jenny, can you hear me?' She swallowed her rising panic and blew out several short breaths. 'Oh God, please, no.'

She picked up Jenny's wrist and felt for a pulse. Nothing. A mirror, she needed a mirror. She rushed to the bathroom and returned with her magnifying make-up mirror, holding it to Jenny's mouth with a trembling hand.

Jenny coughed and pushed the mirror away.

'What on earth are you doing, girl?'

'Oh, thank God, you scared me half to death. Sorry, I couldn't . . . I thought . . .'

She heaved herself into a sitting position. 'You thought I was dead?'

'Well, yes, a bit.'

'I'm not sure how anyone can be a bit dead. You either are or you aren't.'

'I meant . . . Oh, never mind. How've you been anyway?'

'I've been grand, love. I went down to the terrace and had a few of those martini cocktails. They do a chocolate one, if you can believe that. The barman got a little bottle of chocolate sauce and squirted it round the inside of the glass in a flower pattern. Then he poured in the vodka and what have you. It was all very arty. Then I came up here for a lie-down.'

'Bloody hell, no wonder you were dead to the world.'

Jenny indicated a glass on the table. 'Pass us that water,

would you, I'm parched. Oh, and another thing, that phone of yours has been buzzing all afternoon.'

Candice remembered the note and fished it out of her pocket. *Please call Beau Devine. He says it is urgent.*

'Shit,' she muttered under her breath.

'Beau, is it?'

She nodded and reached for her phone. 'Oh Jeez, sixty-eight missed calls.'

'Did you tell him where you were staying?'

She shook her head. 'No, I didn't. He wasn't all that interested in the trip. He knows he can always get hold of me on my mobile. Or he thought he could.'

'I wonder how he found you then,' mused Jenny. 'He must've phoned a hell of a lot of hotels.'

Candice shook her head. 'No, he didn't.' She held up her phone. 'All he needs is this. It has an app that shows where I am at all times. At least it shows where the phone is.'

'You mean he can spy on you?' asked Jenny.

'I wouldn't put it quite like that, but yes, he can see where I am.'

'And you're happy with that?'

'Yes, well, no . . . I mean, it's never bothered me before. I've got nothing to hide, so why should it?'

'Are you going to ring him?'

Candice fingered the paper with Beau's message. 'He does say it's urgent.'

'Mmm . . . I wouldn't mind betting his definition of urgent isn't the same as yours or mine.'

'I'll think about it.' She screwed up the note. 'Anyway, enough about that. I climbed to the top with Stefano.'

Jenny nodded slowly. 'He showed you, then?'

'Yes. Why didn't you tell me?'

She ignored the question. 'What did he tell you?'

'Not a lot. Just that Nico was a hero of the resistance or summat and that he fell to his death from the top of those cliffs.'

Jenny stayed silent as she picked at the buttons on her dress. Eventually she looked up at Candice, her blue-green eyes fixing her with a determined stare. 'Do you know what cathartic means, Candice?'

'Of course I do. I may not have had the best education, but I'm not that ignorant.'

'Sorry, I didn't mean to insult you. Before I shuffle off once and for all, I needed to come back here one last time.' She gave a small laugh. 'At my time of life, most things you do are for the last time. I need to face up to my actions. Time's running out, Candice. I can't put it off any longer.'

'Are you ill?' asked Candice. 'Do you need me to call a doctor?'

'There's nothing wrong with me. Stop fussing. You've already nearly called out a coroner tonight. I'm fine. Just listen.'

'Sorry.' Candice crossed her legs and leaned forward. 'Carry on.'

'Well . . .'

Her phone vibrated on the table and they both looked at it impatiently.

'I'll turn it off,' she said, squeezing a button and throwing the phone onto a nearby chair. 'There. I'm all ears.'

Jenny closed her eyes, her breathing long and deep as though she was meditating. 'Whichever way you look at it,' she began, 'it was a tragedy.'

50

1943

They were protected from the icy winds blowing in from northern Europe by both the Alps and the Apennines, but there was still a bitter chill in the air after the first dumping of snow had settled on the mountains behind Cinque Alberi.

In the month since Nico had retreated to the mountains, life in the village below had adjusted to a different pace. The occupying Germans had helped themselves to the Villa Verde, their jackbooted feet scuffing the polished parquet floors, their sharp elbows showing no regard for the antique china and crystal. The panoramic window afforded them a bird's-eye view of the sweeping bay, ensuring the whole population felt under scrutiny every minute of the day.

Lena was in the back yard, hauling a sack of corn onto a wooden cart. Under cover of darkness, Enzo would take it up to the partisans' hideaway.

'I'm going too,' Jenny declared. It was said with such determination that Lena appeared to accept that argument would be futile.

'If you are sure, then I will not stop you. I know how much you miss Nico and I don't want to stand in your way. We are stronger than they think, you and I, but I'm afraid you'll have to convince Enzo.'

Lena was right. Even though Jenny would never be as fit and able as most of her peers, her health and strength had improved beyond all recognition since she'd left Manchester over three and a half years ago. Her muscles had grown and tightened, her lungs now able to cope with exertion to the extent that she could now run a couple of miles, admittedly with a lopsided gait that made her look as though she'd had more than a few drinks.

'You leave Enzo to me,' she said.

Lena smiled, knowing that her husband had a soft spot for their daughter-in-law. 'He only want to keep you safe. He promise Nico.'

The bell sounded above the front door.

'I'll go,' said Jenny.

The German removed his cap and dipped his head as he crossed the threshold. '*Guten Morgen.*'

Jenny clutched her apron in her hands. It was the first time one of them had ventured into the café, and she wasn't sure what she was supposed to do. They were the enemy now, and yet he seemed so friendly. His tanned face contrasted with his sandy hair, and he had a ready smile that disarmed her. But he could be here on a spying mission. Maybe he had received word that they were helping the partisans; perhaps she would be tortured until she revealed what she knew. They'd all heard such terrible things. She took a few steps backwards, desperate to warn Lena about the danger in their midst. It would be just like her to holler something incriminating from the back.

'*Buongiorno.*'

'Aha,' he said, spreading his arms and switching seamlessly to English. 'It is you.'

The day she had dreaded had finally come. It had taken just one word to give her away. Italian only by marriage, she'd always feared she would be carted off to a camp or deported.

'Have you come to arrest me?'

'Why?' He laughed. 'What have you done?'

'Um . . . nothing. It's just that . . .' She rubbed her wedding ring, twisting it round and round her finger until the metal grew warm.

'Do not be scared. My name is Maxim Fischer.'

She dug her hands into her pockets. 'Jennifer Bernardi, but I expect you already know that.' She nodded towards a table. 'What would you like? There's no coffee, I'm afraid, but . . .'

He held up a small package. 'I have the beans. Can you grind them for me and I will let you keep the rest of the bag?'

Jenny tried to order the thoughts in her head. She was sure this must be some kind of trick. 'I don't know. I . . .'

'You have a grinder?'

She nodded.

'*Kein Problem.*' He sat down and folded his arms, watching her with faint amusement as she tipped the beans into the top of the grinder and turned the handle. The sound brought Lena in from the back.

'What are you doing, Jenny? Where did you get the . . .?'

Jenny fixed her gaze on her. 'Herr Fischer brought them.'

Lena frowned. 'Herr Fischer?' She stared at the German. 'And where did Herr Fischer get them, I wonder.'

Jenny lowered her voice to a whisper. 'Don't antagonise him, Lena. He's the enemy now, remember.'

Lena approached the German with her hands on her hips, her chin tilted upwards. She pointed at the bag of beans. 'I suppose you steal these from the Grimaldi house.'

'From where?'

'The Villa Verde, where you stay uninvited.'

Jenny could feel the colour rise in her cheeks. Why was Lena being so difficult? She turned her back to him and busied herself with the coffee. 'It'll be with you momentarily, Herr Fischer.'

'*Danke, Fräulein.*'

'*Frau,*' corrected Lena. 'She is married to my son.'

'And where is he?'

'Forgive me, Herr Fischer, but are you here on official business or are you just being inquisitive?'

The cup rattled in its saucer as Jenny placed the coffee in front of him.

He afforded Lena a gracious smile before downing his espresso in one gulp. 'Your daughter-in-law makes a satisfactory cup of coffee.'

'I have to go now,' Lena said, turning to leave. 'In the spirit of good relations, the coffee is on the house.'

'Would you like another?' asked Jenny. 'It too will be on the house.'

He laughed. 'On the house? It was I who brought the coffee!'

Lena's bravado had given her new-found confidence. 'The cost of a cup of coffee is made up of many things, not least the time spent making it.'

'Then it would be rude to refuse.'

Jenny returned with his refill and he indicated the chair opposite. 'Please join me.'

'Oh, I couldn't possibly.'

He regarded her over the rim of the cup. 'Not even for the sake of good relations, as your mother-in-law said? I'll bring you another bag of beans if you'll sit with me for a minute.'

She noticed his hands, his fingers so long and slender it would be a travesty if he didn't play the piano. 'Why would you want to talk to me?'

She was going to be grilled for information now, she knew it. She had to tread carefully, maybe give him just enough to avoid a thorough interrogation up at the Villa.

He removed his spectacles and gave them a cursory polish on the edge of the tablecloth. 'I miss the normal things. A cup of coffee with a pretty girl. There is no . . . how is it?' He pinched the bridge of his nose. 'No strings. Is that it?'

Jenny managed a smile. 'Your English is very good.'

'My grandmother, she was originally from Liverpool, so she insist I learn.'

'What is happening, Herr Fischer?' she asked warily. Just talking to him like this felt dangerous. One tiny slip was all it would take to jeopardise everything Nico was trying to do.

'Please, call me Max. Explain, please.'

She stared into his eyes, as green as a blackbird's egg. She hadn't noticed their startling colour until he had removed his glasses. His green tunic certainly brought them out. 'With this country, with the war, there's so much confusion. Nobody seems to know who is fighting who any more. What's it all for?' She clasped her hands together. It wouldn't do for him to see how much they were shaking.

He replaced his glasses and looked down at his palms, splaying his fingers as though the answer was contained right there in his hands. 'I don't know,' he sighed. 'There are many young men on both sides of this war who would rather be at home. I miss my mother and her cooking. I miss my little sister even though she is often annoying, and I miss my dog.' He searched in his pocket and pulled out a photo of a scruffy pooch. 'This is Otto. He is a wire-haired dachshund and my best friend.' He caressed the image with his thumb. 'I was drafted into the Wehrmacht. I'm not here because I want to be.' He stuffed the photo back in his pocket.

Jenny took the chair opposite. Max might be sitting there buttoned up in his German uniform, but he was still human, with a life back home as normal as the next person.

'Is your husband fighting with Mussolini's new army?' he asked.

'He's . . .' She stopped, silently berating herself for almost walking into the trap. He was clever, she'd give him that. All that talk about his family and his dog. She'd almost fallen for it, but it was the second time he had asked about Nico's whereabouts. She could see it now, he was so transparent. He had obviously been sent to butter her up. She rubbed at a stain on the table with her finger, avoiding any further eye contact. 'I have no idea where he is.' She reached for his empty cup. Her tone was stiff but polite. 'Will there be anything else, Herr Fischer?'

He stood and pulled a roll of lire out of his pocket, slapping a few notes onto the table. 'For your time.' He winked, then picked up his cap and ducked out of the door.

Enzo led the way for the final few metres, beating back the foliage with a stick as he tried to clear a path for the cart. His breathing was laboured and his brow coated in sweat in spite of the sub-zero temperature. He was almost sixty years of age; these escapades should really be a thing of the past. Jenny's lungs too burned with the effort, but she would not falter now, not at the final hurdle. She wanted to show Nico she was as strong as any of them.

The mountain hut came into view just as she was about to give in and collapse onto the forest floor. 'We're here,' Enzo whispered. 'Come on, let me push this thing for you.' He took over the cart as she approached the door of the hut. She rapped three times, waited for the count of three, rapped twice more, waited for the count of two, then rapped one final time. The door opened a crack and she was pulled in by Nico. 'Jennifer. Did anybody see you?'

She kicked the snow from her boots. 'No, no one. Enzo's brought the cart. He's taken it round the back. Look, I've brought you this.' She held up a bag of ground coffee.

He untied the string and took a deep sniff of the contents. 'Where did you get this?'

'Never mind that now.' She opened her arms. 'Have you got a hug for your wife? I haven't seen you for a month.'

He seemed distracted. 'Oh, yes, sorry. Come here.' He gave her a cursory squeeze, then turned his attention back to the coffee. 'Well?'

She glanced over at the other partisans in the corner, but they were engrossed in a candlelit game of cards. She dropped her voice to a whisper. 'A German soldier came into the café with a bag of beans.'

Nico held her at arm's length, his expression darkening. 'Are you completely stupid?' he hissed.

312

'No . . . I . . . What do you mean? He was very nice and—'

'*He was very nice,*' he mimicked. 'You don't fraternise with the enemy no matter how nice they may seem, and you certainly don't take anything from them.' He spoke with such venom, a piece of his spittle landed on her lip.

'Nico,' she placated. 'You're overreacting.'

He gripped her arms. 'This is why I wanted you to stay out of it, Jennifer. You're so naïve and trusting, it's dangerous. You could have put everything we are doing here in jeopardy.' He shook her by the shoulders. 'Do you understand? Have you any idea what—'

'Nico, leave her alone.'

Enzo stood in the doorway, flicking snowflakes off his shoulders. 'Don't speak to her like that. That is not how we brought you up. Apologise at once.'

Nico bowed his head. 'I'm sorry, Papà.'

'Not to me, you fool. Apologise to your wife.'

'It's all right, Enzo. Nico's right. I'm an idiot. But I promise I didn't tell him anything.'

Nico pulled her close. 'No, you're not an idiot, *mia cara*. You are a beautiful soul who is just too trusting. I am so sorry.' He kissed her lips. 'Forgive me, please. I just want you to be safe, that is all. You know I could not bear it if anything happened to you.'

'You're in more danger than I am, Nico. What exactly are you up to here anyway? What's all that?' She nodded towards some equipment in the corner.

'We're building a transmitter to communicate with Allied troops in the south. Until communication is established, weapons and other supplies won't reach us.'

'Weapons? But—'

'Shush, that's all you need to know. Any more will put you in danger.'

'But I want to help, Nico. I feel so useless down there.'

'You are helping, Jennifer. You brought provisions, didn't you?'

She nodded. 'A sack of corn. I know you're probably sick of polenta, but it's all we could get.'

'It is fine.' He patted his belly. 'As long as we are full of something, we can work.'

'I made some soup too. It's mainly cabbage, but it'll fill a hole.'

Enzo poked at the cinders in the fireplace. 'Shall I cut you some more wood, son?'

'It is all right, Papà, we have plenty out back. We only use the fire for cooking. The less attention we draw to ourselves, the better.'

Jenny hugged her arms to her chest. 'But it's bitter in here, Nico.' She blew out a breath to demonstrate. 'How can you sleep?'

'We take turns, two-hour slots. It is important to be vigilant.'

Enzo placed a hand on Jenny's shoulder. 'Are you ready to leave? I know it will be easier on the way down, but we really do not want to get caught in another blizzard.'

She stood on tiptoe and kissed her husband on the cheek. 'Bye, Nico. I'll come again, I promise.'

He mimed zipping his lips together. 'You say nothing, okay? Do not be taken in by the Germans, no matter how charming they appear.' He swept his arm around the hut. 'You could compromise the whole operation, this one and the other units in the area.'

Jenny thought about her encounter with Max. He seemed like any other young man who had been wrenched away from his comfortable life to fight in a war he didn't understand and wished to be no part of.

'Please don't worry, Nico,' she said. 'I'm not stupid.'

Max was as good as his word, and appeared in the café the next day brandishing a fresh bag of coffee beans. He held them aloft. 'See? I keep my promise.' He dumped the bag on the counter. 'Now, how about you grind a few for me and then we can enjoy a cup together outside. It may be bitterly cold, but the sun is shining.'

As Jenny made the coffee, she shifted her gaze towards the kitchen. Lena had managed to procure some flour and was making bread for the partisans. She turned her thoughts back to Max. He might be German, but he was definitely adopting the softly, softly approach. Swanning in here all smiles, as though they were the best of friends. Who did he think he was? Nico was right, they couldn't be trusted. As she silently congratulated herself for having seen right through him, the thought occurred that *she* could use *him*. Perhaps she was being naïve, but if she could glean information about what the Germans planned to do next, then this would be of more use to Nico and the others than a sack of corn and a flask of soup.

She pasted a smile on her face and turned round. 'All right then. I'll just get my shawl.'

At last she was going to make a difference.

51

I watch Candice as she stretches out her long limbs, the languid movements reminding me of a cat. She squeezes her shoulder blades together, then loosens them with a series of shrugs.

'Are you bored, Candice?'

The tinkle of her laughter fills the evening air. 'Of course not, Jenny. Just a little stiff, that's all. And hungry. Shall we send down for something?'

I must admit I'm comfortable here on the sunbed with the woollen throw over me. It's still warm out here, and the blanket is surplus to my requirements really, but Candice insists I shouldn't be taking any chances at my age. I don't know. If you can't take chances at my age, when can you?

She's running her finger down the room service menu. 'I'll just have the crostini. I'm not one for a big meal this late in the evening.'

'Make that two then,' I say. 'And order a bottle of the Frascati, too.'

She frowns at me. 'Haven't you had enough, what with all them martinis?'

'I've had enough of you telling me what I can and can't do.'

She goes to defend herself, but my smile tells her I'm only joking.

After phoning down the order, she leans on the balcony, staring at the shimmering bay. She turns round swiftly. 'Hang on. This is it, int it?'

I nod slowly. 'Yes, this is the former holiday home of the Grimaldis from Genoa, if that's what you mean.'

'The Villa Verde,' she says to show she's understood. 'Fancy that. This is where Max hung out then?'

I can't help but give a rueful smile. It's hard to describe exactly what went on here, but 'hanging out' doesn't begin to cover it. I have to smile or else I'd cry.

I've seen from the hotel brochure that the basement is now a gym. From the photographs, it is unrecognisable from the last time I saw it. There are no beams from which to hang people by their feet, no vats of car lubricant for immersing their heads and no tool bench with six-inch nails ready to hammer into knee joints, elbows and hips. It makes me shudder to think about it now.

'Are you cold, Jenny? Shall I fetch you another blanket?'

Her voice startles me, whipping me back to the present. 'I'm fine, love. Where is m'laddo with our room service?'

Right on cue, the buzzer on our door sounds.

'I'll bung him a couple of euros, shall I?' she says, reaching for her bag.

We set the table on the balcony and light the candle in the glass jar. Candice places the silver wine cooler next to it and pours out two glasses of chilled Frascati. I notice she only half fills mine, but I let it go. She helps me into a chair and fusses with the rug around my shoulders.

'*Salute*,' she says, clinking her glass against mine. 'So, you've been inside this place before, have you?'

'Unfortunately, I have.' I reach into my bag and bring out the pebble, rubbing its smooth surface between my fingers before bringing it to my lips. 'Do you remember me telling you where I got this?'

'The pebble? Yeah, sure, that little girl on the beach gave it to you right before Nico came back. I do listen, you know,' she teases.

'It was around November 1943 when Il Duce eventually decided to cooperate with Hitler and round up Italy's Jewish community. Before then there'd been no specific policy on the persecution of Jewish people, but now they were offering a reward for turning them in, can you believe? As much as five thousand lire, double if it was a rabbi.'

'How awful,' says Candice, biting into a slice of crostini. She scoops up the fallen bits of tomato with her napkin and continues with her mouth full. 'I can't imagine anybody would be so mercenary.'

'Plenty were, love.' I sigh. 'They were desperate times.'

'What does all this have to do with the pebble?'

I glare at her. Why is she in such a hurry? She has a piece of basil stuck between her front teeth and I've a good mind not to tell her about it now.

'Some stories can't be rushed, Candice.' I run my finger around the rim of the wine glass, concentrating my thoughts. 'I was outside the shop, rolling out the canopy. Even though it was the beginning of December, the sun was out, but it was so low in the sky it was blinding. I heard the scuffle of boots and then someone clearing their throat. I wobbled on

318

the stepladder and turned round to see Max standing next to another officer, both of them officious-looking and rather intimidating.'

There's a bitter taste in my mouth and I chase it away with a slug of wine.

'"Frau Bernardi," Max began, "I need you to come with me." He'd dropped his affable manner and his formal tone unnerved me. The other officer had a nasty smirk on his face, and my insides turned to water.'

'Oh Lordy. Where did he want you to go?' Candice asks. I can't decide if she's bored with my story and wants to get it over with, or whether she's so enthralled she just can't wait to find out. From the way she's perched on the edge of her seat, her eyes shining, I'll go with the latter.

'Here, Candice.' I point at the floor. 'He wanted me to follow him to the Villa Verde.' I don't wait for a horrified reaction, because it's hard to imagine this place as anything other than a luxury boutique hotel with thousands of five-star reviews on TripAdvisor. 'I told him there was no way in this world or the next that I would go willingly to the Villa Verde. I said he'd have to arrest me or whatever it was they did. I thought about Nico up in the mountains. I didn't know any details of what the partisans were doing, but I was sure that wouldn't stop the Germans from torturing me to find out. It didn't matter to them that I was just a young girl. So I told him straight. I will not go with you, Herr Fischer. I do not know anything, so you can torture me all you like but it would be a complete waste of your time and mine.'

'Wow,' says Candice. 'Standing up to a Nazi, that was so brave.'

319

I shake my head. 'Oh, he wasn't a Nazi. He was conscripted into the German army and was just following orders. He insisted I go with him, promising I'd be safe. He said he would personally ensure nothing bad happened to me. The other officer gave a snort, and Max glared at him and said something vicious-sounding in German.'

I swig the last of my wine and hold my glass out to Candice, who duly obliges, although not without a slight pursing of the lips.

'Lena and Enzo were out, so I said I needed to use the bathroom and took the opportunity to scribble them a note. At least if I disappeared, they would know where to look. We didn't speak for the ten minutes or so it took us to walk here, and I remember Max didn't look at me once. It was as though he knew we were being watched. When we got here, he said we had to go down to the basement.' I steal a look at Candice. 'Nothing good ever comes out of a trip to a basement. I was absolutely petrified. I just knew I was going to be tortured for information. I cursed myself. Nico was right, I was just a silly little girl who'd been duped.

'I was trembling; I felt sick and could barely walk. Max ordered the other officer to leave and guided me downstairs. There were three doors in the basement, but two were firmly closed and bolted. Behind the other door was a room with a massive desk covered with maps and papers, and I remember a metallic smell so pungent I had to cover my nose with my hand. It was the smell of blood.'

Candice visibly shudders. 'Oh God, Jenny. That's so creepy.'

Creepy is one way of putting it; barbaric, depraved and inhumane would be more accurate.

'There was an SS lieutenant standing behind the desk, his uniform starched and uncreased, not a button or a badge out of place. He fingered the buckle on his belt as though he was going to take it off and whip me with it. Just as my imaginings were about to get the better of me, I noticed a woman not much older than myself sitting on a bench, her legs crossed at the ankles, her hands resting demurely in her lap. From her body language she appeared poised and untroubled, but her face was a mask of pure terror. It was Vanda, Eva's mother.'

Candice gasps and her hand flies to her mouth.

'I was ordered to sit on the bench opposite, and then Max and the SS lieutenant exchanged a few words in German before the lieutenant sat down and put his feet up on the desk, a chilling smirk across his face.' I try to adopt a stern German accent. '"You two, no speak," he commanded. Vanda and I looked at each other and both nodded.'

Candice is staring at me, her gaze so intense I feel like I'm back in that basement with the eyes of the SS lieutenant pinned on me.

'I barely had enough spit to swallow,' I continue, 'let alone speak. Then the door opened and a little girl was shoved into the room. She was dressed in what looked like her Sunday-best coat, and her hair was braided into the two neat plaits she always wore.' My fingers instinctively close around the pebble.

'Eva?' whispers Candice.

'Yes, it was Eva. I was so confused but didn't dare ask any questions. The lieutenant spoke in broken Italian to her. He said he was feeling kind and that he was going to give her a choice: to go home with me or stay with her mother.' I have to stop and take a breath as my voice begins to break. 'Can you imagine anything so cruel, Candice? Asking an eight-year-old to choose whether to stay with her own mother or leave her behind and go with a woman whose biggest contribution to her life was the occasional free focaccia.'

I dab at my eyes with a napkin. 'She had been allowed to bring her favourite toy, a doll, which she clutched to her chest. She looked at me first, and then at her mother. It was agony to watch, Candice. I dreaded what would become of her if she made the wrong choice. With her child's innocence, it only took her a few seconds to make her decision, and as she took a faltering step towards her mother, I looked at Vanda's stricken face. She didn't need to say anything. Her eyes said it all. *Do not choose me.*

'Eva glanced at me then, biting down on her lip, her eyes as wide and terrified as a startled fawn's. I looked at the lieutenant reclining in his chair, his hands clasped behind his head, obviously enjoying the hideous spectacle. He knew there was no way she would choose me over her mother. Max was staring down at his feet, and as the lieutenant reached for his cigarettes, I felt in my pocket for the pebble Eva had given me and dropped it on the floor, where it rolled and stopped just next to her. The officer ordered Max to pick it up, and I muttered an apology, but my mission had been accomplished. Eva had seen the pebble and I hoped that she'd remember I'd promised to treasure it forever.'

'She chose you?' Candice asks, her palm laid across her heart. 'Please tell me she chose you.'

'She did.' I nod.

Candice visibly relaxes. 'They were Jewish then, Eva and her mother?'

'Yes, they were. I wasn't able to call out to Vanda as she was dragged from the room by two other SS officers. They took an arm each and manhandled her out of the door. I suppose she sensed she had nothing to lose then, because she turned round and somehow managed to smile at her daughter as she said, "*Ciao, piccolo fagiol. Sii una brava ragazza per Mamma.*"'

Candice frowns and wipes a tear from her cheek.

'It means "Goodbye, little bean. Be a good girl for Mummy."'

'Heartbreaking,' says Candice, dabbing her cheeks with a napkin. 'Did Vanda return to collect her after the war?'

I shake my head. I sometimes wonder what they teach kids in school these days. 'No, she didn't. I later discovered that four days after she was taken away, Vanda was gassed in Auschwitz.'

Candice gasps. 'Oh my God, that's tragic.' She gazes out across the still water of the bay, gentle waves lapping onto the pebble beach, unchanged in seventy-odd years.

'It was a despicable act of cruelty done purely to entertain, a game to satisfy the curiosity of a deranged SS officer.' I can feel my heart rate accelerating in the way it always does when I think about that day. I have never been able to understand how one human being could be so cruel. 'Max accompanied me and Eva back to the café. None of us spoke until we arrived, and then Max took hold of my hand and pressed something into it. "I sense this is precious," he said. I opened my palm. It was the pebble.'

I suddenly feel drained, as though the life has been sucked out of me. I close my eyes wearily, but then my head nods and snaps me awake. 'It's late, love. I think I'd like to turn in now, if you don't mind.'

'Hang on, not so fast. You haven't told me about Nico yet.'

She's right, of course, and I steel myself once more. 'There's stuff you need to know before we get to that bit, Candice.' I pause and adjust my focus to the peninsula in the distance. 'Otherwise none of it will make sense.'

52

1944

They were sitting in the café, the door firmly closed against the snowflakes squalling outside. Eva's tongue protruded in concentration as she wrote out the unfamiliar English words. Jenny turned the paper around. '*Eccellente*, Eva.' She kissed the top of the child's head. 'You are a clever girl. Your *mamma* would be so proud of you. I know I am.'

At the mention of her mother, Eva looked down at the table and covered her face with her hands.

'It's okay, love. You have a good cry. I'm not going to tell you not to cry for your *mamma*.' Jenny rose from the table. 'But I am going to make you some warm toast. My little brother always felt better when his belly was full of toast.'

Eva removed her hands and managed a smile, even though Jenny was sure her own Italian wasn't fluent enough for the little girl to understand everything she said.

'Can I wear my new dress today?' she asked. The bolt of peacock-coloured silk that had languished in Lena's blanket box for nigh on half a century had finally been released from its prison. Lena had always insisted it was only to be used for something special, and when Jenny suggested that nothing would ever be more important than making a party dress for the vulnerable little girl who had been thrust into their lives, she had agreed without question.

'I don't see why not, Eva. You look so pretty in it.'

She wrapped her arms around Jenny's neck. 'Thank you.'

Jenny squeezed her eyes shut. 'You're welcome, my love.'

Nico had been holed up in his mountain hideaway for four months now, working with his comrades on plans to blow up bridges, tunnels and roads in order to destroy or frustrate enemy convoys. Jenny hadn't been told the specifics and neither did she want to know. It sounded like dangerous work and she feared for Nico's safety every minute of the day. He wasn't used to handling explosives and she was terrified he'd blow himself up and end up being maimed or worse.

She knew from Max that the partisans were more than making a nuisance of themselves. They were becoming a feared and effective fighting force against the German occupation, and Nico was high on their wanted list. Since that day in the basement, she and Max had developed an understanding. They wouldn't betray each other's trust. Max didn't ask about Nico, and in return she didn't try to persuade him to divulge anything that might be useful to the resistance. It was safer that way, for all of them.

After an hour's climb at a steady pace, she came to the clearing where she always had to sit down and ponder which way to go. Only a few years ago, this journey would have been unthinkable. She'd brought her cane, but it was primarily used to bat away branches and undergrowth in order to forge a way forward. She looked around for the chestnut tree on which

Nico had carved a mark. Nothing too obvious and certainly nothing that would be of any help to the Germans.

It was another hour before she arrived at the latest hut Nico had commandeered. He was always on the move, always one step ahead of the enemy. She used the coded knock and waited, her heart pounding with exertion and excitement. After several excruciating minutes, Nico opened the door a crack and pulled her inside. He clasped her frozen cheeks between his hands and kissed her mouth. 'Oh Jennifer, I've missed you so much.' He caught hold of her gloved hand. 'Come and sit with me on the mattress, let me warm you up. The others are out collecting wood, so we have a little time to ourselves.' He grappled with the buttons on her coat, so roughly that one of them popped off.

'Careful, Nico.' She laughed. 'What's the rush?' She removed her shoulder sack and opened it for him to have a look. 'I've baked some bread, and there is another flask of soup and—'

He flung the sack to the ground, his breathing ragged as he pushed her down onto the mattress and shifted his weight on top of her. 'Never mind that now. It's not my hunger for food that needs satisfying.' He kissed her neck, his teeth nipping at her flesh, his breath hot in her ear.

'Nico, please.' She wriggled out from under him. 'You're going too fast. I haven't seen you for weeks, I can't just—'

'Shush, Jennifer. You love me, don't you?' He clamped his mouth onto hers, rendering her incapable of answering as he pinned her arms above her head with one hand, the other searching under her long skirt.

She kicked her legs. 'Nico, please,' she breathed.

As his callused hands moved over her body, she froze at

his touch on her bare skin. The fight was lost. She was his wife and he needed this. She kissed him back and succumbed, allowing his urgency to overwhelm her.

Afterwards, she lay in his arms, the contours of his body unfamiliar. He was leaner, harder, and he smelled of sweat and of the outdoors, of the cool mountain air and decaying forest mulch. He stroked her hair with such tenderness she could hardly believe they were the same fingers that had tugged at her so roughly moments before.

He sat up and dragged the sack over to the mattress. 'Let's see what we have here then, *mia cara*.' He took out the bread and soup and fumbled around for the last item. When he pulled out the bar of chocolate, his brow creased with confusion. 'Where did you get this?'

'Isn't it wonderful, Nico? I thought you deserved a little luxury.' She laid her head on his shoulder as he turned the bar over in his fingers.

'I asked you a question.' His voice had taken on a dangerous edge, and she realised her mistake immediately but wasn't quick enough to make up a convincing lie.

'I . . . um . . . Max brought a couple of bars for Eva,' she said in a rush. 'I thought it would make a nice change for you to . . . to . . .' She faltered as she saw the look in his eyes. 'Nico, I . . .'

He picked up the chocolate bar and waved it in her face. 'Are you trying to tell me that that Jewish girl is still living with you in my home and you continue to fraternise with the enemy?'

'I do not fraternise with Max, I—'

'You're on first-name terms with a Nazi and you expect me to believe—'

'He's not a Nazi, he's just a regular soldier in the Wehrmacht.'

He threw his hands in the air. 'Jennifer, you are putting at risk everything we are fighting for here. I told you to get rid of the girl. It's dangerous to harbour Jews.'

'Get rid? Are you insane?'

He exhaled slowly, his voice calmer but no less firm. 'Look, I'm not suggesting you turn her over to the Nazis.' He stroked a finger down her cheek. 'I'm not that heartless. But you need to get her to another place of safety. She can't stay in my house.'

'Why not? They know she is there.'

He laid a tender hand on her shoulder, but his bony fingers were menacing rather than comforting. 'You've got to trust me. It will be used against you. They are just biding their time. They set a trap and you walked straight into it.'

'I can't let her go, Nico, please.' She allowed the tears to fall freely, couldn't have stopped them even if she'd wanted to. 'I know it's only been a couple of months, but I've grown to love her. She trusts me, and she's got nobody else. She's never even known her father, and now her mother's . . . well, who knows what's happened to Vanda. I'm her second chance. Please, Nico,' she ended breathlessly.

'Jennifer, I am telling you she has to go.' He lifted his hand to scratch his head, and she flinched instinctively.

'Don't look so frightened, *mia cara*. I'm not going to hurt you.' He placed his lips against her ear. 'I love you.' He let his hand slide to her stomach. 'We don't need anybody else's child in our lives. We will have our own one day soon.' He looked into her eyes. 'Perhaps even now there is a baby.'

*

The shutters were closed when Jenny returned to the café. The chairs had been turned upside down on the tables and the wooden floor swept clean of the day's detritus. Lena sat in the back room with Eva on her knee, snuggled up against her chest as she read from *The Adventures of Pinocchio*. She looked up when she heard Jenny enter. 'You've been longer than I thought. I was beginning to worry. How was my boy?'

'Fine. Can I talk to you, Lena?'

'Of course. Can it wait, though? Geppetto is about to be swallowed by the Terrible Dogfish.'

'Now, please, Lena.' Jenny reached for Eva's hand, addressing her in Italian. 'Go and put your nightdress on, *tesora*.' She picked up one of the child's plaits, running her fingers along its length. 'I'll be up to comb your hair out shortly.'

With the little girl safely out of the way, she crashed into the chair opposite Lena. The older woman leaned forward. 'You look so tired, Jenny. I don't like the idea of you going up there alone. I know you miss Nico, but it is dangerous.'

'I'm fine, Lena, it's not me you need to worry about.'

Lena leaned forward and patted her knee. 'It will soon be over. The Allies are moving closer every day. You have to keep the faith. It's worrying, but Nico knows what he is doing.' She clasped her hands together in prayer. 'God protect him, he is so brave. My son the warrior.'

Jenny couldn't help herself. 'Your son the warrior says Eva has to go.'

'What? Go where?'

She shrugged. 'A place of safety. She can't stay here any more. He says his word is final.'

'We'll see about that.' Lena pressed herself out of her chair and hollered up the stairs. 'Enzo, come down here now, please.'

He appeared moments later, rubbing the sleep from his eyes. 'What is all the noise? Can't a man have a quiet nap? Your voice could trouble the dead, Lena.'

'It is Nico; he says that Eva has to go.'

Enzo settled himself on the arm of his wife's chair, a reassuring hand on her shoulder. 'Perhaps it is for the best.'

'Pardon?'

'It is dangerous for both her and us. You cannot trust the Germans. They play games.'

Lena drew herself up to her full height and crossed her arms in defiance. 'Over my dead body. Eva stays, and that is the last time we ever have this discussion.'

Jenny's heart swelled with love and admiration for her mother-in-law. 'Thank you, Lena.'

The next morning Jenny crept into Eva's room and sat down on the bed. The little girl stirred in her sleep, her hair spread in dark waves across the pillow. Her mouth twitched at the corner as she sought out her thumb.

'Morning, darling,' whispered Jenny, kissing her forehead.

Eva opened her eyes and rolled onto her back, her voice thick with sleep. 'Is Mamma coming back today?'

'No, not today, Eva.' She had lost count of how many times the little girl had enquired after her mother. They had heard terrible things about the camps, but there was no definite news on Vanda. They had only been told that Jews were a threat to society and had to be removed.

'Let's go to the beach, shall we? See if we can find any

more beautiful pebbles.' She pulled Eva into her arms, revelling in the warm smell of sleep. She buried her nose in Eva's hair and rocked her to and fro. 'I'll never let you go, Eva,' she whispered. 'I've already had to leave my little brother, and nobody is going to take you away from me.'

Eva stared at her, a questioning look in her eye. 'I want to stay with you. I have to stay here so that Mamma will know where to find me when she comes back.'

Jenny managed a smile. 'That's right. You're going nowhere.'

53

2019

I'm staring at the photo of the child I came to think of as my daughter. She looks happy as she beams into the camera. Such a resilient, brave little thing.

'Are you all right, Jenny?' Candice asks. 'Do you want to go to bed?'

I wave her away. 'I loved that little one like she was my own flesh and blood. Everything I felt for our Louis, I poured into her. Seeing the world through a child's eyes again made me miss Louis even more, and I was overcome with homesickness. I was lonely. Oh, I know I had Lena and Enzo, and I was fond of them, but it wasn't the same. I still slept on my own every night, while my husband hid in the mountains. I craved affection and I missed him so much. I fretted about him constantly. No mercy was shown to captured partisans.'

'How did he feel about you not sending Eva away?' Candice asks.

I shake my head. 'Furious, as you might expect. But Lena too was adamant that she should stay, so he accepted it eventually.'

My voice cracks as I remember the joy Eva brought me. 'I taught her to read in English, you know. I'd brought my treasured copy of *Anne of Green Gables* and I was chuffed to bits when she loved that story as much as I did.' I look at Candice, my lips trembling. 'We didn't know it then, but Eva was an orphan herself by that time.'

'Ah, bless,' says Candice, touching her heart with her fingertips. 'What happened to her then?'

Candice is so impatient. Always wanting to skip ahead.

I stare out across the moonlit bay, the peninsula silhouetted against the darkening sky. My voice is barely a whisper. 'It pains me to admit it, but Nico was right. I should have sent her away.'

54

Max was sitting on the wall, a sketchbook laid across his knee. He was so engrossed in his work he didn't realise she was standing behind him. His hand moved freely, the charcoal strokes caressing the thick paper.

'That's really very good, Max. I didn't know you could draw.'

'Oh,' he said, turning round. 'You startled me.' He laid the charcoal down. 'There are many, many things you don't know about me.' He stared at the horizon. 'I have almost forgotten who I am myself. This war, it is tearing me apart.'

She longed to put a reassuring hand on his shoulder, but there were prying eyes everywhere. Nobody could be trusted. Perhaps not even Max himself. She pushed the thought away, knowing instinctively that he would not betray her. She couldn't afford to be wrong about this.

He pointed to the object of his sketch, a seabird perched on an upturned fishing boat. 'It is an *Austernfischer.*'

Jenny looked at the bird's beady red eye and long orange beak. 'An oystercatcher. It's beautiful.'

'Just a few more strokes here and there and it will be finished.'

'I assume you got the paper and charcoal from the villa.

The youngest Grimaldi child is a particularly good artist, I gather.'

'I did, but I don't intend to take it away. I will leave the drawing for them as a gift, you know, a thank you for letting us use their villa.'

'You make it sound like they had a choice.'

He stared at the bird as it flapped its wings and took off, flying low over the sea. 'I'm not proud of my fellow countrymen, Jenny. This is war and I hate it as much as you do.'

She removed her handkerchief from her sleeve, running her fingers over the fine embroidery. 'This war has already taken so much from me, Max. My mother died under the rubble of her own house after one of your bombs aimed a direct hit.' She cast him an accusing glance, as though he himself had been piloting the plane. 'I promised her I would take care of our darling Louis, and yet he won't even reply to my letters. We were so close once, and now there's a chasm between us and I don't know if I'll ever be able to bridge it.' She paused for a steadying breath. 'And Lorcan. I'll never forgive myself for what I did to him. He was the sweetest boy to ever walk this earth. His mother was right. I didn't deserve him.'

Max laid his hand on her arm. 'I doubt that, Jenny, you are—'

She shook him off. 'No, don't feel sorry for me. It's all my fault.' She stared at him through narrowed eyes, unable to keep the bitter tone from her voice. 'But none of it would have happened if your country hadn't started this dreadful war.'

Max looked down at his sketch, nodding slowly. 'As I said, I hate it as much as you do.' He rolled up the sheet and slipped it into his pocket. 'Would you care to take a little walk? There's something I want to talk to you about.' He glanced up at the villa. 'But not here.'

'Oh, I'm not sure that's wise. In any case, I should really get back and help Lena and Enzo in the café, and I promised I'd read Eva some more of her book. She was taking a nap when I left, but she'll be up and about soon enough.'

Max nodded, his downcast eyes betraying his disappointment. 'I understand. You're right, perhaps it is dangerous for us to be out like this.'

She felt herself bristle. She was still at liberty to engage in an innocent stroll with somebody she had come to regard as a friend. German he might be, but if she had judged him correctly, she was safe with him. 'All right, Max, let's take a walk.'

She craved the company of somebody near her own age. Three months had passed since she had last seen Nico, and she was almost crippled with loneliness. His operations had become so clandestine that even she now had no idea of his whereabouts. She missed him every day, longed for his attention, his love, his touch. She wanted her Nico back. Not the embittered, hardened partisan he had become, but the vivacious, adoring man she had fallen in love with. He was still in there somewhere, she was sure of it.

The afternoon sun blazed down as they walked along the shoreline, the glossy pebbles slippery underfoot. She lost her balance and Max steadied her, catching her elbow.

'Thank you,' she said, immediately taking a step away from

him. She could imagine the penetrating stares of the SS officers from the panoramic window of the Villa Verde. She would not give them any ammunition to use against her. They'd already taken enough from her.

Max dabbed at the sweat on his forehead. 'You and I may be on opposite sides in this war, Jenny,' he began, 'and I'm risking a lot just by talking to you like this, but you are my friend and I consider it a risk worth taking.'

She squinted along the bay towards the imposing villa. 'I don't want you to get into any trouble, Max. Perhaps we should—'

He shook his head. 'Let's just walk. Keep your head down and don't react to what I tell you. I know you have your doubts about me and my motives, but I'm going to prove you can trust me.'

They fell into step, side by side, as Max spoke quietly. 'I don't have all the details – I'm not party to the specific plans of the Waffen-SS – but I believe your husband is a wanted man. They suspect he is behind the massacre of a German battalion about ten miles from here.' His voice faltered. 'I think you should expect reprisals, Jenny. I don't know where and I don't know when, but it is happening everywhere. Partisan activity is not to go unpunished and they are exacting terrible revenge. Ten innocent civilians for every German killed.'

She kept her gaze fixed on the beach ahead as instructed. She had no details about what Nico was doing, but she refused to believe he was capable of that level of violence. 'No, that's not right. I believe the partisans are only there to frustrate the occupying German forces.'

'SS intelligence tells them that it was the work of Il Falco. I could be wrong – as I said, they don't tell me anything – but I've heard the name mentioned.'

She didn't even flinch as she heard Nico's code name, the Hawk.

'They also suspect that you and your father-in-law take supplies to him in the mountains,' Max continued, 'and that your mother-in-law works as a *staffetta*, carrying messages between units. It is dangerous for you all, Jenny. Once they catch up with him – and it's only a matter of time – you could all be arrested. I am gambling with my life by telling you all this, so I hope it proves I'm genuine. You saw straight through me from the start. You are right, I was sent to befriend you, to get you to reveal what you know, but you were too smart for me.'

They had reached the tiny square at the end of the harbour-front. Out of sight of the villa now, he caught her arm and led her down a narrow side street.

'I admire what your husband is doing, Jenny.'

She looked at him in shock. 'Really? Surely you don't mean that.'

'I do. It takes courage, with few weapons and little training, to rise up against an occupying force. The partisans are fighting for their freedom, against the invading enemy and also the enemy within.'

'Fascism, you mean?'

He nodded. 'Exactly. Nico is putting his life on the line every day. I've seen what they do, the militant fascists, the Brigate Nere. They quite literally do not take any prisoners; it is only executions for them.' He drew a finger across his throat, shaking his head gravely. 'Your husband is a brave man, Jenny. You should be immensely proud of him.'

She thought of Nico hunkered down in some shepherd's hut in the forested mountains high above Cinque Alberi. The memory of their last meeting still caused her face to colour. The heat of the afternoon sun suddenly felt too oppressive. She leaned against a wall and blew out a few shallow breaths.

'Are you feeling all right, Jenny?'

'Fine.' She sighed. She longed to feel the cool sea breeze on her clammy skin. She pointed to the top of the peninsula. 'Have you been up there yet, Max?'

He followed her finger. 'No, I haven't, but it looks wonderful.'

'Are you game?' She smiled.

'Well, yes, but I thought you didn't have long. What about the café?'

She couldn't actually remember the last time she had done anything approaching fun. There was no harm in it. Lena and Enzo could cope with Eva and the café. It was hardly a hive of activity these days. And if they couldn't cope, she would face the consequences later.

She grabbed his arm. 'Come on then. What're you waiting for?'

By the time they reached the tiny church on the top of the cliff, they were both heaving with exhaustion. The sun still beat down with the ferocity of a blowtorch, but the breeze was more than enough to cool the blistering temperature.

Jenny wiped her brow with the back of her hand. 'You

know, Max, it wasn't so long ago that I wouldn't have been able to manage that climb at all, let alone without my cane.'

'You are an inspiration, Jenny. I am lost in admiration. You are strong and so beautiful it—'

She shook her head. 'Stop, Max, please. You don't know what you're talking about.'

Before he could protest, she gestured towards the door. 'Let's go inside. There's something I want to show you.'

Once inside, Max blinked in the gloom, waiting for his eyes to adjust. He shivered dramatically, rubbing his arms. 'It's like an ice box in here.'

'You'll soon get used to it.' She made her way down the narrow aisle and stepped up onto the wooden pulpit.

'Are you going to give me a sermon?' he asked, removing his steamed-up glasses and squinting at her.

'Believe me, I'm the last person who should be preaching to anybody.' She crouched down and fumbled underneath the lectern before standing triumphantly, holding a key aloft. 'Found it.'

'What are you up to now, Jenny?' Max queried, his eyes shining in quiet amusement.

She inserted the key into an ancient walnut cupboard, the hinges creaking as she opened the door. Underneath a pile of hymn books lay a wooden box. She wrestled it free and sat down on the nearest pew. 'Have a seat, Max.'

He slid in next to her, his body so close to hers it made her skin tingle. 'It was supposed to be for my jewels, but since I don't have any, I use it to keep the things that are most precious to me, things that are more valuable to me than diamonds. Isn't it beautiful?'

He ran his fingers over the lid. 'It certainly is, but what's it doing up here?'

She gave a deep sigh. 'Father Ascarelli looks after it for me. It's safer here. Nico told me to get rid of it, you see. Said it was a part of my past that I had to let go. That it had no place in our lives.'

'Oh,' said Max. 'What's in it?'

She lifted the lid. 'All sorts.' She picked up a photograph, the sudden rush of sadness making it difficult for her to speak.

'Jenny?'

'This is our Louis,' she sniffed.

Max took the photograph, smiling. 'Your brother? He looks so happy.' He squinted at the picture of Louis's beaming face. 'Is that a lamb tucked under his arm?'

She flicked away a tear. 'Yes, he hand-reared it himself.' She brought out the carving. 'He made this for me. There's another part to it, but I gave it to him to keep.' She nodded determinedly. 'One day the two parts will be slotted back together.'

She picked up another photo. 'This is me and Nico on our wedding day, here in this very church.'

Max grinned. 'You look scared to death.'

'Aye, well, I'm not fond of heights and we were standing on the edge of the cliff. Nico's idea.' She picked through the contents again. 'Oh, and here's the pebble that Eva gave to me. Of course you know all about that.'

He glanced at the floor, shaking his head. 'Terrible day,' he whispered. 'I'll never forgive myself for not stepping in.'

'There was nothing you could've done, Max. Please don't be so hard on yourself.'

He inhaled deeply and stared at the rafters. '*Lieber Gott*, I hate this war, Jenny.' He smoothed his hand over the lid of the box, his fingers coming to rest on the carved initial. 'It seems cruel to ask you to part with this.'

'Yeah, well, Nico didn't *ask* me, he told me.' She sneaked a look at Max. 'And a part of me can understand why. He is very . . . um . . . insecure, I suppose. I do love him but he doesn't like to feel threatened by my past and any lingering feelings I may have for the people I was once close to.'

'But still, your own brother?'

'I know.' She shrugged. 'But it's not that simple.' She closed the lid of the box. 'Nothing ever is.'

Light, hazy clouds drifted across the sky, tempering the intensity of the sun and making the walk down more comfortable. Max proved to be engaging company and it was easy to forget that their respective countries were sworn enemies. She hadn't felt this carefree in a long time. He insisted on walking ahead this time, checking for loose stones or invading vegetation, ensuring the path was clear. She was still reflecting on what an unexpectedly glorious afternoon she'd had when he stopped without warning, causing her to barrel into him.

'Oh, sorry,' she laughed. 'What is it? Why've you stopped?'

He stared down at the harbour below. The sparkling sea still lapped against the pebbles, but it appeared that at least one of the buildings was shrouded in thick smoke, choking curls of it only partially obscuring the flash of fire.

'*Nein!*' he shouted. '*Nein.*' He clasped his hands to his head, then dropped to his knees in the dirt, his glasses falling onto the stones, one lens popping out.

Jenny stared at the unfolding carnage, unable to move. 'Oh my God, the café. No, no, it can't be. Eva!' she screamed. 'Please, please not Eva.'

55

I'm shivering now, but it's got nothing to do with the drop in temperature. The colour has drained from Candice's face and her features are frozen in shock.

My voice quivers as I speak. 'This is why I had to come, Candice. It's seventy-five years since that dreadful day, the day the population of Cinque Alberi was massacred. Innocent people, children included, who had done nothing wrong.'

Candice seems to have trouble finding her voice. 'But . . . what happened?'

'A reprisal attack. The Germans and their fascist allies wanted their revenge. They had to send out a message to the partisans; somebody had to pay and they didn't care who. It was indiscriminate and wicked, but the resistance had to be quashed in any way possible. The message was unequivocal.'

She scoops her hand through her hair and her words come out as no more than a breathless whisper. 'And Eva?'

I close my eyes and bite down on my lip. I can do it. I've come this far. 'Max took hold of my hand and we stumbled down the hillside together, neither of us saying anything. It took us, I don't know, maybe another half-hour to reach the bottom, but we could see there was a blockade of German

345

troops, all standing with their weapons poised. I lurched towards them but Max grabbed my shoulder and pulled me back. He knew I would be shot on sight, but at that moment all I cared about was reaching Eva. The noise was deafening, shots were being fired every second, and I thought my head would explode. Screams of pure terror cut through the carnage. The smoke was so thick and noxious that my eyes streamed and I could barely see. The smell of burning flesh made me retch right there on the street. Max led me away to a deserted alley and pressed me against the wall, his face only inches from mine. "I'm so sorry, Jenny," he said. Then he wrapped me in his arms and held me tight as he fought back his own tears.'

Candice picks up her glass and I can see her hands are trembling. 'Were there any survivors?'

'Only the few lucky enough to have been out of town. Every person there that day was rounded up and shot. Imagine being dragged from your house and being forced to watch as your neighbours were summarily executed, knowing that you would be next. The bodies from the café were unrecognisable, some fused together, others completely incinerated. It's difficult to put a number on it, but around a hundred and twenty people died that day, including Lena, Enzo and . . .' I stop and pinch the bridge of my nose. 'And Eva.'

'Poor little thing,' says Candice, the greatest understatement ever uttered.

'If I'd sent her away as Nico had told me to, she wouldn't have perished.'

She nods slowly. 'And if you'd not gone for that walk with Max, you'd have died too.'

I'm annoyed that she has picked up on this so quickly. It makes me sound selfish. I should have been at home protecting Eva, instead of which I was cavorting with the enemy. 'I've had seventy-five years to reconcile my actions, Candice. I don't think I'm quite there yet, but after the remembrance service, I hope my conscience may be able to rest a little easier.'

'Max must've known the attack was coming. Perhaps that's why he took you out.'

I shake my head. 'It was my idea to climb to the top of the peninsula. Max hadn't been told any details of the attack, but he knew of others that had already taken place, so he was well aware of what they were capable of and felt he had to warn me.' My heart swells with pride as I remember the risk he took. 'There were many different divisions of the Wehrmacht and the SS involved in reprisal massacres, but the one based in Cinque Alberi was not responsible for that one.'

'And Nico?' asks Candice. 'What happened to him?'

'He was shell-shocked. Blamed himself, naturally, but he wasn't responsible for the attack on the German patrol that sparked the revenge. To this day, historians are divided on the subject, but without doubt the partisans contributed to winning the country's freedom from both the foreign invader and that home-grown lunatic. They were heroes in my book.'

Candice is nodding along, but I suspect she doesn't really understand the many nuances of this particular subject. I'm not even sure I do. 'These days, Nico would have been diagnosed with post-traumatic stress, but that wasn't a thing back then. He took the death of his parents really hard. It changed him, Candice.' I give her a hard stare. 'And I wish I could say it was for the better.'

56

1946

She stumbled along the rocky path, Nico tightening his grip on her arm. 'Ow, you're hurting me.'

'Stop whining, Jennifer. That is all you ever do these days. I'm sick of hearing it.'

She fought to keep pace with him as he dragged her up the track, the loose stones under her feet as slippery as marbles. His mood had been foul since she'd told him that morning that her period had come and once again there would be no baby.

He had been incandescent when she'd broken the news. 'Why are you doing this to me, Jennifer?'

'Nico, it's not my fault. I—' He had silenced her with a slap to her face. Even though it wasn't the first time he'd raised his hand in anger, she was stunned, the shock obliterating the pain of her stinging cheek.

In the immediate aftermath of the reprisal attack, he had returned from the mountains under cover of darkness to see the devastation for himself. His grief was palpable, his guilt all-consuming. There were tens of thousands of partisans fighting for the cause, but he still blamed himself. He'd taken her back with him to the mountain hideaway, and together with the other partisans they had seen out the end of the war there, existing on foraged mushrooms, chestnuts and whatever villagers from the surrounding area were able to spare. After the war, they had returned to Cinque Alberi to begin the daunting task of rebuilding their lives, but the man she had fallen in love with, the man for whom she had given up everything, was gone. He became withdrawn, unpredictable and impossible to be around. He was like a hand grenade with the pin pulled out, ready to explode at the slightest knock.

She could feel her lungs burning as Nico pulled her along, his grip on her hand as tight as a vice. 'Nico,' she gasped. 'Please stop . . . I can't breathe.'

'Stop it, Jennifer. There is nothing wrong with you. Why do you have to make such a drama out of everything?' He gave her arm a savage tug. 'We're nearly there, so try to stop moaning.'

As the tiny church came into view, Jenny almost wept with relief. Sweat ran down into her eyes and she dabbed at them with the hem of her blouse. The sun's blistering rays burned through her hat without mercy. 'I . . . I need to sit down, Nico, please.'

'You can rest after you have got down on your knees and prayed to God to give you the baby you seem so desperately determined not to conceive.'

'I don't do it on purpose, Nico.'

He let go of her hand and wiped his palm down his trousers as though her sweat disgusted him. His chest heaved with the effort of the climb as he turned away and stared at the horizon. 'Three and a half years we've been married, Jennifer.'

He gestured towards the church. 'Do you remember our wedding day, *mia cara*?'

'Of course I do. It was—'

'Where did it all go wrong?'

Without waiting for an answer, he walked to the edge of the cliff and held out his hand. 'Come and join me.'

'No, Nico, you know I don't like heights.'

'Come on,' he urged. 'I won't let anything happen to you.'

Reluctantly she walked towards him, and fell gratefully into his outstretched arms.

'There you are, see. It's not too bad, is it?' He removed her hat and stroked her hair. 'I've got you, Jennifer. Now . . . look down.'

'No, I'd rather not, Nico, if—'

He grabbed her hair, forcing her to look over the cliff edge at the swirling surf hundreds of feet below. As she watched the waves crash against the rocks, she struggled to keep the terror out of her voice. 'All right, you've had your fun. Can we go back now?'

He laughed. 'You do not appreciate the view?'

With her legs threatening to buckle, she had no choice but to cling onto him. She grabbed at his shirt. 'Why are you doing this to me, Nico? Why are you being so cruel?'

'Cruel? Oh no, Jennifer. It would only be cruel if you didn't deserve it.' He shuffled closer to the edge. 'You have always been too strong-willed for your own good. You have never been the wife I wanted you to be.'

'I've no idea what you're talking about.' She reached out to touch his face. 'Look, I know you're still grieving for your *mamma* and *papà*. I miss them too.'

'How can you possibly understand?' he snarled. 'They were not your parents.'

She could feel her anger rising and fought to bring her voice under control. 'I lost my mother too, don't forget, and our Louis. I left him behind to be with you. That's how much I love you, Nico. I made a huge sacrifice for you.'

He squeezed her arm until she cried out. 'You owe me,' he said. 'Your brother would be dead by now if he'd come with us. Think about that. He'd have died along with Mamma and Papà and that kid you insisted on keeping instead of getting rid of like I asked you to.' He moved his face so close to hers she could feel his fiery breath. 'She paid with her life for your disobedience. You as good as killed her.'

'Please, Nico, don't say that.'

'Why did you always want other people's children in our lives? First it was your brother, and then Eva. I wanted a wife who could give me a baby, but you couldn't even manage that. You're just a useless cripple. A useless, *barren* cripple.'

In spite of her terror, she could hold back no longer. 'And what makes you so sure it's *my* fault we can't have a baby?'

He laughed in her face. 'You cannot be serious. I'm an Italian man. We are known for our virility. There is nothing wrong with *me*.' He grabbed her chin, forcing her to look at him. 'That womb of yours must be a hostile place. Like a desert incapable of supporting life.'

'Oh really?' She smiled at him. 'Are you sure about that?'

'You think this is funny?'

She glanced down at her feet, her toes perilously close to the edge. 'I think it is hilarious, Nico.' The adrenaline surging through her body gave her the confidence to carry on. 'And

351

I'll tell you why, shall I?' Unleashing her pent-up anger, she screamed into his face. 'I know there is nothing wrong with me, because I've already had a baby.'

She felt his grip loosen. 'You're a liar,' he managed, but there was no mistaking the doubt in his eyes.

She seized the opportunity to take a step away from the edge. 'Remember that little boy you told me to forget about? He was my absolute world, but I still chose you over him.' She could taste the anger now as she pummelled her fists into his chest. 'Louis is not my brother. He's my son.'

The world seemed to stop turning as Nico opened his mouth to speak. When no words came, his eyes narrowed and he clenched his teeth. 'You are a whore,' he finally managed. 'A cheap, nasty little whore.' Flecks of spittle had gathered in the corners of his mouth.

'I gave up everything for you, Nico, including my own son. You forbade me to make contact with him and I respected your wishes even though it nearly killed me. And I can't ever forgive you for that. It's over, Nico. Us, I mean. We're finished.'

She turned to leave, but he lunged for her arm, twisting it round her back.

She yelped at the bolt of pain. 'Let go of me!' She tried to wriggle free, but she was no match for his strength.

'You cannot leave me, Jennifer. I will not allow it. You are my wife, you belong to me.'

With her arms restrained, she kicked out at his shin. Her foot connected with his bone to produce a gloriously satisfying crunch.

'Aargh, you stupid bitch.' He loosened his grip for a split second, but it was all the time she needed. She brought her knee up between his legs, and he stumbled backwards, turning away from her as his hands went to cradle his groin. With his pathetic groans resounding in her ears, she shoved him hard in the back.

The earth beneath his feet crumbled, dislodging stones that cascaded into the sea. He lost his footing and slipped over the edge. Twisting his body, he made a desperate grab for a tuft of grass, his knuckles turning white as he literally clung on for his life.

'Jennifer,' he gasped. 'Help me.'

She crawled to the edge and peered over, staring into his wild eyes. Realising the horror of what she had just done, she gripped his wrists and attempted to pull him back.

'Nico, please, you'll have to use your legs. I can't do it by myself.' She felt his hands begin to slide through hers.

'Please, Jennifer,' he begged. 'Don't let me go. I love you. Please, I'm sorry. We can make this right again.'

'I . . . can't . . . do . . . it,' she said, her voice straining with the effort. 'My hands are too sweaty and I'm not strong enough.'

'You are, Jennifer. Please, come on, you *can* do it.'

She shook her head, tears blurring her vision. 'I'm so sorry, Nico.'

'No, no, Jennifer . . .'

Her name bounced off the cliff face as his hands slipped out of hers and his primal scream was carried away on the wind.

57

Candice runs her hand through her hair, her eyes wide with incredulity. It's a lot to take in. 'You . . . you had a son. Louis was your child? And . . . and you killed Nico.'

She doesn't frame those last few words as a question, and perhaps she's right not to. I pushed Nico on purpose; that part was no accident. I may have tried to pull him back when I saw what I had done, but make no mistake, I was responsible. I had to protect myself, though, and I was ever so good at playing the distraught young widow, arriving breathless at the police station several hours later. Although I couldn't see how anybody could've have survived that fall, I had to make sure. Nico was the only person who could have contradicted my account.'

'My God, Jenny,' breathes Candice. 'You killed your husband.'

'It wasn't my intention to kill him, Candice. I shoved him too hard. It was an accident.'

'But . . . why?' She's looking down at her lap, so I can't tell what she's thinking. I know there's no excuse for what I did. Nico may have become cruel, unreasonable and impossible to live with, but he didn't deserve that.

'I just snapped, Candice. He was taunting me over Eva. Making me believe that I was responsible for her death.' I shake my head. 'That was wicked.'

Candice is picking at her nails, studiously avoiding my gaze.

I instinctively rub my cheek as I remember the shock I'd felt as his hand whipped across my face. 'I'm not making excuses for his behaviour, but the war changed him. The boy I fell in love with would never have raised a hand to me.'

She finally meets my eye. 'I know what you're thinking, but Beau is nothing like Nico. He has never once hit me. He wouldn't do that.'

I'm surprised she's made the connection but thankful the spotlight has been turned off me. As tragic as Nico's death was, I don't wish to dwell on this part of my story. 'Are you sure, Candice?'

'Yes, I'm sure. Believe me, if he ever laid a finger on me, I'd be out.'

'Everybody thinks that's the way they would react, but the reality is quite different. Nico only raised his hand to me a few times, but I always managed to convince myself it was my fault. When I was a little girl, before our Louis was born, I had a dog. He was only a mongrel, a stray my father had found quivering under the arches. I loved that dog so much. If ever I was upset, I'd bury my face in the thick fur around his neck. He made everything better.' My eyes mist over. I've not thought about Hector in many a year. 'When he got older, he became snappy and would growl at me if I fussed him. One day he was particularly grumpy, and I leaned down to kiss his head. He suddenly lurched for my face and clamped his jaws around my chin. There was blood everywhere and I had to have stitches. But do you know what, I loved that dog so much I would have forgiven him anything. He died a few weeks later and I tortured myself with thoughts that he might've been ill. What if he'd had a brain tumour or something? Perhaps he was in so much pain he just wanted to be left alone and didn't know any other way to tell me.'

Candice pulls a face. 'Surely you're not making excuses for Nico?'

'No, there is never an excuse for using physical violence against your partner, but when you're in the middle of an all-consuming relationship, when you love someone so much, you'll tell yourself anything.'

'For the umpteenth time,' she sighs, 'Beau has *never* hit me.'

I'd rather not do this now, but I'm in too deep. 'You've heard of the frog analogy?'

She frowns at me, I suppose with good reason. 'What're you on about?'

'What do you think would happen if you plunged a frog into a pan of boiling water?'

'Dunno.' She shrugs. 'He'd leap out, probably.'

'Yes.' I nod. 'The second he feels the heat, he's out of there. Now imagine putting a frog in a pan of cold water and then lighting the gas under it.'

She doesn't even bother to stifle her impatience. 'Go on.'

'As the water in the pan heats up, the frog adjusts his body temperature, so he doesn't really notice the water getting hotter. By the time it reaches boiling point, he has no strength left to jump out of the pan and so he boils to death.'

She wrinkles her nose. 'What's all that got to do with anything?'

'What do you think killed the frog?'

She gives me the 'duh' expression so favoured by young-sters. 'The boiling water, obviously.'

I pause while I consider her answer, tilting my head thoughtfully. 'Or was it the frog's inability to realise until it was too late when to jump?'

I can almost hear her brain ticking over.

Her voice is a whisper. 'Beau has never been abusive towards me.'

'Abuse comes in many forms, Candice. Beau is controlling you. He's trying to make you dependent on him. Look at how he manages your money, tells you what to wear, suggests you lose weight. What was it he called you? *Little Chubster*, wasn't it? He dressed up an insult as a cute little pet name and you thought it was all right. All those things are meant to look like he's looking after you, but that's not what it's about.'

'No, you're wrong, Jenny. He loves me.'

'I'm not doubting that, but it's a toxic love, one that will end up eating away at your self-esteem until there's nothing left of you.' I reach for her hand. 'Just think about it.'

58

The church is situated at the end of a long lane rising steeply out of the village. Visible above the treetops, the bell tower stands out against the cloudless blue sky. Candice sits beside Stefano as he negotiates the rough track, the car's suspension not quite up to the job of cushioning the bumps. She looks over her shoulder. 'Are you all right back there, Jenny?'

'I do feel a bit sick, but don't worry, Stefano, it's nothing to do with your driving.'

'Shall I stop? We only have about a hundred metres to go.'

'I'll be fine, you carry on.'

I'm hot in my heavy black dress. It's the one I wore for my hundredth birthday party, the one from the charity shop, if you've been paying attention. As I said, the tailoring is exquisite and only for special occasions. I wonder how many more of those there'll be.

Stefano brings the car to a halt under the shade of a beech tree and cracks open all the windows. As I try to heave myself out of the car, he offers me his hand.

'Thank you, Stefano. You're a good lad.'

He certainly looks the part today in his dark suit and black tie secured with a silver pin. His shoes are polished to a mirror finish and his hair has been slicked back with some sort of gel. A few people file past, heads bowed, as sombre organ music resounds around the graveyard. Stefano gestures to a woman swathed in black, her hands firmly clasped together. Candice would probably call her elderly, but to me she's young, seventies I'd guess.

'Please,' Stefano says, 'I'd like you to meet my mother, Isabella Buccarelli.'

'Lovely to meet you,' I enthuse. 'Your son has been so kind to us.'

Isabella gazes adoringly at Stefano. 'He is a good boy.' She pinches his cheek.

'Mamma, please,' he tuts. 'Jenny is here for the seventy-fifth anniversary too. She's come all the way from England.'

'Oh,' says Isabella, raising her eyebrows.

I feel compelled to explain my presence. 'I used to live here. I was here that terrible day.' I lean on Candice for support. 'I saw it all.'

Isabella's features have frozen, and it seems an eternity before she speaks again. 'I was here that day too,' she whispers. 'I was a babe in my mother's arms. You'd think that might've saved her, but no, they shot her in the back of the head. I was found days later, huddled under her body, barely alive.'

Bound by our common grief, I feel brave enough to touch her arm. 'I'm so sorry, Isabella.'

She nods towards the church. 'We really should be going in.'

Candice takes hold of my elbow. 'Do you want your frame?'

I straighten my back a little. 'No thank you. Today of all days, I need to walk tall.'

*

Stefano takes his mother's arm and settles her into a pew before dipping his fingers in the holy water and crossing himself. He drops down on one knee in front of Christ on the cross, then seats himself next to Candice and bows his head, his lips moving in silent prayer.

A hush falls over the congregation as the priest takes his place in the pulpit. His address is in Italian, and I'm surprised by how much I understand.

My thoughts turn to Eva, as they have done so often over the course of my lifetime. Whenever I picture her, she's wearing the peacock-blue dress I made for her, her plaits ramrod straight, her trusting smile never far away in spite of her terrible plight. Such a brave little girl. I press my handkerchief to my nose and try to focus on what the priest is saying.

From what I can gather, we're going to listen to a reading by one of the few survivors. I shuffle in my pew, my feelings of guilt that I too survived when so many didn't begins to resurface.

A woman on the end of a pew rises unsteadily from her seat, a sheet of paper fluttering in her hand. She looks elegant in black wide-legged trousers and a black and gold striped tunic. She makes her way to the pulpit, where a young man offers his hand and helps her up the steps. Her voice is surprisingly powerful given her age, but I suspect she's driven on by her emotions. I'm overcome by mine and weep silently into my handkerchief. But I'm so glad I came.

I'm blinded by the bright sunshine as we exit the gloomy interior of the church. The priest smiles as he shakes my hand

and thanks me for coming. He's no idea who he's talking to, of course.

'I'll get the wreath from the car, shall I?' asks Candice. 'You just sit here.'

She settles me on a bench under the canopy of a yew tree and hurries off. There is a memorial stone at the back of the churchyard listing the names of the victims. I know it's going to be tough to see it, but I have to do this.

Stefano carries the wreath and Candice holds my arm as we make our way along the gravel path.

Behind the marble memorial, the Italian flag flies at half-mast, and there is a string quartet of young Italian girls, their hauntingly beautiful faces perfectly capturing the sombre mood. The music is quietly respectful and the mournful tune brings me to tears once more.

Candice squeezes my arm and I feel a rush of love for this young girl who has selflessly given her time to accompany me on this poignant journey. I certainly couldn't have managed it by myself.

Stefano stands next to his mother and they both cross themselves and bow their heads. Isabella takes a step forward and her fingers find the name of what I assume is her dead mother. Stefano fastens his arm around her and she leans her head on his shoulder.

They move along and Candice and I step into their place. It takes me only a few seconds to find them. *Enzo Bernardi* and *Valentina Bernardi*. I shuffle forward and rest my fingers on the gold lettering. I close my eyes briefly before looking for the name I'm afraid to see. The name I loved so much. But . . . it's not there. I can't see it.

I scan the stone anxiously. Why is Eva's name missing? How could they have forgotten her? She was only a child, but she should be remembered.

I'm suddenly unsteady and I feel a hand on my arm. It's the woman who read the poem at the service. She is standing next to me, her huge sunglasses covering half her face.

'Are you all right?' she asks in Italian.

I nod my head. 'I was looking at the names of Enzo and Valentina Bernardi. They were my in-laws. I was married to their son, Nico.'

The woman takes off her sunglasses and looks at me, her eyes narrowing as she scrutinises my face. It seems an age before she speaks again, and when she does, it's only a whisper. 'Jenny?'

I look around half expecting there to be somebody else behind me. 'Yes.' I frown. 'But how did . . .'

She clutches both my hands in hers as she switches to English. 'It's me.' She smiles. 'It's Eva.'

I suddenly can't see. Black dots dance in front of my eyes and the world seems to close in around me, wrapping me in its suffocating embrace. My legs have turned to spaghetti and I know I'm only being held up by Candice. I hear her voice from somewhere far away shouting for help, and then there are solid arms around me and I know it's safe to let go as the darkness descends.

'Jenny, Jenny.' There is somebody tapping my cheeks.

'Oh, thank God,' breathes Candice, her face only inches from mine. 'We thought you were a goner.'

I've been manhandled onto a bench, the leafy shade of a

tree providing respite from the blistering sun. The woman is now sitting next to me rubbing her thumb over the back of my hand. Candice picks up my other hand and presses a bottle of water into it.

'You gave us all quite a fright,' the woman says. Can she really be my Eva? After all this time?

I take a long drink from the bottle.

'I . . . I . . . can't believe you're here,' I gasp.

Her wide, intelligent eyes are locked on mine, and I suddenly see her as an eight-year-old again.

'Just like you, I wanted to pay my respects,' she says.

I shake my head. 'No, I mean I can't believe you're alive.'

She gives me a quizzical look. 'Well, I look after myself. A Mediterranean diet certainly helps.'

I grasp her arm. 'But I don't understand, Eva. You died that day. In the café, along with Lena and Enzo.'

It's her turn to look confused now. 'Surely your husband told you?'

There's ice in my veins and I can barely swallow. 'Told me what?'

She turns to look at the memorial, her hands clasped as though in prayer. 'That morning, the morning of the attack, a man arrived in the café. I was sitting at one of the tables quietly reading my book, and he took the seat opposite. He looked wild and dishevelled, like a caveman. I remember his face was streaked with mud and he smelled of the earth, all dank and musty.'

'Nico?'

'Yes.' She nods. 'His *mamma* came through from the back and she was overjoyed to see him. She flung her arms around him and I remember wondering how she could possibly hug somebody who smelled so bad.' She gives a little snort. 'Such childish innocence.' She brushes some invisible flecks off her tunic before continuing. 'Anyway, he said he'd come to take me away to a place of safety. Well, I was so confused. I thought I was already safe. I started to cry because I knew that if I went away again, my mother wouldn't know where to find me when she came back.'

She inhales a deep breath through her nose. 'Of course, I didn't know it then, but she was already dead.'

'You poor lamb.' It's all I can manage.

'I didn't want to go anywhere without you, so I got off my chair and hid under the table, clutching my dolly. I squeezed my eyes shut as I heard Nico and his *mamma* arguing. I was terrified, and tried to block out the sound with my hands. The next thing I knew, Nico was dragging me out from under the table. He was so strong, and even though I kicked my little legs for all I was worth, I was no match for him.'

I'm simmering with rage now. 'How dare he? I'm so sorry, Eva.'

Somehow she manages a smile. 'Don't be.' She nods at the memorial stone. 'If it wasn't for him, my name would be up there too.' She places a hand on my shoulder, her voice wavering. 'Your husband saved my life.'

59

We're back in the cool sanctuary of our hotel room. The curtains are drawn and I'm lying on the bed with a cool face-cloth pressed to my forehead. There's an untouched cup of sweet tea by the bed, which Candice insists is good for shock.

Whilst I am thoroughly overjoyed that Eva is alive, I cannot believe that Nico let me believe she was dead, and that I was responsible. He knew how much I loved her and saw how much I grieved. How could anybody be so cruel?

'Why would Nico lie to me?' I ask, although I'm not sure how Candice could possibly fathom Nico's motives.

She sits herself down gently on the bed and offers some words of wisdom. 'You told me that he said he didn't want anybody else's kids in his life. First there was Louis and then Eva. Look how he engineered it so that neither of them would be part of your family. He came back that day to spirit Eva away; it was his good fortune that you weren't there.'

I shake my head vigorously. 'There's no way I would have let him take her away.'

'Then you'd both be dead,' Candice says with a slight shrug. 'And then when the massacre happened, he knew that if you believed Eva was dead, you wouldn't go looking for her.'

I prop myself on my elbows. 'But to let me think she was dead . . .' I flop back down onto the pillow. 'It's just plain wicked.'

'He did save her life, though.'

'I suppose so,' I concede. 'But he can't have known the massacre was about to happen, otherwise he would've saved his parents too.'

She squints at the bedside clock.

'I'm sorry, love, I'm keeping you, aren't I.' Suddenly I feel tired, overwhelmed by the events of the day.

'Not at all. You take as long as you need. What time's Eva getting here?'

'In about an hour. I can't wait. We have so much to catch up on. You carry on getting ready for your date with Stefano.'

'It's *not* a date,' she states firmly, but there's a hint of a coy smile.

She's certainly having a hard time deciding what to wear for an outing that isn't a date.

She pulls a cream linen dress out of the wardrobe, holding it at arm's length. 'Look at this, it's creased to glory.'

'Well, that's linen for you, Candice,' I reply absently. It's hard to care about something so frivolous at the moment.

She puts the offending dress back in the wardrobe and pulls out another. 'What about this one? It'll show off me tan.'

'It's perfect, love,' I say, without looking up from Eva's photograph. I caress her image with my thumb. My darling Eva. All these years . . .

Candice interrupts my thoughts again. 'Stefano said we might have a chance to go swimming so I should wear a cossie. Well, he didn't say "cossie", obviously, but you know what I mean.'

She slips off the bathrobe to reveal a jungle-print bikini, the straps as thin as dental floss. After putting on the dress, she takes a long look at herself in the mirror.

'Hmm . . . you can see the bikini through the fabric.'

I resist an eye roll. 'It's fine, Candice, now will you please get out of here and let me have a little siesta before Eva arrives.' There's no chance of sleep, of course, but I need space to think.

She opens the safe and retrieves her mobile. 'Beau's been calling again.' She allows herself a small smile, presumably at the thought of him manically pressing the keys. 'Hang on, that's weird.'

'What is it now?' My patience is hanging by a thread. I just need some peace and quiet.

'Beau. He was calling and calling this morning from around six, and then he just stops. Nothing, no text messages, no voicemails.'

'Good, he's finally got the message then. It's taken him long enough.'

She bites her bottom lip. 'You don't think he's done owt daft, do you?'

'What do you mean?'

'You know . . . hurt himself, or worse.'

'Candice, will you please stop fretting about Beau. I'm sure he's fine.' I tap my temple. 'This is how he gets into your head. Forget about him and just enjoy your afternoon.'

She puts the phone back in the safe. 'You're right, as always.' She scoops her hair up into a high ponytail and props her sunglasses on top of her head. 'I'll see you later then.'

'You take as long as you want, love. Don't worry about me.'

367

60

Stefano had definitely said he would meet her down at the harbour. He hadn't been specific about where exactly, but that shouldn't have been necessary. There were only a couple of bars with tables outside, and he wasn't sitting at either of them. She looked along the breakwater heading out into the bay, but there was only an old man shuffling along with an even older dog that didn't look at all thrilled at being dragged out in the heat.

'Candice, *ciao, bella*. Over here.' Stefano was standing at the helm of a small motorboat, which wobbled from side to side as he flailed his arms to attract her attention.

'Stefano, there you are.' She walked to the edge of the jetty. He'd changed out of the dark suit and into a more nautical ensemble of white denim shorts and navy and white striped T-shirt.

'Welcome aboard,' he said, holding out his hand.

'What's all this?'

'I take you cruising,' he beamed.

She looked at the wooden bench seat that ran around the inside of the hull, a yellow canopy over their heads to shield them from the sun's fierce rays. 'It's . . . it's so diddy. Is it safe?' She took his hand and hopped into the boat.

'Diddy?' He frowned. 'What do you mean?'

Candice laughed. 'Small.' She clutched the side for support as another boat went past, causing a swell. 'Ooh, it's wobbly.'

Stefano patted the bench. 'You sit there and I sit here so that I can steer us.'

With one hand on the tiller, he guided them expertly out of the harbour and into the bay beyond. The water was calm, its glassy surface only occasionally troubled by the wake of other boats.

After a few minutes, he nodded towards a cool box tucked under the bench. 'Drag that over here, please.' When Candice obliged, he prised off the lid and brandished a bottle of chilled Prosecco. 'You like?'

'Who doesn't?' She smiled.

He clenched the bottle between his legs and removed the cork with one hand. Candice held out two glasses, and he slugged in the frothy wine.

'*Salute*,' he said, tilting his glass towards hers.

She took a sip and leaned back against the side of the boat, stretching her arms along the edge. Further out to sea, the water became choppier and the sun's rays danced on the wavelets, making them glitter like a thousand jewels.

'How is Jenny?' he asked. 'She get quite a shock, no?'

'She's a tough old boot. She'll be fine. But I've never seen her speechless before, I'll grant you that. Eva's going to the hotel this afternoon. They have a lot to catch up on.' She turned her face to the sun. 'This is heaven,' she sighed. 'I hope you appreciate living in a place like this, Stefano. You should see where I live back home. A grotty flat with a shared hallway. I have to fight my way past bloody pushbikes and pizza leaflets and garbage. And there's always a dodgy character or two lurking in the street, wanting to know if I "need anything".' She looked at Stefano, his head on one side as he waited for her to continue. 'I'll tell you what I do need. I need to live somewhere like this. I could be happy here.'

'You're not happy at home?'

She took another gulp of her drink, then blew out a long breath as the wine loosened her tongue. 'I dunno. I thought I was. I thought our flat was bloody Buckingham Palace when we first moved in. Compared to some of the places I've lived, it was.'

'We?'

'I'm sorry?'

'You live with someone else?'

She ignored his question and slapped her thigh instead. 'Okay, that's enough about me and my problems. What about you? Do you have a girlfriend?' She cursed the damn Prosecco. 'I'm sorry.' She pointed at her glass. 'Blame this stuff.'

'It's all right. I don't mind. They come and go.'

'What do?'

'Girlfriends.'

'Oh, right. I see.' She could feel herself blushing. As if somebody like him wouldn't have a girlfriend.

'Now, Candice,' he said, 'we are going to go a little faster. We need to get around the headland and into the next bay, and then you will see what paradise is. Hold on.'

She gripped the side of the boat as Stefano gradually increased the speed until it skimmed across the waves, the cooling breeze a welcome relief from the sun's merciless rays. As they rounded the headland, he slowed the boat down, allowing them to glide into the still waters of the sheltered bay. Here the beach was made of finer pebbles, almost sand-like, and the cliffs behind were so densely covered in pine trees, their fresh scent hung in the air.

Stefano reached for a pole and scooped up a buoy, tying the rope securely with deft, expert fingers. 'Ready for a swim?' He pulled his T-shirt over his head and dropped his shorts to reveal a pair of black swimming trunks, the sort usually favoured by Olympic athletes. Candice instinctively averted her eyes and peered into her empty Prosecco glass.

'I will give you a refill after we swim,' he said, rolling his shoulders. 'Ready?'

She stood to slip off her dress, suddenly wishing she'd worn a more modest one piece instead of the brazen animal print, which left nothing to the imagination.

'I go first,' Stefano said. He dived off the boat, his body slicing into the sea, causing barely a ripple. He was gone for what seemed an eternity, as Candice stood alone on the boat, not another soul to be seen, the only sound the gulls squawking to each other on the cliff edge. She scanned the flat expanse, her pulse quickening as she realised that without him she would be stranded.

'Stefano,' she called, keeping her voice light. 'Where've you gone?'

Moments later, like a breaching whale, his head broke the surface. 'Come on, what is keeping you?' He shook his head, sending droplets of seawater in her direction. 'You can swim, no?'

'Yeah, course. It's just . . . Is it cold?'

'No, not cold, only refreshing.' He held out his hand. 'Sit on the edge of the boat and slide in. I will catch you.'

She held her breath as her toes dipped into the sea. 'It's bloody freezing, Stefano.'

'Don't think about it, Candice. Just drop down. I've got you.'

She pushed herself off the side and slid into the chilly water, the shock rendering her speechless. Stefano's hands were round her waist as she kicked her legs to stay afloat.

'There you are, see. I'll race you to the shore.' He let go of her waist and glided through the water in the direction of the beach. Her plodding breaststroke no match for his athletic crawl, she arrived a few minutes after him, stumbling over the pebbles to join him in the shallow surf.

'Has me mascara run?' she asked, flopping down beside him and squeezing the water from her ponytail.

He studied her face. 'A little. Allow me.' He grazed his thumb under her eye, using just enough pressure to smear away the offending make-up. His face only inches from hers, she could smell his minty breath and feel the water dripping off his hair and onto her thighs.

'That is better,' he declared, lying back on the fine stones and putting his hands behind his head. 'Paradise, no?'

She squinted at the perfect blue sky, where two seabirds were performing acrobatic loops, as though putting on a performance just for them. The staggering cliffs embraced the tiny bay on three sides, affording them total privacy from all but the most determined sightseers. 'It's as close as I'll ever get,' she agreed.

61

I'm waiting in the lobby, enveloped in the folds of a squishy sofa, when I notice Eva outside in the gardens. She has her gigantic sunglasses on, but I can see she is staring at the hotel, her mouth slightly open. A gold handbag is slung across her body and she delves inside for a tissue. And then it hits me, and I cannot believe I have been so insensitive. This place holds devastating memories for her. It was the last place she saw her mother. I need to stop her from coming inside, but there is no way I can heave myself out of this ridiculous sofa without assistance.

She pushes through the revolving door, steps inside and removes her sunglasses. Her once-ebony hair is now a perfectly coiffured sweep of silver, but apart from that, and a slight stoop, she looks incredible for a woman of eighty-three.

I give her a feeble wave from my upholstered prison. 'Over here, Eva.'

She comes across, all smiles, and sweeps her arm around the lobby. 'Quite a transformation.'

'I'm sorry. I should never have asked you to come here.'

'Nonsense,' she says dismissively, holding out her hand. 'Come on, let's go and sit on the terrace.'

We settle ourselves at a table and order a bottle of rosé.

'The view's not changed much,' Eva observes, gazing down at the bay below.

At this minute, I couldn't care less about the view. I grasp her hands. 'Tell me what happened that day. I want to know everything. Was Nico mean to you?'

She takes a sip of her wine. 'No, of course not. I'm not going to say it wasn't traumatic. Saying goodbye to Lena was truly terrible. It's a long time ago now, but I can still remember how she fought for me. She was like a woman possessed as she clawed at Nico's arms to try to wrestle me free.'

My heart swells with love for my late mother-in-law. 'She always was a fighter.'

'Indeed.' Eva nods. 'She was never going to win that battle, though. Enzo calmed her down, promising that Nico knew what he was doing and that they should let me go.'

My face colours with shame as I recall where I was at that precise minute: gallivanting with Max on the peninsula, both of us oblivious to the unfolding drama below. 'I should have been there, Eva.' My eyes fill with tears.

'It wouldn't have made any difference. Nico had it all worked out. It was a six-mile walk to the convent, a lot of it uphill over rough terrain, and my little legs were so tired. He had brought bread and some water and he let me rest. When I could go no further, he hoisted me onto his back and carried me the rest of the way. At the convent, he handed me over to the mother superior and thanked her for taking me in. He rooted in his bag and pulled out my dolly, smiling as he pressed her into my arms, then he crouched down and kissed my forehead. "Goodbye, Eva," he said. "You're a brave little girl." Then he stroked my hair with such tenderness, I couldn't believe they were the same hands that had wrenched me away just a few hours before.'

I am so relieved he was gentle with her at the end. 'He was quite a disturbed character,' I tell her. 'When I first met him, he was utterly charming, and he captivated me in a way that nobody else had ever done. I gave up everything for him, I loved him that much.'

She touches the back of my hand. 'I can see why.'

'Looking back, the signs were there, I suppose. Not wanting Louis to be part of our lives, always wanting me to himself, never letting anybody else get close to me. He was incredibly insecure.'

'I think he loved you very much.' I have no idea what Eva is basing this notion on, but I don't push it. None of it matters any more.

'After that day – the day of the massacre – Nico was never the same again. Oh, I'm not making excuses, but it changed him. To see his family, his neighbours, everybody wiped out like that, well . . . it's got to have some effect.'

'I suppose these days he would've had counselling or something.'

'Oh, undoubtedly,' I say. 'Anyway, enough about Nico. What happened to you after the war?'

'Well, I was an orphan, obviously. I had absolutely no family left, so nobody came to claim me. I harboured the hope that you would come back for me, but it wasn't to be.'

This hurts, like a dagger to the heart. 'I would've done, Eva. If I'd known you were there all alone, nobody could've stopped me. You were like a daughter to me.'

She pats my knee and I appreciate the gesture. 'I know you

would've.' She refills my glass without asking and continues. 'I was adopted by a couple from Tuscany and went to live with them on their olive farm. They'd not been able to have children of their own, so they took me and another little girl, Anna-Maria. She's three years younger than me and we grew up as sisters. We're still close to this day, although she's moved to the south now.'

'You've no idea how glad I am to hear that, Eva. My whole life I've tortured myself with the fact that you'd still be alive if I'd listened to Nico. I still can't believe he didn't tell me.'

She wafts away my concern. 'I expect he had his reasons. I have two sons now, and four little granddaughters who are my world. None of them would exist without your husband.' She seems unsure about her next question. 'What happened to him? I assume he is no longer alive.'

I cannot possibly go into all that now. Eva thinks of Nico as a bit of a hero, so there's no way I'm going to tell her exactly how he died. 'He . . . um . . . fell to his death, two years after the massacre.' I nod towards the peninsula. 'Up there. It was a terrible accident.'

She closes her eyes and rests her head against the back of the chair, inhaling a deep breath through her nose. 'I still dream about that day in the basement, the day I chose you over my own mother.' She opens her eyes and looks at me. 'I didn't want to choose you. I wanted to go with my mother, but she knew, didn't she? I don't know how, but she did. The look in her eyes when I took a step towards her . . . I'll never forget it. And then you dropped that pebble on the floor.'

My lips are trembling so much I can barely sip my wine. I press a napkin to my mouth, steeling myself to answer. 'I remember the day you gave me that pebble on the beach. I promised to treasure it forever.'

I reach into my pocket and hold my hand out flat, the pebble balanced on my palm. 'That's one promise I did keep.'

I press it into her hand, and suddenly I feel lighter, as if a weight I never knew I'd been carrying has been lifted.

Eva turns the pebble over in her fingers, marvelling at it as though it's a priceless diamond. 'All this time, Jenny?'

'I couldn't part with it. It would've been like denying you ever existed.'

She goes to give it back to me, but I hold up my hand. 'You must keep it, Eva.'

'Oh, but it's yours.'

'Please. It belongs to you and your children now. Besides, I no longer need it. You are here, in the flesh, and this is the memory I'll keep with me now.'

62

It was late afternoon by the time Stefano steered them into the harbour. Candice could feel her skin tingling with salt, her cheeks glowing with sunburn. Her hair hung in loose, wavy strands, sticky with salt water.

Stefano was watching her, a half-smile on his lips.

'What are you staring at?'

'You look beautiful.'

Her hand automatically went to her hair. 'Give over. I must look a right state.'

He shook his head. 'You look radiant, happy. No, more than that. You look . . . what is the word . . . without cares. There is no tension in your face. It is a look that cannot be achieved with any amount of make-up. It is pure joy.'

She patted her crimson cheeks. 'You're making me blush.'

He finished tying up the boat. 'Come on. Let's eat.'

The restaurant was situated at the end of the jetty, so close to the surface of the water she could hear the waves slapping against the wood. The air was filled with a mouth-watering mixture of barbecued fish, garlic and lemons.

Stefano held out a chair. 'Please, have a seat.'

She tucked herself under the table. 'Me stomach's rumbling. I didn't realise how hungry I was.'

'I can recommend the ravioli.' He kissed his fingers. 'They say it was invented right here in Liguria.'

Candice frowned. 'I thought it was invented by Heinz. I've only ever had it out of a tin.'

Stefano shook his head. 'You have much to learn about Italian food, Candice. On the ships at the end of a meal, all the left-overs were gathered together, chopped up and stuffed into little pasta parcels ready to be served to the sailors at the next meal.'

'Simeon, that's the chef where I work, he does a similar thing with left-over spuds and cabbage and onions and whatnot. Calls it bubble and squeak.'

Stefano laughed. 'You are funny, Candice. Now, we must order.'

The ravioli was certainly easier to eat than the spaghetti she was more used to. All those long strands of tomato-covered pasta had a habit of trailing down her chin in a most unattractive way.

'So,' ventured Stefano, drawing out the word. 'Do you have anybody special in your life?'

Candice almost choked on a square of pasta. She chased it away with a swig of her water. 'Erm . . . yes . . . well . . . no. I mean, sort of.'

He raised his eyebrows but said nothing.

She placed her fork down and blotted her mouth with her napkin. 'I have a boyfriend. He's called Beau and we live together, but just before we came away, I discovered he'd been lying to me.'

Stefano picked up his wine glass and stared at her over the rim. 'He sounds like a fool.'

'Yeah, well. You're not wrong there.'

'He has been cheating on you?'

'No, nothing like that.' She looked at Stefano's expectant face. 'He told me his parents were killed in a plane crash out in Malaysia, in one of those tiny planes as they were flying over the jungle.'

'Oh,' Stefano said. 'That is tragic.'

'Yeah, it would've been if any of it was true.'

'Why . . . why would he lie about that?'

'Jenny thinks it's all about control. You know, getting me to feel sorry for him. He would often mention it, now I come to think about it. He said he had no family and was an only child. That turned out to be rubbish an' all. His brother turned up on our doorstep just as I was about to get in the taxi to the airport. He told me their father had just died of a heart attack and their mother wanted Beau to attend the funeral.'

'Wow,' said Stefano. 'Such deceit. It is incredible.'

Candice swigged her wine. 'You're telling me.'

'Has he told you why he lied?'

'I haven't given him a chance. I've not spoken to him since we got here. I've left my phone off. I just can't face it. I'm having such a lovely time, and he'll only find a way to ruin it.'

'Do you love him?'

She spluttered into her glass. 'Blimey, you get straight to the point, don't you?' She gave the question some thought. 'I suppose I do, at least I think I do, but Beau's quite a sensitive guy. I'm forever treading on eggshells and I always seem to be apologising when I've done nothing wrong.'

'Why do you stay, then?'

'You make it sound so simple. We need each other, that's why. He's not all bad, you know. He loves me so much that he just wants me all to himself. He's so sweet sometimes. I've never had anybody care about me as much as he does.'

Stefano nodded. 'Sounds quite a catch.'

She gave him a long look. 'I'm not a fool, Stefano. I know he's not perfect, but then neither am I.'

'Forgive me, Candice. It really is none of my business.'

Stefano walked her back to the hotel under the orange sky, only a sliver of the sun visible above the horizon.

'I've had a lovely day, Stefano; really, it's been special. I'm not that good with words, but it was damn near perfect. Thank you.'

They stood in the gardens of the Villa Verde, the fading light affording them a moment of privacy. Stefano took hold of her hand and brought it to his mouth. He pressed his lips to her skin and closed his eyes. 'The pleasure was all mine, Candice.' He leaned forward and kissed her cheek. 'I will see you tomorrow.'

She watched him leave, his long stride carrying him effortlessly up the hill. She took a moment to savour the tranquil gardens, only the noisy cicadas intruding on the silence. A movement behind a nearby hedge made her stop and listen hard. She spotted the bushy red tail of the fox as it cast her a sneaky glance before disappearing into the undergrowth.

As she followed the winding path to the stone steps leading up to reception, where two enormous urns planted with yuccas stood guard, she heard another noise, one that made her heart quicken. She had the uneasy feeling she was being watched. 'Hello? Is there somebody there?'

A figure crept out of the shadows. 'Hello, Candice.'

She instinctively took a step backwards from the familiar voice. 'Beau . . . what are you . . . how did you get here?'

'Same way as you did – on a plane.' He held his arms out. 'Got a hug for me then?'

'Yeah, sure . . . sorry.' She gave him a brief squeeze, recoiling from the slight smell of traveller's sweat. 'What're you doing here, Beau?' She stared at his porridge-like complexion. Compared to Stefano, he looked as though he spent his life underground.

'You didn't leave me any choice, did you, babe? You've ignored all my calls and texts and you didn't even ring me back when I left a message with the hotel. What else was I supposed to do?'

'Beau, you lied to me. Telling me your parents had been killed, it's wicked is that.'

'I'll tell you what's wicked, shall I?' He prodded his finger into her chest. 'You not giving me a chance to explain.'

She batted his finger away. 'Don't do that, Beau. Look, I've got to go up and see Jenny. You'll have to excuse me.'

He caught hold of her hand as she turned to leave. 'Wait, we need to talk. Come to our room when you've sorted Her Majesty out.'

'Our room?'

He looked perplexed. 'Yes, I've got a double. No sense in you sharing with that old bat now that I'm here. Room 340. Don't be long, I'll be waiting for you.'

*

She burst through the door as Jenny sat at the dressing table slathering her face in udder cream.

'What on earth is the matter, Candice? You look as if you've seen a ghost.'

'Believe me, a ghost would be preferable.' She paced the room, her hands embedded in her hair as she tripped over her words in a desperate attempt to tell Jenny what had happened. 'He's . . . he's here,' she said breathlessly. 'Beau . . . in this hotel . . . right now. He's followed me here because I wouldn't answer his calls. Can you believe it?'

'Why the little . . . Where is he now?'

'In his room . . . *our* room, as he calls it. He's waiting for me.'

'Are you going to go?'

'What choice do I have?'

'Erm . . . not to go?'

'I can't just leave it like this, can I?'

'No, love, I suppose you can't. Make him wait for a bit, though. Tell me all about your afternoon with Stefano.'

'Oh God, Stefano!' Candice exclaimed. 'Beau's bound to have seen us together. He was in the garden when we said goodbye. Shit . . . what am I going to do?'

'Calm down, Candice. What do you think he saw exactly?'

'Stefano held my hand and kissed me on the cheek.'

'Is that all?'

She gave Jenny a stern look. 'This is Beau we're talking about. Jeez, if he saw that, he'll have a duck fit.'

'What's his room number?'

'Um . . . 340. Why?'

Jenny reached for the phone, halting Candice's protest with a raised palm.

He answered almost immediately. 'Hello?'

'Is that Beau Devine?'

'Yep.'

'It's Jenny here, Candice's friend. I understand you wish her to join you, but I'm afraid I need her here to attend to my bedtime routine. I'm really sorry to inconvenience you, but can it wait?'

'That's fine, tell her there's no rush. I'll be here when she's ready. Goodnight, Jenny.'

She replaced the receiver. 'He's full of surprises, that one.' She turned to Candice. 'Right, I've bought you some time. Think about how you're going to play this – and remember, you've done nothing wrong.'

63

Beau opened the door dressed in only his boxer shorts, his damp hair clinging to his face. 'I thought you'd changed your mind.' He beckoned her over the threshold.

'Sorry, it took longer than I thought sorting Jenny out.'

'What happened to you?'

'What do you mean?

'Your hair. It's all stringy and matted.'

'I . . . I went swimming.'

'Oh, I see. Glad you've been having a good time without me.'

She sat down on the chair in front of the dressing table, studiously avoiding the king-size bed. 'Don't start, Beau. It's you who's got some explaining to do.'

'Me?'

'Erm . . . yes. Your parents were never killed in a plane crash.'

'Oh, that,' he said, lighting up a cigarette.

'Yes, *that*.' She pointed to the sign on the back of the door. 'And this, is a non-smoking room, by the way.'

'I'm estranged from my parents. It's really no big deal; you're making far too much fuss about it.'

'Why didn't you just tell me that then?'

He shrugged and blew out a cloud of smoke.

'Do you want to know what I think?'

'Not really but I suppose that won't stop you telling me.'

'I think you told me that story to get me feeling sorry for you, get me on your side, make out it was just the two of us against the world. Stop me asking any awkward questions about where they lived and that. It was easier to just write them out of your life.'

He sat down on the bed. 'You're right, babe, honestly, that's it. I didn't want you asking questions or trying to get us back together or just your usual general interfering.'

'I wouldn't have done anything you didn't want me to do, Beau.'

He gave her a doubtful look. 'Yeah, right.'

'Why did you fall out with them?'

'They didn't approve of my lifestyle choices.' He indicated the cigarette. 'They didn't even like me smoking, so when I progressed to weed and that, they started clamping down, restricting my movements and my money like I was a little kid. They tried to control me.'

She stiffened at the word, but he seemed oblivious to the irony.

'Anyway,' he continued, 'they didn't care about me. They had their golden child to focus on.'

'Jay?'

'Yeah. I was a lost cause to them, but Jay, well, he was going places, that kid. He was all academic and that. I wanted to concentrate on my music, but to them that wasn't a proper career. Imagine if Ed Sheeran's parents had said something like that.' He flicked some ash onto the carpet before rubbing it away with his bare foot. 'There were just all these arguments every day. The same old thing time after time. *Get a degree, get a career, make something of yourself.* It was exhausting, so I left.'

'I don't know why you couldn't have just told me that.'

'You're my future, Candice, they're my past. They're not important any more.' He reached for her hand. 'You're the only one I care about now. You're all I have left.' He took a deep breath, his voice cracking. 'When you wouldn't answer my calls, I honestly thought I'd lost you. I don't know what I'd do without you.'

She moved over to the bed and sat next to him, her arm around his shoulders. 'I'm sorry, Beau. I was just too annoyed at you to call you back. I felt like our relationship was built on a lie. I wondered what else you hadn't told me.'

He stroked her cheek. 'I'm sorry. Do you forgive me, babe?'

'I suppose so . . .'

He ran his hand through her hair, his nose wrinkling as his fingers found a knot. 'I think you'd better take a shower. Your hair's mingin'.'

'It's the salt water.'

'I don't like the idea of you swimming alone in the ocean. It's dangerous. You could've been carried off by the surf or been caught in a rip tide or something.'

'Oh no, it's okay, I was with . . . um . . . with Jenny.'

'The old bat went swimming?'

'Well, no, obviously she didn't go in the water, but she paddled at the edge and kept her eye on me. It was fine, stop worrying.'

'So let me get this straight.' He shuffled away from her. 'You went swimming alone. There was nobody else in the water with you.'

She pictured Stefano diving off the edge of the boat and slicing into the water, his body a perfect arc. 'No, it was just me.'

He regarded her carefully, his stare so intense she was forced to look away.

'Okay, then.' His words were slow and deliberate. 'You can go and get your shower now.' He bounced on the bed, testing the springs. 'Then we can make the most of this. It's costing enough.'

'Where did you get the money for it?' she asked, slipping her dress over her head.

He stared at her. 'Hellfire, Candice. Look at you.'

She held the dress up to her chest, Beau's scrutiny making her feel exposed.

'That cossie,' he continued. 'I don't remember seeing it before.'

'This old thing.' She laughed. 'I've had it years.'

He reached out and tugged at the bow of the bikini bottoms. 'Why have I never seen it?'

'I'm sure you have, Beau. You've just forgotten.'

He stiffened his lips until they began to turn white. 'I bet there was quite a crowd watching you cavorting in the sea. I can just imagine all those pervy gits staring at my virtually naked girlfriend.'

'I wasn't cavorting and there was nobody staring. Now, where did you get the money?'

'What money?'

'Lord above, Beau. The money for this hotel room, for your flight.'

'Oh, that. I took it out of our savings.'

'The beauty course fund, you mean?'

He lay back on the bed, stretching out his limbs starfish-fashion. 'You gave me no choice, babe. You wouldn't answer my calls. You've only got yourself to blame.'

She watched his skinny body writhing on the pristine sheets and closed her eyes around the image of a frog frantically scrambling to get out of a pan of boiling water. Jenny was right. It was all about knowing when to jump.

Still clutching her dress to her, she stood over him, her voice trembling as she forced out the words. 'It's over, Beau.'

'What is?'

'Us.'

He sat up then, propping himself on one elbow. 'Us?'

There was no turning back now. 'Yes. I don't want to be with you any more.'

He jumped to his feet. 'Don't say that, babe. I'll pay the money back.'

'It's not just the money, it's . . . everything.'

He frowned, genuine confusion creasing his features. 'Everything? What are you on about now, you stupid cow?'

She kept her voice level. 'Don't call me that, Beau.'

He took a deep breath, his eyes narrowing. 'You've got some nerve, Candice, I'll give you that.' He grabbed her arms and manhandled her onto the bed. 'It's you who should be begging for my forgiveness.' He straddled her, pinning her arms above her head.

'Get off me.' She tried to kick her legs, but the weight of

his body across her thighs made it impossible to move. 'Beau,' she panted. 'Please, let me go.'

His face was only inches from hers. 'I saw you,' he snarled.

She stopped struggling. 'Saw me when?'

'Before. Outside with some greasy fuckin' Italian. All over you he was, the smarmy git.'

She turned her head to avoid his hot breath on her face. 'It was nothing, Beau. He's just our . . . um . . . driver. Jenny hired him to—'

'I might've known that interfering bitch had something to do with it. She's always had it in for me.' He closed his hands around her throat, the pressure from his thumbs enough to make her gulp in a panicked breath.

'Beau,' she gasped, clawing at his hands. 'Get off me, you're hurting me.'

'Why are you never satisfied, Candice? All I ever wanted was for you and me to be happy. Just the two of us, nobody else. Why isn't that enough for you?'

She writhed beneath him, panting. 'Beau, I can't breathe . . . please . . . I . . .'

'Candice?' Jenny's muffled voice came through the door. 'Candice, are you all right in there?'

Beau clamped his hand over Candice's mouth. 'Not a fuckin' word,' he commanded, 'or I will kill you. If you're leaving me, I've nothing left to lose.'

'Candice? Answer me. I'm not going away until I know you're all right.'

'Get rid of her. Tell her you're fine . . . now.' He removed his hand from her mouth. 'Go on.'

'I'm f . . . fine, Jenny. I'm just going to take a cool shower.'

'Well you don't sound fine, love. Are you absolutely sure you're okay?'

She gave a dramatic cough. 'I've just got a *frog* in my throat, that's all. I'm off to have that cool shower now. It's *boiling* in here.'

There was a short pause before Jenny spoke again. 'I hear you, Candice.'

Beau cocked his head, straining to hear Jenny shuffling off, her cane banging on the terracotta tiles as she retreated down the corridor.

'Right,' he said. 'Where were we?'

Candice sat up, pointedly rubbing her neck. 'I think you were about to choke me.'

'That was just a warning. You can't leave me, or else I'll . . . I'll . . .'

'Go on. You'll what?'

He forced her back down onto the pillow, pinning her arms above her head as he pressed his lips to hers, forcing his tongue inside her mouth. He spread her legs with his knee, briefly letting go of her hands only to claw at her bikini bottoms.

'Stop it, Beau,' she gasped. 'I'll scream.'

He lay on top of her, the full weight of his body ensuring that she could barely draw breath, and his hands found her throat again, but she could only wheeze a faint protest. Her fingernails raked his back as she tried to bring her knee up to jab him between the legs. As the pressure on her throat increased, the room grew dark and pinpricks of light danced before her eyes. It was the terrible guttural gurgling sound that confused her, like a recently unblocked drain greedily swallowing the water that had backed up. She twisted her head, wondering where on earth it was coming from, before realising the sound was emanating from her own mouth.

The click from the door was loud enough to stop Beau. He froze above her as the door was flung open by the duty manager, a frantic Jenny in his wake. 'You,' he commanded. 'Get off her this moment.'

Beau hesitated for a second, allowing Candice to scramble off the bed and into Jenny's arms.

'Oh Candice, love,' she soothed as the girl sobbed into her shoulder. 'Shush, Candice. You're safe now. I've got you.'

Beau sat on the edge of bed, the sheet draped around his midriff. 'Look, I don't know what you think this is exactly, but you're mistaken, and I'm sure there must be rules about breaking into someone's hotel room, invading their privacy. My girlfriend and I were just making love.' He glanced at Candice. 'Tell him, babe.'

Candice looked away, shaking her head. 'Please Jenny, just get me out of here.'

64

I gaze down at Candice's sleeping form. She looks untroubled and restful, despite the puffy eyelids. We were up half the night just talking everything through. Beau was taken away by the *polizia*, and as far as I'm concerned, they can leave him to rot. Candice is not up to pressing charges, though, so there's a good chance the weasel will be let go.

There's a faint tap on the door and I fumble to open it before the sound wakes her. I manage to take the tray from the room service guy and lay it on the dressing table, lifting the silver dome to inhale the smell of warm bread rolls and buttery croissants.

Candice stirs, and I can see from her expression that for a fleeting moment she doesn't know where she is.

'It's all right, love. I'm here. You're safe.'

She rubs her eyes and stretches her arms above her head. 'What time is it?'

'Quarter past eight. You had a good sleep?'

She blinks several times. 'Not bad . . . under the circumstances.'

'Coffee?' I ask, pressing down the plunger.

'Yes please. You're up and dressed early. I never heard you.'

'Aye, well, dead to the world you were.' I hand her the cup of coffee. 'Let me look after you for once.'

I pick up the tray and carry it out onto the balcony. Candice trails behind me and rests her elbows on the railing as she gazes across the flat sea at the five trees on top of the peninsula.

She takes a sip of her coffee before turning to me, a questioning look on her face. 'And how do *you* feel now?'

'After seeing Eva again?' This brings a smile to my face. I think it always will. 'It was wonderful, Candice. She lived the best life she could in the end. She's happy, and for that I'll always be grateful to Nico.'

She sits down opposite me and picks at the bunch of grapes before speaking with her mouth full. 'There's something else I've been thinking about.'

'Go on.'

'If Louis is your son, who is his father?'

I top up my coffee. I haven't told anyone about this except for my parents, all those years ago.

'I brought shame on my family, Candice. What you've got to realise is that things are different today than they were in the thirties. To have a baby out of wedlock back then was sinful; no one could ever speak of it. Some poor girls were even locked away. Nobody thinks anything of it nowadays – that's called progress. Louis's father was a boy I'd courted on and off, but we weren't particularly serious. I'd first met him in hospital when I was recovering from the polio. He'd had scarlet fever and we were the oldest kids on the children's ward, so we gravitated towards each other.

'I was only fifteen when I got pregnant with our Louis, and

certainly had no intention of marrying Herbie. A family conference was called. Herbie came round with his parents and we all sat at the kitchen table, the mothers all pursed lips and folded arms. There was absolutely no question of me keeping the baby. It was decided it would have to be put up for adoption. I remember glancing over at Herbie, but he was slumped in his chair studiously inspecting his fingernails, obviously wishing he was anywhere else. I put up a spirited fight against adoption, mainly because I didn't want to appear heartless, but I knew I wasn't capable of raising a baby. I was still recovering from the polio. Then my mother had the bright idea of raising Louis as her own. At first we all scoffed, but as she explained how it would work, it seemed like the perfect solution. The baby could stay with our family, and Connie and Fred Tanner, my mother and father, would be named as the parents.'

'And Louis never suspected anything?'

'Why would he? As far as he was concerned, Connie was his mother, and I promised her I would never, ever tell him the truth. It's easier to believe a lie you've heard hundreds of times than the truth you've only heard once. So no, he never suspected anything.'

'But when Connie died, why didn't you tell him then?'

'Apart from breaking a promise I'd made to my mother, imagine telling a little kid that his mother hadn't died but was in fact masquerading as his sister.' I shake my head. 'No, that was never an option.'

Candice seems to be having trouble getting her head around it all. 'But when Louis wouldn't go with you to Italy, why not tell him then?'

'Oh no, that would've been the worst time to do it. Del would never have believed me anyway. She would have seen it as the grossest form of manipulation, and she would've been right.'

'How did she manage to adopt him, though?'

'He was an orphan. There were death certificates for his named parents. There was nobody to dispute it, and I assume Louis would have been all for it.'

'What happened to him?'

I feel the familiar rush of blood to my head when I think about that. 'After the war, after Nico . . . you know . . . I wrote to Louis again. Told him Nico was gone. I wasn't sure what I was expecting, but he wrote back and told me he was sorry to hear that but he didn't want me contacting him again. He would've only been about ten years old at the time. He told me he was happy and that I shouldn't worry about him any more. Del was his mammy now and he loved her.'

I lower my eyes and stare into my lap. 'I can't lie, Candice. That really stung, but it was no more than I deserved.'

'It must have been a comfort to you, though? You knew he'd always be safe.'

'Yes,' I concede. 'And to be fair to Del, she also wrote reassuring me that if Louis ever changed his mind about seeing me, she wouldn't stand in his way, but it had to be his choice. I think she'd mellowed a bit, because she told me he was settled and doing well at school. He could speak fluent Welsh too. She even sent me a photo.' I rifle through my handbag and bring out the faded black and white photo of Louis standing outside the front door of Mynydd Farm.

Candice takes it and cocks her head to one side. 'Ah, bless.' She stares at it for a moment before adopting an apologetic tone. 'He does look happy, Jenny.'

I feel a flutter of relief, so grateful that she has noticed. 'It was reassuring.' I nod. 'Del was just as good a mother as Connie, and a far better one than I would've been.'

'Don't be so hard on yourself. You would've made a wonderful mum.' She hands back the photo. 'I wish I'd had a mum like you.'

'Thank you, love. You're very sweet.' I heave a deep sigh.

She pauses before asking her next question. 'Why did you never have any more children?'

I manage a mirthless snort. 'Max and I tried for years, but—'

As everything falls into place, she slaps the heel of her hand into her forehead. 'Of course, Jenny *Fischer*. God, I'm so dense. You married Max, didn't you?'

I'd forgotten she's yet to hear the details of that part of the story. 'We kept in touch after the war. He visited me in Italy, helped me get back on my feet. I had no one, don't forget, and without Max, I don't know what would've become of me. After what happened with Eva, we had a special bond, and he was easy to fall in love with. So uncomplicated, such a kind man, everything a husband should be. I moved over to Germany in 1950 and we got married. I picked up my dressmaking business and he went into engineering. We had forty-four happy years together before he died.'

'But no kids?' Candice asks.

'No, and it turned out it was my fault after all.'

'How do you mean?'

'Max had all the tests; there was nothing wrong with him. Nico was right all along.'

'But you'd already had a baby.'

'That was my punishment, I suppose. I just couldn't conceive again. Unexplained infertility, they said.'

Candice reaches for my hand. 'I'm so sorry, Jenny.'

I shrug. 'I wasn't exactly a textbook mother for the child I did have. Save your pity for Max. He definitely deserved better.'

'When did you move back to the UK?'

'After I was widowed, twenty-four years ago now.'

'Don't you ever wonder what became of Louis?'

I can see Candice is having trouble understanding it all, and who can blame her? I often doubt my actions myself.

'Louis was fine without me,' I say eventually. 'He'd already had two mothers; he didn't need a third.'

'Hey.' Candice speaks so forcefully I actually jump. 'We could get you on that long-lost family thing, you know, with Davina.' She claps her hands together, her eyes suddenly brighter. 'I bet they'd be able to trace him.'

From the look on her face, it's clear she thinks this is one of the best ideas she's ever had, but there's no way I'm airing my dirty laundry on national television. 'I don't think so, Candice. I've long since come to the conclusion that if Louis wants to find me, he will.'

65

I've been back at Green Meadows just over a week now. The trip has left me so exhausted I can barely lift my head off the pillow. I have no regrets, though. How could I? Learning that Eva was still alive and has led a long and happy life was balm to my soul. It has even made me think about Candice's idea of tracing our Louis.

When we got back from Italy, Candice didn't want to return to the flat she shared with Beau. Luckily, Mrs Culpepper has come through for her and is allowing her to stay in one of the vacant rooms here at Green Meadows until she finds her feet. She's a different girl since she escaped the controlling clutches of that boyfriend of hers.

It's not like me to still be in bed at this hour, but I can't seem to find the energy or inclination to do anything but stare at the ceiling. Perhaps my race is run.

My memory box is next to me on the bed. I've been having a sort through it. I need to make room for the new memories I'm going to make. My birthday card from Her Majesty is in there now, and Eva's promised to send me photos of her family. I smooth my hand over the box, marvelling at the craftsmanship that went into making it. And the love, too. It deserves a careful guardian after I've gone. I'm going to give it to Candice so she can fill it with her own treasures. I have a feeling life's going to be wonderful for her from now on.

There's a gentle rap on the door.

'Come in.'

Frank pokes his head round. 'Are you up to a visitor?'

I wriggle into a sitting position. 'I'm always ready for you, Frank.' I pat my duvet. 'Get yourself over here.'

He sits down on the bed and takes my hand, running his thumb over my mountainous veins. 'I don't like seeing you like this.'

I waft away his concern. 'Frank, I'm a hundred years old. I'm allowed to lie in.'

He casts a look at the clock on my bedside table, but is too polite to point out that it's almost lunchtime.

'Candice is wondering if you want a tray bringing in.'

This does spur me on a little. 'No, I don't, Frank. Lunch in bed is only for old people.'

He laughs as he gets up and wanders over to my dressing table. He leans in towards the mirror, fiddling with his already immaculate cravat, then picks up the framed photo of me in my youthful glory. I notice his wistful smile in the mirror, but he says nothing.

'I'll see you for lunch then.' He leaves without a backward glance.

I manage to get myself out of bed and dressed before Candice pops her head round.

'Frank says you'll have lunch in the dining room. Is that right?'

'Yes, love. I'll just sort my hair out.'

I sit down at the dressing table and Candice comes up behind me, taking the brush. 'Here, let me.'

I stare at her reflection as she concentrates on brushing my hair. 'How are you doing, love?'

She rests her hands on my shoulders. 'Better. I've spoken to Beau a few times, and he's still begging me to go back, promises things will be different, but I'm managing to stay strong.'

The worried knot in my stomach loosens. 'Good for you, love.'

Her gaze shifts from my face to the dressing table, and I notice a quizzical look in her eyes. 'Oh, you had it all along then,' she says.

'Had what?'

'The missing carving of the little boy. The one that slots into the girl's arms. It's complete now.'

My scalp suddenly feels hot and prickly as I stare at the carving. Candice is right: both parts are there; the girl's arms are no longer empty. I'm too stunned to speak as the years roll back and I remember giving the little boy part to Louis, saying he could bring it back to me when he was ready to forgive me. It was the last time I ever saw him.

My hands are shaking as I pick up the carving and turn it over, feeling the smoothly honed contours of the wood, remembering how proud of his creation Louis had been. I stare into the mirror as realisation dawns. 'It's him.'

'What's him?' asks Candice as she fusses with the back of my hair.

'Louis *Francis* Tanner.'

There's a shuffling noise at the open door, and we both

turn to see Frank leaning against the frame, a tattered teddy bear clutched to his chest. He dips his head towards the bear, burying his nose in its fur, before holding it up to me. 'You never did make a skirt for Mrs Nesbitt.'

Candice looks from me to Frank and back again, her forehead creased in confusion. 'C . . . Candice,' I stammer. 'Could you leave us alone for a while?'

'What about your lunch?'

'Please, Candice.'

She trots out, giving Frank an exasperated look as she brushes past him.

He comes fully into the room and sits down in the armchair, crossing his legs.

I can only shake my head. 'Why, Frank? Why didn't you say anything?'

He gives a deep sigh and steeples his hands under his chin. I wonder why it's taking him so long to answer. Presumably he's known who I am since the day he moved in here. It's me who should be lost for words.

'It was Ernest's idea to track you down,' he begins. 'It wasn't that difficult really. You'd had the foresight to leave forwarding addresses in Italy, Germany and here. Ernest said it was so simple, you must have wanted to be found.' He does his trademark one-eyebrow lift and I'm not sure if he's expecting me to answer. I don't say anything. For once, I just need to listen.

'Mammy Del and Tad died within a few months of each other back in 1975. Lorcan and Rhiannon carried on with the farm—'

'Rhiannon?'

He gives me a hard stare, which I probably deserve. 'His wife.'

My mind flashes back to mine and Lorcan's wedding day, and my pulse quickens. The pain I caused him has haunted me ever since. 'Did she make him happy?' I'm surprised by how much I want the answer to be yes.

Frank affords me a smile as he nods slowly. 'Married for fifty-one years until he died in '97. She was a sweet girl, hardworking too. Mammy Del adored her. She gave Lorcan everything he ever wanted, including three kids.'

A whoosh of relief escapes my lips and my conscience is eased a little. 'I'm glad, Frank, truly I am.'

'I think Lorcan forgave you a lot sooner than I did. I know I was only a little boy, but I really hated you for what you did to us.'

His words sting. 'I don't blame you, Frank. Part of me wishes I'd stayed. It would've saved a lot of heartbreak, but then I wouldn't have met Eva or Max.'

'That's the trouble. We can't cherry-pick the parts of our story we'd like to keep. Our lives are a melting pot of regrets, triumphs, sorrow and joy. You have to accept it all.'

He's not wrong there.

'You came to Green Meadows because you knew I was here, though?'

His expression is blank. 'I did it for Ernest. He said he couldn't bear the thought of me all alone after he died, so I promised him that I'd contact you. He was a much more forgiving person than I am. A much better person altogether, in fact.'

I stare at his face, searching for traces of the little boy I left behind a lifetime ago. 'I doubt that, Frank.'

'Once Lorcan and Rhiannon had passed on, I had no family left. Oh, I know they weren't my blood relatives, but that didn't matter to me. The only blood relative I'd had let me down badly.' He looks at me to make sure I understand.

I can't help but bristle, and there's a tightness in my chest. 'I tried to get you to come to Italy. Surely Del gave you my letters.'

'She did, but I didn't want to go. I was happy at Mynydd Farm. Why would I want to travel to some foreign country to be with a sister who cared more for her lover than for me?'

He's not making this easy, and I can't blame him. 'Why did you wait so long before telling me who you were, though?' I do a rough calculation in my head. 'I mean, you've lived here for ten months.'

'It was never my intention to actually move to Green Meadows, but after Ernest died, I couldn't stay in that house without him. I knew you were here and I came a few times for a look round. You probably won't remember, but we did actually meet on one of those occasions. Mrs Culpepper introduced you to me as their oldest resident.' He gives a little laugh. 'We actually shook hands.'

He's right, I don't remember. Mrs Culpepper is fond of introducing me to prospective residents. She sees me as a good advert for the place, as though my living at Green Meadows is the sole reason I've survived to such a great age. She likes to take the credit for that.

My brain feels particularly sluggish as I try to make sense of everything. 'But you still haven't said why you didn't tell me who you were.'

He gives a resigned shrug. 'I suppose I wanted to find out

if you were worth getting to know. I had to make sure you wouldn't disappoint me again. My last memory of you was in the kitchen at the farm, when you handed me my half of the carving. I stared at the door for a long time after you'd gone. I couldn't believe you would actually leave me behind. I thought you were just teaching me a lesson and would reappear, but no, you'd really gone and you never came back. I vowed there and then never to let you back into my life.'

'I think you're being a bit harsh, Frank. We've become best friends over the past ten months. I thought you liked me.'

'I do, which is why we're having this conversation now.'

'But . . . but . . .' I stop as tightness takes hold of my chest, making it difficult to breathe.

Frank notices. 'Jenny?'

I close my eyes and try to focus on breathing in and out, but there's a sharp pain now that causes me to wince. He goes to press the buzzer by the side of my bed, but I raise my hand to stop him. 'I never stopped loving you, our Louis.'

He halts at the mention of his childhood name.

'You are so much more to me than my little brother. More than you will ever know.' It's as far as I dare to go without breaking my promise to our mother. A bolt of pain shoots through me and carries my words away. Everything goes dark and all I can hear are Louis's panicked tones as he gently pats my face. His voice, high-pitched and unbroken, sounds as though it's coming through a tunnel, and I'm being pulled towards it. I can see him as a boy, running through the wheat fields, his skinny tanned arms flailing as he bats away the flies. I can see him diving into the pool beneath the waterfall, disappearing below the surface before rearing up again and shaking the droplets of water from his hair, his face glowing with delight. I can see him with two rabbits slung over his shoulder, proudly walking next to Lorcan, carrying his rifle like a seasoned soldier.

His voice is closer now, and deeper, his breath warm in my ear. 'Mum?' There's a note of panic now. 'Mum, don't you dare leave me again.'

I have never heard anybody call me that before, and the explosion of pure pleasure I feel has been worth the wait. I open my eyes and reach up to touch his face, my words thick with tears. 'Oh my darling boy, my little Louis.'

I squeeze his hand with every ounce of strength I possess. My son, he knows. Perhaps he always has.

Epilogue

I am fussing with the flowers on the counter even though I know they already look perfect. I decide to pluck the middles out of the lilies, the bit that contains the orange powder that stains your clothes. Everything has to be just so.

Fliss wanders in from the back. 'Are you still messing about with them flowers, Candice? They're fine as they are. Come and have your brew before it gets cold.'

I pick up the mug and wrap my hands around it before taking a sip. I gaze around the salon, the smell of fresh paint still in the air. 'I can't believe this place is all mine.'

Fliss gives a husky laugh, one that comes with decades of smoking. 'You'd better believe it, kid. Come January, I'll be off to Fuengirola with my Derek, and then you really will be on your own.'

'Thanks for staying on for a bit, Fliss. I couldn't have done it without you.'

'You deserve it, pet. You'll be brilliant, and you'll have that Level Three boxed off in no time. There'll be no stopping you.'

I smile at her with genuine affection. 'You really are my saviour. That flat upstairs is just the job. And this salon . . . well, I still have to pinch myself.'

Fliss inhales a whiff of the diffuser. 'You've done wonders with the place. What's that pong?'

'Lavender and camomile. It's supposed to be calming and relaxing. I want to create a tranquil atmosphere so that when clients come in they feel like they're being enveloped in a giant hug.'

I can see her trying to resist an eye roll.

'Teach you that at beauty school, did they?'

I give an enthusiastic nod. I know she thinks I'm bonkers. 'The connection between smell and emotion is stronger than any other sense.'

She narrows her eyes as she thinks about this. 'Happen you're right, love. As soon as I get a whiff of egg and chips, I'm right there in Billy Bob's down on the front in Fuengirola. My Derek's favourite, that place. You can have a full English with a bottomless mug of tea for under a fiver. Eh, you'll have to come and visit us once we're settled.'

The thought of travelling to Spain only to pig out on a full English doesn't fill me with joy. 'I'm not thinking about holidays yet, Fliss. I want to make a go of this place first. I have to.'

'You're a different girl since you gave that boyfriend of yours the elbow.'

I haven't seen Beau for months now. Not since that dreadful night in Italy, in fact. Simeon cleared my things out of our flat, not that there was much. There was no money left in our joint bank account either. It was naïve of me to expect there would be. I just wanted out of there in the end, and it was a relief to walk away.

'Candice?'

Fliss's voice brings me back to the present.

'Sorry, miles away. I believe Beau's seeing someone else, though, poor cow. Perhaps I should warn her.'

'You stay out of it,' Fliss warns with a wag of her finger. 'He's not your problem any more. You've got your second chance here. Don't squander it.'

She's right. I slap my hand on the counter. 'Right, back to work. Can you check the shellac stock and let me know which colours to add to this order?'

Fliss gives me a salute. 'Yes, boss.'

'Now that does sound weird.' I laugh. 'I'm so used to being ordered around by Mrs Culpepper. Eh, that reminds me, she's booked in for another facial next week.'

'There isn't enough moisturiser on the planet to erase the lines on that sour face.'

'You are awful, Fliss. Stop it. I miss working at Green Meadows, but it wasn't the same once . . . well, you know.'

She shakes her head, her enormous hoop earrings bashing against her cheeks. 'I wish I'd had a friend who'd left me pots of money.'

'Hardly pots, Fliss, but enough to get me this place.' I glance out of the window at the ominous purple clouds. 'I hope the rain holds off. I'm going to the cemetery this afternoon.'

The clouds still hover menacingly over the horizon, and the late-autumn air hangs heavy with mist and the dank smell of decaying leaves. I pick my way along the gravel path, ancient headstones either side covered with moss and lichen. Holly wreaths have begun to appear in the shops, making a nice change from the flowers I usually bring.

I can see a familiar figure up ahead, standing in front of

the grave, head bowed, collar turned up against the bitter chill.

'Hey there,' I say. 'How've you been?'

'You only popped into Green Meadows yesterday, Candice. I'm still fine.'

'Yeah, well. You know how I worry.'

'There's really no need.'

'Who's brought you?' I ask, looking around.

'Abigail did, but she's waiting in the car to give me some privacy. She's thoughtful like that. Such a sweetheart.'

I wrinkle my nose at the mention of my replacement. 'Good, I'm glad.'

Jenny laughs and pats my arm. 'Don't worry, Candice. You'll always be my favourite.'

'Glad to hear it.' I nod at the headstone. 'I see you've finally got the permanent one. It's beautiful.'

'I went with the Welsh slate in the end. Thought it was fitting.'

'I think he would approve.'

She leans against me, resting her head on my arm. 'All those wasted years.' A small sob escapes her lips and I pull her closer.

'Be grateful for the time you did have instead of regretful for the time you didn't,' I say.

Frank passed away three months ago now. A coronary embolism. When I found him dead in his bed, he looked peaceful, rested, and although I was devastated, the thought of him back in the arms of his Ernest tempered my sadness a little. Naturally Jenny was inconsolable, and my heart broke for her. They made the most of the time they did have together, though. The three of us travelled back to Wales. We had a coffee in what used to be Bernardi's gelateria but is now a café run by a couple from Swansea. We walked through the park and sat on the bench where Jenny and Lorcan had found Louis eating ice cream with Nico. Not the exact same bench, obviously, but you know what I mean. The farmhouse is now a B&B and the cowsheds have been converted into self-catering accommodation. Frank's eyes misted over when we stood by the waterfall at the back of the house, remembering how Lorcan had taught him to swim in the pool beneath. I'm so glad we had that time together. To see Jenny and Louis reconciled was a fitting end to her story.

'It was so kind of Frank to leave me that money,' I say. 'I really wish I could have thanked him in person.'

'You making a go of your business is all the thanks he would want, love.'

That is exactly what I intend to do. I am my own boss and no man will ever have control over me again. I have such a lot to be grateful for. I'm not saying I'll never have another relationship – that would be ridiculous – but I'm in no rush. You're probably thinking Stefano would be a good bet, but the truth is, I need to forge ahead by myself first. Then we'll see what happens.

I turn back to the headstone and read the inscription out loud. 'Treasured memories of Louis Francis Myers. A loving husband to Ernest and beloved son of Jennifer.' My arm is still linked through Jenny's, and I feel her relax. 'Beloved son.' I smile. 'I like that.'

'He was a beloved son to Connie and Fred, and then to Del and Bryn.' She leans forward and lays her hand on the headstone. 'But now I want everyone to know it. Louis was my boy. He was my son. And he was truly loved.'

Acknowledgements

Thanks as always to my editor and cheerleader, Sherise Hobbs, for her patience and enthusiasm, and to the whole Headline team, especially Mari Evans, Jen Doyle, Rebecca Bader, Rosie Margesson, Vicky Abbott and Bea Grabowska.

To my agent, Anne Williams, for her guidance and wise counsel.

To Jane Selley for her attention to detail during the copyediting and her kind words.

To Ellen and Cameron who are as proud of me as I am of them.

And finally, to my husband, Rob, who has read more drafts of this novel than anyone should have to and remains a constant support.

Inspiration for
The Memory Box

The inspiration for *The Memory Box* did not start with an intellectual idea, a striking newspaper cutting or a visit to a deserted monastery. This time, the book was fuelled by an image. An image of a woman at her own one-hundredth birthday party, having outlived everybody she ever cared about. As my character Jenny reflects on her past with her young carer, Candice, she picks through the precious keepsakes in her memory box and finally resolves there is one important, painful journey she has to make before it's too late.

The joy of writing this book came from the fact that it wasn't set in stone. As my research revealed what really happened in the 1940s, the book took some unexpected turns and although it is a work of fiction, the plot was guided by true events.

When Jenny and Louis arrive in Penlan they are billeted with the Evans family and it soon becomes clear that Lorcan Evans develops unreciprocated feelings for Jenny. However, Jenny is captivated by a striking Italian, Nico, and a fledgling romance develops.

It is here that true-life events conspire against them. Ten months into World War II, Italy entered the war on the side of the Germans, leading Winston Churchill to declare all

Italians living in the United Kingdom to be enemy aliens. He ordered every male Italian to be arrested and detained without charge. An alien advisory committee was set up to assess each Italian's threat level. Category A aliens, the highest potential security risk, were to be interned at once. The Isle of Man was identified as being sufficiently removed from military importance, resulting in the requisitioning of boarding houses to incarcerate prisoners. As the island filled up, thousands of Italians were shipped to Canada and Australia to spend years languishing in camps despite having done absolutely nothing wrong. One such ship, bound for Canada, was the *Arandora Star*. Formerly a luxury cruise liner, it had been painted grey but crucially did not have the red cross painted on it to indicate it was carrying civilians. Early in the morning of 2nd July 1940, the ship was torpedoed by a German U-boat. As a luxury liner, she had carried 354 first-class passengers and 200 crew, all of whom had access to the twelve lifeboats. As a transport ship, she carried 1,729 internees, prisoners of war and guards, three times her normal capacity but with the same number of lifeboats. The prisoners' escape was further hampered by barbed wire surrounding the decks. Many of the Italians were doomed as they had originally come from the mountainous areas of Italy and had never learned to swim. Over 850 people lost their lives, 446 of them Italians. There was much confusion as to the identity of the victims and the exact death toll was difficult to ascertain. These poor people were totally innocent of any charges laid against them. They had been dragged from their homes and ordered aboard a ship which would take them to a place of detainment for the duration of the war, just because they were Italian.

Many Italian communities were pulled apart in this way, including in the fictional town of Penlan, where Nico is arrested and sent away. Despite his promise to return, the only communication Jenny receives is a telegram reporting Nico as 'Missing, presumed drowned'.

I see from my original notes that I hadn't planned this turn of events for Jenny and Nico, but history forced me to think again and this led the story in a different direction. A much better one, it must be said!

I was fortunate in that I managed to take a research trip to Italy just before the pandemic cancelled everybody's plans. I needed inspiration for my fictional village of Cinque Alberi and found the perfect place in Camogli, a fishing village situated on the west side of the Portofino peninsula in Liguria. I stayed in a hotel at one end of the bay which had a panoramic view of the village. This hotel became the Villa Verde in the novel.

Camogli, Liguria, re-imagined as Cinque Alberi. Copyright Kathryn Hughes

Whilst familiar with the history of the French Resistance, I was only vaguely aware of the underground battle between Italians, Germans and Fascists. From 1943, after Italy switched sides, and declared war on their former allies, a spontaneous city-by-city uprising began against the occupying German forces. Rather than warfare, their activities largely focused on sabotage, carrying messages between units, hiding Allied escapees and building radios to establish contact with the Allies in the south of the country. Women played a vital part in these activities and I can recommend Caroline Moorehead's excellent

Copyright Kathryn Hughes

book, *A House in the Mountains: The Women Who Liberated Italy From Fascism* for anybody interested in reading more about this fascinating subject.

Whilst wandering Piacenza, we came across this World War II memorial, which interestingly divides the conflict into two parts: 1940 (when Italy entered the war) to 1943 when it surrendered to the Allies, and then the War of Liberation from 1943 to 1945.

Although partisan activities were focused on disruption, perhaps inevitably some German troops were killed by the resistance and reprisal attacks were swift and brutal, with ten Italians killed for every German life lost. These attacks were indiscriminate and often unleashed on innocent civilians. Whole villages were massacred, including women and children who had no chance of escape. Seventy-five years may have passed but these atrocities should never be forgotten.

Kathryn Hughes

THE
LETTER
Kathryn Hughes
THE No. 1 BESTSELLER
guaranteed to break your heart

Tina Craig longs to escape her violent husband. She works all the hours God sends to save up enough money to leave him, also volunteering in a charity shop to avoid her unhappy home. Whilst going through the pockets of a second-hand suit, she comes across an old letter, the envelope firmly sealed and unfranked. Tina opens the letter and reads it – a decision that will alter the course of her life for ever . . .

Billy Stirling knows he has been a fool, but hopes he can put things right. On 4th September 1939 he sits down to write the letter he hopes will change his future. It does – in more ways than he can ever imagine . . .

Available to order

REVIEW

THE
SECRET

The truth she locked away will set another woman free

Kathryn Hughes

Mary has been nursing a secret.

Forty years ago, she made a choice that would change her world for ever, and alter the path of someone she holds dear.

Beth is searching for answers. She has never known the truth about her parentage, but finding out could be the lifeline her sick child so desperately needs. When Beth finds a faded newspaper cutting amongst her mother's things, she realises the key to her son's future lies in her own past. She must go back to where it all began to unlock . . . **The Secret**.

Available to order

REVIEW

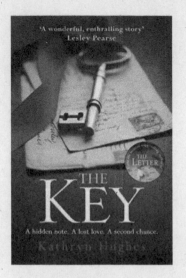

'A wonderful, enthralling story'
Lesley Pearse

THE LETTER

THE
KEY

A hidden note. A lost love. A second chance.

Kathryn Hughes

1956
It's Ellen Crosby's first day as a student nurse at Ambergate Hospital. When she meets a young woman admitted by her father, little does Ellen know that a choice she will make is to change both their lives for ever . . .

2006
Sarah is drawn to the now abandoned Ambergate. Whilst exploring the old corridors she discovers a suitcase belonging to a female patient who entered Ambergate fifty years earlier. The shocking contents, untouched for half a century, will lead Sarah to unravel a forgotten story of tragedy and lost love, and the chance to make an old wrong right . . .

Available to order

REVIEW

Tara Richards was just a girl when she lost her mother. Years later when Tara receives a letter from a London solicitor its contents shake her to the core. Someone has left her a key to a safe deposit box. In the box lies an object that will change everything Tara thought she knew and lead her on a journey to deepest Spain in search of the answers that have haunted her for forty years.

Violet Skye regrets her decision to travel abroad leaving her young daughter behind. As the sun dips below the mountains, she reminds herself she is doing this for their future. Tonight, 4th June 1978, will be the start of a new life for them. This night will indeed change Violet's destiny, in the most unexpected of ways . . .

Available to order

REVIEW

To keep in touch with bestselling author

Kathryn Hughes

and sign up to receive her newsletter

Visit
www.kathrynhughesauthor.com

Find her on Facebook
f @KHughesAuthor

Connect on Twitter
🐦 @KHughesAuthor